The Heiresses

Lord Mountjoy's jaw dropped in shock. 'What the hell was wrong with them, begatting only girls?' he demanded angrily. 'Mountjoys *always* had sons. That's how the line existed for so many centuries.'

'Perhaps it was the foreigners' fault, sir,' Swayne suggested helpfully.

Lord Mountjoy sighed. He was beginning to think he had opened a Pandora's Box for his birthday present. Instead of finding the heir he had hoped for: some decent, impecunious, malleable young man who could be trained to follow the Mountjoy traditions, he was ending up with three females, each of whom sounded worse than the other. 'If only they were men,' he said wistfully, 'then we would be talking. But a French bluestocking, a horse-mad Yorkshire gel and a Texan woman who works the land? What can I make of that, Swayne, I ask you?'

About the author

Elizabeth Adler was born in Yorkshire. She is married to an American lawyer and has one daughter. They have lived in Brazil, the USA, England, France and Ireland.

The Heiresses

Elizabeth Adler

CORONET BOOKS
Hodder and Stoughton

First published in Great Britain in 1995 by Hodder & Stoughton
A division of Hodder Headline PLC
First published in paperback in 1996 by Hodder and Stoughton
A Coronet Paperback

British Library Cataloguing in Publication Data

Adler, Elizabeth
Heiresses
I. Title
823.914 [F]

ISBN 0 340 61781 0

Printed and bound in Great Britain by
Cox & Wyman Ltd, Reading, Berkshire

Hodder and Stoughton
A division of Hodder Headline PLC
338 Euston Road
London NW1 3BH

For my mother.
With love, as always.

PART I

CHAPTER 1

It all began one cold January day, in 1937. Lord Mountjoy was sitting in a first-class carriage on the Bath to London express, holding a copy of *The Times* in front of his face, opened at the business section. He was not reading it; it was merely a screen against the other soberly pin-stripe-suited men, on their way, as he was, back to London after a long weekend in the country.

William Edward Mountjoy was tenth Earl of Mountjoy and a very rich man. He was master of all he surveyed from the windows of his stately home, Mountjoy Park in Wiltshire, and from his Scottish Castle, as well as owner of the vast Mountjoy House on Curzon Street in London's Mayfair. And he was celebrating his seventieth birthday. Alone.

The fact was, he thought, peering over the top of his newspaper, every other fellow in his carriage was younger than himself. 'Not one of 'em over forty,' he thought, gloomily, remembering when *he* was young, a mere sapling of eighteen, green as grass and randy as hell and just out of Eton. Then, his life lay spread out before him like an ever-unrolling red carpet. Forty seemed eons away, and seventy was still lost in the mists of the improbability that he would ever grow old. At eighteen there was no such thing as 'old'.

Not that there was anything wrong with him now, other than the usual problems of ageing; the touch of gout now and then that forced him to lean a little more heavily than he liked on his silver-topped malacca cane; and the failing eyesight that was causing havoc with his August grouse shoot, up in Scotland. Then there was a lifetime's surfeit of good food and wine, and the excellent brandy of which he was inordinately fond. Though of course, he never overstepped the mark and drank too much. A gentleman never did.

And then there was the other problem. Loneliness.

The rolling green Wiltshire hills, dotted with cows and horses – for this was a horse county with many fine training establishments near Newbury racecourse – slipped by the window, but he did not notice. Still behind his newspaper screen, he inspected his reflection in the carriage window. He saw a tall, upright, silver-haired man with the pinkish complexion of the fastidiously-shaven; a small dark-grey moustache and beetling dark brows over faded blue eyes. He was impeccably suited by Huntsman of Saville Row, and, as always, thanks to his valet, immaculately turned out. His dark blue overcoat lay neatly folded on the rack above his head, along with his black bowler hat and his tightly furled black umbrella.

He was, he thought wryly, every inch the English gentleman.

William Mountjoy had inherited the title through an unfortunate series of circumstances. His eldest brother had been killed in a train crash, and the second brother, Georgie, had been disinherited by his father because of his dissolute ways.

William Mountjoy was thirty-five, then. He saw his duty clearly. He married Penelope Latimer the following year and did what was expected to produce a Mountjoy heir. Unfortunately, nothing happened.

It couldn't be his fault, he had told himself then, regarding his naked image in the oval cheval mirror in his immense green-marble bathroom at the Curzon Street mansion. He was still in the prime of his life, and he looked it. Ramrod straight back, only a slight thickening round the waist, muscular chest and arms, strong legs and well-endowed with perfectly functioning sexual equipment. No, the lack of a son and heir was definitely not his fault. It must be his wife.

He sent Penelope to the best gynaecologist in London, who subjected the poor, delicately-brought-up woman to any number of embarrassing questions and unspeakable tests. And then the answer came back. His wife was in good health. She was perfectly able to conceive a child.

William still remembered sitting in the doctor's rooms in Harley Street, hearing him say, 'The fault must lie with yourself, Lord Mountjoy. Perhaps I could recommend a colleague, an expert in such matters. Maybe he will be able to help you.'

Of course, he had not gone to see the colleague. There was no way he could ever admit, even to himself, that he was unable to father a child. 'Nonsense,' he told Penelope brusquely. 'Of course, the fellow has made a mistake. You know there is nothing wrong with . . . with our private life.' He phrased it delicately, but even so, his wife blushed.

She was a plump little woman with a constantly worried expression, always in fear of upsetting him. 'Of course he has, my dear,' she agreed, accepting the blame. 'I'm terribly sorry, though.' She looked him bravely in the eye. 'I shall quite understand if you wish to seek a divorce, William,' she added. 'I know how important it is that you have an heir.'

For a moment, he had toyed with the idea of having his freedom, but he knew it was imperative he had a son. No, he had decided. He had to stay married to Penelope. He had to keep trying. Maybe the poor woman would conceive soon and he could breathe a sigh of relief at having done his duty.

Penelope had never conceived, but she had stuck by him, a loyal wife to a rather testy and often absent husband. She died of a heart attack, sitting quietly at her favourite place overlooking the immense lake installed by Capability Brown, who had re-designed the grounds of Mountjoy Park in 1760. William had been in Monte Carlo at the time. He had of course, taken the train straight back to Paris, and then onto Calais and London.

Penelope was buried in the Mountjoy mausoleum, alongside William's father, mother and brother, and generations of past Mountjoys. He commissioned a specially nice carved Carrara marble tombstone, and held a memorial service, a month later, in the Chapel Royal at Windsor, by special permission of their Majesties, King George and Queen Mary. He found himself surprised by the number of friends and acquaintances who came to remember Penelope. He had always thought her such a shy little mouse, but she had run his houses and hosted the lengthy country weekend house parties, and attended the functions and dances and dinners that went along with a man in his position in life.

She was gentle and unselfish and, sadly, it was not until she was dead that their friends recalled how kind she had always been to them, how gracious a hostess, how willing to lend an ear to their problems. They told William they would miss her, and William missed her too. More than he had thought possible. Somehow, Penelope had always been there for him, and now she wasn't, and he found himself at a loss.

So it was with relief that, when war had been declared a few months after that, on August 4th, 1914, he buckled down to the desk job at the War Office. He closed up the great London house, sending most of its treasures – the Goyas and the Gainsboroughs, the Watteaus and Vermeers, the silver and jewelled ornaments given to them as gifts over the centuries, and the precious souvenirs and mementos amassed by Mountjoys, and placed them safely in storage in the country. He adjusted quickly to the economies and hardships of war, putting in long hours at his desk and sleeping at his club, gloomily discussing the battles of Verdun and the Somme, and the battle of Jutland and the British naval blockade which Germany failed to crack. And finally, he cheered with the others, when the Central Powers sued for peace, celebrating the Armistice, on November 14th, 1918.

It had been, he thought, as he oversaw the restoration of his treasures into Mountjoy House on Curzon Street, the War to end all Wars. The dead on both sides totalled eight and a half million. The youth of Britain, an entire generation of young men, was gone.

The years after the war had sped by contentedly enough, but he had never found a woman who understood him the way Penelope had, and he had never re-married. Now he was seventy years old and set in his ways, and it was too late.

The Bath to London express, belching steam, pulled into Paddington Station with a clanking of wheels and scraping of steel, then jolted to a stop. Lord Mountjoy folded his *Times*, put on his overcoat and his bowler, nodded a distant goodbye to his fellow travellers and stepped smartly away down the platform.

Bridges, the chauffeur, was waiting with the maroon Rolls Royce Silver Ghost. The Mountjoy crest was engraved discreetly on the doors, surmounted by the curlicued initial 'M'. The interior was of the finest leather; the silver bud-vases by the windows each contained a single perfect burgundy rose and there was a burled-walnut bar fitted with hand-carved crystal decanters filled with fine brandy and sherry, and the appropriate crystal glasses.

'Good morning, my Lord,' Bridges removed his cap and held open the door for his employer. 'Home, sir?'

William sighed. 'I expect so,' he said morosely. He wondered what to do with his day, though of course he knew it would be exactly like all the others, even if it was his seventieth birthday. He would go home to Curzon Street; he would bathe again, for he was a fastidious man and even in first class one was subject to the soot and grit of train travel. He would change his clothing, then stroll through Mayfair to his club where he would have a glass of the fine dark ale many of the members despised, but to which he had taken a liking over the years. He would look around, see who was there, perhaps find a crony to lunch with and gossip about the old days over a bottle of claret and shepherd's pie, a nursery favourite.

He would walk it off later, strolling through St James's Park and down the Mall, swinging his tightly-furled umbrella jauntily and eyeing the guardsmen at the palace, envying them their youth. Then he would make his way back home, take a nap for lack of anything better to do, and see what invitations he had for that evening.

The sky had clouded over and the wind was chilly as he mounted the steps of his splendid, lonely house. The butler was expecting him. He flung open the door, standing back respectfully. 'Good afternoon, my Lord,' he said.

'Afternoon, Johnson,' William handed him his umbrella and his hat and coat.

'The housekeeper ordered a fire to be lit in the library sir,' Johnson said. 'She thought it was a bit chilly and you might like to take a glass of sherry in there, sir.'

'No sherry, Johnson, thank you,' he replied, walking into the library and closing the door.

He sank wearily into the big green-leather wing chair, propping his feet on the brass club-fender with its leather cushions, and gazing round the room. Shelves made of finest Brazilian rosewood soared to the ceiling with their cache of leather-bound books. A priceless collection of ivory miniatures painted in Moghul India was ranged along one wall, next to portraits of the family dogs, through the years: Jack Russells, Labradors and Retrievers, Pomeranians and Pekinese. All had been loved by a Mountjoy and remembered in

7

paint. Photographs and bibelots were scattered on small tables, and Chinese Export lamps in blue and white with pleated burgundy silk shades, somehow blended in with the forest-green fringed-velvet curtains and the carpet in the Mountjoy red and green tartan.

It was William's favourite room in all his homes; he was at his happiest here, these days, reading the newspapers or dozing over the pages of a book after dinner. But today was different.

He got up and began to pace the room restlessly. Back and forth he went, staring at the green and red squares of the carpet. The Great War had decimated the Mountjoy family, killing all the cousins and second cousins and third cousins twice removed, until there were no more. Not even any long-lost relations in foreign parts. Except maybe that black-sheep Georgie Mountjoy's bastards, supposedly scattered across Europe and America.

'I am a lonely old man,' he said out loud. 'My friends are dying. I have no son to inherit all this. This beauty, this tradition. *This name.* When I die, it will all be dispersed. Mountjoy Park will be sold off to pay death duties. Inchkyre Castle will be neglected and fall into disrepair. And Mountjoy House will be pulled down to make way for a new hotel or a department store.'

Turning on his heel, he strode to the massive leather-topped desk and unlocked the centre drawer. He took out the papers it contained and sat for a while studying them. Then he picked up the telephone and dialled the number of his solicitors in Lincoln's Inn Fields. He spoke briefly to his man there, discussed what he needed and told him to call him back immediately he had the information. He would be waiting for his call.

He got up and paced the carpet again, his hands behind his back, thumbs twitching impatiently. Every now and again he stopped by the desk, glaring at the telephone, but it did not ring.

'Damn the blasted thing,' he growled angrily, sinking back into his chair and putting his feet up again. The telephone shrilled and he leapt to answer it. 'Mountjoy,' he said abruptly. Picking up a pencil he wrote down a telephone number, thanked the solicitor, and replaced the receiver.

He stared at the number. This just might be the answer to all his problems. Taking a deep breath he dialled the number of Swayne and Marshall, Private Detectives, of the Strand, London, WC1.

Jerome Swayne jumped when he heard who his caller was. 'I shall come right over, your Lordship,' he said, already buttoning his coat.

By the time he got there, William had organised his thoughts. He knew precisely what he wanted. 'What I want you to do, Swayne, is to find the missing Mountjoys,' he said crisply. 'I want you to seek out Georgie Mountjoy's bastard offspring, in Italy, France and the United States of America.'

Swayne whistled, impressed. He was a tall, slightly-built man with a thin black moustache, receding dark hair and an ex-policeman's flat feet. Lord Mountjoy glared at him and he coughed, covering up the amazed whistle. 'That sounds like a lot of work, sir,' he said guardedly.

'You will be well-paid for it, Swayne, I can assure you. And there will be a substantial bonus; shall we say twenty per cent of your fees, if you are successful.' He handed him a file of papers. 'Here is all the information I have. As you can see, George Mountjoy left a trail behind him, in Paris and Florence. He was finally dis- inherited and banished to Texas, to the old Mountjoy Ranch near San Antonio. No one knows what happened to him after that. He was never heard from again.'

Lord Mountjoy handed Swayne a cheque drawn on Coutts Bank. 'This will take care of your per diem fees for one month, plus your anticipated expenses. And by the way, Swayne, when you find them, you might mention that they *may be hearing something. to their advantage.*' He smiled at his own good idea, thinking how clever he was, and that that should lure them to tell their secrets. 'You are to report back to me at the end of the month and advise me of your progress,' he added. 'Is that clear?'

'Yes, sir, your Lordship.' Swayne leapt to his feet, clutching the cheque. 'You can count on me, sir. If they are still there, Swayne will find them for you. I guarantee it.'

William smiled, delighted with himself, as the door closed be- hind Swayne. 'It's my birthday present to myself,' he said, rubbing his hands in anticipation. 'In fact I think I shall open a bottle of the 1925 Krug, to celebrate.'

The butler carried in the silver tray with the ice bucket. He opened the bottle without spilling a drop and poured it expertly into a heavy crystal glass. 'Will there be anything else, sir?' he asked, standing patiently, waiting.

'Thank you, Johnson, nothing more.' William raised his glass in a silent toast to himself.

'Then may I wish you a happy seventieth birthday, my Lord. And many more of them,' Johnson said.

William gave a great shout of laughter, 'You may, Johnson. Indeed you may. And thank you for your kind wishes.' And he quaffed his champagne, still smiling as he thought of the 'son and heir' Swayne would find for him. His future suddenly took on a pleasing rosy glow. Perhaps seventy wasn't such a bad age, after all.

CHAPTER 2

Jerome Swayne had never made it all the way up to Chief Inspector at Scotland Yard, but he had been a detective there for ten years before he retired. He had his contacts in the French Sûreté, and the Italian Polizia, and with the information Lord Mountjoy had given him, he knew where to start.

He opened the door to his dusty office in the Strand, glancing round as he flicked on the light switch. Everything was as he had left it an hour ago. He unlatched the wobbly sash-window and heaved it upwards a few inches, letting in a waft of freezing damp air that sent the single overhead light, in its cheap glass shade, trembling on its chains. Then he sank into his worn windsor chair, took a crumpled packet of Woodbines from his shirt pocket, shook one out and lit up. He inhaled deeply, coughing. 'Begin at the beginning, Swayne,' he told himself, picking up the phone.

He placed a call to his old friend, Enrico Bastiani of the Rome Polizia. While he waited for the call to come through, he read the information Lord Mountjoy had given him.

Apparently George Albert Arthur Mountjoy had been a young and lowly lieutenant in the Guards when he had inherited a bundle from his doting Aunt Agatha. He had thrown in his career with a whoop of joy, and left immediately for Paris and a life more to his liking.

From the photograph he could see that Georgie was tall and blond and handsome, and apparently he had had a taste for women and the good life. He had cut quite a swathe through Europe, leaving behind him a trail of broken hearts, angry parents and, it seemed, a couple of children, before his own father had disinherited him and banished him to Texas.

Two names featured in the information Georgie's father had collected on his son. One was an Italian woman, Adriana Fioraldi. The

11

other was French, by the name of Marie-France d'Aranville. There was no information on Texas because nothing had been heard from Georgie after he had gone there.

The phone jingled and Swayne picked it up on the first ring.

'Enrico, my old friend,' he bellowed because he didn't trust telephones. 'It's Jerome Swayne here, your old colleague from Scotland Yard. Yes, yes, I am well, and you? I have a puzzle for you, Enrico. Something I know only you could find out, because the woman comes from your home town, Florence.'

He told Enrico Bastiani the story of Lord Mountjoy and his search for his brother's illegitimate offspring. 'The girl with whom he was supposed to have had an affair was named Adriana Fioraldi,' he said finally.

'Fioraldi is a very grand name in Tuscany,' Enrico said, sounding shocked. 'It would seem unlikely that a daughter of that house would kick over the traces.'

'Women are strange and mysterious creatures,' Swayne commented darkly. 'Who knows what they might do?' He sighed like a man of the world, though his own love life had been limited to his pet spaniel and his wife of thirty years, in that order.

'I shall leave the matter in your trustworthy hands, Enrico,' he said finally. '*Arrivederci*,' he added, feeling very cosmopolitan.

Swayne replaced the telephone receiver on its hook. He propped his large flat feet in their polished black boots on his flimsy desk and shook the last Woodbine from the battered packet. He leaned back in his chair, blowing smoke through his nostrils and coughing at the same time, glancing round his small office with a satisfied smile.

From where he sat, he could see the frosted-glass door panel engraved with the title *Swayne and Marshall, Private Investigators*. Of course there was no Marshall. He had just thought it looked better somehow if there were two names, sort of more prosperous. Still, he did all right, he thought, satisfied. There were plenty of society capers to keep him in business. All those beautiful women cheating on their rich husbands, and all those rich men cheating on their dull wives. All those shady hotel-room assignations to be arranged as evidence for the divorce courts, where Lord so-and-so had been found in bed with a floosie who certainly was not his own wife. The upper-classes kept him in business, but he had never been involved in anything as potentially profitable as the Mountjoy case.

Bastiani's response came a few days later. '*Have traced Fioraldi/ Mountjoy child to England. Please telephone to discuss,*' the telegram said.

Swayne could hardly believe his luck. He unhooked the receiver, dialled the overseas operator and placed a call to Rome. His luck was holding: there was only a fifteen minute delay.

'That was a tough assignment you gave me,' Enrico Bastiani complained, but there was a smug note of pleasure in his voice as he recounted his success.

'The old family servants are still loyal,' he said, 'even though most of the family is long since dead; including Adriana. None of them would talk, even when offered money,' he added sounding astonished. 'You know my countrymen, Swayne? They will confide their mother's innermost secrets in return for *lira*. Such loyalty can only be described as feudal.

'Anyhow, Adriana was married to Paolo Torloni, a rich man with estates in the Veneto. It was a very grand wedding and it was reported in all the newspapers. Interestingly, they also mentioned that the wedding had been postponed for a year, "due to the bride's illness". The exact nature of the "illness" was unspecified, but I think, Swayne, you and I can guess her complaint.

'Since I had drawn a blank at the Fioraldi estates,' he continued, 'I decided to go to Torloni, Adriana's husband's estate, where she lived after she was married. I was lucky, I found an old woman who had worked as Adriana's personal maid. She told me she was a wonderful, sweet woman and that the only sadness in the *Signora* Adriana's life was that she had no children. The maid thought it was odd, therefore, that Adriana kept a secret from her husband. A secret she had discovered herself, quite by chance.

'There was a hidden drawer in her vanity table. The maid discovered it when she was dusting. She must have pressed the right spot and the drawer slid out. Inside was a silver box. And inside the silver box was a tiny lock of hair. A mere wisp of a curl. A *baby's* hair, Swayne.'

Swayne drew in a pleased breath. 'The Mountjoy baby.'

'Exactly. And that was not the only item in the drawer. There were also accounts of financial transactions. Of monies transferred abroad, on a regular basis. Until the very year that Adriana died.'

'To the person bringing up her child,' Swayne said quickly.

'To Mrs Jeannie Swinburn, of Swinburn Manor, Yorkshire,' Bastiani finished triumphantly. 'I have the documents right here in my hands. The maid took them after her mistress died, fearing that whatever Adriana's secret was, she certainly would not want anyone else to know.

' "I was no fool, *Signor*," the old woman said to me, "I have children of my own, and now grandchildren. Every mother knows what a baby's first lock of hair looks like. Don't I have them too, treasured in glass frames to keep for ever? I loved the *Signora* Adriana, she treated me like a friend. But she is long since dead. Times are hard in Italy and the money you offer me is most welcome. You tell me it is only good news for her descendants and I believe you; I only want good things for my poor dead *Signora* Adriana." And she crossed herself, kissing the rosary dangling from her fingers.'

Swayne sighed a deep satisfied sigh. 'You have outdone yourself my old friend. I knew I could rely on you. Mountjoy will pay well for this information.'

'Let me know what happens, *amico vecchio*,' Bastiani said.

'If the child is there, Swayne will find it,' Swayne replied, already putting on his hat. 'Trust me.'

Swayne wasted no time. He hurried home to Clapham, patted the brown and white, floppy-eared spaniel who greeted him ecstatically, said a quick hello to his wife and told her to pack his bag with clean underwear and a fresh shirt, starched stiff as a board just the way he liked it. He drank another cup of tea along with his favourite dinner of steak and kidney pie, picked up his bag and headed to the door and King's Cross station where he intended to catch the night train to Leeds.

He hesitated at the door. He turned and looked down at the spaniel. It gazed back at him, with the reproachful eyes of a deserted spouse.

'Er, I think I'll take him with me,' he said, looking at his wife. 'He'll enjoy a bit of a jaunt in the countryside.'

She turned away with a sniff that said he was a silly old fool to carry on so about a dog, and he hastily clipped the lead onto the dog's collar and opened the door. '*Arrivederci*, then. Expect me when you see me,' he called cheerfully. She sniffed again as the door slammed behind him; what else did he expect her to do?

Swayne sat upright, and sleepless, in a third-class carriage, swaying with the movement of the train that stopped at every milk station on the way, grinding through the night until, at last, it pulled into the sooty, grey-granite city of Leeds.

Stifling a yawn, he woke the dog, who had demolished the bacon sandwich he had picked up when the train stopped at Grantham and then slept soundly for the rest of the journey. It bounced from the train, dragging Swayne enthusiastically along the platform until it found a suitable lamp-post to make a stop for the call of nature, then looked expectantly at its exhausted master.

'What time's the next train to Harrogate?' Swayne asked a passing porter.

'Two minutes, platform four. You'd better look sharp,' he was told.

They just made it, the dog puffing and grumbling as Swayne dragged him along. At least this journey was a short one. In no time they were in the charming small spa town of Harrogate, though they could scarcely see it under the swirl of snowflakes. The hell with the investigation, Swayne thought. He needed nourishment and rest.

He made directly for the Old Swan Hotel, a lavish oak-beamed establishment where he booked a room, then headed for the dining room, where he put away a large breakfast of bacon, sausage, eggs, tomatoes and fried bread, and copious amounts of hot sweet tea. He felt like a new man.

He walked the dog, then retreated to his cosy room, removed his shoes, climbed onto the bed, put his hands behind his head and contemplated the ceiling and the mysterious Mrs Jeannie Swinburn. The spaniel eyed him for a moment, then it leapt onto the bed and lay beside him, its devoted, drooping eyes fixed on his face. They were still fixed on him when he awoke two hours later.

'My, my,' Swayne said, pulling his watch from the pocket of his waistcoat, hand-knitted by his wife. 'One o'clock already. Time for a pint I think. And maybe a bite along with it,' he added, patting his stomach and remembering with pleasure that Lord Mountjoy was paying for all this.

'And then we shall pursue our enquiries,' he told the dog. He smiled and the dog barked enthusiastically at a sign of action.

'I swear you understand every word,' Swayne said admiringly as he clipped on the lead.

There was a roaring fire in the bar and a good pint of Tetley's best dark bitter with a roast beef sandwich to accompany it. Swayne looked at the swirling snow outside the window. 'I wish we could leave our enquiries for tomorrow,' he told the dog wistfully, handing him half his sandwich. But duty called.

An hour later he had hired a car and was on his way to Swinburn Manor.

CHAPTER 3

Jeannie Swinburn was an old lady when Swayne came calling at her house in Yorkshire, that freezing January afternoon. She was smaller and thinner than she used to be when she was young, with a comfortably rounded bosom, pink cheeks and silver-white hair piled on top, the way she had worn it since she was a girl. And though her blue eyes had dimmed with age, her intellect certainly had not.

Snow was falling lightly and she peered interestedly from behind the curtains as the little black Austin 7 skidded up her driveway and jerked to a stop. Swayne stepped cautiously out, closing the door on the spaniel who gave a resentful bark. He stood looking at the house, and Jeannie looked at him through the window.

'Gladys,' she called to the housekeeper who had looked after both her and the house for the past ten years. 'Who is this remarkable looking man, standing on my doorstep?'

Gladys peered through the curtains with her. 'Damned if I know, Mrs Swinburn,' she said cheerfully. 'But I'll go and find out.'

She came back minutes later. 'He says he's a Mr Swayne, and he needs to talk to you. *Private business*,' she added with a disparaging sniff, because everybody thereabouts knew everything about everybody else anyway.

'Show him in,' Jeannie said, tickled to have such a mysterious visitor. 'We'll soon find out what this *"private"* stuff is all about.'

'Good afternoon, madam,' Swayne said, standing in the doorway, clutching his hat and his overcoat.

'Come in, for goodness sake,' Jeannie called. 'My eyesight's not too good any more and I can't see you clearly, over there in the shadows.'

Swayne stepped forward and Jeannie looked him up and down appraisingly. 'My goodness,' she said finally, 'you look like a policeman.'

17

'Twenty-five years on the force, madam.' Swayne smiled proudly. 'Retired now. But still in the investigating business, you might say. I'm a private detective.'

Jeannie laughed delightedly. 'It sounds just like an American gangster film,' she said. 'My granddaughter sees them at the picture-house in Harrogate. She tells me all about them. Acts them out for me, with all the proper accents and so on. She's quite a little actress herself, I always tell her, but she's going to marry Haddon Fox and become a racehorse-trainer. Imagine? A girl who looks like Laura, a trainer?' She laughed again, and Swayne's dour face cracked into a smile too.

'I'm afraid I do not have the pleasure of knowing your granddaughter, madam,' he said, 'but she is the reason I am here.'

'Oh, for goodness sake, Swayne, there's no need to be so pompous just because you're a "cop".' She grinned at him, pleased with herself for knowing the American jargon. 'Just tell me why you are here, that's all.'

She listened eagerly while Swayne told her about Lord Mountjoy, and the story of Georgie and how his investigations had led him to Swinburn Manor, and to her. And very probably to her granddaughter, Laura, who, he said importantly, 'would shortly be hearing *something to her advantage*'.

'Well, well,' Jeannie said when he had finished. 'The cat seems to be out of the bag all right, and since poor Adriana is dead now, there seems no point in trying to keep it all a secret. So yes, Mr Swayne, it seems that my Laura *is* Georgie Mountjoy's granddaughter. And now that Lord Mountjoy will know, what exactly does he propose to do about it?'

'I'm afraid I do not have the answer to that, madam,' Swayne stood up and put on his overcoat. 'I must get back to Harrogate before it gets dark, Mrs Swinburn,' he said, thinking longingly of the comfortable bar at the Old Swan; of the roaring fire and a pint of Tetley's Best Bitter to wash down a good dinner, and all paid for by his Lordship.

'Well, tell Lord Mountjoy, whatever he expects from Laura, he will have me to deal with,' Jeannie said tartly. 'And make no mistake about it.'

'I'll tell him, Mrs Swinburn,' Swayne promised. The snow had stopped and he prayed it would hold off until he made it back.

Jeannie looked thoughtful as she watched him go. She knew her time was running out, and so was the Swinburns' money. The farm barely paid its way any more, what with wages being so high, and tied cottages for the help. Sending Laura to school at Queen Ethelburga's had cost a small fortune too. Laura had not wanted to go, but Jeannie had known it was wrong to keep her at Swinburn, virtually alone with her, for ever. It had been the right thing – the only thing – to do.

The Marchesa Fioraldi's money had kept the Swinburns in reasonably good style for many years, but it was long since gone. Perhaps this time, the *Mountjoy* money will save us, she thought, as Gladys came in with her evening glass of sherry and a Bath Oliver biscuit. Though it's a safe bet that old Lord Mountjoy does not know what he's taking on when he meets my Laura. And she laughed again, delightedly, thinking of how it had all begun, so many years ago.

Swinburn Manor, where Jeannie and Laura lived, in the tiny hamlet of Swinburn in the Yorkshire Dales, was not really a manor house at all. It was a Bradford wool-merchant's house. Sometime in its past it had belonged to a local man who had made a quick, but quite small, fortune in the woollen mills. He had elevated its status, and his own, by calling it 'The Manor', dubbing himself 'The Squire', and taking on the name of Swinburn.

The land was beautiful: deep rolling green hills dotted with fine old oaks and chestnuts, and the brown, thick-fleeced Jacob sheep that the wool merchant had kept as a hobby rather than a business. The house was not so charming. The downstairs reception rooms were over-large and the ceilings too high, making them impossible to heat, and the upstairs rooms were pokey. In the harsh Yorkshire winters, the view from the mullioned windows was permanently obscured for weeks, sometimes months on end, by a coating of hoar-frost, even though fires roared continually in every grate, fuelled by the good Yorkshire coal brought from the open-cast mines not too many miles away.

But, a couple of generations later, when the Marchesa Fioraldi and her pregnant daughter Adriana arrived, the long-dead wool-merchant's fortune had dwindled considerably and the cost of living had risen. Ends simply were not meeting for Swinburn's grandson and his wife, Jeannie, who had inherited the old place. Bad investments had been made and vast amounts of money spent on improving the house, including installing a cumbersome system of central heating that clanked and rattled and shuddered terrifyingly, but at least took the deathly chill off the rooms.

The decor had not been changed in years and was *haute* Victorian, all red velvet, bobble fringes and heavy mahogany furniture. The plush sofas were stuffed with scratchy horsehair, and dusty aspidistras mouldered in ornate china containers in the windows. Two things saved Swinburn Manor from choking on its own fraying, outdated luxury. One was its kitchen, and the other the sunny disposition of Jeannie and Joshua Swinburn, and their two children: Agnes, aged six, and Freddie, aged nine.

Joshua ran the farm well enough but he could not afford much help and relied mostly on his sheep, many of them descendants of the original Jacob flock. Jeannie ran the house with the aid of a lady from the village, who seemed to spend most of her time mopping muddy paw prints from the floors. There were five dogs, all black and white border collies, specialists in sheep-herding. They were supposed to live outside in the cowbarns or the stables, but would sneak in the door, slinking low to the ground, imagining they would not be noticed. Of course, they always were and after a few half-hearted attempts to throw them out, which both they and Jeannie knew were merely for show, they lolled happily in front of the roaring fire, lifting their noses to sniff the delicious smells coming from the old, black cast-iron stove. Because Jeannie was a superlative Yorkshire cook.

Jeannie's shepherd's pie, her stews and hotpots and her Sunday roasts, could not have been bettered by a French chef. Her Yorkshire puddings floated to stellar heights under their burden of rich brown onion gravy. Her baking was not to be sniffed at either – except to enjoy the aromas of fresh bread, scones and baps, crusty apple pies and rich fruit cakes, stuffed with sultanas and dates and cherries. And then of course, there was her trifle, always the centrepiece of the sideboard at family occasions: a cut crystal bowl filled with sherry-soaked sponge cake with layers of home-made raspberry jam, fresh berries, rich vanilla custard, and, topping the lot, a thick layer of whipped cream – fresh from their own cows.

'You could always get a job as a cook,' Joshua joked, when

times were hard. 'Those rich wool merchants in Leeds or Bradford would hire you away from me in a minute. Or else you could open a hotel.'

Jeannie thought about what he had said, sitting at the big square, scrubbed-white kitchen table, shelling peas into a colander the following afternoon. Of course she could not get a job as a cook, Joshua was just joking. And she certainly could not open a hotel. But they *were* awfully short of money and there must be something she could do to help. The house was big enough to accommodate a few more people besides themselves. Perhaps in the summer months, when people wanted to get away from their factories and offices for a bit of a holiday, she could take in a few paying guests. Just two or three. It wouldn't be much extra work; after all she cooked for her family anyway, and the bedrooms were going spare.

She was excited when she spoke to Joshua about it that evening, and there was appreciation as well as love in his dark eyes when he looked at her. 'You're a grand lass, Jeannie Swinburn,' he said, smiling. 'But a man should be able to take care of his own wife and family.'

The two children sat opposite them at the kitchen table, munching thick slices of bread, fresh from the oven and slathered with butter and home-made blackberry jam. Their eyes, blue like their mother's, were enormous with interest, but they knew better than to interrupt the grown-ups.

Jeannie's face turned pink at her husband's compliment. She was a bonnie woman, small and brown-haired and bustling, and always on the move. Even as she spoke, she was busy whisking eggs and sugar into a batter for a Victoria sponge, to be sent with the children to Mrs Hodgkiss in the village, who was recovering from a bad fall. Jeannie's hands and her mind were never idle.

'It's worth a try, Joshua,' she said quietly. 'After all, times are bad. We all have to pull our weight. Even you children,' she added, smiling at them. 'You will be a big help to me, won't you.' They nodded amiably, their mouths full. 'I thought perhaps an advertisement in the newspaper,' she suggested.

'You mean the *Yorkshire Post*?'

'That, and *The Times*.'

He laughed, 'Nobody in these parts reads the London papers.'

'That's exactly it,' she said eagerly. 'Locals won't want to come here. Oh, maybe a few, but I thought people from the big city, stuck in all that smoke and fog all year, well they might welcome a break in fresh country air. And besides, Swinburn Manor sounds quite grand. Grand enough to tempt a few of those snobbish city folks, I'll bet.'

Joshua was not sure he ever agreed to her scheme, but anyhow the advertisement duly appeared in *The Times*.

> *Comfortable accommodation offered in private home. Remote Manor House in beautiful Yorkshire Dales. Excellent home-cooked fare with fresh produce from own farm. Beautiful walks, stables, boating on nearby river. Ideal for relaxation and fresh air. Apply, Swinburn Manor, Swinburn, Yorkshire.*

And that was the ad Adriana Fioraldi's frantic mother leapt upon like a saviour from heaven, when she picked up a copy of the London *Times* in the tearoom of Brown's Hotel in Dover Street, London, where she had fled with her daughter after discovering the tragic truth about her condition, and about Georgie Mountjoy, the man who had seduced her.

CHAPTER 4

They were at their palatial country home in Florence when the Marchesa Fioraldi found out her daughter was pregnant. Her first thought was to get Adriana out of range of her father's wrath, *and* out of sight of her inquisitive friends and neighbours, as well as the servants, who were always quick to pick up on these things. And particularly, to get her daughter away before she spoke to her fiancé Paolo and told him the truth. That she loved Georgie Mountjoy passionately and wanted to marry him, but unfortunately he did not love her.

'You silly little fool,' her mother said to her for the hundredth time, at Brown's Hotel, pouring tea elegantly, the way she did everything. 'Adriana, how could you do such a thing?'

'It was easy Mama,' Adriana replied calmly. 'I loved Georgie. And I don't love Paolo. Oh, maybe I do, but it's different. *Oh Mama,*' she wailed loudly, '*you must know what I mean.*'

The Marchesa, who had married according to the wishes of her family and whose life had been calm and content, uncluttered by passionate outbursts and wild love-affairs, certainly did *not* understand. 'Kindly keep your voice down, Adriana,' she ordered, 'and listen to what I am about to say to you. I have brought you to London for your own good.'

Then she lowered her own voice until it was scarcely audible, even to Adriana. 'Paolo and his family have been told that you are not feeling well. You have been brought to London to see a Harley Street specialist; you are fatigued and unexpectedly weary. You need a change of air, *fresh country air*, to ensure you do not succumb to tuberculosis. The wedding will be postponed. You will have your child in secret, here in England, where no one knows you. The child will be found a home and you will return and marry

23

Paolo. This whole disgraceful episode will be put behind you and never referred to again.'

She glanced piercingly at her daughter. Adriana's dark head was bowed and a tear trickled down her pale cheek. 'Is that quite clear, Adriana?'

Adriana nodded numbly. What choice did she have? Georgie had loved her and left her. She had thought him so handsome, so debonair, so vibrantly attractive, when he strode into the Villa Fioraldi that first day. He was different from the dark, saturnine Paolo; Georgie was lusty and full of life and laughter. Minutes spent with Georgie meant more to her than days with her fiancé. And she had sensed he liked her too, that very first day.

'How lovely you are, *bella* Adriana,' he had said admiringly, holding her eyes with his own. But Georgie had not been the seducer; Adriana had met him half way, flirting with him, leading him on, then withdrawing. She was a pretty girl, with long smooth dark hair, enormous brown eyes, and a flawless olive-toned complexion. She was not too tall, but she had beautiful posture, a long graceful neck and pretty legs. And she was an expert flirt.

It was by no means all Georgie Mountjoy's fault, and her father knew that. 'I would make the scoundrel marry you,' he had thundered, pacing up and down the *gran salòtto* of the Villa Fioraldi, 'if I didn't know that he was no good. And wicked as you are, I do not intend to marry you off to a worthless younger son with no prospects, a man whose own family are ready to disown him.' And then he had left matters in the hands of his capable wife, the Marchesa.

In fact Georgie had offered, reluctantly, to marry Adriana when she had told him her news in a long soul-searching letter to him in Bavaria, where he was visiting friends. But she knew his heart was not in it. And she knew too that he had loved her only for the moment, and that he would be endlessly unfaithful and cause her deep unhappiness. After a lot of thought, she wrote back, refusing him. Georgie promised if she ever needed him, he would be there and he asked her please to give the child his name. After that, Adriana agreed to do as her mother told her.

'I think I have found just the place,' the Marchesa said, re-reading Jeannie Swinburn's advertisement, thoughtfully.

24

'*Swinburn Manor . . . Remote . . . Countryside . . . Home-cooking . . .* Yes, this place certainly sounds worth investigating. I shall telegraph them immediately and arrange a visit.'

Adriana listened glumly to what she said. All the things that appealed to her mother sounded like a death knell to her. '*Remote*' meant she would never see anyone at all. And she hated the country-side; even in Italy she preferred the urban pleasures of Florence or Rome. And in her condition she could barely even look at food, no matter how good it was. 'Yes, Mama,' she agreed listlessly, facing up to what she was about to endure and wondering whether she would not have been better off marrying Georgie, after all. At least, she thought, wistfully, it would have been fun. For a while.

Jeannie Swinburn had the house scrubbed and brushed and polished from top to bottom for her distinguished visitors. 'An Italian Marchesa, no less,' she told Joshua, impressed.

He said thoughtfully, 'And what, I wonder, brings a grand Italian Marchesa out to the wilds of Yorkshire? I should have thought Paris or Biarritz more her style. Anyhow, just tell me when she's coming, and I shall stay out of your way.' He grinned. 'It wouldn't do for the farmer to come clomping in to say how d'you do, in his muddy boots, reeking of cow manure, and the dogs jumping all over her and the furniture. Not quite what she expects of Swinburn Manor, I'll bet.'

He roared with laughter and Jeannie joined in, and the children laughed too, because their parents were laughing and the dogs barked just for the hell of it. Jeannie hoped that the Marchesa was the kind of woman who did not mind a bit of noise, and mud, and animals, because, truthfully, she did sound a little grander than Jeannie had bargained for when she had placed her advertisement in *The Times*.

A jolting old hansom cab brought the Marchesa and her daughter from the nearest railway station, a journey of more than fifteen miles. It was pouring with rain and they had to stop every five minutes so Adriana could be sick, and the Marchesa gritted her teeth, thinking her spine would crack if there was one more jolt. Then the cab got stuck in the mud near the gate and she and Adriana were forced to walk up the rutted gravel drive, for half a mile, to the Manor.

At first glance, she thought they must have come to the wrong place. '*This* is an English *Manor House*?' she said, staring at the four-square, grey-stone Yorkshire mill-owner's dwelling. '*This* is how the English upper-class lives?'

She tugged on the brass bellpull and they waited, listening to the sonorous drip-drip of rain on the shrubbery. 'And this is only September,' she thought, shivering in the damp air. 'Oh my poor, poor daughter.' But she hardened her heart. Adriana had done wrong. She was completely unrepentant. Her daughter had to be punished.

'Hello, hello. Oh please, do come on in, out of the wet.' Jeannie Swinburn stood in the doorway, smiling broadly at them. Her face was pink from baking and excitement, and her shiny brown hair was escaping from its bun, trailing in little curling wisps round her face.

Adriana found herself smiling back, despite the fact that she was determined not to like this place and had planned to storm and rage and shed tears if necessary, to get her mother to take her back to Italy.

The Marchesa swept inside, glancing to the left and right as Jeannie led them to the drawing room where tea was already set. A fire roared in the iron grate and Adriana sank thankfully into the chair closest to it.

'You look dreadfully pale, my dear,' Jeannie said, looking worriedly at her. 'I know it was a long journey, and the country roads are so bumpy. Perhaps a hot cup of tea will set you up again.' And she poured tea from a massive silver Victorian pot, brought out from its green felt-lined case and polished up specially for the occasion. Normally, the family used the big brown kitchen pot that Joshua swore made better tea than any fancy silver one. And the cups she used today, were old Royal Doulton, so fine and transparent you could see through them, and the silver spoons were worn thin from generations of use, but they were 'good'. They were all brought out for this special tea. *And* she had been up half the night, baking and preparing.

'Don't be so daft, woman,' Joshua had teased her. 'They are too posh for the likes of us. They'll never stay for more than five minutes.'

But here they were – and they had stayed, because already ten minutes had passed and the Marchesa was sipping her tea and looking thoughtful. And the daughter, such a pretty girl, though she did look unwell, was relaxing. She was even reaching out for one of Jeannie's shortbread biscuits.

'Well now,' Jeannie smiled encouragingly at them, 'isn't this nice. I'm sorry about the weather, but it *is* late in September. Though my husband says we are due for an Indian summer this year.' She laughed gaily. 'Now that would be just right for your holiday, wouldn't it?'

The Marchesa said nothing. She placed her cup on the table that had been polished so she could have seen her face in it, had she cared to, while the daughter nibbled on her biscuit and stared sadly out of the window at the dripping landscape. Jeannie heard a scratching at the door. She glared as a dog poked its nose through. '*Out*,' she hissed. Thankfully, for once, the animal obeyed; all she needed was the dogs jumping on the sofa and the Marchesa.

'Mrs Swinburn,' the Marchesa said suddenly. 'I am sure you have realised that your home, charming though it is, is not the sort of place to which a woman like myself would normally come for a holiday.'

'Oh . . . I'm sorry, Marchesa,' Jeannie said, flustered. 'I hope my advertisement didn't mislead you in any way. I know we are a little out of the way, but I did mention it was remote.'

'You mistake my point, Mrs Swinburn,' the Marchesa said firmly. 'And the fact that your home is *remote* is one of the reasons it appealed to me.' She leaned forward, inspecting Jeannie's face intently.

Jeannie felt herself flushing again. She wished she did not always blush when she was flustered. 'Perhaps another cup of tea,' she offered, brightly.

'I think you are a woman I can trust, *Signora*. I am sure that by now you understand that there is another, quite different reason for my being here.' The Marchesa inclined her head towards Adriana, who was still staring broodingly out of the window, ignoring the conversation.

Jeannie followed her glance. 'Your daughter?' she said. Then quickly, 'Oh, I do hope she is not ill, she is so pale and quiet.'

'My daughter is suffering from a malady familiar to most females, *Signora*,' the Marchesa said abruptly. 'But it is, I am afraid, a malady that usually affects only *married* women.'

'Ohhh,' Jeannie said, as the Marchesa proceeded to tell her the sorry little story.

'So you see, the reason I am here – the reason Adriana must stay here, is so that she can have the . . . the event can take place quietly.'

'In secret,' Jeannie said, helpfully.

'Precisely.'

Jeannie looked at Adriana. The girl's sad dark eyes met hers imploringly. She hesitated, remembering her own happiness when she was pregnant with her first child. She could only imagine how terrible it was to be in Adriana's situation.

'Well,' she said hesitantly, still unsure, 'it is a bit more than I had bargained for. I mean I had thought only of paying guests . . .'

'This guest would pay you very well, *Signora* Swinburn,' the Marchesa said briskly. 'Money is not an issue. I shall pay you extravagantly to care for my daughter, and see her through this dreadful time.' She leaned forward and added, in a lower voice, 'And I shall pay you a great deal more money, more than you have ever dreamed of having, *Signora*, if you will take the child into your own home. I promise, on the honour of my family, the child will lack for nothing. And nor, *Signora*, will you and your family.'

Jeannie did not know what to say at first. Then she thought about Adriana, whose life had been ruined by a scoundrel, and about her fiancé in Italy and the wonderful life that awaited her as his wife; and then about the poor unwanted baby.

'I shall have to speak to my husband,' she said at last. But the Marchesa could tell she had already made up her mind. And, if she was any judge of character, the husband was going to agree to whatever his charming wife wanted.

'I shall feel quite confident, leaving my daughter in your hands, *Signora* Swinburn,' she said, accepting another cup of tea. 'Perhaps, afterwards, we might take a look at Adriana's rooms? I should like her to be comfortable.'

The Marchesa was right about the husband, of course, and Adriana was left with the Swinburns for the duration of her pregnancy.

For the first few days, Adriana kept to her rooms, and Jeannie was kept busy running up and down the stairs with trays. Breakfast trays, elevenses trays, lunch trays, tea-trays, dinner trays, supper trays . . . 'Does the girl do nothing but eat?' Joshua wondered.

Finally, unable to bear it any longer, the first day the sun came out, glinting on the wet grass and steaming the dampness from the earth, Jeannie sent the children and the dogs in to cheer Adriana up.

Adriana came down an hour later, preceded by the rushing dogs and hand-in-hand with Freddie and Agnes. 'We are going for a walk,' she told Jeannie, who was sitting on the steps outside the kitchen door, stringing beans for lunch.

'Good,' she said calmly. 'See if there are any blackberries left on the bushes near the long meadow. There may be wild raspberries too, further along. I shall make a pie for supper.' But there was a pleased little smile on her face as she watched them go.

From that day on, Adriana became one of the Swinburn family. She was treated as if she were their own daughter; no better, no worse. Jeannie bossed her the way she bossed all of them, and Adriana thrived on it. She told Jeannie all about Georgie, and how she knew she could not marry him because he would be unfaithful to her; he would make her miserable and then she would feel like killing herself.

'This baby will be yours, Jeannie,' she said, 'and I cannot think of a better mother. Better than I would be myself.'

Even though Adriana was not yet aware of it, Jeannie knew what it would cost her to give up her child. 'It is the price of your freedom, Adriana my dear,' she told her, when, helped by the local midwife, Adriana's son was born six months later. Adriana wept bitter tears, but she knew Jeannie was right.

A few weeks later, Jeannie and Joshua drove her to the railway station and put her on the train to London. 'I shall never see you again, *cara*, Jeannie,' she wept, flinging her arms round her and clinging tightly. 'Nor my little son. I don't know which is worse,' she added, because she had come to love Jeannie more than her own mother.

'I shall think of you,' Jeannie promised. 'And I shall tell your son how lovely you were, and how you loved him.'

'And that I died giving birth to him,' Adriana added, tragically.

'If that is what you wish,' Jeannie agreed. Her own eyes brimmed with tears as the engine puffed steam and the guard began slamming doors. Adriana climbed into the first-class carriage. She leaned from the window, staring tearfully at them as the train chuffed its way out of the station, and Jeannie took her little white handkerchief and waved it until the speck in the distance that was Adriana, finally vanished into the mist. For ever.

29

CHAPTER 5

Lorenzo Mountjoy Swinburn was christened in the little Norman church of St Swithen by the vicar, the Reverend Mr Oates, at a ceremony attended by almost the entire hamlet of Swinburn, all sixty inhabitants, the exception being Mrs Hodgkiss whose hip was still bothering her, and Ethel Aykeroyd, who was visiting her sister in Barnsley and who, to her chagrin, missed the whole thing.

Everyone knew the story of course – it was impossible, in such a small community, to keep an event like this a secret. But they did not know Adriana's true identity, nor the facts of what had happened. Just that the girl had been in trouble; Jeannie and Joshua Swinburn had taken her in, and, out of Christian charity, they were adopting her child. Adriana had spent the long winter months amongst them; she had celebrated Christmas in this same tiny church, and they had come to like her. Besides, they could tell she was a lady, and they were sorry that she had been 'wronged' by a man. So, in a way, little Lorenzo belonged to all of them, and they were thrilled when Jeannie chose two of their members to stand as his godparents, along with her own brother.

Lorenzo did not look in the least bit like his father, Georgie. He looked just like Adriana; olive-skinned and dark-haired with brown, long-lashed eyes. He was stockier than Georgie too, and he would never be as tall, but he certainly was a handsome lad. And a happy one.

Lorenzo always said no one could ever have had a better childhood than he did. He loved Swinburn, where he was the apple of the eye of all the villagers. He was always welcome at their cottages where they offered him whatever was fresh from their ovens, and a glass of milk, still frothing from the cow. Or, if it were Sunday and close to lunchtime, a tiny sip of rich brown ale from a pint mug, followed by a glass of lemonade, sitting in the sunshine on a wooden bench outside the diminutive Red Lion pub.

Jeannie always said she never knew where to find Lorenzo; the whole village was his home. But she never worried about him; she knew he would come to no harm with so many willing friends to look after him.

Lorenzo knew that he was not Joshua and Jeannie's own child. They had thought it wrong to lie to him, but they had kept their promise and he did not know his birth-mother's name. 'It doesn't matter,' he told Jeannie, gladdening her heart, 'I would have chosen you over all the other mothers anyway.'

Lorenzo attended primary school in the nearby village of Moorcroft. Then the local Grammar School where he was a weekly boarder, and then he won a place at Cambridge.

Jeannie was so proud of him the day she and Joshua accompanied him to his college to see him safely installed. She thought about Adriana and wished she could have seen her son, but she could not even write to her and tell her how wonderful he was. It was forbidden, in her agreement with the Marchesa.

Still, each year, when Lorenzo's birthday came around, she wondered if Adriana might succumb to a longing to know about him, half-expecting to see her walking up the drive to the house. But she never did. And Jeannie kept her part of the bargain punctiliously. In her heart, Lorenzo was as much her son as her own boy, Freddie, was.

But then Lorenzo did something quite out of character. After two years at Cambridge, he chucked it all in and joined the Navy.

'Dearest Mam and Dad,' he wrote them. 'I find I am too restless for this static way of life. I always thought I would end up farming our acres anyway, and not teaching snotty-nosed little brats how to parse a sentence in some out of the way little prep school. Or, at best, tutoring foolish young men like myself, in a venerable old Cambridge college, dining too well and savouring fine wines and enjoying the sound of my own voice too much, as I became a pompous and respected Fellow. I need to live. They always say "Join The Navy And See The World". So here I go. "Forgive me, dear parents, for I know not what I do",' he misquoted airily at the bottom of the now tear-stained page, because Jeannie had read it six times.

'Oh, Josh, he's gone and joined the Navy,' she wailed.

Josh looked up from the farm accounts. He thought about it for a moment. 'Don't worry,' he said confidently, 'he'll be back.'

And he was, though much later than they thought. It was at the end of a long harsh war, and it was minus a leg and with a brand-new bride.

But Freddie, her first-born and keeper of a special portion of her heart, was not so lucky. He had been killed in the trenches at Ypres and buried with hundreds of others in a cemetery in the French countryside that she knew she would never see. It was a tragedy she knew she would never overcome, but she did not allow it to diminish her joy at seeing her other 'son' again.

It was the same old charming Lorenzo all right, standing there in the front hall of Swinburn Manor, stocky and dark-haired, his brown eyes dancing with laughter. Jeannie felt a tug at her heart for her maimed son, so brave and carefree, accepting his disablement as he had always accepted everything: stoically and with grace. 'Oh Adriana,' she thought again, 'you would be so proud of our boy.'

Lorenzo looked at her. He knew she was thinking about what had happened to him and he gave her a cheery grin. 'It's okay, Mom,' he said, enfolding her in a giant hug. 'Now, I want you to meet my wife, Marella.'

He took the young woman's hand and drew her into his charmed family circle. She stood there, smiling shyly at them. 'As you can see,' Lorenzo said, laughing, 'she is small and blonde and very pretty. And though she speaks good English, she is, of course, Italian. Like myself.'

'Welcome, my dear,' Jeannie said, embracing her new daughter-in-law. Joshua followed suit, and then Agnes, who had married an engineer and was about to join him in South Africa, where he was building new bridges.

'We met at Forte de Marmi, a little seaside resort on the Adriatic coast,' Lorenzo told them, over lunch. 'Lots of good Italian families take their children there for the holidays. I happened to be convalescing in a nearby hospital, and Marella came in to cheer up the poor soldiers. And as you can see, she succeeded mightily.' He laughed and dropped a kiss on her cheek. 'I think it was my Italian name that caught her interest,' he added.

'And what was *your* name, my dear?' Jeannie said, pressing another helping of fluffy bread and butter pudding onto her son.

'My family name is Fioraldi,' Marella said shyly. 'We are from Tuscany.'

Jeannie put down the dish carefully. The blood pounded in her ears, deafening her, as she met Josh's eyes across the table. She noticed he had turned pale, and for the first time in her life she could find nothing to say.

'Fioraldi,' Josh said, breaking the silence. 'That is quite a distinguished Italian name, is it not? I seem to remember reading about a Marchese? Or am I wrong?'

'You are correct, *Signor*.' Marella gave him her shy little smile. 'The Marchese is my uncle. He was the eldest brother; he inherited the title and the land, and is rich. My father always jokes that he is just a poor *paesano*, tending his vines in Chianti, but in fact he is almost speaking the truth. Of course he is not a peasant, but he is certainly not rich, and he works hard in his vineyard.'

Marella shrugged, spreading her palms upwards expressively, as she continued. 'Some years his vines do well, some years they do not; but Papa says he makes a living and he eats and drinks well. He invested all his money in the vineyard, but it was neglected in the war and a lot of damage was done. Papa married late in life; he is an old man, now, and failing in health. And, sadly, Mama died young. So you see,' she added, sweetly, 'it is so nice for me to join Lorenzo's family, because I never really had one of my own. My father and his brother had not spoken for twenty years, and I was brought up alone.'

Jeannie passed some comment that seemed to be appropriate. Her head was full of the Fioraldis. She looked at Josh and knew he had already figured out that Lorenzo had married his cousin. Of all the girls in the world he might have chosen, she thought worriedly, he had to choose Marella Fioraldi.

Later that weekend, when she and Lorenzo were alone on a rainy walk through the quiet hills, she broke her promise to the Marchesa and Adriana, and told him the truth. Then she waited, with terror in her heart, for what he might say.

Lorenzo limped slowly along, staring into the distance, before he spoke. 'I met Adriana,' he said at last. 'She came to my wedding. It was a very small affair because things were still chaotic in Italy, so soon after the war. Of course, a family like the Fioraldis who seem to be closer to God, and certainly to the Pope, than the rest of us, arranged a splendid ceremony with my own minister sent specially from Rome, and her priest, and a Cardinal or two. So Marella did not have to make do with merely a civil ceremony and, in the eyes of God, we are properly married.'

Jeannie stopped and looked at him and he gave her a wry little smile. 'It's raining hard now,' he said. 'Do you want to go back?' She shook her head and they walked on.

'*Signora* Adriana arrived early with her husband, Paolo Torloni. She brought Marella a very extravagant present. A diamond necklace. I could tell Marella was surprised and, to tell the truth, so was I. Marella only ever saw her at family gatherings, you know, funerals, baptisms, weddings – occasions like that. Anyhow, *Signora* Adriana Torloni came over to me. She put her hands on my shoulders and looked into my face, sort of . . . well, searchingly, I thought. "What a fine young man you are, Lorenzo," she said, in a very quiet little voice. I could tell she felt emotional and I didn't understand why. Then she kissed me twice on each cheek and held me close for a moment, and that was that.'

Lorenzo walked on for a while, then he said, 'I've thought a lot about her since then. Wondering about her. And I think I had already arrived at the truth. After all, I look just like her, don't I?'

Jeannie nodded. 'She was a lovely girl.'

'And now she is a very beautiful woman.' Lorenzo took Jeannie's arm and pulled her to him. 'But she is not as lovely as my mother.' He was smiling as he said it but Jeannie knew he meant it and the great cloud that had seemed to shroud her ever since she knew, lifted and dispersed as though it had never been. Especially when Lorenzo gave her a resounding kiss and said, 'And when they finally let me out of the Navy, I'm coming home to help farm these glorious acres. I shall never roam again, I promise you. Why should I, when everything I want is right here, in these beautiful Yorkshire Dales?'

Lorenzo was true to his word and later, when their baby girl was born on a glorious early summer morning, he and Marella, his family and the entire village celebrated the occasion. Of course the baptism was a little tricky, but they compromised on the village church for the time being, with the promise of a later Catholic ceremony when their daughter was old enough to visit her aged grandfather in Italy.

Unfortunately little Laura Lavinia Mountjoy Swinburn never did get to go to Italy, nor did she see her Italian grandfather. The old man died peacefully in his bed a year later, and of course her parents set off on the journey to Tuscany for his funeral.

Their cross-channel ferry collided with a freighter in dense fog and sank within minutes. They were just off Cherbourg when it happened and help was quickly to hand. More than sixty people were rescued, but Lorenzo and Marella were not among them.

So once more, Jeannie and Joshua were left to care for a small child who was not their own. Then, ultimately, when Joshua died, it was Jeannie who brought up Laura, alone at Swinburn Manor, from which she had rarely strayed more than fifty miles in her life.

At that same moment that Jeannie was speaking to Swayne, twenty year old Laura Swinburn was standing in the swirling snow in Foxton Yard, a well-known racehorse training stable owned by the wealthy Fox family. She was staring into the treacherous eyes of Haddon Fox, the man she had believed loved her. The man she had planned to marry, one day, when his snobbish aristocratic family finally got used to the idea of his marrying 'beneath him' as he not-so-delicately phrased it.

Laura had known Haddon all her life. She had worked as a stable-girl at Foxton Yard in the school holidays, riding his magnificent horses. She thought she must have been in love with him since she was thirteen. There had been kisses; promises of being together always; of being his wife. And now Haddon was walking towards her, holding the hand of a rather plain, unsmiling young woman, dressed in expensive country tweeds.

'Oh Laura,' Haddon said, dropping his bombshell as casually as if there had been nothing between them, 'I would like to introduce my fiancée, Lady Diana Gilmore.'

Laura's luminous whisky-brown eyes widened with shock. In the space of a minute her whole future went down the stableyard drain. She shook her head as though he had struck her a blow, sending her glossy chestnut brown hair swinging round her shoulders. 'I just bet you would,' she cried scornfully, when she finally caught her breath. 'You . . . you *worm*.' She stamped her foot. Unfortunately she was

36

standing in a puddle and droplets of dirty water splashed all over Lady Diana's immaculate skirt.

Laura's eyes blazed angrily. 'I'll bet you didn't tell her about us, did you? Of course not,' she answered herself. 'Well, Haddon, you did well for yourself. Your parents always wanted you to marry money – and now you've got a title to go with it.'

She glared at him, eyes flashing, chin up, back arrow straight; then stalked away across the yard. At the gate, she turned for one last look. They were watching her, still holding hands, and there was a superior little smile on Haddon's face. At that moment Laura decided she would get even with him if it was the last thing she ever did. She would show that treacherous bastard, Haddon Fox. One day, she vowed, she would have her revenge. And she knew exactly how. She would beat him at his own game.

'I wish you luck, Haddon,' she yelled as they disappeared into the swirling snow. 'And believe me, you are going to need it.'

Tossing her head proudly, she stalked out into the lane. She climbed into her tiny, battered old Morgan, and for once oblivious to the icy wind and the snowflakes howling in through the broken isinglass side-vents, she drove off into the storm. She cried all the way home.

CHAPTER 6

Swayne and the spaniel took the early train back from Leeds, arriving in London before noon. He heard the telephone ringing as he climbed the four steep flights of wooden stairs to his office, and he ran the last two, dragging the protesting dog behind him.

Puffing, he unlocked the door, leapt across the room and grabbed the phone. 'Swayne here,' he said in the most dignified voice he could muster, being so out of breath.

'Where have you been?' Lord Mountjoy barked, irately. 'I've been telephoning all morning.'

'I'm afraid I was in Yorkshire, sir, pursuing my enquiries,' Swayne replied.

'Yorkshire?' Mountjoy snapped. 'What about Paris? Italy? For goodness sake, man, stop wasting your time and my money and get on with the job properly. And remember, I need your report by the end of the month.' And he slammed down the receiver, making Swayne's ears ring.

He sighed as he took a seat. He emptied the brimming ashtray into the wastebasket, lit up the usual Woodbine and propped his feet on the littered desk. The exhausted spaniel subsided on the floor next to him, still panting from its exertions. It lay there, watching resentfully as Swayne placed a call to his old friend, Inspector Murat at the Sûreté in Paris. This time the call went through immediately.

'Michel, my old *ami*, it's Jerome Swayne here,' he said, beaming, 'Your colleague at Scotland Yard? We worked together on the Lesage case; the headless body in the trunk in the left luggage at the Gare du Nord.' He laughed, 'Will I ever forget, my friend. Quite a caper, eh? But now I have something even more interesting for you.'

He told Inspector Murat about the Mountjoy case and gave him

39

the name of the woman in Paris, with whom Georgie was known to have had a liaison: Marie-France d'Aranville.

'It says here,' he said, studying the documents Lord Mountjoy had given him, 'that she was an actress.'

Murat gave a scathing laugh. 'Weren't they all? *Eh bien*, rest calm, my old friend. Inspector Murat is on the trail.'

Swayne smiled as he put down the phone. Murat was like a truffle-hound: just give him the scent and he would dig up the buried treasures.

Satisfied that the next phase of the Mountjoy case was in good hands, he began to write up his report on the Fioraldi family, and the granddaughter, Laura Swinburn. He sighed as he did so. He knew Lord Mountjoy would not like it. He would not like it one little bit because he was expecting to find a great-grandson, not a great-granddaughter. The Earl of Mountjoy wanted an heir who could inherit the title and carry on the Mountjoy line that had lasted since doomsday. Until now.

A few days later, Inspector Murat called him back.

'*Mon vieux*, here is Murat,' he said, 'bringing you good news. Marie d'Aranville certainly did live in Paris. In fact, by an odd coincidence, she also died here. Just a few weeks ago. At her home on the rue Bonaparte.'

Swayne groaned. He had hoped he might meet her, get the story from the horse's mouth, so to speak.

'Don't worry,' Murat said confidently. 'The *comtesse* Marie was a popular woman. She had many friends – men friends, you understand – who were only too happy to share their pleasant memories of her. And, *mon vieux*, it seems Marie had a son.' He paused to let the information sink in and then added, dramatically. 'She named him Antoine *Mountjoy* d'Aranville.'

Swayne took a deep breath. Murat had not let him down. 'Did Georgie marry Marie?'

'There is no record of any marriage. In fact, Marie never married anyone, though she had a succession of gentlemen friends, who kept her in the style to which Georgie Mountjoy accustomed her. It was Georgie who gave her the apartment on the rue Bonaparte. They said he was a generous man. And Marie told all her friends he was an excellent lover. Unusual, for your countrymen, eh Swayne?'

Murat laughed and Swayne laughed with him, hot under the collar at discussing such intimate matters. He changed the subject quickly. 'What about the son, Antoine?'

'Also dead. He was a respected army officer. They said he was a cold fish. Icy as the north wind, was what I heard about him. He and his mother had not spoken for years. *And* he was estranged from his wife.'

'His *wife*?'

'Suzette. Now Madame Suzette, of the famous millinery shop on the Faubourg St Honoré.'

'That's it then? The end of the line?' Swayne thought despondently of his promised bonus if he delivered the goods. It looked as though he had drawn a blank first time out.

Murat laughed. He had saved the best till last. 'There is a daughter. By the name of Anjou. She is nineteen years old and at a cramming school, just outside Paris. The École Mérite, in Passy. Apparently she wishes to get a place at the Sorbonne.'

Swayne breathed a sigh of relief. He could deliver the goods after all. He thanked Murat and arranged to visit him the following day, at his office in the rue Balzac.

He walked round to Thomas Cook in the Strand, and booked himself a seat on the Golden Arrow, leaving from Victoria station for Paris that evening. Then he went home to pack his bag and say a reluctant goodbye to his dog. And to his wife, of course.

The Channel crossing was rough. Swayne spent the night sitting at the bar with a glass of brandy in front of him, watching the amber liquid slop from side to side and praying for it all to end. He staggered off the ferry and onto the train for Paris, stifling his groans as he was bounced around on the second-class wooden seat, breathing the garlic fumes of the man opposite, and turning his eyes hastily from the ham and cheese baguette the woman next to him was feeding her noisy children.

He climbed thankfully from the train at the Gare du Nord, wondering what people saw in foreign travel. In his opinion, they were far better off staying at home. He walked round the corner to the small hotel Thomas Cook had arranged for him. It was clean and comfortable and filled with English voices and he began to feel better.

Half an hour later he was in a taxi on his way to the Faubourg St Honoré.

Madame Suzette's famous hat shop occupied a tiny corner, within striking distance of the Ritz and the Hotel Crillon, as well as the British Embassy and many of the grand private houses and apartments located in that very chic neighbourhood.

Its proprietor, the *comtesse* Suzette d'Aranville, had chosen her premises carefully, selecting the pricey corner shop in the best area, over larger premises in a less prestigious location. Her hats were expensive, her clientele was exclusive, and so was her shop. A person could not simply walk in off the street; it was necessary to make an appointment to visit Madame Suzette. Occasionally, some stranger did, of course, but one raking glance from Madame's sharp dark eyes and she had instantly assessed their social position, their financial standing and their breeding. And she let them know when they had not passed her test.

She had set herself those standards long ago, when she was in her early thirties and had found herself left alone with a child to bring up, and with very little money. She had made the surprising discovery that it was easy not to think about money when you had it. When you had none, you thought of little else.

She was tall and very slender with dark hair and dark eyes. She was not beautiful, but she was devastatingly chic.

She was standing in her little jewel-box of a shop, re-reading a letter she had received that morning about the death of her mother-in-law, Marie d'Aranville.

Suzette glanced up from the letter. She noticed for the second or third time, the man standing on the sidewalk opposite. He held a piece of paper in his hand and he was staring intently at her window. She peered at him from behind the lace curtain. He was tall and gaunt and so badly dressed, it made her shudder. His gaberdine raincoat was clasped round his thin middle with a stringy belt; the sleeves were too short, and his dingy check muffler was knotted tightly at his Adam's apple. He had enormous feet in thick black leather boots but, worst of all, was his hat: brown, snap-brimmed and made of cheap felt. *And* he wore it pulled low over his eyes.

'*Exactly like a criminal*,' she thought nervously. As she watched, he pulled his dreadful hat even lower and paced slowly away down the street.

Suzette sighed with relief and turned back to the letter from the

42

lawyer, about Marie d'Aranville. Antoine's mother had finally died and the letter brought back a host of bitter memories.

'The family property, the Chateau d'Aranville now becomes yours, *chère Madame*,' the Notaire informed her in his letter. '*Comtesse* Marie requested that her apartment on the rue Bonaparte and all its contents be given to her granddaughter, Anjou d'Aranville, who she thought of often, with great tenderness. If you would be so kind, *chère Madame*, to make an appointment to discuss these matters in more detail, we can complete our business.'

Suzette shuddered delicately, remembering the last time she had seen the crumbling old chateau. It had been at her husband Antoine's funeral, years ago, and the last of the mourners had just left. She had fed them brandy and sweet biscuits. She had shaken their fine-boned hands and kissed their withered cheeks, thinking that, though everyone around seemed as ancient as their houses, they were still clinging to life, though she didn't know how, since the winter wind had cut through the graveyard and her own warm coat like a knife.

Suzette had walked through the dim rooms making a list of their contents, noting which items of furniture she would require shipping to Paris. Then she put on her hat, buttoned her coat and stepped out into that freezing wind. She turned for one last, hate-filled, look at the Chateau before she closed the door of her little motor car and drove off, never to return.

On the long drive back to Paris she had tallied up her assets. First, was her breeding, or rather, her husband's breeding. Her own background was more bourgeois, but with her chic and *savoir-faire*, she had managed to eliminate any trace of that. Her second asset was her talent for fashion, especially hats. Her third, her wise business head – something she had not even suspected she possessed.

At that time, Suzette had been patronising the Paris couture houses for more than a decade. She attended the fashion shows regularly, and she knew the chief vendeuses at every salon, though her own favourites were Patou and Worth. At each collection, hats were a very important part of the outfits shown, but Suzette had never bought a single hat. She had found she had a talent for creating smart little topknots from wisps of net and ribbons and silk flowers and veiling, and everyone had always admired her creations. She hated the idea of being 'in trade' but she had no choice. She approached her acquaintance, the head vendeuse at Worth, who discussed it with the designer, who then discussed it with Suzette. He suggested she make a few trial samples and then he would see.

Two weeks later, she returned with six delicate examples and he was so charmed, he immediately bought them and designed dresses to go with them. He ordered more from her, for his autumn collection, and she felt a thrill of achievement, sitting in the back row of little gilt chairs, watching the models sweeping gracefully around the room in 'Madame Suzette's' pretty little hats.

'Madame Suzette' was an overnight success. 'What luck, *chérie*,' her 'friends' said, amused.

'Luck,' Suzette said bitterly to herself, thinking of the long days and nights of hard work, her ingenuity and her desperation. She would far rather have married a rich man, like they had, and led a pampered, easy life, but no man wanted to take on a widow with no money and a small child.

That had been fifteen years ago.

Suzette was still far from rich, but her clothes came from the top salons. They gave her items to wear for advertisement, because everybody who was anybody came into Madame Suzette's shop at some time or other. Everyone knew how smart she was, and they always asked, 'But where did you get that wonderful dress?' Of course, Suzette was quick to tell them, so the couture house gained a new customer and Suzette gained another new outfit.

Suzette folded her letter thoughtfully. She supposed she could always sell Marie's old apartment. As she remembered there were some fine antique pieces in there. With a little money of her own, Anjou might fare better in the marriage stakes, and heaven knew the girl would need all the help she could get.

Though Suzette and Marie had barely spoken in years, Anjou had spent a great deal of time with her grandmother. Far more than Suzette approved of. But it had been part of their arrangement. Antoine had left almost nothing and Suzette had been forced to ask Marie for money to start her business.

'It's yours,' Marie had said, smiling as she sipped her aperitif. 'But in return, I want my grandchild.'

And that had been their bargain. Anjou had spent every weekend with her grandmother, and she had adored her. She was the only one to cry when Marie had died, and the only one to attend her funeral.

Unfortunately, it seemed Marie's money had almost run out and all she had to leave her granddaughter was the apartment. Suzette frowned; she had been counting on that money. She sighed. Money was an eternal problem. The only thing left was for Anjou to make a good marriage.

But all Anjou seemed to think about was her studies, and whenever Suzette telephoned the expensive school, a combination of finishing school and college crammer, outside Paris, where her daughter was a boarder, she always seemed to be 'studying' and 'unavailable', whatever time of the day or night.

Good school reports never got a girl a rich husband, Suzette knew that. Anjou was going to have to become better groomed, to learn to dress well, to be sociable and how to charm a man.

She swung round, startled, as the little bell over the shop door tinkled warningly. The criminal from the street in the gaberdine raincoat and brown snap-brim hat was standing there, looking at her. Her hand flew to her mouth to stifle the potential scream.

Calm yourself, Suzette, she warned, do not make any quick moves. Talk to him. Placate him. Run into the street when you have the opportunity. Then you can scream as loud as you wish . . .

'Madame Suzette d'Aranville?' Swayne said with a thin smile.

She gasped in surprise. 'You know my name.'

'I do, Madame. I am Jerome Swayne of Swayne & Marshall, Private Investigators, of the Strand, London.'

'Private Investigators?' Suzette repeated, watching him nervously.

'I am representing an English gentleman, the Earl of Mountjoy, in some investigations he asked me to make on his behalf. To be specific Madame, my client is interested in tracing the possible descendants of George Mountjoy. From certain documents he gave me, and from my investigations, I have finally arrived at "Madame Suzette".'

Swayne shifted uncomfortably from foot to foot as she gave him her steeliest gaze. 'And why do you suppose I shall answer your questions?' she asked imperiously.

'I understand from my client, Madame, that it might be *to your advantage*.'

Suzette's dark eyes narrowed as she contemplated what that might mean. 'I think we should discuss this in private, Monsieur,' she said finally, swinging aside the heavy silk curtain that separated her tiny shop from the even tinier back office. She settled herself in her chair behind the little gilt table, but she did not offer Swayne a seat. He glanced down uncomfortably as she inspected him, then she said, 'Tell me, Monsieur Swayne, what is all this, about the Mountjoy family?'

She listened, unsmiling, while Swayne told her of the Earl's quest for George Mountjoy's descendants.

'I have traced the line from George Mountjoy, to your husband, the late Antoine Mountjoy d'Aranville, and finally to your daughter, Anjou.'

'And what exactly is Lord Mountjoy proposing, now you have discovered this highly personal information about my family?'

He shook his head. 'That is not for me to say, Madame. I was only to inform you that your daughter might be hearing *something to her advantage*. No doubt you will be hearing from the Earl himself in due course. I thank you for your time, Madame d'Aranville.'

'*Comtesse* d'Aranville,' she said icily. 'You can put that in your report to Lord Mountjoy. I think he would like to hear that his relatives are also titled.'

'Pompous little man,' she thought as Swayne folded his papers and pushed them into his raincoat pocket. He tightened his belt, replaced his dreadful hat, and then he bowed to her.

'Good day, *comtesse*,' he said, backing towards the curtain, fumbling with the heavy silk fabric, trying to find his way through it. She watched him making a fool of himself, not offering advice or help. He finally pushed his way out and she heard the bell tinkle and then the door slam.

Suzette took matches from the drawer and lit a scented candle, breathing in the delicate fragrance as if to remove Swayne's unpleasantness from her exquisite little shop. Then she sat, staring into space, thinking about what he had said, and the opportunities that might suddenly open up to her.

'And all thanks to Marie,' she said out loud, 'who was no better than she should be.' And flinging back her neat, dark head, she began to laugh. She laughed until tears ran down her cheeks, thinking how ironic it was that Marie's sexual escapades might make a fortune for her granddaughter.

CHAPTER 7

Georgie Mountjoy had met little Marie d'Aranville at the races in Deauville. It was a glorious spring day with a brisk breeze blowing in from the Atlantic, and it had blown Marie's straw-cartwheel-hat, trimmed with pink silk roses and a satin streamer, off her beautifully coiffed head and into Georgie's arms, where she herself had followed not very many days later.

It was love at first sight for Marie. She was petite with dazzling red hair, a pouting red mouth and greenish eyes with long dark lashes. She was twenty-one years old and a terrible flirt and the look she gave Georgie Mountjoy as she thanked him for catching her hat, promised more than she intended to give. But she had not reckoned on Georgie. He found out that her family was almost as ancient and well-bred as his own; and that her father had disowned her when she had kicked over the traces and decided to become an actress.

She was 'resting' as they call being out of work in that profession, at the time he met her, and was only too happy to be pursued by a handsome young man with flowers and trinkets, and dinners *a deux* in intimate little restaurants.

When she returned to Paris, Georgie followed her. He took her out of the dingy little room she lived in and set her up in an apartment near the Jardins des Luxemburg. It was not too big, she thought, but a good address, with tall windows overlooking the gardens, and very light for a French apartment. Georgie helped her to choose furniture from the antique shops along the Quai d'Orsay and she filled her little home with oversized quality pieces: enormous gilded mirrors, and marble and giltwood consoles, Aubusson rugs and Louis XIV chairs, and a vast Empire bed that she was told had once belonged to the Empress Eugenie. Instead of making her apartment look smaller, the few enormous pieces made it look striking and interesting.

Georgie was generous: the day she moved into the apartment, he handed her the legal documents with her name on them stating that she was the owner. 'Just a small "thank you", for being such a charming lover,' he told her with a regretful smile. And then he said goodbye. He was off to Vienna the following morning. It was unlikely they would meet again.

Marie could not pretend to be broken-hearted. After all, their liaison had lasted only a few months. Georgie had never remotely suggested marriage, and she had hardly come out the loser. Except a month later, when she began to suspect that she was pregnant.

'Give the child my name,' Georgie instructed her, when she contacted him at the Schloss Kronenfeld where he was staying with friends. 'I shall send you money right away.' But he never suggested marriage.

To save shocking her only living relative, her grandmother, the old *comtesse* d'Aranville, Marie invented a convoluted tale of marriage and abandonment. With Georgie's generous settlement in the bank, she returned home to the crumbling Chateau near Bergerac.

Marie's grandmother, the *comtesse*, was old, and it was easy to pull the wool over her eyes. And she was pleased when Marie told her she preferred to give the child their family name. Marie thought it was a good way of getting round the problem that she was not married, but she did not forget generous Georgie's wishes either, and she named her son for him.

Antoine Georges Mountjoy d'Aranville was born at the Chateau six months later. Apart from the mop of flaming red hair, he was the spitting image of his father. The same bright blue eyes, the slightly hooked Mountjoy nose, and as he grew into a young man, the same strong wiry body. The resemblance ended there. In temperament, Antoine was the complete opposite of the carefree, lusty, generous Georgie.

He was brought up by the old *comtesse* at the Chateau, while Marie returned to her Paris apartment, and her 'career', though she was the first to admit, laughingly to her friends, that her 'roles' consisted more of playing the 'lover and mistress', than acting a part on stage. But she was enjoying herself. 'And isn't that what life is all about?' she would ask, gaily.

The old *comtesse* was proud of her lineage. She was distantly related to the royal families of Romania and Spain, and the d'Aranville name was listed in the French directory of blue-bloods. She ruled her decaying chateau like an autocratic old princess, with a few remaining servants who were almost as old as she was. She reminded Antoine daily of his status in life and the importance of his name, and his duty to his family, and to France.

It was a solitary upbringing for a boy. As he grew up and his great-grandmother grew even older, some days she remembered who he was, and some days she did not. Antoine simply accepted it. He just shrugged and got on with his life.

When he was fourteen, his great-grandmother sold the last of the family jewels – a particularly wonderful diamond tiara that had been in the d'Aranville family for four generations; and she sent Antoine off to the École Militaire at Saint Cyr.

Antoine knew what she had sacrificed to send him to the exclusive military school. It wasn't only the tiara; the *comtesse* was a very old lady and she knew she might not have much longer on this earth. He admired and respected her for it, and he determined to do well to make her sacrifice worthwhile. But Antoine was not an emotional young man; he did not love his great-grandmother, nor did he love his mother, whom he saw rarely and whom he despised for her silliness and her wanton way of life.

He had learned his lessons well from his great-grandmother though. His name and his military career meant everything to him. The old *comtesse* lived long enough to attend his graduation at St Cyr, looking regal as a queen in her old-fashioned lilac silk, her tiny shrunken face almost hidden beneath her bonnet. Unexpectedly, his mother showed up too, looking like a music-hall soubrette in yellow silk with an enormous hat, trailing ribbons and scent behind her. Antoine felt his strongest emotion to date when he surveyed all that was left of his 'family'. He respected his great-grandmother, and he was ashamed of his mother.

Until that point, he had never given much thought to his father's family, but now he determined to find out more about them. After the old *comtesse* had been deposited safely in her room at the hotel where they were staying, and left in the care of her personal maid, he took his mother down to dinner. Over the bottle of Pommery champagne that she ordered, and the austere bordeaux that he preferred, he questioned her about the Mountjoys.

Marie regarded her son with amused green eyes. '*Eh bien*, I can tell you this, Antoine,' she said, quaffing the champagne and stabbing enthusiastically at her sole *bonne femme*, 'the Mountjoys make the d'Aranvilles look like *arrivistes*. Their family goes back all the way to the Norman Conquests – and probably earlier. *And* they are rich. Not merely land-rich, the way the d'Aranvilles were. They had money as well as property. They were cleverer than us too. They invested their money. They grew richer every decade, instead of poorer.'

She sighed, rolling her green eyes dramatically to heaven and clutching her fork to her ample breast. 'Ah, if only you had the Mountjoy money, my dear son, you would have every well-bred virgin in this dining room chasing after you.'

She glanced critically at the daughters of the visiting families of the St Cyr military graduates. 'As it is, you will have to rely on your looks. I'm afraid a title cannot compete with money in the marriage stakes these days. Unless you marry an heiress, of course. Perhaps an American,' she added thoughtfully. 'There are so many of the poor creatures around. Lumpy and unlovely most of them, I agree. But *rich*, my dear son. Rich, as they say, as Croesus.'

Antoine blushed a fiery pink that clashed with his red hair. His mother spoke so loudly in her actressy voice, he was sure everybody had heard what she said. Besides, he was a virgin himself, and he blushed even deeper as he caught the amused glance of the pretty girl at the next table.

He bent his head closer, speaking in a low voice. 'But if the Mountjoys are so rich, *Maman*, why is it, that we are so poor?'

Marie gave him a sceptical glance. 'I cannot believe you have not thought about this before, and that you have not arrived at the obvious conclusion, Antoine.'

'Obvious conclusion?' He looked blank.

She lifted her shoulders in the tiniest shrug that explained better than words ever could, that she did not give a damn. 'Well, of course, Georgie Mountjoy and I were just lovers.'

Antoine's jaw dropped. She watched him silently. A malicious little smile curled the corners of her lips. Her son was such a prude, such a stuffed shirt, she wondered how she had ever bred him.

'But I thought . . . you always said . . . the *comtesse* told me you had married the Englishman, that he had abandoned you . . . that you preferred to use our family name because of that . . .'

Marie thought it was typical of Antoine that he should refer to his great-grandmother snobbishly as 'the *comtesse*'. Signalling the waiter to refill her glass, she said impatiently, 'Well of course I told your great-grandmother I was married. Do you think I wanted to give her a heart attack? Use your brains, Antoine, for heaven's sake.'

His eyes filled with horror as he looked at her across the table. 'Then you must mean I was . . . I am . . .'

Marie's mocking laughter would ring in his ears as long as he lived as she said in a loud stage whisper, '*A bastard*. Why yes, my dear son. That is *exactly* what you are.'

Antoine folded his napkin and placed it carefully on the table. He stood up and a waiter hurried to adjust his chair. He clicked his heels and bowed to his mother. Then he turned and strode rapidly from the room. He never spoke to her again.

Marie returned to the Chateau d'Aranville for the old *comtesse*'s funeral a year later, but it was impossible for Antoine to attend since he was with his regiment in Indo-Chine at the time.

When the news was broken to Antoine by his Commander, he set his mouth in a firm line. The Commander offered his condolences. Antoine thanked him, saluted and marched out of the door.

The Commander watched him go, a thoughtful look on his face. 'I would say that young man is made of steel,' he commented to his Aide de Camp. 'Not a flicker of emotion crossed his face, and I happen to know that the old *comtesse* brought him up. Ah well, each man is different when faced with grief.' Nevertheless, he thought Antoine d'Aranville was a pretty cold fish.

Antoine was not a virgin when he married Suzette Marigot at the age of thirty. He had taken care of that little matter immediately after he had graduated from the École Militaire, and attended punctually to his needs once a week ever since, patronising the same discreet bordello and, more often than not, because it saved time, the same girl, in whatever city he was billeted near. He looked upon the act as a man's relief, nothing more, and preferred to channel his energies into advancing his career.

He had served his country well in the early years of the 1914–18 war, sustaining an injury to his leg while rescuing a comrade under fire. This act of valour earned him the Croix de Guerre and left him with a limp that made further combat impossible. He was promoted from Captain to Major and seconded to the War Ministry in Paris.

He turned out to be a brilliant political games player, as well as good at his job, and he was rapidly made Colonel. So, he was the well-known and extremely handsome, brave young Colonel d'Aranville when he met Suzette.

She was young but not too young; attractive but not too pretty, though she gave the impression of being prettier because she was so stylish. And she was almost as tall as he was, close to six foot in her high heels. She had smooth dark hair, cut in a fashionable bob, wary brown eyes and a firm mouth.

She was twenty-seven years old and still unmarried because she had lost her fiancé in the war. Temporarily heartbroken, she had contemplated taking vows and entering a convent, until her father told her not to be so ridiculous, and that she had better get married soon, because he was tired of keeping her in luxury and paying all those outrageous bills for her couture clothes.

Their marriage was not exactly one of convenience; more of a misunderstanding. Antoine thought the Marigots had more money than they actually did, since they were such lavish spenders. And Suzette's father, who should have known about these things, was so overwhelmed by paying his daughter's bills that he never questioned the financial circumstances of the d'Aranvilles. And even if he had known Antoine was poor, he would have allowed Suzette to marry him anyway, just to get her and her expenses off his hands.

Antoine's mother Marie was not invited to the wedding, held at the bride's home, near Lyons. In any case, she would not have come. She was far too busy enjoying her life to waste time on her pedantic, boring son.

'Just look at him,' she said scathingly to her long-time lover, pointing to the photograph in the newspaper, of Antoine, standing stern and ramrod-straight next to Suzette outside the Cathedral. 'I just hope for his bride's sake his pecker is as stiff as his back.' And she fell into her lover's arms amid great peals of laughter.

Antoine proved a disappointment to Suzette. He was handsome all right, with his reddish hair, blue eyes and upright military carriage, and his uniform added a dashing touch of glamour. Too late, she found he had no sense of humour, and that he lived for his work. They made love, as was his custom, once a week and she was almost surprised when she found she was pregnant.

'*Mon amour*,' she said firmly, when he returned from a long day at the Ministry, 'we must find a new home.' She glanced disparagingly round their small apartment on the Champ des Mars. 'Now that we are having a child.'

'We are?' Antoine said, looking dumbfounded.

'It is usual, you know, when one is married,' she retorted, a little acidly, he thought.

He sat for a while, considering the possibility of a child in his life. *His son.*

'You must go to the Chateau d'Aranville at once,' he said. 'I will make arrangements. Our child must be born there. It is the family tradition.'

'But I am only three months pregnant,' Suzette protested. She knew the old chateau: it was falling to pieces, there was no heating and worst of all, there were no chic interesting neighbours. She would die of boredom there, if not the cold. 'What I meant was, we shall need a new apartment,' she repeated.

'But why?' Antoine was genuinely puzzled. 'The child must be brought up at his family home, the way I was. Of course you will stay there to supervise his upbringing, and I shall visit whenever my work permits.'

Suzette stared at him, horrified. 'Are you out of your mind, Antoine?' she cried. 'Do you really think you can send me to moulder in that freezing lonely chateau, while you live in Paris?' And she burst into tears and ran from the room.

Antoine sat silently for a while, thinking over what she had said. Then he walked to their bedroom. He knocked on the door and went in.

'You married a d'Aranville, Suzette,' he said calmly. 'You promised in your marriage vows, to obey. This is the way it has always been done in our family and as my wife, I expect you to do the same.' He turned and walked stiffly out of the door. He turned again, 'Besides,' he added coldly, 'we cannot afford to buy a larger apartment. So you have no choice.'

Suzette's look of horror was not because of his command that she must obey him. It was for what he had just said about not being able to afford a bigger apartment. She already knew, from the bills piling up on his desk, that they were not rich, but she had never had to curtail her spending, and she did not intend to do so now she was married.

She went to his desk, bundled up all the bills and put them in an envelope. Then she rang for the maid and told her to mail them to her father in Lyons, along with the note she had written asking for money to purchase a new apartment, now that she was about to give him a grandchild.

Antoine did not come home that night but she did not care. She did not care if he was taking his un-amorous weekly exercise in a house of ill-repute, instead of with her. She didn't care if he had a mistress, or even two mistresses. But she did care about the awful possibility that, married to Antoine, she might be poor.

Her father returned the bills a week later with a curt note stating that he would no longer be responsible for her debts. He would have nothing more to do with the matter.

Suzette found herself with no choice but to go to the dreary old chateau to have her child. She had no money of her own, and Antoine was adamant that his son must be born there. She put it off as long as she could, pleading the bitter winter cold, but when the spring came, she could delay no longer.

After the three most miserable months of her life, on a wild, stormy morning, amid flashes of lightning and great peals of thunder, her child was born.

'A daughter,' Antoine said quietly, regarding the flame-haired scrap in her lace-trimmed bassinette. 'You must do better next time, Suzette.'

Suzette was lying back on her pillows, exhausted after a long and painful labour. She stared at him, open-mouthed with shock. Her dark eyes grew bitter and her mouth curled contemptuously. '*You bastard,*' she snarled.

Antoine said nothing. It was the second time in his life that someone had called him a bastard. His face turned white as the sheets and he stared at the frescoed angels on the ceiling as though searching for an escape. Suzette watched him, curiously. She had never seen Antoine at a loss for words before.

Finally, he looked at her. His blue eyes were as cold as ice chips. 'Goodbye, Suzette,' he said. And then, just as he had with his mother, he turned and without a backward glance, walked out of the door. He never spoke to her again. And he never saw his daughter again.

Suzette christened her Angélique, but always called her Anjou. She passed the next three years, stuck at the chateau, existing on the small amount of money Antoine sent scrupulously, every month. Her own father died but there was no money left, and even his properties were sold to pay off the creditors.

Then suddenly, one dreary February day, an officer from Antoine's old regiment appeared on her doorstep. He said he had sad news to bring her. Her husband had suffered a riding accident. Well, not exactly a riding accident. Antoine was not actually *riding* at the time. He had been inspecting the cavalry regiment when one of the horses took fright. It reared up, lashing out with its hooves, just as Antoine was passing. It struck him on the temple and he fell to the ground. He died instantly.

The officer assured her that the horse involved had been put down immediately. There was to be a military ceremony, with all the honours, in Paris in two days' time. Then Antoine's body would be returned to his family chateau for burial. A fellow-officer would be sent to escort Suzette to Paris. He proferred his deep condolences, and assured her the Army would make some financial recompense for her deep loss.

Suzette quite enjoyed the military funeral. She took three year old Anjou with her because she thought the young widow and her small child would make an appealing sight to those hardened professional army men – one they might remember when assessing the compensation for Antoine's death. Anjou's red curls were hidden under an unbecoming little black velvet porkpie hat and she laughed and waved at the horses as they trotted by. She stared silent and uncomprehending as her father's coffin was paraded past, and patted the folded French flag that had draped it, when they gave it to her mother.

Immediately after the ceremony, Suzette went to visit Marie. 'You know where I have just come from,' she said, accepting a seat by the fire.

'I do,' Marie said, observing that Suzette's busy eyes were taking in every detail of her apartment: the fine antiques, the paintings, the Venetian mirrors and the wealth of little bibelots and ornaments.

'But you did not choose to attend your own son's military funeral ceremony?'

Marie noticed Suzette's dark eyes were accusing, and she smiled.

'You are correct. I did not choose to attend Antoine's funeral. He would not have expected it of me. In fact, he would have hated it. I always embarrassed him, you know. And I thought it was inappropriate to embarrass my son on his final public outing.'

The maid brought in a tray with glasses and bottles of Pernod and cognac. 'May I offer you a glass of cognac to warm you up?' Marie asked. 'You look a little *cold* to me,' she added with a malicious smile.

Suzette refused. 'I think we should talk about financial matters,' she said abruptly.

'What about them?' Marie sipped the Pernod then licked her lips delicately.

'I am your son's widow. There is a child.'

'A child I have never seen,' Marie said, suddenly icy.

'Antoine left very little money . . .'

'No doubt the Army will compensate you. The military took the place of his family, *chérie*, long, long ago.'

Silence fell between them. The fire crackled and Marie sipped her Pernod, watching her daughter-in-law. 'Don't you think it strange,' she said finally, 'that you have been married to my son for almost five years and we meet only now? Over his deathbed, so to speak? You made no attempt to see me when you announced your engagement. I was not invited to your wedding. I was not informed of the birth of my grandchild; in fact, I would not have known about it, had I not read the announcement in the newspaper. You have never offered to bring the child to see me. And you did not invite me to the funeral. So tell me, Suzette, why should you come to me for money?'

Suzette looked helplessly at her. She was defeated. 'Because there is no one else,' she admitted.

Marie nodded. 'At least now you are being honest. Now let me tell you what I propose. I will give you money, but on one condition. That you use it to start some kind of business. I don't care what it is, but it must be able to keep you and your daughter, without coming to me for help. I am not a rich woman. *I* have always had to look out for myself, and I shall expect you to do the same.'

Suzette hung her head, saying nothing.

'One more thing,' Marie said softly. 'I want my grandchild.'

Suzette's head shot up. 'What do you mean?'

'You are about to become a working woman,' Marie said briskly. 'You will not have time to bring up your child properly. I propose that she come and live with me.'

Marie watched Suzette closely. She saw the conflicting emotions playing across her face: relief, fear, indecision.

Suzette was thinking about the sheer relief of not having responsibility for Antoine's child; about her fear of what the future might hold; and the insecurity of working for a living. But she knew she had something Marie wanted. Anjou was the trump card in her game with Marie and she must play that card wisely.

'I'm sorry, I cannot allow that,' she said at last, 'though perhaps I could allow Anjou to visit you.'

Marie laughed. 'You have more guts than I gave you credit for. The money will be in your bank account next week. Use it wisely. In return, send my granddaughter to visit me every weekend without fail.' And with that, she called the maid to escort Suzette to the door.

And that was how Suzette d'Aranville became Madame Suzette, and how Marie's little infidelity had paved the way for young Anjou Mountjoy d'Aranville's future fortune.

CHAPTER 8

Suzette decided she would telephone Anjou at school and tell her the news. She sighed impatiently as the phone rang and rang. Finally one of Anjou's friends answered.

'I'm sorry, *comtesse*, but Anjou is studying,' she said. 'The exam is tomorrow and she left instructions not to be disturbed. It is so very important to her, you understand?'

There was a hint of laughter in the girl's voice that Suzette certainly did *not* understand, and she put down the phone with an angry sigh. In her opinion Anjou spent far too much of her time at the École Mérite studying, and not nearly enough on being 'finished': learning how to be a social asset, in other words. Really, if it had not been that Anjou's grades showed that she must work very hard, she might have suspected her of running around with men. But her report cards had always shown A's in every subject, even maths for heaven's sake, so obviously Anjou was just a dedicated bluestocking.

Suzette put on her most charming smile as she answered the doorbell and permitted her next client to enter the shop. The woman was a rich American, related to the Rockefellers, and she expected to persuade her to spend a great deal of money today. Perhaps she would buy half a dozen hats for spring, and they would also talk about purchases for the summer. She sighed again, this time with pleasure. It would be a satisfactory day.

Meanwhile, young Anjou d'Aranville, as flame-haired, green-eyed and piquantly pretty as her beloved grandmother, Marie, from whom she had learned more than her mother suspected, was wrapped in the arms of a young artist. They were keeping out the icy January cold of his garret with the heat of their bodies. And, like her mother, Anjou sighed too. But with quite a different kind of pleasure.

Much later that night, Anjou clambered agilely back over the

59

white stucco wall surrounding the École Mérite. The guard dog, waiting as usual on the other side, wagged his tail expectantly as she fished in her pocket for his bribe – a lump of steak stolen from the kitchen earlier, on her way out.

'Good dog,' she said, patting his head. Then she glanced quickly round. All was still and silent. She sauntered coolly through the trees, round the corner of the building to the french window she had thoughtfully left open. Within minutes, she was inside and back in her own room.

Escape from the École Mérite was an art she had perfected through much practice. Anjou Mountjoy d'Aranville might not resemble her grandfather Georgie, but she was like him in spirit: she loved life and having a good time, and the opposite sex. And no school could hold her.

Her friend, Cécile, sat up in bed as Anjou crept into the room. 'Tell me what happened?' she said eagerly, rubbing the sleep from her eyes.

Anjou smiled mischievously at her. 'What exactly do you want to know? You want to hear the words he used as he made love to me? Or how virile he was? Whether he was rough or tender?'

'All those things,' Cécile said breathlessly.

Anjou laughed. 'Yes,' she said, 'he *was* all those things. My poor starving artist is quite delicious, Cécile.' She sighed deeply. 'Alas, it is a pity I shall not see him again.'

'But why not?' Cécile leaned forward, hugging her knees anxiously, 'If he is so wonderful?'

Anjou shrugged carelessly. 'He has no money, dear Cécile. And I fear he is a very, very bad artist. His portrait of me has a green face. Green! *Mon Dieu*, I ask you.'

She inspected her lovely face in the mirror, surprised as she always was, that there were no tell-tale signs of her evening's activities. Apart from the shadows under her eyes, of course, but they could always be explained away by too much studying. She hauled off her dress and her single undergarment, dragged a brush through her long red hair and put on a robe. Then with a sigh she settled down at her small desk to study. After all, the calculus exam was tomorrow. She could not afford to fail if she were to go onto the Sorbonne, and college was the only way she could see to 'freedom'.

'Your mother called,' Cécile remembered suddenly. 'She said it was urgent, and that you should call her when you got through studying.' She winked at Anjou. 'She must think you're a real bluestocking, with your nose buried in your books.'

Anjou laughed, 'It's a good thing she doesn't know where my nose was really buried. And a good thing I don't have to study too hard to get good grades. I'm the lucky one. Lucky in love and work, anyhow.' Her smooth forehead creased in a frown and her jewel-green eyes grew troubled. 'But what I really need is to be lucky with money.'

Money, or not enough of it, had always loomed large in Anjou's life. Suzette might look like a fashion plate, and she made a good living, but expenses always seemed higher than their income and life was a constant series of small economies. There was the maid who came only twice a week instead of every day; the inexpensive dinners at home and too rarely at a restaurant; cheap clothes for Anjou because no one in fashionable circles ever saw her anyway and Suzette said she must wait until she finished school when good clothes would be an investment.

An investment in the marriage market, Anjou thought rebelliously. All her mother wanted to do was find her a rich husband and then both their lives would change. Her mother would finally have the security and prestige she craved. But Anjou knew that when the rich husband got bored with her, he would take a mistress; the mistress would be dressed to kill in couture, paid for by him. She would be escorted to the theatre and all the smartest restaurants and parties, while Anjou mouldered at home with the children.

Anjou knew it was true because she had already been the mistress of exactly a husband like that. Briefly, of course, as were all her affairs. But at least it had been fun. And fun was exactly what Anjou craved. She did not care how many wives or girl-friends she had to trample over to get it: she would have fun at any cost – except to herself. As well as that important place at the Sorbonne, because right now going to college was the only way she could think of that would get her out of her mother's clutches. If she went to college, she could rent a cheap room of her own, lead her own life. Anjou smiled. She might even go to a few classes, if they interested her enough.

'Brains are not my problem, Cécile,' she said with a sigh. 'Money is. I have to find myself a rich man. But I'm like my grandmother Marie; I would rather be the mistress than the wife.'

She glanced at her watch. Two o'clock. Too late to call her mother. She would speak with her tomorrow. She sat at her desk, opened her books and began to study.

Suzette called again at six-thirty. Anjou sat up groggily, then staggered down the hall to the phone. '*Allo*,' she said, yawning.

'Anjou, thank heavens I've reached you, at last.'

Anjou groaned, then changed it into a yawn, only half listening as her mother rambled on about a private investigator and the Earl of Mountjoy.

'The Earl is your great-uncle, Anjou, and he is rich. He sent a private investigator specially to look for you. He says you will soon be hearing *something to your advantage*.'

Anjou could hear the smile in her mother's voice as she rambled on about the Mountjoys. '*Au'voir maman*,' she said, hanging up the receiver.

She crawled back to bed and lay, with her hands behind her head, thinking of the possibility that she might be old Lord Mountjoy's only heir, and that she would inherit his fortune. She gave a small, satisfied sigh. Her dreams were finally coming true. Somehow, she had always known they would.

Anjou was downstairs before anyone else that morning; a 'first' in her entire school life. Moreover, she was neatly dressed in a grey pinafore and prim white blouse, long black cotton stockings and sturdy black shoes. Her hair was neatly brushed and tied back from her face with a black ribbon and she looked as scrubbed and innocent as a girl with a sound night's sleep behind her.

Anjou earned an A in her calculus exam that day.

CHAPTER 9

Swayne was thankful to leave Paris behind. He thought he had never seen anything more welcoming in his life than the white cliffs of Dover, looming out of the mist and rain. The Channel crossing had been stormy. Feeling decidedly queasy and unable to bear the stuffy atmosphere below, he had spent the past few hours on deck in the rain, closing his eyes so as not to see the great green waves rolling past; quelling his heaving stomach with strong mint humbugs and the occasional glass of brandy.

Foreign parts were not for him. There was nothing abroad better than what Britain had to offer and why the upper classes were so keen on it beat him. He wanted none of their *vin rouge* and smelly *fromage*. Give him good old Blighty, a pint of draught bitter and a ploughmans lunch any day.

He thanked heaven he had not been forced to go to Italy in search of the Fioraldi/Swinburn branch of the Mountjoy family, and thought glumly about what to do about Texas. He shuddered as he thought of a civilized fellow like himself set down in a land of cowboys and sharpshooters, thousands of miles from his home. Besides, there was no time. He would have to get on the telephone to America, sharpish. As soon as he got to London in fact.

He shook the drops of rainwater from his new brown felt hat before replacing it firmly on his head. His dingy raincoat was soaked, but he was so glad to be back in 'England's green and pleasant land', he scarcely noticed.

Swayne's legs scarcely seemed to belong to him as he wobbled into the railway station snackroom, took off his hat again, and ordered a cup of tea. He added three heaped spoons of sugar and a slug of milk, stirred it thoroughly, and gulped down the strong, dark brew, wincing with pain as it burned its way down his gullet and into his stomach. He put back the cup and breathed deeply. He paid his threepence, replaced his brown felt hat, tightened his raincoat belt and smiled at the waitress. There was nothing like a good strong cup of English tea. He felt like a new man.

As the train clickety-clacked its way to London, Swayne contemplated the small pleasures of returning home. He would go immediately to his office in the Strand; first he would place a call with the overseas operator to Houston in Texas, but that might take days to go through. Next he would write up his report and see if there were any messages. Then he would take the bus back to the small terraced house in Clapham where his wife would have a good hot dinner waiting. But before that, he would take the dog for a long walk. He knew the spaniel would have missed him and his wife wasn't much for dogs, nor for walks. In fact he would take it for two walks tonight; one before dinner and one after, when he would drop into the Nag's Head for a pint and a chat with the lads. Swayne's eyelids drooped; it had been a long night. There was a faint pleased smile on his face as he dozed off, and he didn't wake up until the train pulled into Victoria.

It was raining harder in London than it had been in Paris or Calais, but Swayne didn't even notice; it was just London weather, that's all. He hopped on a bus to the Strand and climbed the stairs to his fourth-floor office with the spring in his step of a reprieved man.

He heaved open the sash window, emptied the ashtray, lit up the Woodbine and placed his call. To his amazement he was put through immediately to the Houston Police Department. He asked for their assistance: he needed to find a reputable private investigator to help on a case. They gave him the name of Edgar Smallbone.

It took another few days to reach Smallbone, due to a faulty cable, and when he finally did get through, there was so much crackle and echo on the line he could hardly hear himself think. Anyhow, eventually he managed to convey his story to Smallbone, and asked for his assistance.

Financial matters were discussed and agreed upon and Smallbone said, a little too jauntily, Swayne thought, 'I'm already out the door and on my way to San Antonio.'

Swayne put down the telephone and lit up another cigarette. He puffed, uneasily, hoping he had done the right thing. He was only one step away from claiming his bonus, and he hoped Smallbone was the right man for the job, so he could claim it.

Edgar Smallbone was a lean, hard-faced giant of a man. Six foot seven in his stocking feet and weighing in at two hundred and fifty pounds of sheer muscle. Smallbone was more used to seeking cattle rustlers and bank robbers than long-lost relatives, but when Swayne offered him the job, he figured it was a change. And anyhow it was easy money. Finding the Mountjoy Ranch outside San Antonio was a piece of cake, but getting anybody there to talk to him about the family was another matter.

He rolled up one brisk blue morning in his old, mud-spattered black Chevy saloon. It had a faulty ignition, dented fenders and a bullet hole in the back window, shot by a fleeing bank robber whom he never caught, because, when the bullets came that close, Smallbone knew it was time to quit.

He was surprised, therefore, when he strolled up to the rickety porch of the little log ranch-house, to be greeted by a bristling black lady toting a shotgun, and a wary-eyed mongrel whose throaty growl caused him to halt.

'State your business, mister,' Aliza Jefferson said coldly, shouldering the ancient shotgun.

Smallbone tipped his Stetson politely. 'Don't mean to trouble you, ma'am. But the sign at the end of the lane says this is Mountjoy Ranch, and I'm looking for the Mountjoys.'

'Which Mountjoy?' Aliza stared suspiciously at him.

'Why, any one of them, ma'am. Any one at all will do. There's a relative in London, an Earl of Mountjoy, who is anxious to find the descendants of his long-lost brother, Georgie. That's my job, ma'am, to find them, and that's why I'm here, asking your help.'

Aliza's eyes opened wide in astonishment. She lowered the gun, ordered the mongrel to hold his growling and said, 'There's no Mountjoy here wants to talk to an Earl. The Mountjoys left this branch of the family to struggle along on their own all these years. They don't want no fancy Earls knowing their whereabouts and their business.' She glared at him, then curiosity got the better of her. 'Besides, why does he want to know?'

Smallbone shrugged, 'He said something about it being "*to their advantage*".'

'Huh,' Aliza snorted disdainfully. 'More like to their own, from what I've heard of that bunch. Probably just want to get their hands on this ranch. Yes sir, that's it, I'll bet. They want to take back their ranch. Well, you can tell them from me, mister, they ain't gonna get their hands on this property. Not if Aliza Jefferson has anything to do with it.'

She simmered with indignation and the mongrel growled a warning. Smallbone backed away, keeping his eyes on the dog. 'I think you've got it wrong ma'am,' he said placatingly. 'Just tell me when Mr Mountjoy will be home, and I'll come back and speak with him.'

'Ain't no Mister Mountjoy here, feller,' Aliza retorted, 'so don't you bother coming back again because it ain't gonna get you nowheres.'

Smallbone climbed hastily into the Chevy, gunning the engine as the mongrel hurled itself down the porch steps. It chased him all the way down the rutted lane leading to the highway, its claws scratching at the paintwork as it barked a ferocious farewell.

Smallbone did a little more research before he returned to the Mountjoy Ranch. He took a room in a boarding house in the nearby small town of Kitsville. He made it his business to patronise the local general store, where he asked some questions, and in the evening he hung around The Lonesome Steer Saloon chatting with the barkeeper and some of the customers. He was surprised to learn that the owner of the Mountjoy Ranch was a young woman by the name of Honeychile Mountjoy Hennessy.

'Odd kinda name for David Mountjoy's girl,' the barkeeper informed him. 'Rumour is David was never married to the mother, though she always called herself Rosie Mountjoy.' He grinned, knowingly. 'She was quite a character, that one. Quite a woman. Legs that never quit and a walk that gave you a boner just watching her step down the street.' He laughed. 'Used to be "Rarin' Rosie, the Sexiest Stripper on the Circuit", once upon a time. Before she married David Mountjoy, that is. Yes sir, there was always a man sniffin' round Rosie Hennessy. Just you check around San Antonio and you'll find out for yourself. That's where she worked, in the Silver Dollar Saloon. Until she died, that is.'

Smallbone ordered another beer. 'Rosie's dead?' he asked, interestedly.

'Yeah. Shot, outside the Saloon. Never did find who did it. David had died years before, and that just left the girl. Honeychile. She lives at the ranch with the help. They act like they're family, and I guess maybe for her they are, because she sure as hell ain't got nobody else round here. Sometimes see her at the movie-theatre, here in Kitsville. She loves all those romantic Hollywood musicals. You know, with the fancy women in fancy places wearing fancy dresses. Though I ain't never seen Honeychile in nothin' but blue overalls in her entire life.'

Smallbone thought of the shabby log ranch house with the corrugated tin roof and sagging porch, and the arid acres, spreading away into infinity. He ordered a whisky for the barkeeper and asked, casually, 'How's she make a living then? That ranch don't look worth a row of beans, to me.'

The barkeeper shrugged as he tossed back his drink. 'My guess is she don't. Leastways, only barely. Scrapin' a livin', like a lot of other folks round here, after the big drought. Before that, Mountjoy Ranch was a good spread. Ten thousand acres, a few thousand head of cattle – and good cattle too. Angus and Longhorns. Prime meat on the hoof.' He shrugged again. 'The Mountjoys were unlucky; their well dried up same year the drought struck. They lost all the cattle. The cowhands left to look for jobs in other states, and Honeychile was left with just Tom Jefferson, Aliza's son, to look after the place.

'They were just on the edge of going under when young Tom found a patch of green. He hired machinery and drilled for water. Now, y'gotta admire a young fella like that. Nothing was gonna stop him. He drilled day and night for weeks. For a while there was a rumour that he had found oil on the land; a big oil company came out and drilled around, but nothing came of it. Anyhow, Tom found an underground spring. He dug a well, but they don't know how long it'll last. They have a small herd now, not prime stuff this time, though. Honeychile works the ranch with Tom. They say she does the work of two men.'

He sighed contemplatively. 'A young woman like that should be thinkin' of gettin' married, raisin' a family instead of dreamin' about movie-stars. I guess she'd be passable-looking, if she tried a bit. Good enough for some of the horny old ranchers hereabouts, anyhow. And who knows, maybe she learned a thing or two from that sexy mother of hers.' He winked lewdly at Smallbone, who ordered him up another whisky and bade him goodnight.

He had a lot to think about, tossing and turning in the narrow iron boarding-house bed that night. At least he knew he had found his quarry. As he finally drifted off to sleep, he figured that it should be a hell of a lot easier dealing with a woman than a man.

He could not have been more wrong. Honeychile Mountjoy Hennessy did not want to speak to him, Aliza informed him icily, when he returned the next day. She was out on the range and didn't know when she would be back, and would he kindly get off her property before she set the dog on him.

Smallbone was used to such tactics. He went back to the general store, bought himself a loaf of bread, some cold-cuts, mustard and a couple of bottles of beer, then drove out to the ranch again. He parked under the shade of an ancient chestnut tree beside the rusty sign announcing that this was the Mountjoy Ranch, and prepared to wait it out. At some time or other, Honeychile would have to come out of this gate, and he intended to be there when she did.

He sat in the shade of the chestnut, eating his sandwich and swigging the beer, wondering idly how long it would take. Not that it mattered, he was being paid by the day plus all reasonable expenses, so it was no skin off his nose how long it took. Glancing round, he noticed a dusty old mason jar with a few wilting wild flowers, placed in a little hollow under the tree. Like some kind of shrine, he thought, puzzled. The sort of thing a kid would do.

The day was warm and he grew sleepy, listening to the wind moaning over the arid plains, sending the tumbleweed spinning down the empty highway, and the Mountjoy Ranch sign swinging squeakily back and forth. Gradually, he drifted into a doze.

Tom Jefferson honked the horn of Rosie's ancient fire-engine red Dodge, furiously, jolting Smallbone from his sleep.

'What the hell you blockin' my road for, mister?' Tom demanded irately.

Smallbone slowly unfurled his length from under the chestnut tree as Tom watched in amazement. He was a tall man himself, but this stranger was so tall he thought he would never quit. Then he realised.

'You must be the fella Ma told us about. The one askin' all the questions about the Mountjoys. I thought she told you to leave Honeychile alone. We don't want to hear about that skinflint old Earl. He ain't never done nothin' for Honeychile and her guess is he's not about to start now. Wants to get his hands on her ranch, more likely. Well, I'm telling you straight, mister, that girl has put her heart and soul into this place. She works harder than most men. And so did her Pa before her, and her grandfather.'

Smallbone eyed the irate Tom, uneasily. He was a good-looking young man in his late twenties. Tall, strong-limbed and muscular with a bronze skin, dark-brown eyes and a mouth that looked more used to smiling than the grim line it was set in now.

'Her grandfather,' Smallbone replied in his long Texas drawl. 'That would be old Georgie Mountjoy, wouldn't it?'

'What if it was?'

'And her father would be George's son, David?'

Tom glowered, saying nothing.

'I don't mean to be upsettin' no one,' Smallbone said, placatingly. 'It's just I was given a job to do, and now I guess I've done it. But I have a message for Miss Honeychile from her great-uncle – that's Georgie's brother. And I would surely like to pass it onto her personally.'

He glanced up at the sound of horse's hooves. 'Well, I'll be darned,' he drawled, with a pleased grin. 'If I ain't about to get my chance to do just that.'

Smallbone considered himself to be an expert on horseflesh, as well as on women. The horse was a magnificent Appaloosa: strong, with a proud head and a flowing white tail, and it was groomed to perfection. Its coat was glossy as fresh paint, its hooves were so clean they looked manicured and the silver on its bridle glittered in the sunlight.

He wished he could have said as much for the young woman riding the horse. She was tall and slender, and she was a mess. Her long blonde hair was plastered to her head with sweat and caught in a straggling tail at the back. She was wearing men's bib-front, blue work overalls with a grimy undershirt and scuffed cowboy boots. A layer of fine dust covered her from head to toe, giving her skin a greyish look, even her face from which her startlingly-blue eyes blazed angrily at him.

'I can guess who you are,' she said abruptly. 'I have nothing to discuss with you. Y'all leave my property. At once.'

'Excuse me, ma'am.' Smallbone tipped his Stetson, acting the perfect gentleman. 'But I'm not on your property.'

Honeychile glared at him. He was standing on the highway next to his car. 'Your automobile surely is. It's blocking my entrance. Kindly move it before I call the Sheriff and ask him to do it for you.'

'I assume I'm speaking to Miss Eloise Georgia Mountjoy Hennessy? More usually known as Honeychile? The daughter of Mr David Mountjoy and Miss Rosemary Hennessy?'

Honeychile turned white under the layer of dust. She looked like a frightened ghost.

'Don't you dare say anything about my mother,' she hissed menacingly. 'Don't even let my father's name cross your lips. How dare you push yourself onto us. I've heard you were asking questions around Kitsville. Why don't you just go away and leave me alone.'

'I'm sorry, ma'am, if I've upset y'all. I surely didn't intend that. My job was just to find you. Now I've confirmed your identity, I'll be on my way. I thank you for your trouble ma'am, and I apologise once again. No harm intended. In fact, exactly the reverse.'

Honeychile and Tom watched as Smallbone walked round his car and climbed in.

Honeychile turned her horse towards the car. She leaned forward in the saddle, looking down at him in the driver's seat. 'What do you mean – *the reverse*?'

'It's my understanding, ma'am, that Lord Mountjoy wishes to contact the descendants of his long-lost brother Georgie. The message I got was to tell you that you would hear "*something to your advantage*", and that Lord Mountjoy himself will be in touch with you. As soon as he gets my report, that is.' Smallbone touched his hat again politely. 'I'll be on my way now, so there's no need to call out the Sheriff. Thank you ma'am, for your time. Good day to y'all.'

Honeychile watched the battered bullet-scarred Chevy cough its way down the road, until it picked up speed and became a mere black dot on the long, shimmering white highway.

She glanced at Tom, her best friend since childhood and her confidant. Tom knew everything there was to know about her. A worried frown creased her dusty forehead. 'What do you make of it, Tom?'

'When legal folks talk about "*learning something to your advantage*", it usually means you're coming into money.' He glanced over his shoulder at the arid acres that were what was left of the Mountjoy Ranch. 'Seems to me, you cain't get no poorer. Maybe you *oughtta* see what old Lord Mountjoy has to offer.' He shrugged as he climbed back into Rosie's old red Dodge. 'Seems to me, you ain't got nothing much to lose.'

Honeychile did not want to believe it, but she knew Tom was right. They were poor. Dirt poor. Mountjoy Ranch was the driest, dustiest ranch in the area. It had the poorest grass, the stringiest cattle and the lowest water table. No matter how hard they worked, nothing was ever going to change that.

She sagged defeatedly in the saddle as she walked the horse slowly back down the lane to the ranch house. Tom had suddenly forced her to come to terms with the facts of her life and it hurt so badly she wanted to cry. Except she didn't cry much any more. She had disciplined herself not to ever since her father died, leaving a gap in her life that no one could ever fill.

When David Mountjoy had been in charge of the ten thousand acres that were the Mountjoy Ranch, they were fertile, prosperous, alive with the lowing and bellowing of his magnificent herd of Texas Longhorns and the prize Aberdeen Angus cattle he had imported specially from Scotland. The horses he loved, the Tennessee Walkers, the quarter horses and the Appaloosas, roamed the corrals, and in the evening the sound of the cowhands playing their guitars, singing and whistling as they barbecued their suppers down by the longhouse, drifted on the warm, deep-blue evening air.

They were the sights and sounds of Mountjoy Ranch that Honeychile had never forgotten. They kept her father alive in her memory. Inevitably though, when she thought about David, she thought about Rosie, her mother. And Rosie had left behind quite a different set of memories.

CHAPTER 10

When Eloise 'Honeychile' Mountjoy Hennessy was still only a child, she swore she could remember being held in her father's arms the day she was born. No one believed her, of course. But even when she grew up she could close her eyes and feel the blissful sensation of his strong arms enfolding her, feel the warmth of him and the sharp prickle of his citrusy cologne in her nostrils. It would be many years before she would know again that warmth and security, and total undemanding love.

Honeychile didn't know much about her father's family. She never even met her grandfather, Georgie Mountjoy, because one day, long before she was born, he was thrown from his startled horse on Dentelles Pass and had the misfortune to land on top of the irate rattler. He was only forty-three when he died. Papa was still a lanky boy of seventeen and Honeychile was only a starlike glimmer in the blackness of his future. But history said that as a young man in England, Grandpa Georgie Mountjoy had been a gambler and a rake. His English family had given him a one-way steamer ticket to America, and the thousand acre ranch near San Antonio, and they had told him never to return.

To his surprise, Georgie had found he liked Texas. He liked the easygoing manners and frontier lifestyle. He looked good in the ten-gallon hat and fringed chaps astride a spanky black stallion. He enjoyed carousing in the saloons where booze was cheap and the women were pretty enough, and available. But most of all, he loved the land.

He was lucky at cards, and when he won a few thousand dollars from a rich rancher, he added another couple of thousand acres to his Texan holdings; better land this time, rich with grasses and water. The cattle he bought thrived; he became prosperous and bought more land.

He also fathered a child with a pretty young woman named Connie Devine, a dancer at the Stagecoach Saloon in El Paso. He never married her, but he took good care of her. He bought her a little wooden-frame house in San Antonio, and he named his son David, not after anyone in his family, but because he liked the name.

Connie died when David was six years old, and Georgie found himself in a dilemma. He liked his freewheeling independence and had no wish to be tied down by a child. But this was *his* son. David was, after all, a Mountjoy, so he came to live with his father.

With Georgie as his role-model, it was a case of like father, like son. David looked like him: he was tall, wiry and whippet thin, with fair hair bleached gold by the strong sun, piercing blue eyes under bushy blond brows, and a firm chin. The slightly hooked Mountjoy nose added arrogance to his face, and his sensuous mouth gave him a sexy allure that, when he was older, women found irresistible. David was truly a chip off the old block.

Georgie Mountjoy was a jolly, lighthearted fellow. He lived his life with gusto and died with a curse on his lips for the rattler that struck him right between the eyes as he lay, stunned, on the dry stony outcrop overlooking his land.

David was seventeen when it happened, but he already knew how to run a ranch. He knew all about cattle, and grasses and legumes and diseases. He rode like a man born in the saddle and he knew how to handle the cowboys and the workers. He was clever but uneducated, having left school at the age of fourteen, and he was a pushover for a pretty face, a good pair of legs and a soft bosom. Women always fell for him, just the way they had for his father. And Rosie Hennessy was no different.

Rosemary Hennessy was the daughter of a travelling preacher. When she was fifteen, tired of being constantly on the road and at his beck-and-call, she had dug in her heels and refused to trek another mile. Instead of her preacher father abandoning her, she abandoned him.

Rosie quickly got herself a job at the grain and feed store on Main Street in San Antonio. She took a room at the Widow Martinez's grey wooden lodging house, with a breakfast of fresh corn *tortillas* and a substantial supper of *pozole* soup, *fajitas* and *frijoles* included in the small weekly rental. She was soon bored with the soup and the *tortillas*, but it was cheap and the house was clean and besides, she met a lot of interesting people at the store.

Every rancher and cowboy passed through Elias's Grain & Feed at sometime each month. And every woman in the neighbourhood, which in that part of Texas meant the surrounding few hundred miles, drove into town in their new Ford automobiles, or, the richer landowners in their smart Stutz roadsters, to patronise the drapery department next door, where Rosie now worked under the eagle eye and disdainful nose of the snobbish Miss Drysdale.

Miss Drysdale, grey and astringent, certainly knew how to keep a person in her place, and she certainly knew her own status – far superior to Rosie and most of the customers, but smarmily inferior to the richer women.

Rosie stuck it for almost two years. Then she woke up one fresh spring morning feeling the tingle of her own blood rushing through her veins and a restless spirit of excitement permeating her ripe young body. She threw off her flannel nightdress and, balancing precariously on an old wicker chair, she inspected herself, inch by naked inch, in the small wall mirror. She had to contort herself into unimaginable positions to do so, but what she saw was pretty good.

'Enough of dried-up old Miss Drysdale,' she decided, leaping gaily from the chair. She was young and beautiful and too good to waste behind the counter measuring out lengths of spotted voile for summer blouses. The whole world awaited her. Somewhere out there, beyond San Antonio.

It was an odd coincidence then, that like Georgie's mistress, she ended up in El Paso dancing two-steps with cowboys for a living. There she met the manager of a burlesque troupe, travelling the southern states performing in tents and small theatres, and he talked her out of her virginity and into his troupe of girls. And she became 'Rarin' Rosie, the Sexiest Stripper on the Circuit'.

The first time David Mountjoy saw Rosie Hennessy, she was fully clothed. She was strolling down Main Street in Houston, window shopping. She didn't even notice him, but he noticed her all right. Even dressed, she managed to look half-naked.

It was late September. The city was broiling under a heatwave and Rosie was wearing a flowery summer dress that clung to her every curve. The low-cut neckline revealed the faint sheen of sweat across the top of her round breasts and every now and then a swirling little wind flipped up her skirt, giving a quick tantalizing glimpse of pretty legs in shiny silk stockings.

David slowed as he approached her. Rosie was gazing into the department store window at a display of furs. Her eyes were riveted on a white ermine stole. She coveted it so badly, she thought she would do anything to have it. She could just see herself wrapped in it, arriving at some grand restaurant on the arm of a rich handsome guy. He would be wearing white tie and tails and she would be in a silver-spangled dress, as glamorous as any Broadway star. And they would be in New York, a city she had yet to see; yet to conquer with her lovely body.

She noticed the man next to her for the first time. They were both reflected in the plate glass window and she saw he was looking at her. Taking her in, was more like it. He was almost drinking her with his eyes.

Rosie smiled at him, a small conspiratorial smile that told him she knew just what he was thinking. She always enjoyed a man's admiration, it made her feel secure somehow. After all, her looks were her stock-in-trade. She liked the way he looked too. He was attractive and sexy. So sexy she could almost feel the heat coming off him. He was wearing denim pants and a workshirt and cowboy boots, and he looked as though he didn't have two cents to rub together. She heaved another sigh. He surely didn't look like the kind of guy who could buy her that ermine stole.

She turned from the window and met his eyes. Blue, and deep with longing. He was young too, not much older than she, and soooo cute. She felt that pleasant answering little tremble inside her as he held her eyes. Then, with another sly, seductive smile, she strode off down the street, swinging her hips in the walk she had practised in a thousand rented rooms and on a hundred dusty stages, in burlesque houses across the country.

She knew he was watching her; those blue eyes burned into her butt like a torch, and she turned to look at him again, laughing this time as she sauntered round the corner and headed for the theatre.

Rosie was a good stripper. She had quickly learned how to strut, how to bump and grind and dip, and how to use her fan to cover what she wanted kept covered. She knew how to shake that black feather fan just enough to give the audience, out there in the darkness beyond the footlights, a tantalizing glimpse of her soft, rounded white nakedness.

She learned just how far to go to keep within the city codes of decency, and exactly what daring things she could get away with beyond that. And that extra bit of daring was what had taken her from the flea-bag theatres and shared, roach-ridden boarding houses, to the bigger city theatres, her own small but clean hotel room, and her private curtained-off space in the strippers' dressing room.

She liked to make that space her own and her dressing table was covered with her collection of fluffy animals, her figurines of bunnies and bears and playful puppies, her swansdown powder-puffs and Tangee lipsticks, and her giant-size cobalt-blue bottle of Evening in Paris scent. Dozens of strings of bright glass beads and faux pearls were slung over a corner of the mirror and her 'costumes', black, white and red, *her* colours, were flung across her black tin trunk, printed with her name *Rosie Hennessy* and a host of little gold stars.

As the English gentleman his father had always reminded him he was, at first David had not liked to follow Rosie. Until she had flung him that tantalizing smile as she disappeared round the corner. Then nothing could stop him. He had watched her swing her way through the stage door and stood for a few minutes, hoping she would come out again.

The doorman watched him dourly. He was used to guys hanging round his doors. All kinds of guys. Young and old; fat and thin; rich and poor. They all wanted one thing. He tipped his derby over his eyes, stuck the half-smoked dime-store cigar between his teeth and tilted back his chair, watching him watching the doors.

David quickly tipped him five bucks and learned that she was 'Rarin' Rosie, the Sexiest Stripper on the Circuit', and that the next show was in two hours.

The roses arrived half an hour later. One hundred of them. They stood in galvanised-tin fire buckets in the strippers' dressing room, exhuding a faint hot-housey scent. And they were all white.

The other strippers crowded round Rosie, demanding to know who her admirer was, telling her she'd better hang onto him and to watch out for JoJo who was a notorious man-stealer. JoJo shrugged her shoulders, hitching up a satin strap and glaring at Rosie.

'He's just after your cute little ass, baby,' JoJo said nastily, slashing magenta lipstick across her wide mouth.

'How did he know my favourite colour is white?' Rosie said, ignoring her. 'I wonder who he is?'

'Whoever he is, he'll be out there tonight. In the front row,' JoJo told her. 'Taking it all in for the price of a ticket. Maybe he's a millionaire come to take you away from all this,' she added with a sceptical laugh.

Later, when Rosie stalked the stage in a black satin teddy and fishnet stockings – with about half a yard of bare flesh in between, the girls crowded in the wings, whispering and giggling, peering into the dim recesses of the auditorium for a glimpse of Rosie's mysterious admirer.

She couldn't see him, but David was there all right; in the aisle seat, third row centre. He hadn't expected anything like this: Rosie looked sensational in that underwear. He cast an irate glance at the guy in the next seat who was watching Rosie's every move through a pair of binoculars; he already felt as though Rosie was 'his girl'. David felt himself tremble with excitement as she strutted across the stage, switching her hips provocatively, the way she had done walking down the street, knowing he was watching her.

With one slow, lingering movement, Rosie slipped out of the black satin teddy. The audience gave a collective gasp, laughing as she covered herself quickly with the fan. Rosie smiled seductively at them. She enjoyed what she did; she liked them to like her, admire her, want her. Especially the unknown admirer in the audience. It gave her a special little thrill. As though she was dancing just for him. *As though she were making love to him.*

Slowly, she lowered the fan, caressing herself lingeringly as she slid her hand away, allowing them to see her glorious breasts, tipped with spangled tassels. She stretched herself taller and swung her tassels for them, laughing as they whistled and applauded. She could feel their eyes burning into her as she stood there, naked but for the spangled, flesh-coloured scrap of chiffon between her legs, and the sequinned tassels. Then, giving them a sexy little shrug of the shoulders, she sauntered, breasts bouncing, to the footlights.

Rosie had one daring little trick left. She had to be careful in case any of the city morals inspectors were watching, but tonight she didn't even think about it. This was for him. Her unknown admirer. The guy who had sent her one hundred white roses deserved a little bonus, after all.

She stalked the footlights, first downstage then back up again, giving them her famous strut, her biggest smile, her sexiest poses. Then, knees demurely together, prim as a schoolgirl, she flipped aside the chiffon G-string. Dipping first to one side, then the other, she gave her audience a quick glimpse of the soft, pale, naked triangle beneath.

They were on their feet, hollerin' out her name. 'Rarin' Rosie', they yelled. 'Do it again, babe . . . you're the greatest, I love ya Rosie . . . do it for me . . .'

Smiling, she turned her back on them and sauntered slowly from the apron. The spotlight focused on her pearly rump, twitching enticingly beneath the black feather fan. She paused, legs apart, hands on her hips, and gave them that one last over-the-shoulder smile they would surely remember in their dreams that night.

CHAPTER 11

That was Rarin' Rosie's final performance. The Sexiest Stripper on the Circuit never did make it to New York City. The city morals and decency inspector was waiting for her backstage, with a summons to appear in court on corruption charges.

Wrapped in her shabby chenille robe, Rosie sat hunched over her dressing table, looking scared. JoJo leaned against the wall, glamorous in black chiffon and not much else, smoking a pink cigarette in a long black holder, with an 'I told you so' little smile on her face. The other girls quickly flung on robes and sat around, trying to look innocent and inconspicuous, while the black-suited official harangued Rosie. Red-faced with anger and self-righteousness he told her in no uncertain terms, what a trollop she was and that she was a disgrace to the community and his fine city.

David stood in the doorway, taking in the situation.

'You are a disgrace to womanhood,' the official ranted on, 'exposing your naked . . . your *nakedness* to every man in the audience . . .'

'Including you, fella,' David said. 'Weren't you the guy sitting next to me, the one with the binoculars?'

'Binoculars . . . ? I don't know what you mean?' The man's face turned beet red and he looked suddenly flustered.

'Sure you do, fella,' David replied calmly. 'I saw your hands trembling.'

The man took out a white handkerchief and mopped the sweat from his brow. 'It's my job,' he blustered, 'I have to know exactly how naked she is . . .'

'Sure you do. It's the nature of your employment. We all understand that. Don't we girls?' They nodded silently, watching in the mirror to see what would happen.

'Why don't you and I have a little talk about this,' David suggested, laying a genial arm across the shaken man's shoulders. 'Out in the hallway, so these young ladies can get dressed in private.'

Rosie's frightened blue eyes followed him. He turned and gave her a cheerful wink as he led the official, still red-faced and blustering about his job, out into the corridor.

Five minutes later there was a knock on the door. Rosie bit her lip anxiously. Was she going to jail? Or had her unknown admirer saved her? 'Come in,' she said in a tremulous little voice. Every eye in the room was on the door as it opened.

'Miss Rosie,' David said, smiling confidently, 'I would be a proud man if you would do me the honour of dining with me tonight.'

His eyes – almost as blue as hers – were drinking her in. In a room full of beautiful half-naked women, she was the only one he saw.

Rosie smiled back at him. 'I'd be charmed,' she replied demurely.

Heads turned again when David Mountjoy escorted Rosie Hennessy into the oak-panelled, potted-palm grandeur of the Warwick Hotel dining room. He thought she looked stunning in a black velvet hat and a clinging red dress with one of his white roses tucked between her perfect breasts. And she thought he looked even cuter than when she had first seen him reflected in the department store window.

'Everybody's looking at me,' Rosie said, hesitating nervously on the top step.

'I don't blame them.' Taking her arm David followed the maitre d' to a discreet corner booth.

'It's like I always dreamed about,' she said breathless with excitement. 'Being in a fancy restaurant, the maitre d' recognising us – well, *you* at least. Except I always thought you would be wearing tie and tails. And I'd have on a white ermine stole and we would be in New York City.'

He laughed. 'Sorry I didn't live up to your dream.'

'Oh, you did. You *do*.' She took his hand across the table, feeling him tremble as their eyes locked again, sending the same urgent message.

The waiter coughed discreetly. David beckoned him closer. 'I know it's difficult these days,' he whispered, 'with Prohibition. But

I'd surely like to order some French champagne.' He slid a large denomination dollar bill into the waiter's palm.

The waiter took in Rosie's charms in a quick glance. He smiled. 'A wise choice sir.'

'I've never tasted French champagne,' Rosie confessed. 'Most guys just buy you bathtub gin.' She giggled, nervous again. 'What did you do to the morals inspector? Bump him off or something?'

David shrugged nonchalantly. 'Money always talks.'

She studied him, hardly believing her luck. He was handsome *and* sexy. *And* he had money. 'You must be very rich?' He looked steadily at her, saying nothing. 'I mean all those roses and the French champagne . . . and everything.'

'I have a ranch. South of San Antonio.'

'Ohhh, your own ranch.' Rosie smiled, pleased. Ranchers were rich guys: they owned acres and acres of land and millions of cattle. She knew that from her days in Elias's Drapery Department. 'I'm kind of from San Antonio myself,' she said as the waiter poured champagne discreetly into two water glasses.

David lifted his glass to hers. 'Here's to us, Rosie,' he said.

'To us,' she repeated, thrilled.

David ordered dinner for them, but they hardly ate: they were too busy holding hands and gazing at each other over the tops of their champagne glasses. It seemed no time at all before they were in the elevator and on their way up to David's room.

'Oh God, Rosie,' he said, closing the door and looking at her. 'I don't think I can wait.'

'Me neither,' she said, hauling her dress over her head. She stood in front of him, naked but for the spangled chiffon G-string she had worn on stage. 'I thought you would like it,' she said with a pouting mischievous smile.

His eyes lingered on that famous triangle. 'Why did you do it? Show all those guys your sex like that?'

'In my business, you do what you can get away with. That's how you get to the top. Minsky's and New York City.' She stood, legs apart, hands on hips in her sexiest stage pose. 'And now I'm gonna do it again. Just for you.' And she did.

With a great shout of laughter he swept her into his arms and onto the bed.

Rosie was no sexual innocent and neither was David. He loved the way she yelled out instructions to him, telling him exactly what to do, what she liked. 'Do this, do that . . . no, here, oh more more, please, more.' He loved the way she yelped her pleasure with each thrust, and she liked what he was doing to her all right. 'Ah, Ah, Ahhhhhh do it to me, Dave,' she yelled.

He paused. Lifting himself on his arms he looked at her. '*David*,' he corrected her. Then he continued what he was doing.

'Do it to me there, yes, yes, ohhh yessss . . .' She was a girl who knew exactly what she wanted.

'Rosie, ohhhhh Rosie, I think I love you,' he shouted as he finally came inside her in a great tumultuous shuddering climax.

Lying beneath him, her sweat mingling with his, Rosie pondered on that remark. '*I think*' was not the phrase she wanted to hear. '*I love you*' was. She resolved to do her damndest to change it.

Late the next afternoon, when they finally got out of bed, she went back to the theatre.

'Soooo? How was Prince Charming?' the girls demanded, crowding round.

'Terrific,' she replied, airily, sweeping her collection of fluffy animals and figurines from the dressing table and into her trunk. 'We drank French champagne at the Warwick with all the other rich folk.'

'Lucky you weren't in jail, *Miss* Hennessy,' the stage manager said angrily from the door, 'and me with you. You'd better not try that again, or you'll be out on your famous ass.'

Rosie tossed her head haughtily as she flung a tangle of lacy garments on top of the toys and figurines. 'You should think yourself lucky. You'll see, you'll have a full house tonight.'

'What are you doing?' JoJo asked, watching her through a haze of cigarette smoke.

'Packing.'

'Packing? Why . . . who . . . where?'

'San Antonio,' Rosie lifted her chin triumphantly. 'I'm getting married.'

'*Married*. Who to? Prince Charming?'

The stage manager grinned sceptically. 'Somebody's fooling you, kid. Strippers don't get married. They just get old.'

Rosie threw him an angry glare. 'Well this one's getting married. And to a *rich* guy. A rancher.'

'Oh yeah. Just wait till he gets you back to that ranch and you find out he's only a cheap cowhand.' He laughed coarsely, 'That is if he hasn't left town already; now he's had all you've got to offer.'

Rosie's heart missed a beat. Was it true? Had David left town? Left *her*? He had promised her he would be waiting, but she was lying when she said she was getting married. *'I can't leave you,'* David had said. *'Come with me Rosie, back to San Antonio.'* But there had been no mention of marriage. She just figured that when she got there she'd make him feel so good he wouldn't be able to live without her. He would have to marry her then. Besides, he was *sooo* cute and so sexy, just thinking about him made her shiver with pleasure.

Oh Lord, she prayed, flinging her old chenille robe on top of the rest of her stuff and slamming down the lid, please let him be waiting. Please, *please*, let him be there.

She kissed all the girls goodbye, and even cynical JoJo, relieved to see the back of her rival, wished her luck, waving as the cab wafted Rosie and all her worldly belongings in the old black tin trunk, off to her new life.

'Lucky Rosie,' they sighed enviously, turning reluctantly back to the mirrors and the make-up and the bump-and-grind music, and the first performance of the evening.

Rosie's heart leapt with relief when she saw David, waiting in the hotel foyer. He was sitting in a big leather chair next to a potted-palm, reading a newspaper, and she thought he looked as though he owned the place.

There was a large shiny red box tied with a scarlet bow on the table in front of him. She stared at it, then up at David, questioningly.

'A present,' he said, grinning nonchalantly.

Rosie couldn't remember the last time she had received a present. *Payment* was more usual. Her face was alight with pleasure as she ran her fingers over the tempting red satin ribbon.

'Go on. Open it,' he said, smiling at her look of childish delight.

'Open it *now*?' She looked at him, wide-eyed, smiling, pretty. Then she ripped off the red ribbon and flung open the box.

'Oh,' she said, 'Oh! Oh! Ohhh . . .' He thought she sounded just the way she did when he was making love to her.

She lifted the white ermine stole with the little black tails from its box and flung it round her shoulders. She held it to her cheek, feeling its softness, inhaling its scent, its luxury.

'Let's go Rosie,' he said, taking her arm.

This time the doorman held the door for her, and a porter hefted her gold-starred black trunk into the boot of David's brand new Ford motor car, that she knew must have cost a fortune.

'We're on our way, Rosie,' David said, squeezing her knee, as they sputtered off down the street. On their way to San Antonio, and the Mountjoy Ranch. And, Rosie hoped, a life of rich, wedded bliss.

CHAPTER 12

It didn't work out quite like that, but then, Rosie told herself, life never did. David Mountjoy was an indefatigable lover; he was affectionate towards her and he cared about her. She knew, because he told her so. But even when, a couple of months later, sitting up in bed on an unusually chilly November morning, she told him she was pregnant, he did not ask her to marry him. He just grinned with surprise and pleasure and said, 'It'll be a boy, I just know it.'

'It'll be a bastard,' she retorted, 'unless you marry me.'

He threw back his head, laughing heartily and said, 'Like father, like son.'

Tears spurted from her eyes, and he gazed remorsefully at her. Rosie was fun but he just wasn't ready for the full commitment yet. Maybe it was in the genes, he thought, remembering the bastards his own father, Georgie, had supposedly sired in Europe. And then himself, another illegitimate brat.

'Rosie, don't cry,' he said, anxiously. 'I told you, I think I love you. Maybe we'll get married one day.'

'What about the baby?' she sniffed tearfully. 'He'll need his father.'

'He's got a father,' he said gently. 'I promise you I shall always look after him. And you. You have my word, Rosie. Only I just can't marry you right now, this minute. I have to think about it.'

'Well, don't take too long,' she warned him, mollified. 'He'll be born before you know it, only seven months.'

His eyes met hers questioningly. 'Seven months?'

She nodded, smiling at him. 'It must have happened that first night. The first time we did it. Remember?'

He took her in his arms and kissed her lingeringly, remembering that tumultuous climax. 'How could I ever forget,' he whispered, climbing back into bed.

The Mountjoy Ranch was big all right. Acre after lonely acre of flat prairie, dotted with scrub brush and Texas Longhorns and fine Angus cattle, leading monotonously into infinity. The house, such as it was, was in the south-western corner, surrounded by barns and stables and corrals filled with David's fine horses. It had been built, or more accurately – flung together – before Georgie Mountjoy ever got there, and he had seen no reason to alter the simple one-storey log structure, with three steps leading up to a porch that ran all the way round the house. There was a rocker on that porch, and an old-fashioned pot-bellied stove in the kitchen that was also the living room, and the 'facilities' were in an outhouse at the back. Rosie hadn't been there a week before she realised that when the wind was in the right direction, there was no mistaking where those 'facilities' were.

The kitchen was presided over by plump, cheerful Mrs Aliza Jefferson, a black lady from Galveston who lived with her young son, Thomas, in a two-room 'cottage' down the dusty, rutted lane. She had looked after David for ten years, and Rosie had no cause to interfere with that arrangement, but something had to be done about the facilities – and the rest of the place.

David had told her the story of his father, Georgie, and his aristocratic family in England, and she demanded to know how he could live in such squalor. 'You should know better,' she scolded him, 'with your background. Whatever would those Lords and Ladies think if they came visiting?'

'Don't worry Rosie,' he replied drily. 'The Mountjoys haven't visited in fifty years. I hardly think they're going to show up now.'

But the following week a crew of workmen appeared at her door with instructions from David to carry out whatever Rosie wanted done. Even he was astonished by the scope of her plans: she wanted a proper bathroom and water closet; a bedroom for the baby; and a new kitchen for Aliza, with a decent cookstove. Fans were installed in the ceilings to stir the hot sluggish summer air, and a bigger stove to warm the place in winter.

Brand new furniture was chosen from a Sears catalogue and Rosie was almost sick with excitement when it finally arrived by train, all the way from Grand Rapids. And, with her pregnant belly sticking jauntily out in front of her, she returned to Elias's Drapery Department in San Antonio on a shopping expedition.

Miss Drysdale was still there and Rosie took great pleasure in placing her large order with her.

'Just charge it all to Mr David Mountjoy's account,' she told Miss Drysdale loftily. '*I* am Mrs Mountjoy.' Of course it wasn't true, but she *was* wearing a ring. It was David's signet ring with the Mountjoy crest that used to be his father's. Twisted round, it looked exactly like a gold wedding band and over it she wore the other ring David had given her: two bright small diamonds on either side of a pretty little ruby.

She could tell Miss Drysdale was impressed, even if all she said, sniffily, was, 'Come up in the world, haven't you, miss.'

'You betcha,' Rosie retorted with a cocky little grin as she strolled from the store.

So, all was in readiness on the warm humid night in April when the baby was born, early. The pains came on quite suddenly at four o'clock and by nine o'clock the baby was there, aided on her way by the experienced Aliza.

'She just popped right out,' Aliza told David, amazed. 'It must have been all that bumpin' and grindin' did it.'

'She?' David asked, standing by the bed, smiling down at Rosie.

'It's not a boy,' Rosie explained, as Aliza appeared holding the infant wrapped in a soft white shawl.

'Oh my, oh my, this little honeychile is gonna be a beauty,' Aliza said. 'Blonde and blue-eyed, like her Ma and Pa. Yes sir, this is one little honeychile all right.'

David took his daughter in his arms. He stared down at her funny little face. Her blue eyes, still opaque with the newness of birth, fastened on his and he felt his heart suddenly lurch with true love for her. He touched her cheek with one finger, feeling its softness; and he hefted the small weight of her in his arms. Then he bent his head and kissed her. 'A "honeychile", that's what you are,' he whispered. 'Daddy's little honeychile.'

And that's why they always called her Honeychile; even though she was baptised Eloise Georgia Mountjoy Hennessy in St Michael's Episcopal Church in Dallas. The ceremony was in Dallas because

Rosie didn't want anyone in San Antonio to know that she still wasn't married to David Mountjoy, though she had hopes.

David went out and bought his little Honeychile the cuddliest, softest teddy bear he could find. 'Here, my little girl,' he said tenderly, as he put it next to her in her crib, 'here's teddy for you to hug when your Papa's not here.' And darn it, if she didn't throw her arm round that teddy and rest her cheek against his softness. She gave a happy little sigh as her eyes closed. And so did David. Somehow, now he had Honeychile, his life was complete.

As the weeks crawled by and the arid heat of summer struck the flat Texas plains, a strange emotion stirred in Rosie.

'You're just plain jealous, that's all,' Aliza told her bluntly. She hovered over her new cookstove, anxiously inspecting the simmering pots of chicken and the hominy grits which were David's favourites. 'It's natural enough, after a woman's given birth, to feel that way. Kinda left outta things. Babies always come first,' she added wisely.

'Ain't that the truth,' Rosie said bitterly. Babies had to be fed first; bathed first; *kissed first*. Honeychile always got first kiss when David came striding up the steps in the evening, calling out her name. It was always Honeychile, Honeychile, Honeychile . . . 'Goddamn it,' she thought sulkily, 'what about me?'

The years slid slowly past. Rosie never did learn to ride a horse, the way David wanted her to, so she could ride out with him and share his life. Instead, she learned to drive. She would take off in David's Ford for San Antonio and yet another shopping expedition, and then lunch at a fancy restaurant where she had a chance to show off her new clothes. Sometimes, she would not get home until late, when it was already dark.

Aliza always stayed with Honeychile until Rosie returned and she would breathe a sigh of relief when she saw the headlamps jumping up and down as the car bounced over the ruts in the lane that led from the highway. Somehow she always wondered whether Rosie would come home or whether, this time, she had gone for good, back to the burlesque theatres she missed so much.

Laden with new lipsticks and scent and frou-frou little dresses, Rosie threw down her packages, kicked off her high heels, and started to tell Aliza all about the movie she had just seen; the new fashions the women were wearing in town, and what local celebrities she had noticed in the restaurant, with never a question about her own, already-sleeping little daughter. And Aliza could swear she caught a whiff of liquor on Rosie's breath.

It was different with David. 'Hey Honeychile,' he would call as he strode up the steps to the porch at the end of a long day. 'Where are you baby?' And from the time she took her first steps at the age of thirteen months, Honeychile would come running towards him as fast as she could, her blonde hair flying, her eyes alight with excitement, and a big adoring smile on her sweet face.

Rosie would rock sulkily back and forth on the old porch swing, smoking a cigarette – a new habit she had adopted – watching silently as David lifted Honeychile high into the air. The child squealed with delight as he pretended to drop her, then he clasped her to him and gave her a big kiss.

'How's Mom today?' he asked, coming over to Rosie. She offered her cheek for his kiss and he breathed in her perfume and said appreciatively, 'Mmmmmm, that new?' And he gave her a broad wink that told her she could expect more from him later. But Rosie knew his heart belonged to Honeychile.

David first put Honeychile on a horse – a proper horse, not a pony because David never liked ponies, he thought they were too snappy and temperamental – when she was two years old, strapping her into a special saddle with a little wicker seat, just so she could get the feel of it. Honeychile yelled with joy as the horse paced round the corral on a leading rein. By the age of three she had dispensed with the wicker seat and learned to ride in an English saddle, and when she was four David gave her her own horse.

Lucky was an Appaloosa, grey and white spotted with vertically striped hooves, a flowing creamy mane and the longest tail of any horse Honeychile had ever seen. She loved her on sight and the feeling was mutual. Honeychile rode Lucky out on the range with her father, sometimes spending the whole day with him. Rosie didn't seem to miss her but Aliza was afraid for her.

'No need to worry,' David reassured her. 'Lucky's the most sure-footed animal I've ever owned. When Honeychile gets tired, we stop and she eats her lunch and takes a little nap. Besides, it's good for her to learn about the ranch. After all, it will all be hers some day.'

And that's the way things stood the day David Mountjoy drove his Ford out of the lane onto the highway, and under the wheels of a speeding cattle truck taking a load of heifers to market. He was flung from the car and the last thing he saw as he hit the ground was the Mountjoy Ranch sign, swinging above him. And the last thing he heard was the terrified bellowing of the cattle stampeding from the truck, as they trampled what was left of the life out of him.

Two days later, Rosie stood at the graveside wearing a clinging black silk crêpe de Chine dress and a smart black hat with a veil, crying tears of rage at David Mountjoy for dying before he married her. Her only consolation was that she realised none of the neighbours knew she was not really 'Mrs Mountjoy'. But she was concerned because she thought his lawyer might know the truth. As David's widow, she would inherit the ranch. As Rosie Hennessy, she would get nothing.

Honeychile clutched her mother's hand tightly. Her blue eyes were dark with horror as they lowered the handsome polished oak coffin with its silver handles into the gaping black hole in the churchyard. They had told her her father was in there and she screamed out loud when the preacher threw handfuls of earth after the coffin.

'Hush, child,' Aliza said softly. 'Your Pa's all right now. He's in heaven with Jesus.' And young Tom Jefferson, Aliza's son, gripped her hand comfortingly in his, wiping away his own tears as they walked slowly from the grave.

Honeychile stopped at the top of the small grassy slope and turned back to look. 'I'll remember you, Daddy,' she called out in her high clear voice. 'I'll always love you. I promise.'

But the biggest blow was yet to come for Rosie. She had gone to see David's attorney about the Will. She took Honeychile with her, not because she wanted her company, but to reinforce her position as David's 'wife'. Still, she crossed her fingers and prayed the lawyer would not demand to see her non-existent marriage certificate before he handed over the Mountjoy Ranch, and the money.

She planned to sell the ranch; buy herself a big new house with a white pillared portico in Houston, where there was some real action. Then she'd have a grand time as the 'rich widow Mountjoy'. At last, she would have some fun.

When the lawyer, who was as old and doddery as Methuselah and had looked after Georgie Mountjoy's affairs from the beginning, told her that she had not inherited the ranch, Rosie's heart skipped a couple of beats.

He said, 'Georgie Mountjoy left the ranch "in trust" for his heirs. That means it cannot be sold; it stays in the family for ever. David inherited the ranch for his lifetime, and now his daughter, Honeychile, inherits it for hers.'

He smiled at the little girl who looked as small and lost in her big leather chair as he did himself. 'It's sort of like being a caretaker,' he said. 'Honeychile, in turn, will pass it onto her own children. And so on, and so on, in perpetuity.'

Rosie didn't know what perpetuity meant, but she did understand the ranch wasn't hers to sell after all, and now the big new house with the white pillared portico would never be hers either.

'*Goddamn it*,' she snarled, 'David left the ranch to the kid.'

The lawyer flinched at the curseword. He wasn't used to such language in his discreet, dark-panelled office with its generations of files overflowing from every cupboard, and its shelf after shelf of heavy leather-bound legal tomes.

'Not exactly, Mrs Mountjoy,' he said crisply. 'And don't forget you get the money. The sum of fifty-nine thousand dollars in David's account in the Bank of Texas is yours alone.' He pushed a legal document across the desk to Rosie. 'If you would just sign here, I shall witness your signature, and our business is complete.'

Rosie perked up at the mention of the money. She gave him the kind of smile that made him understand what David Mountjoy had seen in her, then signed, '*Rosie Mountjoy*,' with a flourish. 'Is that all?' she asked, smoothing down her skirt as she got to her feet.

'That's it, Mrs Mountjoy.' She gave him that all-embracing smile again as she strode to the door with the provocative swing of the hips that was automatic to her.

'Mrs Mountjoy,' he called as she stepped out the door.

'Yeah?' She popped her head back in.

'*Your daughter.*'

Rosie stared, surprised, at Honeychile, still sitting on the edge of the slippery leather chair. 'Goddamn,' she said, laughing, 'I forgot all about the kid. Come on babe, hurry up, why don't ya.

Now you're a rich rancher you've got to look after your Mommie. And don't you ever forget that.'

Rosie bought a couple of bottles of illegal bourbon from her 'connection' on the way home. Then she left Honeychile waiting, alone in the car, while she stopped off to have a 'little drink' in a speakeasy she knew, returning two hours later, slightly the worse for wear. She drove erratically home and retired to her room with the bottles.

'You goddamn fool, David,' she muttered to herself later that night, after the first bottle was finished. 'Gettin' yourself killed like that.' Tears ran unchecked down her face as she thought about him. She was bored and lonely.

'You had the best years of my life, David Mountjoy,' she sobbed drunkenly. 'You didn't even marry me and then you went and left the ranch to your kid, instead of me.' And she hurled the empty bottle at the wall, flinching as it exploded into a thousand sparkling shards.

'Mommie?' Honeychile was standing in the doorway in her white cotton nightgown, looking frightened. 'Why did you break the bottle?'

Rosie stared at her. 'It's all your fault,' she yelled, flinging herself back onto her pillows. 'If it weren't for you, the ranch would be mine. Oh, get outta here you little brat,' she sobbed. *'Get the hell outta my life and don't bother to come back.'*

Honeychile ran back to her room. She went to the window and stared into the night as though she might see her father out there, coming home, calling her name. A trembling feeling of desolation made her knees weak and she sank to the floor. 'Why did it happen Daddy?' she asked. 'Why did you have to go away and leave me?'

She knelt there for a long time, oblivious to the cold. When the dawn light finally tinted the horizon with grey, she stood up stiffly and put on her old blue bib-overalls. She walked silently down the hall, past her mother's room, through the kitchen and out onto the porch. She sniffed the cool clean early-morning air for a moment. It was too early even for Tom Jefferson to be at the stables and she was too small to saddle up Lucky herself, so instead she walked up the long rutted lane, leading from the ranch to the highway.

She stood in the shifting shade of the old chestnut tree at the entrance to the property, the same tree they said had blocked her father's vision for a fatal instant as he drove out into the road. She stared at the place where he had died. There was no blood; no tyre marks or lumps of twisted metal; no evidence left that a tragedy had taken place here. There was nothing left of her father.

Honeychile walked from the shade into the already blazing sunlight. She stared left, then right, along the silent highway, shimmering into infinity across the flat horizon. Then she sat down in the middle of the road, legs crossed, waiting for the cattle truck to come and get her too. So she could be in heaven with her father.

It was Tom who found her, a couple of hours later. Her own mother hadn't even missed her, but Aliza had.

He rode down the lane, slowing down when he saw Honeychile, sitting cross-legged in the middle of the road. His heart missed a beat when he looked at her; at the way her head drooped wearily on her slender neck; at her knobbly knees and stick-like limbs, and the way the sun bounced off her golden hair. He was fourteen years old and he knew then he would always love Honeychile Mountjoy. It was a moment he would never forget.

Dismounting, he hitched his horse to a low branch on the chestnut tree. 'Honeychile,' he called softly, walking over to her. 'What you doin' here, baby?' He crouched next to her and she looked at him with weary, sun-dazzled blue eyes. 'I know,' he said holding up his hand. 'You're just waiting for your Daddy to come and get you, ain't you?'

Honeychile nodded, still gazing at him. He sighed as he took her small hot hand in his. 'Well, baby, I have to tell you it just don't work that way. The Lord only takes those He wants. And He takes them exactly when *He* wants them. And right now, Honeychile, He just wants your Daddy, and not you.'

'Nobody wants me then,' she said with a sudden ragged sob. 'Not even the Lord.'

'The Lord wants you all right.' Tom stroked her hair gently back from her tear-stained face. 'He just don't want y'all right now, Honeychile. And I do. All of us at the ranch do. They're all out there looking for you, half out of their minds. My Ma is goin' crazy with worry. So let's you and me go on back there now, and tell them you're fine.'

He helped her up and they stood together for a moment looking at the place where David had died. 'Tell you what, Honeychile,' he said suddenly. 'Why don't you and me go and pick some flowers. Ma will give us an old mason jar and we'll fill it with water to keep those flowers fresh. Then we'll ride back here together and you can set it right here, under the tree. In memory of your Pa.'

Honeychile looked up at him with fathomless blue eyes. 'Yes,' she said simply. Then, as he swung her up in the saddle in front of him, 'Thank you Tom. You're my best friend.'

'Sure,' he said, holding her tight in front of him. And he hoped in his heart he always would be.

CHAPTER 13

Rosie soon remembered the fifty-nine thousand dollars, and that she was an heiress after all. She went to San Antonio and bought herself a brand new bright red Dodge automobile and a whole lot of new outfits. Silk dresses, kid-leather shoes with high heels and half a dozen of the latest hats. Then she took the train to Houston and a suite at the Warwick, and she did a little more shopping, buying herself the full-length mink coat she had always promised herself one day. Daringly, she went to the beauty parlour and had her long blonde hair cut in the latest short bob, and she scoured the stores for whatever was the newest in lipstick shades and powder and rouge, and treated herself to the biggest size bottle of French perfume in the store.

Dizzy with pleasure, she returned to her hotel suite and flung her purchases onto the bed with a happy sigh. Then she ordered a bottle of expensive bourbon and some ice from the bell-boy who had 'connections', and sat down to contemplate where she might go to wear all her new finery.

'There's just no one to appreciate me,' she sniffed tearfully into her glass. 'No one at all, now David's gone.' That familiar pleasant thrill ran through her body as she thought of David and their lovemaking. She really missed him. What she needed, she decided after a couple more drinks, was a man.

She wore black, that night, because after all she was in mourning. Soft and clinging, with a low V-neckline, fastened with her diamond bunny pin. She flung a couple of ropes of her old *faux* pearls round her neck because without her long hair, somehow she felt a bit naked, and she wore a chic little black cloche hat covered in satiny black feathers. It was much too warm, but she wore her new mink anyway, and she felt a little thrill of power when the doorman leapt to find a cab for her as she left for the burlesque theatre.

That's what money does for a girl, she thought, satisfied. If only David had treated her like this more often, maybe she wouldn't have been so bored. And just look where staying home got him. Under the wheels of a truck and all those goddamned heifers.

But she wasn't going to think about David tonight. Nor about Honeychile owning the ranch when it should have been hers. She had fifty-nine thousand bucks – well, maybe a bit less after today's shopping spree, she thought, with a giggle. And she was gonna forget all her troubles and have herself a good time.

She studied the pictures outside the burlesque theatre intently, but the only face she recognised was JoJo's. 'Wouldn't ya just know it,' she said resignedly.

The woman in the ticket booth stared hard at her. 'Don't I know you?' she asked, puzzled.

'I certainly don't think so,' Rosie replied haughtily, pulling her mink closer around her shoulders and striding into the theatre.

She glanced from side to side as she took an aisle seat near the back. She smiled as she saw that, of course, she was the only woman in the audience. The men glanced sideways at her, taking her in and she tilted her nose aloofly in the air, reading the advertisements on the safety curtain, for Dr Carter's Little Liver Pills, and Gramma Hotchkiss's Cough Linctus, and Scholls Bunion Relievers.

'Lord,' she thought, despondently, 'can all the guys here be that old and decrepit?'

The guy on the row behind and three seats along certainly wasn't. He was tall and well-built. He had black hair brushed back from a widow's peak and he was good-looking if you liked those dark Irish sort of looks. And, she told herself with a giggle, that if she thought about him any more she might find herself suddenly becoming quite fond of Guinness and shamrock.

Then the lights went down and the band struck up a squeaky overture, and the comic came on with his familiar patter to make the intros. Rosie was soon so wrapped up in the old show-biz glamour of it all, it was as though she had never left. Her heart sank as she noticed how young the strippers looked, though. *As young as she had been, when she played the circuit*, she thought with an envious pang.

In the interval, she lit a cigarette and sat moodily blowing smoke rings and thinking about her future. The stage lured her like a child to ice cream, but she knew it was too late. She was too old.

She stubbed out the cigarette viciously, glaring over her shoulder as a male voice said, 'Excuse me?'

It was the good-looking 'Irishman'. 'I saw you were alone and . . . well, I wondered whether I might buy you some refreshment?'

He gave her a polite smile while she studied him. He was well-dressed and in good shape and he did not have a moustache. Rosie couldn't abide men with facial hair.

'No strings attached,' he added with another smile. 'I promise.'

He had nice teeth, she noticed, white and strong, and as he bent over her she caught a whiff of eau de cologne. He's a gentleman she decided, because in her experience only true gents wore cologne. Her spirits rose as she looked at him. 'Why not?' she agreed, standing up.

He held her arm as they walked up the aisle and into the bar that sold only soft drinks. He asked her what she would like, then ordered two plain sodas. He took a silver flask from his pocket and looked enquiringly at her. 'Bourbon?' he asked. She nodded, smiling as he discreetly doctored their drinks.

'My name is Jack Delaney,' he said, looking into her eyes.

'Rosie Hennessy,' she said. Then quickly, 'Rosie Mountjoy, I mean.'

He took a sip of the bourbon. 'You're married?'

'Widowed. That's why I'm wearing black. Naturally.'

'Naturally,' he agreed solemnly. 'That's a mighty pretty mink coat you're wearing. Isn't it a bit warm for furs though?'

Rosie smiled with pleasure. 'I just bought it. Today, as a matter of fact. I wanted to wear it so bad, I thought the hell with the weather. Who cares what the temperature is anyhow?'

He laughed with her. 'Who indeed, Mrs Mountjoy.'

'Oh, Rosie, please. And why don't I call you Jack. Somehow it's just more natural that way.'

'Naturally,' he said and they both laughed again.

He sat next to her for the second half of the show and Rosie thought approvingly that he behaved like a gentleman. He didn't even try to put the make on her – no hand on the knee or anything like that. But she knew his eyes were on her and not on JoJo, strutting her stuff on stage and looking not a day older than she had six years ago, unless you looked close and saw how much make-up she was wearing. Still, Rosie thought with a deep sigh, her body looked terrific. JoJo had always said her 'ass was her greatest asset', and it still was; quivering sexily as she strode back from the catwalk and gave them a final pose, legs apart, smiling at them over her shoulder as the curtains swished together.

'Why, that bitch stole my act,' Rosie cried indignantly. 'That's exactly how I used to close. Jeez, is nothing sacred these days?'

'I guess not,' Jack said. 'I didn't know you knew JoJo. That you were in the business?'

'Not any more I'm not,' she said, striding up the aisle beside him as the lights went up. 'I married a rich guy, a rancher. I don't need to work the circuit any more.'

'I'll tell you what,' he said, outside the theatre. 'I had a date with JoJo tonight, but I'd rather be with you. How about if I take you out to supper instead?'

Rosie laughed, thinking of JoJo being stood up by her date. 'It kind of gets back at her for stealing my finale,' she decided, linking her arm in his.

'Let's go to Victor's. They know me there,' he said.

Victor's was an intimate little speakeasy in a dark alley off Houston Street. Rosie was thrilled to see it was so intimate and exclusive they had to ring a bell and be inspected through a little grill, just to get in. 'How do they know you?' she whispered, as the door swung back and they stepped into a dark foyer. He pressed the button for the elevator, taking her arm politely as she stepped into the dark, mirrored cab. 'I'm one of their suppliers,' he told her lightly.

Rosie had never been in a speakeasy like this. All she had known in the old days when she was on the circuit were the cheap places where you got cheap booze along with cheap guys. She had never enjoyed them: they were so low-class and the booze was always so bad it just about cut your throat. But this was different: soft lights, a band, couples dancing, and prime bourbon served in little china teacups – 'To fool the Feds,' Jack told her, 'though we don't have to worry tonight. Those who matter are all here, enjoying themselves along with the rest of us.'

They drank a cup of bourbon and then they danced. Rosie liked the way he moved and the way his body felt, and the roughness of his cheek against hers. 'He's all man,' she thought happily.

In the cab on the way back to her hotel, she asked him where he lived. She was surprised when he answered, 'Right where we're going. The Warwick. I always take a suite there when I'm in town.'

'Okay Jack,' she said breathlessly in the hotel elevator, smiling in anticipation. 'Your suite? Or mine?'

Honeychile was happiest when her mother was away, and she seemed to be away most of the time now. 'In Houston,' Aliza told her when she asked where she was. 'Gallivantin'.'

Honeychile didn't know where Houston was but it sounded very far away, and she didn't know what 'gallivantin'' meant either, but she thought wistfully it sounded like fun. Every now and again Rosie would surprise them, driving her bright red Dodge automobile too fast down the lane, honking her horn and sending the startled horses careering round the corrals and the jack rabbits scurrying and the rooks squawking from the trees.

Aliza would emerge from the kitchen and stand, arms akimbo, her face grim, with Honeychile standing quietly beside her. 'Let's hear what she's been up to this time, baby,' Aliza would say. 'And you can just bet your sweet life it's no good.'

Rosie always bought presents – her 'sweetener', she called them laughingly. Fussy, frilly new frocks for Honeychile; a flowery cotton dress for Aliza, and shirts and shorts for her boy.

'Maybe she ain't all bad,' Aliza would say, mollified by the gifts for her son, but the fancy dresses did not suit Honeychile who was as whippet-thin as her father had been, and growing taller by the minute. They were always too short and her coltish legs and scratched knees stuck out ludicrously from the layers of ruffles.

She said thank you, politely, but she flinched from Rosie's critical frown.

'Well, you're sure not growin' up to be a beauty, Honeychile,' Rosie said with a laugh. 'Ain't that the truth.'

Honeychile asked Aliza what 'a beauty' was, and when she told her it was ladies with nice regular features and good complexions and silken hair, Honeychile looked in the mirror and knew that her

101

mother was right. Her face was boney, her blue eyes looked sunken, there was a bump in her nose, and her hair was a mess.

So Aliza hung the new dresses in the closet and Honeychile wore her bib-overalls with the legs rolled up and, mostly she went barefoot, the way Tom did. She wished she looked like him too, so brown and strong and handsome. And she wished she was a boy so she would never have to wear stupid frilly frocks and dangling beads and sticky red lipstick, like her Mom.

Honeychile loved Aliza; she was big and round and comforting, and she was always there. Aliza sang as she worked around the house; she cooked rice and pork and chicken and collard greens for them to eat and she made the best peach ice cream in a little wooden drum with a handle that she allowed Honeychile to turn, until her arm got so tired she thought it might drop off. But Aliza's arm never got too tired, and her lap was always there for Honeychile to snuggle on when she wasn't feeling good, or was just plain lonesome.

Aliza smelled of sweet fresh linen dried in the sun, with a hint of rosewater from the pomade she used to smooth her thick, black curly hair. To Honeychile, it was the most comforting scent in the world. To her it meant 'mother', because Aliza was more nearly her mother than Rosie with her French perfumes and her long absences ever was. Honeychile loved Aliza best. After Aliza, she loved Tom. But she would never love anyone quite the way she had loved her father.

The months passed slowly. Honeychile rode every day; she fielded softball with Tom and the ranchhands; they mucked out the stables and fed the horses and rode the trails together. Sometimes Tom took her out on the range with him, the way her father used to. She helped Aliza bake cookies and bread and she never wore shoes anymore.

And once a week, without fail, she walked up the long lane to place her bouquet of wild flowers under the chestnut tree, for her father.

'It's high time you were going to school, young lady,' Aliza said worriedly.

Honeychile was coming up to six years old but she did not want to hear about school. She wanted to stay exactly where she was, doing the things that made her happy. The fact that she rarely saw other children, except when she went to the Kitsville market with Aliza, didn't worry her one jot. She felt safe with Aliza, and the highlight of her year was the May stampede and round-up for the cattle auctions.

Then, Honeychile polished up her saddle and the silver trim on Lucky's bridle until they gleamed. She wore fringed leather chaps, a crisp white cotton shirt with a red bandana tied at her neck, tooled-leather boots with silver spurs, and a miniature version of her father's Stetson. With her golden hair tucked under the hat, Aliza said she looked exactly like a boy.

'*A thin starving boy*,' she added severely, because no matter what nourishing food she managed to get down her, Honeychile never gained those nice rounded limbs that would have satisfied Aliza. 'You're built like your Daddy,' she added resignedly. 'I never could put an ounce on him neither.'

It was the middle of the May cattle round-up when Rosie brought Jack Delaney home to visit. The Texas Longhorns were being corralled and Honeychile was watching with Tom, hot and happy after a long exciting day on the range. Tom had kept her safely to one side and out of the action, but he was proud of her.

'Y'all just hung in there, Honeychile, like a real cowhand,' he told her admiringly, because he didn't know any other kid, especially a girl, who could handle a horse the way she could and who had that kind of stamina.

They rode their horses companionably back to the stables. Honeychile talked excitedly about the stampeding cattle and the dust-cloud their thundering hooves made that covered them and almost choked her. The sun was setting and she was contemplating standing under the pump in the stableyard to cool off, when she heard the familiar hoot of the horn and her mother's fire-engine red Dodge came bouncing down the lane towards them.

She and Tom reined in their horses, watching silently as Rosie spun the car round and squealed to a stop in front of the house. They heard her shriek of laughter as she flung open the door and climbed out. Honeychile stiffened warily as a man climbed out of the other door, and stood, looking round.

'This is it, Jack,' Rosie said loudly. 'Mountjoy Ranch. My ancestral home.' And she burst into more peals of laughter.

'Who do you think he is?' Honeychile whispered, edging closer to Tom.

He shrugged. 'Just a friend, I guess.' But he looked anxious. Rosie had never brought anyone home with her before.

103

'Honeychile? Is that you out there on the horse?' Rosie shaded her eyes with her hand, staring hard at her daughter. 'My God, I thought it was a boy. Come on over here and say hello to my friend.' She gave a short irritated laugh. 'Kids,' she said in an aside to Jack, 'just when you want to show 'em off, they look as though they've been rolling in the dust.'

Honeychile rode Lucky slowly across the yard. She slumped sullenly in the saddle, avoiding her mother's eyes.

'Jack, this is my little girl.' Rosie smiled apprehensively at him; you never knew how men would react to kids and Honeychile was acting up again. And just look at her, filthy and smelling like a steer and looking ugly as sin. Wait till she got her alone, she would let her have it all right. *And* Aliza for letting her get into this state.

'Hello, Honeychile,' Jack nodded at her, unsmiling.

'Hi,' she muttered, her head averted. She threw him a quick glance from the corner of her eye. She thought he looked odd, dressed in a city suit and tie instead of regular blue jeans like everybody else. As she watched, he put his arm round her mother's waist. His hand wandered upwards to her breast, and he whispered something in her ear, making her laugh.

Honeychile felt the hot blush sting her cheeks. She nudged Lucky round and trotted back across the yard.

'Hey,' Rosie called half-heartedly after her, 'where are you going?'

'The stables,' Honeychile said, over her shoulder.

'Well, just make sure you're back in time for supper with me and Mr Delaney.' Rosie walked up the steps into the house, looking for Aliza. 'And make sure you take a bath first,' she added, and she and Mr Delaney laughed again and Honeychile's cheeks burned with shame and resentment.

Aliza disliked Jack Delaney on sight. She thought he was flashy and citified and he acted too smarmy, calling her Aliza and putting his arm along her shoulder, as though he were her friend.

'And friend you ain't, mister,' she muttered under her breath, watching him looking round, taking in every detail of the shabby ranch house. 'As though he's figuring on buying the place,' she thought angrily.

She set the table on the porch for supper, but tonight she did not set places for herself and Tom, the way she usually did when Rosie was away. They would eat later, at her own house, a quarter of a mile away across the pasture. She knew if that fella was fixin' to stay the night, there was nowhere else for him to sleep except with Rosie, and she wasn't staying round to listen to that racket all night.

Honeychile stuck her head in the kitchen door. 'Has he gone Aliza?' she asked hopefully.

'Uhuh, that fella's not goin' nowhere tonight,' she replied, adding under her breath, ''Cept in your Momma's bed'. She glanced at Honeychile, covered in dust up to her eyeballs. 'Better get yourself bathed, young lady. And quick about it. They're expectin' you for supper any minute.'

Honeychile stared agonisedly at her. 'Do I have to?' she pleaded.

'Well, baby, this time I guess you just do.' Aliza smiled appeasingly at her. 'Never mind, it'll soon be over. Besides, I've made fried chicken and biscuits and gravy. Just the way you like it.'

'I'm not hungry,' Honeychile said stubbornly. 'In fact I think I feel sick.' She stuck her tongue out for Aliza to inspect. 'See? And feel my head, it's hot.'

Aliza sighed sympathetically. 'I'm sorry girl, it just won't work. You're havin' supper with your ma and her friend and that's all there is to it. You've got fifteen minutes.'

Honeychile's silver spurs jingled as she dragged her feet across the room. It had been such a fun day. Why did her mother have to show up now? And with that awful city man. She didn't want to have supper with him. She hated him.

Slamming her door, she stared dispiritedly at the dress Aliza had ironed and placed on the bed. It was white voile with red spots. It had a peter-pan collar and puff sleeves and a red satin sash. *And* it had ruffles round the neck and hem. She knew she would look ridiculous in it, she always did. And then they would laugh at her again.

She flung off her boots and her clothes and stood under the drizzle from the big shower-rose that Tom had fashioned from an old tin watering-can, luxuriating in the feel of the cool water on her hot dusty skin. The minutes were ticking by and when she knew she could put it off no longer, she dried herself and put on the spotted frock, tying the red satin sash in a sloppy bow. She flicked the brush through her long wet hair and walked sullenly out onto the porch.

'There you are at last,' Rosie examined her critically. 'Lord that dress is too short already,' she exclaimed. 'And where are your shoes, girl?'

'Don't have any,' Honeychile muttered, eyes lowered. 'I grew out of the last pair weeks ago.'

Rosie glanced nervously at Jack, covering her embarrassment with a quick giggle. 'Honeychile, don't say such things. Mr Delaney's going to think I'm a bad mother. Really, a daughter with no shoes. Aliza should have told me, I would have bought you two pairs.'

'She looks fine to me, Rosie,' Jack said genially. 'And is that fried chicken I smell? My, I haven't had fried chicken in too long a time.' He gave Honeychile an ingratiating smile. 'I'd be willing to bet it's one of your favourites too, Honeychile. Isn't that so?'

'No,' she lied. 'It's not.'

Rosie flung her an angry glance. The little brat was going to be difficult. 'It's amazing how charmless children can be when they want to,' she said bitterly to Jack. 'After all you do for them, a little gratitude and humility would be appreciated.'

He shrugged, uncaring. He took the flask from his pocket and set it on the table. He removed his jacket and rolled up his shirt sleeves, then he poured a couple of drinks.

'Pretty nice spread you've got here, Rosie,' he said, looking into the distance, past the barns to where the Longhorns were corralled, bellowing nervously, pawing the ground and twitching their tails. 'And that's a fine herd of cattle you have ready for auction.'

'They're only part of the herd,' Rosie told him eagerly. 'There's plenty more out there, a few thousand I think. Plus the Angus. I forget how many of them there are though.'

Jack helped himself to chicken and biscuits. He poured gravy liberally, nodding his head in approval as he tasted the food. He said, 'I'll bet Honeychile knows how many head of cattle there are.'

Honeychile lowered her eyes, staring at her empty plate. Rosie put a piece of chicken on it and a couple of biscuits and poured gravy over the lot. It smelled wonderful and Honeychile was so hungry she could almost taste it. She gulped back her hunger and shut her mouth in a firm line. She would rather starve than eat with that man.

Rosie glared at her. 'Don't waste your time talking to her, Jack,' she said angrily. 'She's just acting up.'

'You don't know what you're missing kid,' Jack said with a grin, biting into a chicken leg.

Oh yes I do, Honeychile thought bitterly, and it's worth it just not to have to eat with you.

'Oh for goodness sake, why don't you just disappear and leave us in peace to enjoy our supper,' Rosie finally said, exasperated.

Honeychile didn't need telling twice. She was out of her chair before Rosie finished the sentence. She ran inside and hid behind the window-shade, listening to her mother telling Jack all about the ranch, how big it was and how many head of cattle and how profitable it was.

'I'm lucky,' Rosie said finally, leaning back and lighting a cigarette. 'My husband was a good rancher. He left me a rich woman.' She added with a giggle, 'Though it's amazing how quickly money just seems to slide through my fingers.'

He said, 'Still, you always have the ranch to fall back on. It must bring in a fine income.'

She nodded, inhaling deeply, looking at him. 'I guess so,' she agreed.

Aliza cleared off the dishes and began washing them in the huge pot sink in the kitchen. Honeychile ran in after her. She took the cloth and began to dry them silently. 'Your supper's there, still on the plate, untouched.' Aliza said over her shoulder.

'Don't want it.'

Aliza caught the tremor in Honeychile's voice. She always stayed at the house with her when Rosie was away but now she said, 'How's about you sleepin' over at my place tonight. We can have our supper there, along with Tom.'

Honeychile threw her arms round Aliza's waist, sagging against her in relief. 'Oh Aliza, can I really?'

'Course you can, baby,' Aliza replied, adding to herself, 'As if I'd leave you here with them, drinkin' and then goin' at it, yelpin' like hound-dogs on heat in the other room, no doubt.'

She went to tell Rosie she was taking Honeychile with her. 'Go kiss your Mom goodnight, Honeychile,' she ordered.

She stepped forward dutifully and kissed her mother's cheek.

'That's better sweetheart,' Rosie hugged her tightly, suddenly smothering her with kisses. 'She looks just like her father,' she told Jack, with a sentimental little sigh.

Honeychile did not look back as she ran down the steps, skipping along next to Aliza.

The ranch house was certainly no mansion, but Aliza's cottage was little more than a two-room shack with a lean-to for a kitchen and an outhouse at the back. Its wooden boards were weathered to a silvery grey and Honeychile loved it best when there was a storm. Then the rain drummed down on the corrugated-tin roof and the lightning flashed outside the window, and she felt cosy and safe curled up next to Aliza's warm comforting bulk. She didn't even mind when Aliza snored; just as long as she was there.

She and Tom and Aliza sat on the porch, eating fried chicken and chattering about the round-up and nobody mentioned Rosie and Jack. It was as if they had just gone away, Honeychile thought relieved.

And the next morning at seven o'clock, when she walked reluctantly back home with Aliza, to her surprise and delight, they were gone.

Jack Delaney had made expert and enjoyable love to Rosie that night. When she finally fell asleep, he had lain awake for a long time, thinking about things. He was a moderately successful man. He had good connections and he supplied whisky to speakeasies in several cities, but competition was tough. He was in with the Mob and the right people, but in this business the 'right people' often changed without warning. A man could find himself on the outs without even knowing what happened. Besides, there was a persistent rumour that Prohibition would be repealed before too long. He had to think about his future.

Rosie was not too bright, and she was older, but she was still pretty and sexy. And she was rich. The Mountjoy Ranch was a fine spread, and he could see himself in the role of the Texas rancher. With his know-how, he could improve this place no end. And the first thing he would do was build a proper house, instead of this ramshackle log cabin that looked as though it would blow away in the first good gust of wind.

'Rosie,' he said, digging her in the ribs. 'Why don't you and I get married?'

Rosie was awake in an instant. 'You really mean that?'

Her eyes were round with amazement and in the half-light she looked very pretty, lying there naked. 'I sure do,' he said. 'I've been thinking it over and it'll be good for both of us.'

'Oh, ohhhh Jack,' she said, winding her arms round him, and then her legs. 'Where shall we go for our honeymoon?'

He woke her up again, before dawn. 'Come on, let's get out of here,' he said, slapping her still pert behind playfully.

He took her to the finest store in San Antonio and told her to pick out a gown. Rosie was in her element, surrounded by attentive salesgirls, trying on every dress in the place. She finally chose a girlish peach-silk with a narrow ruffled skirt. Each ruffle was edged with satin ribbon, and she bought matching T-strap satin shoes and a cloche hat with an enormous bunch of peach blossoms at the side.

He took her to the jewellers and she tried on several diamond rings before he made the decision, choosing a single round stone that was more than twice the size of David's little ruby and diamond ring; as well as a gold wedding band. Rosie paid for all these items. 'Just until we get to Chicago and my bank,' he told her. Then he drove her red Dodge to the city hall where they took out a licence.

They were married by the Judge that same afternoon and left immediately for a honeymoon in Chicago, where he happened to have business to attend to, and which also happened to be one of Rosie's favourite cities.

CHAPTER 14

It was six months before Honeychile saw her mother again. She came driving down the lane at her usual speed, only she wasn't honking the horn this time and Honeychile noticed there was a big dent in the side of the red Dodge and the running board was broken off. Still, her heart lurched with sudden unexpected tenderness when Rosie stepped from the car and she noticed she was limping.

'Mommie, Mommie, you're hurt,' she cried, racing towards her.

'You bet I'm hurt,' Rosie retorted bitterly.

Honeychile stared horrified at the big bandage strapped round Rosie's ankle, and at her bruised face. She took her arm protectively. 'I'll help you Mommie,' she said. 'You can lean on me.'

Rosie laughed, a short sharp sound that had nothing to do with gaiety. 'Thanks kid,' she said. 'I could use someone to lean on.'

Aliza appeared on the porch. She stood with her hands on her hips, looking silently at the dented car, then at Rosie. 'Somebody hit you?' she asked finally.

Rosie met her eyes. 'They sure did, Aliza,' she said tearfully. 'Oh they sure did.'

She looked so forlorn and vulnerable that even Aliza's heart was touched. 'Maybe she's done gallivantin' this time,' she told Honeychile as she fixed a pot of coffee. 'Maybe she's turned over a new leaf.'

'You mean maybe she's going to stay home now, Aliza?' Honeychile looked apprehensive. A repentant Rosie with a sprained ankle was one thing, but who knew how long her mood would last. She might revert to her old self and Honeychile couldn't bear that. She wanted things to stay exactly the way they were.

Sitting on the porch, Rosie sipped her coffee in silence, staring out across the range. Honeychile perched on the top step, her arms clasped round her knees, watching her. Fisher, the shaggy black pup

Tom had found abandoned on the roadside crouched by her side, its pink tongue lolling as it panted in the heat.

'You'd have to look hard to find an uglier dog,' Rosie commented testily, still staring out across the scorched-looking prairie. 'Where on earth did you get it?'

'Tom gave it to me.' Honeychile put a protective hand on the dog's head and it turned and licked her.

'Well, you should have given it right back to him. That dog's not worth a damn.' Rosie took another sip. 'Coffee's bitter,' she said to Aliza.

'Seems to me, so are you,' Aliza retorted shrewdly.

Rosie burst into tears. She could hold it back no longer, the whole sorry story spilled from her trembling lips: of what a gent she had thought Jack Delaney was; how successful he had said he was. How he had wooed her, and how she had married him.

'You got *married*?' Aliza said, stunned. '*To that city slicker?* Why, I could've told you that first night he was no good, looking round this place like he already owned it. Why that man was so slippery it's a wonder he didn't just slide right outta here.'

'Pity he didn't,' Rosie commented bitterly.

Honeychile's astonished blue eyes fastened on her mother as she told how she had married Jack in San Antonio and gone on a wonderful trip to Chicago. They had taken a huge suite at the Drake Hotel, dined at all the best restaurants, taken in all the shows and drank and danced the nights away at speakeasies, where the dancebands and the gangsters and glamorous people – all in evening dress and sparkling jewels – were more entertaining than all the stageshows she had ever seen. Jack had even introduced her to Al Capone.

A wistful expression crossed Rosie's face as she remembered. 'It was the most wonderful time of my life,' she whispered with a sigh for what might have been. But her tone hardened as she remembered the truth. 'When the bills came in at the end of the month Jack told me he was "temporarily embarrassed". He said would I take care of it, just for now. He would pay me back later.'

She threw up her hands, looking helplessly at them. 'I mean, the guy lived like a prince: the best clothes, the biggest suites in the best hotels, the best booze. You name it, Jack bought the best. Who wouldn't have believed him? So of course I paid. And I kept on paying. In Peoria and St Louis and Indianapolis. In Cincinnati, Ohio and Pittsburgh, Pennsylvania. He gave me a break in New Jersey, said he had suddenly come into money – a payment or something.' She paused, staring wistfully into the past. 'He treated me like a queen that night, a *real* queen. Bought me a new evening dress, red chiffon with panels that floated from my shoulders when I danced . . . everybody was looking at me, admiring me.'

Honeychile imagined her mother dancing in the red dress with the floating scarves trailing from her shoulders. She imagined the men watching Rosie, staring at her, and she clutched the pup closer, for comfort.

'When we got back to the hotel suite that night, Jack asked me about the ranch,' Rosie continued. 'He said, "Whoever's running that spread for you is surely not doing a good enough job. The place looks run down and you can bet your bottom dollar they're cheating you. Now we're married, it's time I took charge."

'It seemed like a good idea to me. After all, he was my husband. So I said, "Why not?" Then he asked me all sorts of questions about the ranch, the size of the property, how many head of cattle, how much it was worth. I told him I didn't know. I said David's attorney, old John Parker Grant dealt with all that. Next thing I know, he's called the attorney and asked a whole load of questions. Old Grant refused to answer; said he didn't know him from Adam, and that anyway I didn't own the Mountjoy Ranch. Honeychile did.'

Rosie's eyes were frightened as she looked at them and said, 'Jack went crazy. He said I'd cheated him: pretended to be a rich widow; told him I owned Mountjoy Ranch when I didn't.

' "I *was* rich," I told him, "until I started paying all your bills." ' Her voice broke and she put her face in her hands. Tears spilled through her fingers as she whispered, 'Jack beat me up. He called me a cheating, lying bitch. And then he walked out.' Rosie choked on a sob. '*He left me.*'

'Stuck with the hotel bill again no doubt,' Aliza said tersely. 'Well, Rosie, you'd just better stop feelin' sorry for yourself and get on with livin'. There's no use cryin' over a man that treats you bad and steals your money as well.'

Honeychile didn't understand at all, but she knew Jack Delaney had taken her mother's money and he had beaten her up. Nobody had ever struck Honeychile in her life; she only knew gentle things: the animals on the range; her small 'family' circle; and the cowboys who treated her as though she was someone really special and called her jokingly 'ma'am', tipping their hats to her. 'You're the boss,' they would say to her, laughing.

'Mommie,' she said, uncovering her ears. 'Is the ranch really mine?'

Rosie threw her an angry glare. 'Yes, goddamn it, it is,' she said sullenly. 'What do you think I've been talking about? If I'd have owned the ranch the way I should have, none of this would have happened. It's all your father's fault.'

Honeychile shrank back against the steps, clutching the pup. 'It's not David's fault,' Aliza intervened, 'nor Honeychile's. That's just the way Georgie Mountjoy wanted it. And a good thing for all of us he did, else it seems to me Jack Delaney would own it now, and then where would we all be? Out on the street, Rosie Hennessy. And don't you forget that.'

Rosie stayed in her room, lying on the bed, staring at the ceiling. Aliza tried to get her interested in running the house, even in running the ranch, but Rosie was indifferent. Fancy clothes and furs spilled from her closet, eternally reminding her that she had no place to wear them, and she didn't even bother to put on powder and lipstick and the French perfume that sat in giant-size crystal bottles on her dresser, any more. She never went into San Antonio, not even to go to the beauty parlour, and her wavy bob soon became a straggling unkempt mess.

Honeychile kept out of her mother's way. Sometimes she almost believed Rosie wasn't there. Most nights Aliza slept over because she was afraid to leave her alone with Rosie in such a state. 'I don't know whether she's gone crazy, or what,' she told Honeychile, mystified.

Honeychile knew it was too good to last though, and one day, a few weeks later, Rosie emerged onto the porch, looking gaunt and haggard in the sunlight. 'Aliza,' she yelled as she passed the kitchen, 'bring me some coffee and quick about it. I'm going into town.'

A short while later they watched Rosie drive off and both of them wondered whether she was coming back. But of course she did. She had nowhere else to go, and not much money left to do it with. But, she still had her fancy clothes and with her hair freshly cut and waved, and wearing her 'war paint', Rosie looked pretty good. And she still had that sexy swing to her hips that men never failed to notice.

She spent more and more time in San Antonio, often staying away for weeks on end. And whenever she returned, it was always with a supply of 'hooch' stashed in the back of the Dodge. Then she would shut herself in her room and maybe not come out for twenty-four hours.

'Rosie,' Aliza yelled one day, hammering angrily on her door. 'Get yourself out here, woman. I know what you're doin' in there. Drinkin' yourself crazy, that's what. And with never a thought for your little girl and your responsibilities.'

Rosie flung open the door. Her face was blotchy and her eyes red and she stank of liquor. She thrust her face into Aliza's. 'Y'want to know *why* I drink? Because I'm bored. Goddamn *bored out of my skull*. That's why.' And she stepped back into her room and slammed the door.

Honeychile watched as Aliza took the key from her pocket and locked it. 'I took all those bottles of liquor out of your room, Rosie,' Aliza yelled. 'And now there ain't none. So you can just sit and stew for a while, woman, and think over your sins.'

Rosie shrieked. She battered at the door with her fists. 'You conniving bitch Aliza,' she yelled. 'You're fired. Get outta here. Out of my house.'

'This here is Honeychile's house, woman, and don't you forget that,' Aliza yelled back. Then she took Honeychile by the hand and led her away into the kitchen.

Honeychile could not eat her supper that evening and as a matter of fact, nor could Aliza. Rosie had stopped hammering and hollering and the silence was frightening. But neither one of them mentioned it. Aliza made Honeychile go to bed at the proper time and she even allowed the pup to curl up next to her, though she still doubted the girl would sleep. Then she took a chair and sat guard all night outside Rosie's ominously silent room.

There was a polite tap on the door early the next morning. 'Aliza?' Rosie said in a subdued voice. 'Can I have a cigarette? Please?'

'You sober?' Aliza glared at the door as if she could see her.

'Yes ma'am.'

Aliza unlocked the door and they stared at each other. Rosie looked swollen-eyed and chastened. 'I'm gonna be good from now on, Aliza,' she said. 'You'll see.'

But Rosie's promises were always temporary. She was soon back in her old ways, living it up in San Antonio and Houston, and the rumours gradually filtered back to the Mountjoy Ranch.

'There's always a guy sniffin' round Rosie Hennessy,' they said.

CHAPTER 15

Honeychile was eight years old when the great well that had supplied water to the Mountjoy Ranch for more than a century, suddenly began to dry up. It had been a grilling summer the year before and this one looked like being the same. Tom told her that the miles of pipelines linking the cattle's drinking troughs were reduced to half their normal flow, and she overheard him telling Aliza he was worried.

Rosie wasn't concerned though. 'That well's always been there,' she said carelessly, sitting smoking on the porch. 'All we need is a good storm and it'll fill up again.'

Even Honeychile wondered how she could be so stupid. She knew that without water the cattle would die. 'And without water, so will we,' Aliza muttered apprehensively.

Tom drove Honeychile the ten miles to school every morning, across the highway to the small town of Kitsville. He drove Rosie's old Dodge, except when she had done one of her regular disappearing acts; then they rode horseback.

Honeychile blushed with shame when she first overheard the other children's mothers talking about Rosie. 'What kind of upbringing is that child getting?' they said to each other. 'Just look at her, barefoot and in those old bib-overalls, like a farmboy. And Rosie Mountjoy with one of the biggest ranches around. I hear she's spending all their money in Houston and San Antonio, living it up. All the men talk about her and what she gets up to.'

They looked knowingly at each other, glancing proudly at their own gingham-skirted children with their neatly braided hair, and pristine white ankle socks and clean shoes, and they whispered to them to keep away from Honeychile, as though they might get contaminated by her mother's sluttish habits.

Honeychile felt ashamed for her mother but it was different when they talked about Tom. Then Honeychile's red face burned with anger. They stared at her and Tom, and one woman said loudly how scandalous it was that she was left in the care of a black boy to bring her to school.

Honeychile turned and confronted them, tossing back her wild blonde hair, blue eyes blazing. 'Don't you dare talk about Tom,' she shouted angrily. 'What do you know about him anyway? Tom Jefferson is my best friend. And that's the truth. So there. Now go and gossip all you want.' And with another toss of her head, she turned and strode into the schoolhouse. She darted out again a second later.

'Listen up, you gossipy women,' she shouted from the steps, 'Aliza Jefferson is my *real* mother. I'm the same colour as they are only you're too blind to see it. Now go put that around town, why don't y'all.'

Sam Waterford, Honeychile's teacher, hid a smile as she stalked past him, still simmering with anger, all gawky elbows and spindly legs. She took a seat at her desk at the back of the class, where he had placed her because she was head and shoulders taller than the other girls. He liked Honeychile's spirited innocence and her defence of her mother and her friend. And he also admired her intellect.

Honeychile Mountjoy was the brightest child in his class. She took a book home every afternoon and when she brought it back the next morning, he knew she had read it. Devoured, was more like it. She was hungry for tales of far-away places, of great feats of daring and adventure, of history and famous men and women: presidents and actors, rodeo champions and ballerinas. And especially anything about England because, as she told him proudly, her grandfather Georgie was English. She lived in an escape dream-world of books, and the movies she attended every Saturday afternoon in Kitsville. And Sam did not blame her one bit. Nobody envied Honeychile Mountjoy Hennessy's life.

Now, however, Sam was forced to say reprovingly, 'Honeychile Mountjoy we cannot have that kind of behaviour in this school. Kindly do not raise your voice that way again.'

'*Bitches*,' Honeychile muttered under her breath, causing shocked gasps from the girls and titters of laughter from the boys.

Sam decided to pretend he hadn't heard. Honeychile had a tough enough time from the other girls. She didn't look the way they did, didn't dress the way they did, and she didn't live the way they did. Honeychile was unconventional in every way and he had high hopes of a college education for her, when all these other silly little rabbits were getting married and having babies, just the way their mothers had done.

'You will do extra homework this afternoon,' he told her severely. 'You will take home the volume of Shelley's poems and read the first twenty pages. Then I want you to learn one poem by heart. You may choose which one, but you will stand in front of this class tomorrow and recite it. Is that clear?'

'Yes, sir.' There was a smile in Honeychile's voice though. Mr Waterford knew how much she loved poetry. His so-called punishment would be a treat for her. Except the recitation when she knew all the boys would stare her out and the girls would whisper behind their hands about the way she looked.

School was an on-going love-hate battle for Honeychile, and so was her relationship with her mother. Sometimes when Rosie was at home, Honeychile would watch her sitting on the porch, rocking back and forth, staring into space. She would look so forlorn and lonely, Honeychile's heart would almost break. She would go sit beside her and lay her head against Rosie's knee, wishing she knew how to calm the restless demons that seemed to eat at her mother. Until the whole sequence of 'gallivantin'' as Aliza called it, inevitably started again and Rosie would disappear into her own world, with her 'friends'.

That same year that the Mountjoy well began to dry up, so did America's fortunes. The Wall Street Crash reverberated like a seismic shock throughout the country, echoing across Europe and the rest of the world.

The Mountjoys had never lived like rich folk, except for Rosie of course, and she was not truly a Mountjoy; but they had never been poor. Not since Georgie Mountjoy had won that first couple of thousand dollars at a card game and invested it in more land and finer cattle. Now their cattle were dying for lack of water and there was no market for them anyway, because nobody had any money to buy them.

The ranch manager told Rosie she would have to drill for new wells if the ranch were to survive, and it was then that Rosie informed them there was no money left to drill for wells, or to pay cowhands to tend dying cattle that nobody wanted to buy anyway.

'You mean you spent all David Mountjoy's money?' Aliza asked, shocked. 'And all the money earned since he died?'

'You know money goes nowhere these days,' Rosie blew a nonchalant smoke ring and studied her garnet-lacquered fingernails.

'Well, that money certainly went *somewheres*,' Aliza retorted. 'Now what we all gonna do?' Her broad forehead creased in an anxious frown and she pursed her lips angrily together. She had counted on that money to get them through the hard times that she knew always came, as inevitably as spring rains. Only this year there had been no spring rains.

'Don't be such a grouch,' Rosie retorted. 'Mountjoy Ranch makes enough money to keep hoity-toity little Miss Honeychile in overalls. As well as you and your boy.'

Aliza's voice was tight with anger as she said, 'I never expected to say this to you, Rosie Hennessy – oh yes, *I know* you're still Rosie Hennessy, even though I may be the only one left that does. And I ain't about to split on you on account of that poor fatherless child. Still, I never did expect to say this, but you ain't paid my wages since Mr David died. My boy earned his own keep on the ranch. And thank the Lord he did, at least *he* got paid. So don't you come queenin' it over me Rosie Hennessy. I've looked after your little girl since she was born. And this house. *And all for nothin'.*'

Leaving Rosie staring open-mouthed after her, she stomped back into her kitchen and began rattling pots angrily around the stove, preparing supper. 'Soon there won't be no chickens in this household,' she muttered to herself, 'it'll be mustard greens and nettle soup and pork scratchin's, *if* we're lucky.'

Somehow though, they scraped through that year and the next. *Just.* The sunbaked land cracked until it looked like a huge, crazy jigsaw puzzle. Cracks so wide Honeychile thought they must go all the way through to the other side of the world. Every day was the same: the grilling heat; the flat, dead blue sky and the tumbleweed blowing across the dusty, barren landscape.

Honeychile lay in bed at night, unable to sleep, hearing the terrible sound of the starving cattle bellowing in the hot black nights, desperate for the cool water and the rich nourishing grasses that used to be so plentiful on Mountjoy Ranch. She heard the hot wind humming in the telegraph wires and, in the distance, the hoot of a far-away train, heading out of this dusty hell-hole to civilisation, where water flowed from faucets and nobody even thought twice about it.

She covered her ears, filled with a deep, desperate loneliness. 'You shouldn't have gone away, Daddy,' she whispered into the darkness. 'You shouldn't have left us.'

The dog, as long and lanky as she was herself, stretched out on the bare floor next to her, scratching at his fleas and panting in the dry dusty heat. He heard her crying and he put his paws on the bed, whimpering in sympathy, trying to lick away her bitter, lonesome tears.

Then Prohibition was repealed and Rosie took herself into San Antonio, to celebrate. She took with her the trickle of dollars from the sale of the last of their cattle, which, since there was no grass to feed them on, seemed a logical move to her, and not the tragedy Tom and Aliza and Honeychile knew it was. They were not the only ranchers to have suffered in the long drought, but theirs was the only spread on which the well had just about dried up.

Honeychile was curled up in the rocker on the porch, thinking about the train and where it was heading.

'Don't you ever wish you could see New York, Tom?' she asked.

He was leaning against the porch rail, staring at the sky, and he turned and looked at her. 'No, Honeychile, I don't. I don't care if I never see New York. All I ever wanted was to be here on this ranch. It's my life,' he said, spreading his thin, long-fingered hands helplessly. 'I don't know nothin' else, and I don't want to. I love this place and it just about breaks my heart knowing there's no more cattle out there. And that's the truth.'

'It would never have happened if my father had been alive.'

'Even your father couldn't have done nothin' about this weather. He was just a man, Honeychile. As helpless as the rest of us when the Lord wants things *His* way.'

'He would have saved our money, not spent it like my mother did,' Honeychile said. 'He would have drilled the new wells and put in new pipelines and our poor cattle wouldn't have died and we wouldn't be nearly starving . . .'

'You're not starvin' yet, miss,' Aliza shouted from the kitchen.

121

'Supper's just 'bout ready, so get your hands washed and come and set the table.'

They ate their supper in silence. Tom forced down the thin soup, avoiding his mother's eyes, wondering what was going to happen to the ranch. It had just about died on them by now. 'There's nothin' left but this old house and the barns and farmbuildings, and some machinery,' he thought tiredly. 'There's no work for me any more 'cept tendin' the two horses and mindin' Honeychile.'

He glanced at her out of the corner of his eye. She was staring at her plate, but he knew it wasn't the soup she was seeing. She had that empty, lonely look she always got when she was thinking about her father. With her hair dragged back from her face in a tight golden braid, and her lost blue eyes, he thought she looked older than her twelve years.

Childhood's already leavin' her, he thought sadly. And what little is left, her Mom is gonna take away. Rosie had no right spendin' all that money, without a thought for her daughter. Now what's to become of her?

He put down his spoon, unable to eat. His mother glanced questioningly at him, but she didn't say anything. She didn't have to; she knew what he was thinking. The same thing she was. There was no grass and no water and no cattle – and no money. What would they all do now?

Aliza had brought up her son on her own. It had been a long hard struggle and she wasn't afraid of hard work, nor of poverty. But she surely was not looking forward to the kind of poverty she remembered only too well; the bitter, desperate soul-destroying kind with no work to be had, wondering where your next meal was coming from, and when the landlord would evict you from your rotting, roach-ridden room. Aliza had been there; before David Mountjoy took her on as his housekeeper. And now, thanks to Rosie, it seemed she would be going there again.

'You should have made Rosie pay you your wages, Aliza,' Honeychile said angrily. 'All she did was squander the money anyway. On moonshine and furs and beads and dresses and . . . oh I don't know what she spent it all on.'

She looked despairingly at Aliza, with her sweet, round face and her plump bosom, and her stately carriage; the woman who had loved her and cared for her all her life. And at Tom; so tall, long-limbed and strong; his brown eyes were so dark they reflected her own despairing image as he looked at her. He was her true friend, her *only* friend, her mainstay in life. Aliza was the buffer between her and Rosie; and Tom was the buffer between her and the rest of the world – meaning school and the other children.

Now they would both have to find other work to earn money to live on, and she was desperately afraid of losing them. Her hand trembled with anger as she slammed down her spoon.

At that moment, she hated Rosie with such a passion, she wished her dead. It was *Rosie* whose funeral she should have attended, not her father's. It was *Rosie's* coffin they should have thrown clods of earth on; *Rosie* who should have gone to be with Jesus – instead of to the rowdiest saloon in San Antonio, spending the last of their money, earned from selling their few remaining half-starved cattle.

'I wish Rosie would never come back,' she hissed through clenched teeth. 'I *hate* her. I never want to see her again.'

'Hush up, child. What a thing to say,' Aliza admonished. But she did not look shocked. The good Rosie, sitting in the old chair on the porch, rocking back and forth looking lonesome and vulnerable was one thing; but the Rosie who had frittered a fortune on worthless fripperies and men and moonshine was unforgivable.

Tom got up from the table. He leaned against the porch rail, his hands in his pockets, watching the black clouds banking over the distant horizon. He had seen clouds like this many times in the past few years, and the most that ever happened was a few sprinkles, barely enough to dampen down the everlasting dust. A gusty wind sent balls of tumbleweed scudding across the yard, swirling the dust again and he shrugged and turned away. There would be no storm tonight. And no reprieve for the Mountjoy Ranch.

He was twenty-two years old and his future looked bleak. Once, he had hoped to become the manager of the Mountjoy Ranch. Now he knew that he would have to leave. Tomorrow or the next day or next week, he would have to hit the road and seek work. Just like the hundreds of thousands of other men who were all looking for the same non-existent jobs.

Tom glanced over his shoulder at Honeychile. She was curled up in the old rocker, her knees hunched under her chin and her eyes

123

closed. The dog lay next to her, his muzzle resting on her feet and she draped her hand across his head, smoothing his rough black fur. *'Tomorrow, or the day after, or next week,'* Tom told himself bitterly again, *'he would leave Honeychile. Maybe for ever.'*

'Let's you and me go for a ride, baby,' he called to her, smiling as she leapt to her feet in a single reflex movement. She didn't bother to put on boots; she just sped barefoot across the yard, whistling to Fisher, and he could tell she had forgotten all about their problems for the moment.

They rode for a long time. They didn't gallop the horses hard because there were no lovely cool watering holes to refresh them at any more, but they trotted companionably along the familiar trails, speaking only to point out a withered tree, the latest victim of the rainless years; or the way the dry grasses rattled in the strange hot wind; and the puffy black clouds that seemed to sit eternally on the horizon, promising an end to the terrible drought, but never keeping that promise.

Later, when she was in bed, in the very darkest hour of the moonless night, Honeychile lay awake, listening to the hot wind singing in the telegraph wires, and that distant, familiar, lonely train whistle across the miles. And she cried for Tom who would never achieve his life's ambition to run Mountjoy Ranch, and for Aliza who had never been paid and was now a poor woman again; and she cried for herself because she did not know what would happen to her. But she swore she would never shed another tear for her feckless, selfish mother.

Honeychile got up with the dawn and ran down to the stables as she always did. She noticed there was barely enough hay and oats to feed Beaut and Lucky, the only two horses they had left, and she was suddenly filled with panic as the reality of having no money was brought home to her.

'Don't worry,' Tom said, coming into the stable, 'there's more in the barn. Plenty to feed them both, for a couple of months at least.'

'And then what?'

Her eyes were frightened and he said as jauntily as he could, 'Oh, the Lord will provide, Honeychile. Don't he always?'

They both glanced up as thunder rolled suddenly across the heavens. Tom grinned at her. 'What did I just tell you? That must be the Lord himself, agreeing with me.'

Honeychile ran outside, staring at the lowering sky. Her face lit up and she jumped excitedly up and down, her straight corn-coloured hair bouncing round her shoulders. 'It's coming Tom,' she yelled excitedly. 'It's really coming this time. The storm is finally here. Just look at it.'

He scanned the horizon eagerly, but it was only sheet lightning and even as he looked the black clouds began to soften into grey. Except in the east, where there they seemed to be caught by the wind and were spiralling upward into the sky. Into a tight, whirling funnel.

'Grab Lucky,' he yelled, leaping bareback onto Beaut. He whistled for Fisher and the dog gambolled eagerly to his side, expecting another run. 'Hurry up why don't you girl,' he yelled again. 'Honeychile, for God's sake, move.'

'Why Tom? What's up.' She vaulted easily onto the horse's back. 'Where are we going?'

'To the house,' he shouted, glancing nervously over his shoulder. 'We're gonna get these animals and us along with 'em into that basement. There's a twister coming, and it looks like it's headin' straight at us.'

Honeychile had never seen a tornado before, but she had read about them at school. She knew how dangerous they were; how they destroyed everything in their path, sweeping up houses and automobiles and people and tossing them into the sky. She was afraid, but she just had to look back. She had to see it.

When she did, she wished she never had. A great black evil-looking column was whirling across the flat prairie, twisting first this way then that, gathering speed and height as it came closer. Kicking Lucky into action she closed her eyes and galloped after Tom.

He was already wrenching open the trapdoor behind the house that led into the cellar where Aliza kept her winter apples and root vegetables and the neat rows of jars filled with summer fruits and jams. David Mountjoy had built it specially for her when she complained there was no place to keep her stores cool, and he had built it properly, with strong wooden support beams and a stone flagged floor, and decent stairs so she would have easy access. Aliza thanked David now, as she stepped down into the cool darkness, followed quickly by the dog. She turned to watch Honeychile and Tom struggling to get the nervous horses to walk down the steep steps.

The wind increased into a breathy roar and the panicked horses scrambled suddenly down the steps, whinnying and showing the whites of their eyes. Tom slammed the trapdoor into place over his head and turned the big old iron key in the lock. He looked at his mother standing against the wall in front of the neat shelves, holding a cast-iron cookpot over her head for protection, and at Honeychile, hanging onto the horses' bridles, trying to soothe them.

'Not much more we can do now, 'cept wait,' he said, trying to sound confident.

'Wait – *and pray*, son,' Aliza said, sinking to her knees.

'Well I'm not praying,' Honeychile yelled, suddenly angry. 'I'm damned if I'm gonna pray to a Lord who does this to us. After all we've been through, everything that's happened. What's the matter with Him? Isn't that enough?'

But a terrible noise drowned out her voice, a great screeching roar that hurt her ears. She screamed, 'He's come to get me. The Lord has come for me because I took His name in vain.' Her screams mingled with Aliza's loud praying and Fisher's nervous barking, and Tom's voice commanding her to be quiet and help with the terrified, rearing horses. And then there was the sound of the whole world being ripped apart in one great crashing roar as it came tumbling down on top of them. And after that, only silence.

CHAPTER 16

The silence seemed to drum against Honeychile's ears. She knelt on the stone-flagged floor, staring upwards, waiting for what would happen next. She heard Aliza conversing with the Lord, telling him they were going to die and that she was ready to meet her maker.

Honeychile thought about dying. It seemed remote, something that happened to other people, not to her. And not Rosie either, she thought with a sudden flare of anger that Rosie, out gallivanting in San Antonio, was not trapped with them in the cellar, waiting for the ceiling to cave in and to be whisked up to heaven by the tornado. Rosie always got lucky, she thought bitterly, and the good people, like Aliza and Tom were the ones who were always left to carry the burden. Or in this case, to die.

Silence fell. Aliza had stopped her praying and even the horses and Fisher were quiet. Tom climbed the wooden steps and stood, listening. The twister had passed. He turned the big iron key in the lock, put his hands under the trapdoor and gave it a push. It did not move. He put his shoulder to it and gave another mighty shove. Nothing.

He turned to look at them. 'It's stuck,' he said matter-of-factly. 'Must be something blown down across it.'

'Oh Lord, oh Lordie,' Aliza whispered. 'We're trapped.' Sweat beaded her forehead and she gripped her hands tightly together, repeating the Lord's name in an endless murmur.

Honeychile flung her arms comfortingly round her. She said, 'It's all right Aliza. Somebody's sure to come and get us out soon.' And then she told herself they had just better, because she was surely not ready to die just yet. Life had not even started for her: there were all those magical far-away countries yet to visit, and ballets and opera concerts, and about a million books she absolutely needed to read.

'Oh my,' Aliza said suddenly, 'just look at those no-good horses.' They turned to see Lucky and Beaut nuzzling their way through the racks of apples and carrots. 'They're surely not gonna starve,' Aliza added with a heart-felt sigh.

'Honeychile's right, Ma,' Tom said encouragingly. 'Soon they'll find us and get us out of here.' But he glanced anxiously at the trapdoor; for all he knew the entire house had collapsed on it.

Honeychile took an apple and sat on the floor next to Aliza. The dog flopped, panting beside her, and they watched Tom manoeuvre the horses to the far end of the cellar, away from the stores. He stood holding them. Nobody spoke. They just waited.

Five hours later, Rosie turned the old red Dodge into the lane, driving blithely over the place where her husband had died so violently, with never a thought for him. The car bounced over the hardened mud-ruts as she drove. She was thinking about the guy she had met the other night. He had told her he was new in town and he was planning on opening a late-night bar and grill.

'The kind of place where a fella can come on his own and get a bite to eat and a good drink,' he had said. 'And a woman like you, with your looks and savvy, would look great behind the bar. Y'know how it is, sometimes a fella would rather look at a woman than at another man. Chat with her, give her a bit of a line. Now you could handle something like that, couldn't you, Rosie?'

Rosie had thought of the ten bucks left in her purse and she had smiled at him. 'How much?' she asked, cautiously.

'Thirty a week and the tips are yours.'

Manna from heaven, she thought. 'Make that thirty-five,' she said, not wanting to look too easy.

'Done.' They shook hands and Rosie agreed to start work in three weeks' time, when The Silver Dollar Saloon would open for business. It wasn't exactly star billing at Minsky's or the chorus line at the Zeigfeld Follies, but she was a working woman again. And who knew what it might lead to? Who she might meet?

She glanced up from her dreaming and slammed her foot suddenly on the brake. The car skidded to a stop, and she sat there, staring. She looked around her, wondering if she had come to the wrong place, because where the log ranch house had been, and the barns and stables and the longhouse, now there was just a heap of lumber.

She looked back down the lane where she could see the familiar chestnut tree and the Mountjoy Ranch sign, and with a cry of terror, she leapt from the car and ran towards the heap of rubble that had once been her home.

'Oh God,' she whispered, awed by the devastation. Aliza's cookstove lay on its side in the field, and the white bath tub gleamed in the sunlight where the stable used to be. And all across the range, as far as the eye could see, were scattered shattered remnants of dishes and mirrors and furniture, and bright pieces of clothing.

Rosie gave a howl as she ran across the yard into the field, searching the dusty brown grass for her possessions. 'My mink coat,' she screeched hysterically, 'my ermine stole, my silver foxes . . . all my good dresses . . .' She sank to her knees and the tears coursed down her cheeks as she clutched a string of red glass beads to her heart. 'All I worked for all these years,' she whispered, anguished, 'now, it's all gone.'

She looked back at the place where her home had been. Her eyes widened with horror as she remembered her daughter and Aliza. She clambered to her feet and began to run towards the pile of logs and debris. 'Aliza,' she whispered. 'Oh my God, Honeychile . . .'

Rosie must have been the only person in San Antonio not to have heard the tornado warnings. She had no idea what had happened. She stared at the wreckage and then she began to scream hysterically.

'Honeychile,' she screamed, 'Aliza . . .' She tugged at a log and sent a heap of others crashing to the ground. 'Aghhhhh . . .' she yelled, imagining an explosion, imagining Aliza and Tom and Honeychile blown into a thousand bloody pieces . . . 'Aghhhhhh.'

She ran hysterically in circles, her arms flapping, screaming. Then she heard the sound. She stopped and stared, bewildered, around her. There it was again, a hammering sound. And wasn't that a dog barking?

'Fisher,' she cried, 'Fisher, good dog. Where are you?'

The barking was coming from the back of what used to be the house. Rosie took a step closer, peering cautiously at the rubble. Then she heard the thumping again.

'Aliza,' she yelled. 'Is that you?'

'It's Tom. All of us. We're down here, in the cellar, Rosie.'

'Oh thank the Lord,' she said sagging with relief. But she still couldn't find the trapdoor leading to the cellar because it was covered in a heap of logs and roof shingles and debris. 'The house has fallen down on top of you,' she wailed, tugging vainly at a massive beam.

'Go get help, Rosie,' Tom shouted. 'We've been down here a few hours now, so better make it snappy. It's gettin' a bit stuffy, we could use some fresh air.'

'Yes, yes . . . I'll go right now. I'll get help.' Rosie ran to the car. She turned the ignition with shaking hands and swung back down the lane, driving fast and erratically.

Kitsville looked so normal: a sleepy little Texas town sizzling under the afternoon sun, that she could hardly believe what she had just seen.

She ran to the General Store and stood in the doorway, clutching her hand to her heaving breast. '*Help*,' she cried hysterically. '*Help, help, help.*'

The store was full of women, picking out their groceries and knitting patterns and sewing thread. They turned as one to stare at her. Their mouths dropped open in astonishment. Rosie's dress was filthy, her hair was dishevelled and her tears had left mascara tracks down her cheeks.

'Why, it's Rosie Mountjoy,' they whispered to each other. 'Whatever is the matter with her?'

The store-owner hurried from behind the counter. 'Mrs Mountjoy, what is it? What's wrong?' He took her arm and led her to a chair.

'My house . . . it's gone . . . they're all in the cellar. Buried alive. Honeychile, Aliza, Tom. I don't know what happened.'

'Must've got caught in the twister.' He grabbed the telephone receiver, jiggling the dial-tone up and down. 'Operator, get me the Texas Rangers,' he said urgently. 'There's an emergency out at Mountjoy Ranch. It caught the twister and there's people buried in the cellar there.'

'Imagine,' the women whispered to each other, 'Rosie Mountjoy must be the only person in the entire neighbourhood didn't know there was a tornado. And it touched down on her own home. Where was she, I wonder, that she didn't know?' And they raised their eyebrows and looked at each other. Everybody knew where Rosie spent her time.

'Poor child,' they whispered, thinking of Honeychile. 'Imagine her, buried alive in the cellar.' But not one of them went to Rosie to offer their sympathy or their help.

And hours later, when the drama was over and the prisoners were finally released, the stories flew around, about how shiftless Rosie Mountjoy hadn't even known her own house had blown away. And how Honeychile Mountjoy had ridden her horse bareback out of that cellar, followed by Tom Jefferson on Beaut, and then Aliza with the dog.

'Just like Noah's Ark,' they said, with a contemptuous snigger.

Rosie paid a visit to Mr John Parker Grant the very next day. The attorney looked older and even more frail, but he was still sharp and thankfully for Rosie, he knew what he was doing.

'What happens now, Mr Grant?' she asked, crossing her legs and looking him boldly in the eye. 'Everything's gone. The grass, the well, the cattle. And now the house.'

'As well as all the money.' He glanced at Rosie over the top of his wire half-spectacles. 'I feel it is my duty to tell you, Mrs Mountjoy, that I have never seen an estate so badly mismanaged in my entire career. All that money gone, and nothing to show for it.'

'Not one damn thing,' Rosie agreed. 'So now are you still gonna tell me I can't sell the ranch? Or that Honeychile can't?'

'Mountjoy Ranch is virtually worthless. You wouldn't get a row of beans for that property right now. And I told you several times that, valuable or worthless, the ranch is in trust. It can never be sold.'

'So what am I going to do now?' Rosie glared at him. 'How am I supposed to rebuild my house? With a row of beans?'

Grant sighed deeply, shuffling through the papers on his partner's scarred old mahogany desk. 'Once again, you're a lucky lady,' he said, giving her the benefit of the word lady, because trollope though she was, she was still his client. 'I kept up the insurance on the house, paying it annually from the fund set aside for that purpose. I have already contacted the insurance company and they are willing to rebuild the house and pay your claim in full.'

'In full?' Dollar signs danced through Rosie's mind. She would be rich again. She smiled at him. 'How much?'

'Twelve hundred dollars.'

'*Twelve hundred*. That's all? What about my furs and all my good clothes, and . . . and the dishes and stuff?'

'Only the structure was insured, Mrs Mountjoy. Not the contents. That was your personal responsibility. I only act for the estate in trust.'

She gave him a contemptuous glance. Where did he get off telling her the insurance was her responsibility? 'When do I get the money?' she said curtly.

'I have already filled in the claim form. If you sign here, the company will, I am sure, pay promptly.'

Rosie signed and then with a huge sigh, she got up and walked out. 'Thanks Mr Grant,' she called over her shoulder. 'Thanks for nothing.'

He shook his head, watching her as she sauntered out of the door and down the street past his window. 'Poor Honeychile,' he said sorrowfully. 'If ever anybody needed a father, that girl does.'

As usual, Rosie worked things out her own way. She gave Aliza two hundred dollars on account of her back wages, and told her she would have to find new employment. She told them the insurance company would rebuild the house, but she had rented a house in San Antonio and she was moving in there right away because she had gotten herself a job at the new saloon, opening next week. Honeychile would have to come with her. She would be starting a new school and she would also have to take care of things around the house because with her working, she surely was not going to have the time.

Honeychile said horrified, 'I'm not going with you to some awful rental park in San Antonio. I'm not going to stay home and keep house while you're out gallivanting, and I'm not starting any new school. I'm stayin' here with Aliza and Tom.'

'Oh yeah? And how will that make things look for me? All those old biddies will be gossiping again about how Rosie Mountjoy left her kid to live with the black help.' Rosie tossed her head angrily. 'Forget it, Honeychile. You're coming with me.'

Aliza said sadly, 'Your mother's right, girl. You're just gonna have to do as she says. At least for now. It was all right livin' here on the ranch, because that was your home, but it wouldn't be right for you to live in town with me and Tom. And it'll take ages for the house to be rebuilt. Anyways, we may have to travel miles from here to find ourselves new employment. I'm sorry, Honeychile, but that's just the way it is. For now,' she added gently.

Her heart was breaking and so was Honeychile's, but there was nothing either of them could do about it.

Honeychile said a tearful goodbye to Tom and to Aliza. She did not know when she might see them again; it was the goodbye of all good-byes, and it broke her heart for the second time in her young life.

It was almost as heart-rending parting with Lucky, the beloved Appaloosa her father had bought for her, because her mother said a city rental park was no place to keep a horse, and anyhow they couldn't afford it. But Tom said he would hang onto Lucky and Beaut as long as he could, and that if he got a job, he would keep them right here on the ranch and Honeychile could come and visit whenever she wanted.

Only the dog went with her, standing on the back seat of the battered red Dodge, wagging his tail and barking excitedly as they drove off down the lane, past the spot where her weekly bunch of wild flowers wilted in the mason jar in the shade of the old chestnut tree, and over the place where her father had been killed by the cattle truck. On down the long shimmering-white highway, to San Antonio, and her new life.

Honeychile's new 'home' was a small flimsy-looking wooden shack in the Silver Birch Rental Park. The once-white paint was peeling, the two windows were small and tightly closed and three rickety wooden steps led up to the only door. It was surrounded by other small, battered shacks, some with thin mangy-looking dogs tied to the steps. They barked at Fisher and he stared nervously at them.

The Park had once been grassy, with neat gravel walks. Now, like everywhere else, it was just a sea of dust. A solitary birch tree drooped tiredly in one corner and their shack sagged beneath it.

'We got lucky,' Rosie said sarcastically. 'We got the only bit of shade. My oh my,' she added, 'if your father could only see what we have come down to, he surely would regret not having left the ranch to me. I'd have sold it years ago and we would be living like kings right now.'

Honeychile knew Rosie believed what she had just said. She still believed she would have been living in that white porticoed mansion on a smart street in Houston – if only she had inherited the ranch and not her daughter.

Rosie unlocked the door, and a great waft of hot stale air greeted them as they stepped inside and looked around.

'I guess it's not too bad,' she said uncertainly, though it had definitely looked better late one evening last week, after a few drinks. Then, in the lamplight it had had a kind of Bohemian charm. Now it just looked shabby and worn.

'There's only one bedroom,' she said, opening a door at the far end and peering in, 'so I'll take that. I'll be working late most nights and I don't want you disturbing me, getting ready for school. I shall need to get my beauty sleep. In fact, I'll need all the rest I can get since I am now the sole provider in this household.'

Rosie stared critically at her daughter. 'How old are you now? Twelve? Going on thirteen? You had better hurry and grow up, Honeychile. Another two years of school and you can get a job and bring in some money.' She had a sudden thought. 'Say, maybe you could do some baby-sitting? There's bound to be kids in a place like this, and it'll keep you busy, nights, when I'm away.'

Honeychile sank dispiritedly onto the greasy chintz sofa. She looked at the small battered wooden table and the two rickety chairs; at the metal sink and the ancient gas ring. The brown linoleum covering the floor was stained and cracked, and tattered orange and brown curtains drooped over the two tiny windows. The kitchen/living area that was also to be her bedroom, was no more than twelve by nine and Rosie's was even smaller with just enough room for a bed, a dresser and a chair. She felt suddenly trapped.

'We'll fix it up real nice,' Rosie said, tossing her hat onto the bed. She lifted her hair from her neck, fanning herself. 'Mercy, this heat. When will it end? I'm going out shopping Honeychile, so just make yourself at home.' She glanced around. 'Maybe you could clean the place up a little. Then go to the grocery store on the corner; get some milk and cornflakes and bread and things. I'll be eating out mostly, at the saloon, so you don't have to worry about me.'

Honeychile stared, speechless, at her mother. They had only just arrived at this awful place and she was already leaving her.

'Oh come on,' Rosie cried impatiently, 'Give me a break, why don't you. The trouble with you, Honeychile, is you've always been cossetted by Aliza. You've never had to do a hand's turn. You're more than old enough to take care of yourself now.'

She strode to the door, then turned back and looked at her daughter, still sitting on the greasy sofa, staring numbly at her. Her face was ashen and her blonde hair, damp with sweat, hung in limp strands around her shoulders. She looked older than her age, fourteen, or even fifteen; but her blue eyes were those of a frightened child.

'It will do you good. Build your character,' Rosie said firmly. 'Just what you need, if you ask me. God, I only wish you had half my get-up-and-go.' She flounced back and threw a couple of dollars on the table. 'See y'all later,' she called as she swung out the door.

Life at the Silver Birch Rental Park was just as bad as Honeychile had known it would be. It was off a main highway with a bus depot at one end of the street, and a pawn shop at the other. Down the street was a cheap grocery, a butcher, and a string of closed-down stores with white-washed windows, a symbol of the depression. Lakewood Junior High was three blocks away, though there was no lake and not a single tree to account for its name. The brick structure had seen better days and the children who attended it were as shabby as the area, so at least Honeychile didn't feel different, in her tacky flowered skirts and blouses.

All the girls at Lakewood High knew each other and had already formed tight little groups. Honeychile was shy and awkward; she had always been the outsider at Kitsville and she had never had any girl friends. She didn't know how to approach these new girls, or even what to say to them, so she kept to herself, hugging her books to her chest and eating the brown-bagged sandwich lunch she had prepared, alone.

After a while, some of the girls said 'Hi' and smiled, but Honeychile still kept her distance. She knew their lives were different from hers. True, they were not rich, but they had real families, and they lived in proper homes. Their mothers did not work in the Silver Dollar

Saloon, and she bet they were always home when their daughters got back from school. Not like Rosie, who sometimes didn't even come home at all, until the next afternoon. And then only to change her clothes and get ready to go out again.

And there were no babies for Honeychile to baby-sit for in the Silver Birch Rental Park; only rheumy-eyed old men who drank and looked her up and down appraisingly; and tired, blowsy women who peered at her from their windows. And nobody ever called 'good morning', or said 'how are you today'.

Every afternoon, after school, Honeychile ran the three blocks home, clutching her precious books. Poor Fisher had to be kept tied to the steps all day, just like the other dogs, and the minute she came running up the path, he would dance on his hind legs, barking delightedly. She knew he missed the ranch: she saw how he twitched in his sleep, chasing jackrabbits in his dreams. Fisher missed it as much as she did.

She took him for a long walk to a small park she had found a few miles away. Then she unhitched his lead and let him run off his energy.

They always dawdled on the way back home, reluctant to return to the squalor of the shack. When they got back, Honeychile gave him his dinner, and, occasionally, a bone she had begged from the butcher. Then she fixed herself a bowl of cereal, or a Velveeta cheese sandwich with a glass of milk, propping a book in front of her on the table while she ate, devouring the words more eagerly than the food.

Afterwards, she did her homework, then she went and sat on the steps with an apple and her book. The dog dreamed lazily next to her, while she read about wonderful Medici villas in Italy and Renaissance Cathedrals in France, and great stone castles in England that had been built in the Middle Ages. She read about King Henry and Anne Boleyn; about Louis and Marie-Antoinette, about Leonardo and Lucretia Borgia.

Later, sprawled uncomfortably on the sofa that was her bed, she punched her pillow, trying to make it softer, sighing in the hot darkness and dreaming of the day she would somehow, miraculously, be freed from this stifling sordid life she led, and of how she would travel the world and see all these wonderful far-off places with her own eyes, instead of just reading about them.

One afternoon, when she got home from school, there was a letter waiting for her. She recognised Tom's writing and she ripped it open eagerly.

Tom said they were rebuilding the ranchhouse, and it was coming along just fine. He had fixed up Aliza's house almost as good as new, though she wasn't there much since she had gotten herself a job thirty miles away, working in the kitchen of a restaurant. She was managing all right, but she was lonesome and she missed Honeychile badly.

'I'm a lucky guy,' Tom wrote. *'I'm helping out at the gas station and general store on the highway, near Kitsville. It doesn't pay much, but it's a job and I'm thankful for that. Best thing is, it means I can still live in our old house at the ranch, and that means I can keep the horses ready for when your fortunes pick up and you get to come home again. They will be waiting for you, Honeychile, I promise you. And so will Mountjoy Ranch, because I'm surely keeping an eye on things here for you.*

One day this drought has to be over, and the grass will grow again and we'll find a new well. I know just the place – there's fresh, new grass growing on that patch of land, Honeychile, and that means sure as anything, there's water under there. I'm borrowing myself a drill and a bit from a friend, and I intend to have a go at it. Meanwhile, Lucky and Beaut have a patch to graze on, and I exercise them every day, and we all miss you.

We will see each other again one day soon, Honeychile. You can count on it. My Ma says she's no good at writing, she never learned how, but to tell you she loves you and thinks about you.'

He signed it simply, *'Tom'*.

Honeychile held the letter to her face. She kissed his signature, as though it were Tom himself she was kissing. At least something was right in her world. She just ached to be back on the ranch though. She considered simply telling her mother she had had enough and that she was going home. Or just taking the dog and disappearing without saying a word. But she knew neither one would work. She was doomed to live for ever in the Silver Birch Rental Park with Rosie.

The months passed emptily for Honeychile, but Rosie was having herself a good time. If she couldn't be on the burlesque stage, then a saloon was where she belonged. She knew how to mix a cocktail as well as how to pull draught beer. She was no chicken any more, past forty now, but she still had a good body and a wide smile and a come-on walk that the male customers appreciated. And if ever a girl liked to be 'appreciated' it was Rosie Mountjoy Hennessy. She also liked a drink and more than a few bourbons on the rocks passed her lips during the course of an evening.

When her shift was over, around midnight, there was usually a guy willing to take her onto the next place for another drink. Or, now and again, (because after all, as she was careful to point out to them – she was no hooker, just a girl working for her living) if she took a fancy to a guy, she went to a hotel with him. And every now and again, that little extra money came in real handy.

She needed to look good for work, didn't she, she said to Honeychile, showing her the bright new dress she had bought, or a new rope of 'pearls' and 'rubies' and 'diamonds'. 'After all,' she added, 'if your father was alive, he would be buying me the real thing.'

Rosie's bedroom in the shabby little home was cluttered with cheap knick-knacks; little bunny statuettes and celluloid kewpie dolls. She bought lamps with dangling bead fringes and dozens of pillows in red and mauve and pink plush. Ropes of cheap glass beads and imitation pearls were slung over the posts of her dresser and skimpy black underwear spilled from the drawers. Her dresses hung on pegs around the walls, and her fluffy satin mules with puffs of swansdown on the toes were scattered across the floor, next to high heeled T-strap shoes in black patent with rhinestone buckles, and flimsy scarlet sandals.

It was after midnight and Rosie was home early, for once. She was sitting at the table with a bottle of bourbon and a half-filled glass in front of her. The ice was melting, leaving a sticky wet stain on the already stained table and the bottle was almost empty.

'It's just like my dressing room in the old days, when I was a star,' she said to Honeychile, glancing at her room. She lit a cigarette and poured another slug of bourbon. 'You didn't know your mother was famous, did you,' she said, with a reminiscent smile. 'I was the best stripper in the business. Everybody said so. *And* I had a better ass than JoJo, even though she always claimed "her ass was her greatest asset".' She laughed, 'Get it Honeychile?' she asked, with a broad wink.

Honeychile nodded wearily. She had heard it all before.

Rosie thrust her feet into her high-heeled satin mules, sashaying across the floor clutching her Celanese print robe round her. '*Whispering while you cuddle near me,*' she sang. She struck a pose. '*Dum de dum de dum, boom,*' she hummed, flinging open the robe and giving a little bump and grind. '*Da dah, de dah, dedah.*' She laughed, flicking ash casually across the floor as she strutted her stuff for Honeychile.

She stuck the cigarette in her mouth and struck a final pose. 'What d'ya think?' she asked. 'Still pretty good huh?'

Honeychile looked away. 'I don't know. I never saw you before. *When you were a star.*'

Rosie glared suspiciously at her, suspecting sarcasm. 'Yeah, well,' she said finally, flopping back onto the sofa and dragging on the cigarette. 'Just you remember, girl. It's the truth. Your mother was a star. And that's why your father fell for me. All of a heap, he fell. He just saw me walking down the street and that was it.' She sighed and stubbed out the cigarette, then took a long drink.

'I was heading for New York City, headlining at Minsky's and Zeigfield, and I gave it all up for love.' She gave a cynical snort. 'Young fool that I was.'

Rosie refilled her glass, not bothering with the ice any more. She took a gulp and said, 'Ah, Honeychile, your father and I drank French champagne in those days – and you have no idea how much it cost in Prohibition times. I never drank cheap stuff then.' She took another sip and lit another cigarette, talking half-to-herself now.

'He bought me an ermine stole, so white, so soft . . .' She touched a hand to her cheek, remembering how it had felt. 'God, he was attractive though,' she whispered, 'and soooo sexy . . . I thought, this is the man for me. Young, rich and sexy. What more could a girl want?'

Her head fell back against the cushions. 'I might have known there was a catch,' she said drunkenly, looking straight at Honeychile. 'And there were two. The ranch that ruined my life. *And my daughter.*'

Honeychile didn't wait to hear any more. She ran to the door and the dog ran with her. She took off, through the silent shacks into the street. She walked aimlessly for hours, her hands thrust into her pockets, her head down, oblivious to the occasional passerby, and the lateness of the hour and the potential danger. She didn't even know where she was walking, or where she ended up, except that it was on top of a hill with some trees.

She stared at the black night sky, unsilvered by moon or clouds. There was no heaven up there, she thought bleakly. Her father was not watching over her. There was just nothing. She was nowhere. No one. She did not exist.

The months crawled by. Surprisingly, she was doing well in school and her teacher said she was college material.

'College material,' Rosie scoffed when she told her about it. 'Soon as the law allows, you're leaving school. I'll find you a job. Even if it's washing dishes at the saloon, at least you'll be bringing in some money.'

Money was very much on Rosie's mind. It still slipped through her fingers like water; there was always something she needed, or fancied, or just plain *wanted*. And Honeychile never seemed to quit growing, she was always having to buy her a new skirt, and Lord knows that girl had no taste. Rosie would pick out something nice and colourful for her, with pretty flowers and ruffles, and she would refuse to wear it.

'Hey Honeychile,' she called, 'what d'ya hear from Tom these days?'

Honeychile looked warily at her mother. She never usually asked about Tom, or Aliza.

'Aliza's still working out at Brotherton. Tom's living at the ranch. He borrowed a drill from the man at the garage where he works, and he's drilling in the green patch near where the longhouse used to be. He thinks he'll find water there, with it being so green and all.' And please God let him find it, she prayed silently. Because then I can go home and never, *never* have to see the Silver Birch Rental Park again.

Rosie waved the ash casually from her cigarette onto the floor, watching Honeychile. 'Tom's a fool. There's no hidden spring under that land. It's as dead as a dodo, whatever that might be. And it's all yours, my darling daughter. Every worthless acre of it.'

Honeychile went outside and sat on the steps, her chin propped in her hand, staring at the scabby landscape. She hated every minute of her life here. And she hated Rosie. She sat for a long time, planning how she could escape and return to live at the ranch, but she had no money, and there was just no way.

Strangely, the very next day Rosie came hurrying home from work early. Really early. Like ten o'clock.

Honeychile looked up from her book, startled, as the door was flung open and her mother stepped in. There was a flush on her cheeks and a sparkle in her eyes and her first thought was 'uhuh, she's drunk again'. But Rosie wasn't drunk this time.

She flung herself into the chair opposite, lit a cigarette and said, 'Guess who I've just had a phone call from?' She threw back her head and blew a perfect smoke ring, smiling at Honeychile.

'I don't know. Who?' Honeychile replied warily.

'From the office of Parker Grant & Andersen, smart-ass attorneys-at-law, right here in San Antonio. That's who.' She grinned at Honeychile, waiting for her to ask why.

'Why did they call you?' she obliged.

'They called Mrs David Mountjoy because, dear daughter, they wanted to inform me that oil has been discovered on our land.'

Honeychile sat up straight. 'On the Mountjoy Ranch?'

Rosie nodded. 'That's exactly right, baby. On our ranch. It seems young Tom fooling round with that drill came up with something. He called the attorney, old John Parker Grant, but he's long dead. Mr Andersen spoke to him instead. He liked what he heard and he sent a team out there to investigate.' She laughed delightedly, thinking about it. 'They say there's a fortune under there, just waiting to be tapped, and they're waiting for our permission to put in a rig.'

She sat back, smiling at Honeychile. 'Your Mama's gonna be rich at last, girl,' she whispered. '*Really, really rich.* How does that saying go? . . . *beyond the dreams of avarice* . . .'

Rosie heaved a huge contented sigh. 'Imagine, I did marry a rich man after all,' she said, taking a fresh bottle of bourbon out of the brown paper bag she had been carrying. 'And boy, am I gonna celebrate.'

She glanced suspiciously at Honeychile. 'What's the matter? Cat got your tongue? Don't tell me you're not pleased?'

'Of course I'm glad. If it's really true,' she added doubtfully.

'Oh, it's true all right. And we're going to Mr Andersen's office at ten o'clock tomorrow morning to sign the papers for the oil company to explore our land as soon as possible. "The sooner the better,"

Andersen said. And he's right, because I can almost feel those lovely silver dollars jingling in my pocket.'

She poured the bourbon and took a long swallow. 'Only the good stuff from now on, Rosie,' she complimented herself. 'No more cheap hooch for you.'

Honeychile left her mother to her drinking and went outside. She sat on the steps, the place she always went to think. What if Rosie was right, and there was oil on Mountjoy Ranch? They would be rich. She could go home again. *At last.*

She called the dog and strode off into the night. '*Finally*,' she thought walking up the lonely hill and staring at the midnight blue sky, lit by a full harvest moon. '*Finally, I am going to be happy.*'

The next morning they went to sign the papers at Andersen's office. Rosie wore her best black dress and a little cloche hat with a long feather, and Honeychile wore a clean gingham skirt and a white blouse that was too tight.

Mr Andersen was a tall, stout man with prominent blue eyes and cold hands. Honeychile took stock of him silently, while Rosie gushed on like the oil well about how thrilled she was, and how it was only her due after all these years of struggling, because David Mountjoy had left her just about destitute.

'He did not leave you destitute,' Honeychile said angrily. She was sitting in the same slippery leather chair she had occupied eleven years ago, when her father had died and Mr John Parker Grant had informed her that *she* was the owner of the Mountjoy Ranch, and not her mother. 'He left you a fortune. Fifty-nine thousand dollars. And you spent it all.'

Rosie's face flushed a deep red. 'Why, how dare you, Honeychile. What a thing to say. You know whatever money there was went on you, and on living and . . . well money just goes nowhere, does it, Mr Andersen?' She gave him a beseeching little smile. 'It just never did with me, anyhow.'

He nodded, then told them about the company that would look for the oil. 'They will pay a fee for the permission to explore your land,' he said. 'They will also put up the necessary investment money and do all the work, and if there is oil there, you will reap the rewards,' he added, with a smile.

'So when do we get the money?' Rosie interrupted.

'First we have to see if there is oil,' Honeychile explained patiently.

'It could be a couple of months, or a couple of years,' Andersen told her.

'Jeez.' Rosie bit her lip, annoyed. 'I planned on buying myself a house, moving right away.'

'Let me remind you, there is no money yet,' Andersen explained, hastily. 'We are talking about investigating the possibility of oil on the Mountjoy Ranch.'

But he didn't know Rosie. The word 'possibility' was not in her vocabulary. In her mind, gushers were already spouting dollars into her eager hands, and she was ready to spend them.

CHAPTER 17

Rosie went out to celebrate. She didn't come home that night, nor the next. She had never been away this long before and Honeychile was worried. Then suddenly, she came striding up the dusty path, past the sagging old shacks, wearing a new red dress and a fancy little feather hat, looking like a flamboyant bird of paradise in a ghetto of grey pigeons. And she was carrying half a dozen boxes and bags, all with smart labels.

'I've been shopping,' she announced, flinging her packages triumphantly onto the bed. Sinking down next to them, she stuck a foot in the air and flipped off her sandal, then she repeated it with the other one. She heaved a sigh of relief. 'Wheee,' she gasped, pulling off the hat and wiggling her toes. 'Oh the relief of it. Honeychile, don't ever let anyone tell you shopping's not hard work. Believe me, it is.'

'Where did you get the money, Rosie?' Honeychile almost wished she had not asked, she was so afraid to hear the answer.

Rosie grinned as she lit a cigarette. 'There are ways and means,' she said primly. 'Ways and means.' Then she laughed and said, 'Oh well, if you must know, I went to Victor, at the Silver Dollar. I told him we were gonna drill for oil on Mountjoy Ranch. I said if he didn't believe me, all he had to do was call Mr Andersen. So he did. And baby, you should have seen his attitude change. He said, "Sure, we can advance you some money, Rosie." So I signed a form, giving him ten per cent of my share and he gave me a lot of money, and now I can have whatever I want.'

'What if they don't find oil? How will you ever pay him back?'

Rosie shrugged. 'Of course they'll find oil. Look, it says so, right here, in the newspaper.'

She tossed a newspaper across to Honeychile. 'See that,' she said, 'on the front page no less. All about us and the Mountjoy Ranch, and how rich we're gonna be.' She threw back her head, laughing gleefully. 'I'm finally famous. Rosie Mountjoy, the wealthiest widow in Texas.'

'Aren't you forgetting something?' Honeychile corrected her. 'Jack Delaney. The man you married? You never got divorced, so you are still Rosie Delaney.'

Rosie glared at her, then began busily unwrapping her parcels. 'Yes, well, nobody else knows about that. So let's just let sleeping dogs lie, shall we. Anyhow, me and Victor are throwing a party at the Silver Dollar, to celebrate. And *I* shall be on the right side of the bar this time, along with the other paying customers. No more tips for me,' she added triumphantly, 'I'm doing the tipping from now on.'

Honeychile sighed. She could see the way it was going to be with Rosie. Exactly the same as before. If ever the phrase 'easy come easy go' was coined for anyone, it was her mother. And there wasn't even any guarantee they would find oil.

'I got you a present,' Rosie said, rummaging under the pile of new dresses. 'I meant to get myself a real mink stole, you know – like the movie stars wear, but I guess I'm just gonna have to wait until I go into Houston for that.' She found the bag she was looking for and handed it to Honeychile. '*There.* Now you can't ever say your mother doesn't think about you.'

Honeychile took out the dress. Bright blue chiffon with a low V-neck and a short skirt, dipping into little handkerchief points at the hem. It was garish and meant for someone ten years older than she was.

'Well?' Rosie asked, exasperated. 'Don't you like it? I thought it would bring out the blue of your eyes.'

'Thank you, Rosie,' Honeychile replied, surprised that Rosie had even thought about the colour of her eyes. 'It's very nice,' she added quickly, 'but I don't go to the sort of places I could wear it.'

'That's just the point,' Rosie retorted gleefully. 'You can wear it tonight. To my party. I thought it was time you were brought out a bit, into Society.' She laughed. 'Your *début*, you might call it. Now you're gonna be an oil heiress.'

'No thanks.' Honeychile put the dress back in the bag.

Rosie looked exasperatedly at her pale-faced, lanky daughter. 'It's about time you got out more, met some people. You're gonna be a rich girl now, Honeychile. We shall have to launch you into Society. Properly, I mean. Not just tonight.' She heaved a sigh, looking at her, 'We'll fix you up a bit and you'll look okay. Who knows, you might be a real knockout.'

Staring at her, she laughed and laughed until she almost choked. Then she lit a cigarette and said, 'And tomorrow, we're outta here. I've rented an apartment on Grand Avenue, one of the best on that fancy street.'

She stepped out of her dress, letting it fall to the floor. 'Only thing is,' she added casually, putting the cigarette between her lips and tying her robe, 'they don't allow animals. You're gonna have to get rid of Fisher.'

Honeychile flung her arms around the dog. It wagged its tail and licked her face, hoping for a game. 'How can you even say that,' she cried. 'You must have lost your mind.'

Rosie shrugged. 'Don't blame me. Those are the rules, that's all.'

'Well, they're not *my* rules and I'm not going to live any place where I can't have Fisher. I'd rather stay here.'

'Oh, then stay here on your own, you stupid girl,' Rosie snarled, suddenly angry. 'For God's sake, I try to do my best for you and this is all the thanks I get.'

Rosie went into her room and a moment later Honeychile heard her singing the latest tune in her sexy, cigarette-rasped voice, as she prepared for her party. Nothing ever bothered Rosie for very long. Not when she had money to burn.

Honeychile took Fisher for a walk and she did not return until she knew her mother would have left.

She opened the door cautiously and peered in. The shack smelled of Evening in Paris scent and pungent Turkish cigarette smoke and the sweet-sour aroma of bourbon. She looked into Rosie's room, at the new dresses and lingerie flung on the bed and the clothes she had stepped out of, half-submerged in the tissue-paper wrappings on the floor. At the chaotic tangle of beads and Tangee lipsticks and swansdown powder-puffs and spilled rouge and red nail polish.

She felt badly that she had been so ungrateful for the dress. Rosie had tried hard to please her. She told herself she would apologise when Rosie got home. But still, it bothered her, Rosie had meant well; she had really tried to give her something nice. Honeychile decided to go to the saloon and find her mother. She would tell her she was sorry, and thank her for the present.

Loud jazz music and laughter spilled from the Silver Dollar Saloon's open doors. Honeychile held Fisher's lead tightly, hovering uncertainly outside.

Finally, she walked to the entrance and peered over the top of the swinging doors, just as the music changed to a different rhythm. It was a tune she knew.

'They're playing my music,' she heard Rosie call, and then she saw her mother being lifted onto the bar by half-a-dozen willing men.

Rosie stood with her hands on her hips, smiling down at her audience. Her new scarlet dress was shirred up the front like cinema curtains and it clung lovingly to her curves. Her breasts, white as a dove's spilled from the top and as Honeychile looked, she hiked her short skirt even higher, wiggling her hips provocatively as she called out, 'So, who's still the Sexiest Stripper on the Circuit, fellas?'

'You are, Rosie,' they yelled back. And they laughed and applauded as she shimmied along the counter in time to the music, pausing here and there to give them a bump and grind, and a gleeful little smile.

Honeychile fled down the street, dragging Fisher behind her, not even stopping to let him sniff a lamp-post.

'How could you, Rosie,' she said through gritted teeth. 'How could you do that. How could you, *how could you*?' And she didn't stop running until she reached the Rental Park.

The next morning, early, she took the bus into town and went to speak to Mr Andersen. She reminded him that Mountjoy Ranch belonged to the Trust, and asked him if she could have some of the two thousand dollars the oil company had paid them for permission to drill.

He said, as long as it was for the ranch, he didn't see why not. So Honeychile went with him to the Bank of Texas and withdrew five hundred dollars from the Mountjoy Trust account. Then she said goodbye to Mr Andersen and took a bus to Kitsville. From there, she and Fisher walked the ten miles to Mountjoy Ranch. Then she sent Tom to fetch Aliza and wrote a note to Rosie telling her she was not coming back. Finally, she was home.

A couple of months later, Rosie's body was found in a pool of her own blood, in the alley outside the Silver Dollar Saloon. And a couple of weeks after that, Jack Delaney returned to claim Mountjoy Ranch.

Honeychile always left her memories at that point, because she couldn't bear to think about what happened next. It lurked somewhere in the dark recesses of her mind, like a time-bomb, waiting to explode.

She never spoke about Rosie and Jack Delaney, and if Edgar Smallbone had not come calling that day, and told her that her great-uncle was looking for her, she probably never would. But the mention of Lord Mountjoy had triggered her memory.

As she rode back to the ranch, she wondered exactly what old Lord Mountjoy had up his sleeve. What did he mean, *'she would learn something to her advantage'*? She hoped it was good, because they surely could use a spot of luck right now.

She wondered, wistfully, what her father would have thought about it all, and she cast a smile to the wind-blown blue sky. 'Pray for me, Papa, up there in heaven,' she said. 'And remember, I still love you.'

PART II

CHAPTER 18

'A hat maker?' Lord Mountjoy said incredulously. 'You mean she is *a woman who makes hats*?'

Swayne was standing in front of his Lordship's desk in the library of the London house, where he had come to deliver his reports on George Mountjoy's descendants. The butler had taken his raincoat, and his brown felt hat, and he stood to attention, hands clasped behind him, listening attentively as Lord Mountjoy repeated his amazement that a relative of his actually made hats for a living.

'Madame Suzette is a very *exclusive* hat maker, my Lord. She only deals with the best people. Her shop is very successful.'

Mountjoy glared irately at him. 'How successful could a hat shop be? Tell me that, Swayne, since you are so knowledgeable about milliners.'

Swayne coughed nervously behind his hand. He had thought Lord Mountjoy would be happy with his success. 'Madame Suzette is also a countess, sir. She said you would be pleased to know that.'

'A *French* countess,' he said contemptuously. 'Besides, she is only related by marriage. Now, tell me about the child.' He looked expectantly at Swayne.

'The *comtesse* has a daughter, sir.'

'A *female*?' He sank back in his green-leather chair; it had never occurred to him that Georgie's possible descendants would be anything but male.

'By the name of Anjou, sir. She is almost twenty years old and has been educated away from home, at a school in the countryside. A good school, as you will see from my notes. It seems she is intelligent and an excellent scholar. A quiet girl, was the report I got.'

'A bluestocking,' Lord Mountjoy said glumly. This was getting worse and worse.

Swayne brought him up to date on the story of Marie and Georgie, and he heaved a despondent sigh.

'Is that all you found? Just the French woman?'

'We had a more difficult time in Italy, sir. The little "episode" had been covered up by the Fioraldis. A very aristocratic bunch, if you don't mind me saying so, your Lordship. The family line goes back a long way. Not quite as far as your own, of course, but there are several Papal Knights amongst them.'

'Humph,' Mountjoy commented, looking interested.

'The family's servants were very loyal, sir. They refused to answer my associate's questions, despite being offered substantial sums in bribes.'

Lord Mountjoy gave a disbelieving grunt. 'Servants always take bribes. Especially in Italy.'

'Not these, sir. Still, my associate was able to discover that when she met George Mountjoy, Adriana Fioraldi was engaged to be married to Paolo Torloni, a wealthy young man with large estates in the Veneto. He had been hand-picked by Adriana's father and she had no say in the matter.'

'Quite right too,' Mountjoy muttered approvingly. 'Well, go on, go on.' He waved his hand impatiently at Swayne, listening intently as the detective told him the story of Adriana and Georgie; and about Jeannie Swinburn.

'Yorkshire,' Mountjoy observed gloomily. 'The very back of beyond. Still, there's some damned fine shooting.' He sighed, foreseeing trouble. 'There's only one creature more stubborn than a Yorkshireman, Swayne. And that's a Yorkshire woman. Well, go on then, tell me his name?'

'*Her* name, sir. Laura Lavinia Swinburn, also aged twenty years.'

For once in his life, Lord Mountjoy was speechless. He stared uncomprehendingly at Swayne for a few silent minutes. Swayne shifted uneasily, afraid that Lord Mountjoy might renege on his promised twenty per cent bonus just because Georgie's grandchildren were girls.

'What happened to Adriana Fioraldi?' Mountjoy asked finally.

'She married Paolo Torloni, sir. At the *Catedrale del Duomo* in Florence, a few months after she returned. I understand it was a very grand ceremony, attended by many of Italy's finest families.

It seems the union was a happy one, though there were no children. They were married for over thirty years and died within months of each other. They were devoted.'

'*Devoted*, hmm,' Lord Mountjoy said, reflecting that what a man did not know apparently did him no harm.

'What next?' he asked, hoping for better luck.

'Good news, your Lordship,' Swayne permitted himself a smile of triumph. 'I have also located Georgie Mountjoy's descendant in Texas, in the United States of America.'

'Damn and blast it, man, we all know where Texas is located. Get on with it, why don't you.' Mountjoy glared, irritatedly, at him.

'I'm afraid it's another young woman, sir,' Swayne allowed himself a moment's pleasurable anticipation before he added, 'By the name of Honeychile.'

Lord Mountjoy's jaw dropped in shock. He swallowed hard. 'Honeychile,' he repeated, shaking his head. 'Surely it must be some kind of joke? No one – especially a Mountjoy – can possibly be called *Honeychile*.' Then he realised his hopes for a male heir to inherit the Earldom had disappeared like smoke in the night. 'What the hell was wrong with them, begatting only girls?' he demanded angrily. 'Mountjoys *always* had sons. That's how the line existed for so many centuries.'

'Perhaps it was the foreigners' fault, sir,' Swayne suggested helpfully.

'I dare say you are right,' Mountjoy nodded, conceding that certainly his family could not be to blame.

Swayne then told him about David and Rarin' Rosie and their terrible deaths.

'Honeychile still lives on the old Mountjoy Ranch with the woman who brought her up, Aliza Jefferson.'

'Her nanny, you mean?'

'In a way, sir.'

Lord Mountjoy sighed. He was beginning to think he had opened a Pandora's Box for his birthday present. Instead of finding the heir he had hoped for: some decent, impecunious, malleable young man who could be trained to follow the Mountjoy traditions; he was ending up with three females, each of whom sounded worse than the other. He glared at the detective as though it were all his fault.

Swayne shifted uncomfortably from one enormous foot to the other. His black boots squeaked loudly and Lord Mountjoy's brows knitted into a scowl.

'One more thing, your Lordship,' Swayne said quickly. 'Honeychile is poor. *Very* poor, sir. The Mountjoy Ranch was devastated by drought several years ago. They are struggling hard to survive. They tell me Honeychile does the work of two men. She is devoted to her land and thinks of nothing else.'

Mountjoy looked thoughtful; he admired hard work in the young. 'If only they were men,' he said wistfully, 'then we would be talking. But a French bluestocking, a horse-mad Yorkshire gel and a Texan woman who works the land? What can I make of that, Swayne, I ask you?'

Swayne waited patiently while Lord Mountjoy stared into space, thinking about Georgie and his granddaughters.

'Is that all, Swayne?' Lord Mountjoy said, at last.

'It is, sir. Here are my written reports on the girls. May I point out one strange coincidence, sir. That they were all born in the same year.'

Lord Mountjoy riffled through the reports, checking the dates and finding Swayne correct. 'Remarkable,' he said. 'Extraordinary.'

'Almost as if they were triplets, sir,' Swayne said with a grin.

Lord Mountjoy suppressed a shudder. 'They are Mountjoys,' he said stiffly. Then, thoughtfully, 'The Mountjoy girls.' The phrase rolled off his tongue as though it were tailor-made for the society pages of the *Bystander* and *Tatler*, and the court circulars in *The Times*.

Swayne shifted from one creaking boot to the other, wondering, now his job was done, if he had the nerve to remind Lord Mountjoy about the bonus. 'I trust my work was satisfactory, your Lordship,' he said finally, when it seemed he was never going to return from his reverie.

'What . . . what? Oh, indeed, yes. Very good work, Swayne. Of course, the bonus will be forwarded to you.'

Swayne smiled broadly. You never knew with aristocrats. Not that they would ever cheat a working man like himself, but sometimes they just forgot what they had said. 'One other thing, sir, while I think of it. About the young American girl. Her proper name is Eloise Georgia Mountjoy Hennessy.'

'But you said *Honeychile*,' Mountjoy exclaimed, dumbfounded.

'Just a nickname, sir.' Swayne permitted himself a satisfied little smile at having put one over on his Lordship. 'A nickname, that's all.' He failed to add that no one in her entire life, had ever called Honeychile, *Eloise*.

Lord Mountjoy spent a long time, after Swayne had departed, reading and re-reading the reports. He thought angrily that his brother, Georgie, had scattered his seed far and wide and with criminal carelessness. To get one girl into trouble, might be understandable. But *three*? Remembering Rarin' Rosie the Sexiest Stripper on the Circuit, he groaned out loud.

He pushed his chair away from the desk, and began to pace the red and green tartan carpet again, his hands behind his back, thumbs twiddling as they always did when he was agitated.

'*Anjou d'Aranville*,' he said out loud. '*Laura Swinburn. Eloise Hennessy*.' He paced some more, thinking about them. He stared out of the window at the swirling snowflakes. The blizzard had whipped up from nowhere while he was not looking and all traffic had stopped. No one was on the streets and the snow whirled down on the icily silent city.

'Laura *Mountjoy*,' he said tentatively. 'Anjou *Mountjoy*. Eloise *Mountjoy*.'

He began to pace again, stopping for a while in front of the mantelpiece to check his invitations for that evening: there was just one, to a dinner party in Belgrave Square.

He stared as though mesmerised at the piece of engraved white pasteboard. Suddenly, before his eyes it seemed to change into an invitation he had penned himself . . . an invitation to a ball he was giving for his great-nieces, Laura, Eloise and Anjou.

Lord Mountjoy shook his head; it would be impossible to foist Georgie's bastards off on Society. 'I mean,' he said out loud, 'the daughters of a French milliner, a half-Italian Yorkshireman, and an American striptease artiste?'

He thought about it for a minute more, then a smile twitched at the corners of his mouth. It spread into a grin, then a bigger grin, then he burst into laughter. He laughed the way he could not remember laughing in thirty years; great hearty peals of laughter that echoed in the snowy silence.

'Well, well,' he chortled, when at last he was able to speak, 'perhaps my birthday present to myself will be better than I ever thought it would be.'

He sat down at his desk and, before he could change his mind, penned a letter to each of his great-nieces.

'My dear Eloise,' he began. *'You may recently have been aware that investigations were being made on my behalf, to trace the descendants of my brother, George Albert Arthur Mountjoy. I feel it better, under the circumstances, to gloss over the matter of my brother's indiscretions, and those of the women involved. Suffice it to say that, at my time of life – I am seventy years old – I am facing a circumstance no Mountjoy has ever faced before. I am the last of a line that has existed, in unbroken male succession, since the Norman Conquest.*

I am therefore inviting you, my brother's granddaughter – and my own great-niece, to visit me in England. I should like you to come to stay at Mountjoy Park, your grandfather's childhood home and the place where he was born. And to be introduced to English Society, at a ball I shall give for you, at Mountjoy House, in London.

I am sure you are unaware, as I was until recently, that there are two other granddaughters; one in Paris and one in England and by an odd coincidence, you are all twenty years old.

I feel sure that your grandfather, George Mountjoy, would have wished you to take this opportunity of meeting me, his brother and the sole remaining member of his family, and of being presented properly at Court, as Mountjoy girls always have been.

Needless to say, all expenses for your visit, and for your Presentation, as well as everything necessary; travel, clothes, jewels, etc., will be taken care of by myself. In return, I would expect you to place yourselves completely in the hands of a chaperone, my relative by marriage, Sophie Mountjoy, who will guide you in matters of dress, deportment and the social niceties.

I need hardly add that, since there are no male Mountjoys left to inherit the Earldom, the title will alas, die out with me. But of course, the decision as to which one of you will inherit the Mountjoy money, will be entirely mine.'

He signed it with a flourish, *'Mountjoy'*, then sat back, enjoying the little stinger he had put in the tail of his letter.

'That bait will get those gels here faster than a hound after the fox,' he thought, rubbing his hands together gleefully. Each hoping she will be the one to inherit the Mountjoy money. And who indeed would that be, he wondered, as he wrote a similar letter to Madame Suzette, and to Mrs Jeannie Swinburn.

When he had finished, he tugged the tapestry bellpull by the fireplace and waited for Johnson to arrive. 'See that these are posted, will you, Johnson,' he ordered. He took out his watch. 'And there's just time before I change, for a glass of whisky.'

Johnson handed the letters to the footman to be stamped and mailed, then he carried the decanter of the single malt Mountjoy preferred into the library.

Lord Mountjoy savoured the first mouthful slowly, drawing its flavour across his tongue. 'There's nothing like a drop of good whisky on a cold winter's night, Johnson,' he said appreciatively.

'Indeed not, sir,' Johnson said impassively.

The library clock ticked into the silence, the snowflakes patted against the window-panes and a log shifted in the fire amid a crackle of sparks.

'Better make the most of our peace and quiet, Johnson,' Mountjoy commented with a mischievous grin, 'I have a feeling things are going to change around here.' And he laughed heartily again. He couldn't wait to get to the dinner party so he could tell them he was going to present his three long-lost Mountjoy great-nieces at Court this season. Because it never occurred to him for an instant that they might refuse.

CHAPTER 19

A few weeks later, on a cold blue March afternoon, Honeychile was in a yellow cab on her way to the West 70th Street Pier, and the luxury liner that would take her to England.

Manhattan and Wall Street passed by the window in a late afternoon blur of ivory towers and shadowy canyons, then suddenly the great white liner soared above her.

She paid off the cab and stood, clutching her suitcase, looking at flags and buntings fluttering in the wind, and the brass band in smart dark blue uniforms, playing songs from the latest Broadway shows; and at the Redcaps wheeling giant trolleys, loaded with enormous cabin trunks, to the hold at the side of the ship. She stared enviously at the beautiful women, clutching alligator jewel cases, with orchids pinned to the lapels of their smart tweed travelling suits, trailing furs and perfume and surrounded by laughing friends who had come to see them off. 'See you later, for cocktails,' they called to each other, and Honeychile felt plain and dowdy in the camel-hair coat that had looked so smart in the Sears catalogue.

Loneliness and fear of the unknown overwhelmed her; she longed for the security of the ranch, and Aliza and Tom. But then she reminded herself of what the Mountjoy money could do: it could pay to irrigate her land; it could pay to plant new grasses; it could buy prime Longhorn and Angus cattle. Then Mountjoy Ranch would come into its glory again, the way it used to be when her father ran it. And besides, she knew her father would have wanted her to go. Taking the first-class ticket from her purse, she walked determinedly towards the gangway.

There was a sudden commotion behind her and she turned to look. Photographers were crowding round a tall dark-haired man and his companion. Their flashbulbs illuminated the sternness of the man's face and the familiar beauty of the woman he was with, and she gave a gasp of amazement as she recognised her from her long afternoons at the Kitsville Roxy. With her platinum hair, startlingly red mouth and sultry gaze, it could only be Viva Molson, the famous Hollywood star. One of the photographers, eager to grab a picture, suddenly darted in front of Honeychile, knocking her to the ground.

'Enough,' a male voice thundered above her. 'Get out of my way, you idiot. Can't you see what you've done?'

The stern-looking man was bending over her and his light-grey eyes were looking anxiously into hers. 'Are you all right?' He helped her to her feet. 'If that fool hurt you, I'll have him fired.'

'It was an accident,' Honeychile said quickly, shocked by the idea that someone could be fired just because he knocked her down. 'I'm not hurt.'

'Then please accept my apologies, Miss . . . ?'

'Honeychile Mountjoy Hennessy.' She remembered Lord Mountjoy's instructions and corrected herself quickly. 'I mean, I'm really Eloise. Eloise Mountjoy.'

His face lost its sternness as he smiled, and she thought he looked suddenly a lot younger, almost boyish. There was a hint of laughter in his voice as he said, 'My apologies again, Miss Mountjoy.'

From the corner of her eye, Honeychile caught Viva Molson's angry pout and the impatient tapping of her beautifully shod foot. Embarrassed, she said, 'I'm okay, really I am. Thank you for helping me,' and she walked quickly up the gangway.

'For God's sake, Alex, let's get a move on,' Viva called. 'It's getting late.'

Frowning, he escorted her up the gangway, standing back as she posed again on the deck for the photographers. 'See you for cocktails, Alex, darling,' she called as he left her to her audience.

'Not if I have anything to do with it,' he said to himself as he strode through the corridors of the enormous ship, to the florists on a lower level.

Alexander Andreos Scott hated cocktail parties. He had no time for press photographers and gossip columnists, nor for celebrities, though he had earned himself that doubtful title, along with the headline, 'Mystery Man', that seemed to haunt him. And he had no time for women like Viva Molson.

He had met her at a dinner a few months ago, and then he had bumped into her again last night at the Stork Club, where he had been entertaining business associates. Viva was bored with her escort and she had attached herself to him, clinging like a limpet to his arm. She had demanded he take her home and when she found they were both sailing on the Queen Elizabeth the next day, she had asked him for a lift.

'Why take two limousines, darling,' she had murmured in her sexy contralto, squeezing his hand meaningfully. And then she had given him that famous smouldering look, and whispered, 'This promises to be an exciting voyage, Alex.'

Her thick-skinned assumption that all she had to do was beckon and any man would come running, angered him. He could not stand unintelligent women, and the voluptuous Viva held no charm for him.

Alex Scott was thirty-eight years old, and the debate was open whether you considered him attractive or not. His face was long and narrow, some jealous critics even said 'cadaverous'; his nose was strong and his firm mouth had a sardonic twist to the lips. He had thick dark hair, already streaked with silver; his eyes were the same silvery-grey but with darker flecks in the iris, and there were lines of strain around them, evidence that he had led a tougher life than his present one of ease and success. He was tall and lean with a well-muscled body that looked good in the custom-tailored Saville Row clothes he wore. And he had a formidable reputation with women.

They said when Alex Scott wanted you, he let you know it. He sent flowers, and somehow he always managed to find out your favourite. He suggested dinners *a deux* in discreet expensive restaurants. He gave jewels and sent books, with no thought to the extravagance of one gift, nor the inexpense of the other, merely the pleasure it would bring. Women said Alex Scott gave you everything except his heart. And a window onto his soul, and his mysterious past.

At the florists, he ordered two dozen yellow roses to be sent to Miss Mountjoy. He enclosed his card, with the message, 'My apologies again. I trust there are no bruises.' Then he went to the enormous suite on the upper deck where his valet was already unpacking his bags, and a white-jacketed English steward awaited his command.

163

Alex was always scrupulously polite and considerate to servants. He thanked the steward and said there was nothing he needed. He flung off his jacket, rolled up his expensive blue Sea Island cotton shirt sleeves, and sat at the corner desk with the large windows overlooking the busy dock. He placed two ship-to-shore telephone calls: one to his Manhattan office, and one to the Secretary of State in Washington. Then he summoned his assistant, Stavros, who was installed in a smaller cabin on a lower deck.

When he arrived, Alex dictated three cablegrams: one to the ship-builders in Glasgow, enquiring about the progress of his new oil freighter; one to his wine merchant in Bordeaux, about the 1937 vintage; and one to a woman in Rome that said simply, '*Happy Birthday, You have my love as always.*'

The ship's siren blasted, announcing their departure and he went to stand by the window, watching the tiny tugs manoeuvring the great ship out of her berth and into the river. The band played loudly, people waved and threw streamers and shouted 'Bon Voyage' across the widening gap of water. They were on their way at last.

Alex put on his jacket and a muffler and walked to the Promenade Deck. As he had expected, it was deserted; the jaded first-class passengers had seen it all before, they had no interest in the view and were more concerned with getting ready for the cocktail parties that would take place in a little while.

He strolled round, watching the tugs doing their job and the Manhattan skyline diminishing in the distance. Alex loved the sea; it was in his blood. Had he been born a hundred years earlier, he would have been a cabin boy on a six-masted sailing ship, climbing the rigging and battling the winds and storms and pirates. Instead, he was the owner of one of the largest freight shipping lines in the world, and suspected of being a bit of a modern-day pirate himself.

Scott vessels traversed the globe with precious cargoes of grain and lumber, oil and machinery. And, it was rumoured by some, with car-goes of illegal armaments. Everyone knew the Scott ships, and about Alexander Andreos Scott. They knew how rich he was, how powerful and how remote. What they did not know, was how he had done it.

The more charitable rumours said he was a member of the aristo-cratic Italian Scotti family; but others said he was a child of the Roman gutters who had clawed his way up, using whatever illegal or criminal path he could. One report claimed he was the illegitimate son of Greek royalty, though no one named any names. They said that was how he had got the money and his start in shipping, and it did explain why he had a Greek middle name.

One fact was certain: Alex Scott had started out in shipping, but now his business interests had spread to aircraft in the US, automobile factories in Italy and France, and his own private bank in England. But at the core of his empire, and the part he loved best, was his fleet of ships. Plus his own one hundred and eighty foot yacht, the *Atalanta*, berthed in the South of France, at Cannes. The *Atalanta* was not the largest yacht afloat, but he considered her, foot by sleek, beautifully-engineered foot, the finest.

And that was why he could not resist the sight of the enormous liner inching her way out of the Hudson river. The sun was setting in a fiery orange glow when he saw the girl again, leaning against the rail and clutching her cheap coat around her to keep out the chilly wind. She flung back her head and closed her eyes, breathing in the smell of the ocean. Her blonde hair was beaded with spray and he guessed she had been there since they left. The look of rapture on her face, made him smile. He knew exactly how she felt.

She sighed, snuggling deeper into the collar of her coat as the wind hit them, and then she laughed out loud. It was such a spontaneous, joyous sound, he found himself responding.

He said, 'It's a marvellous feeling, when you hit the open sea like that; seeing Manhattan disappearing into the horizon. No matter how often I do this trip, it always lures me on deck.'

She swung round, surprised. 'I thought everyone would be out here. How can they bear to miss it?'

'Too busy getting ready for dinner.' He offered her his hand. 'We were never properly introduced. I'm Alex Scott. And I know you are Eloise Mountjoy, sometimes known as Honeychile.'

She smiled, embarrassed. 'Honeychile was my father's name for me, I've always been called that. Only now my great-uncle says that in London I shall need to be called Eloise.' She laughed, 'I guess I won't know who they're talking to at first.'

He noticed how amazingly blue her eyes were; he thought she was so young and naïve he could almost see stars in them. But she was so dowdy in her cheap unfashionable coat, he guessed, sympathetically, that she probably worked as a nursemaid, looking after a brood of spoiled kids with an even more spoiled society mother to contend with; or else she was a paid companion to some demanding old lady in first-class.

'It was pleasant meeting you, Miss Mountjoy,' he said with a courtly little bow. Then he turned and strode back along the deck.

'Mr Scott, it's my very first time on a ship,' Honeychile called after him, impulsively.

He turned and looked seriously at her, arms folded. 'Is that so?' he said. 'Even more reason to enjoy yourself, Miss Mountjoy. A first voyage on a great ship is a milestone event.' Then he continued on his way.

CHAPTER 20

Honeychile had expected a modest cabin, but Lord Mountjoy was a man who only bought the best. Her luxurious suite was on the top deck, and its walls were panelled in rare woods from trees native to every country of the British Commonwealth. It had Lalique sconces, the latest in Art Deco furnishings, a brocade-canopied bed and a gleaming marble and gold bathroom. Honeychile felt as though she were living in a movie, instead of as she usually did, dreaming and longing, in the very front row of the Kitsville Roxy.

Movies and books were her great escape from her harsh, threadbare life at the ranch. They took her into worlds so different from the one she knew, she had never believed they really existed. Until now. She stared at herself in the bathroom mirror, and, disappointed, knew she did not belong. This elegant suite was meant for women like Viva Molson, glamorous in satin and diamonds.

There was a knock at the door and a steward came in carrying a vase of yellow roses.

'Good evening, Miss Mountjoy,' he said, cheerily; 'I'm your steward, Bill.' He assessed her in a quick, surprised glance; she was not the kind of woman who usually travelled in first. 'I thought you were going to be the only passenger on my deck with no farewell flowers, Miss,' he said, recalling the extravagant bouquets that transformed his other suites on the exclusive top deck into veritable bowers.

He smiled as she buried her nose eagerly in them. 'They're hothouse blooms, Miss, they don't smell like garden roses.' He handed her the accompanying card and told her a stewardess would be along shortly to unpack for her. 'If you need anything, Miss Mountjoy, you just give me a call,' he added as he left.

Honeychile counted the roses. *Two dozen*. No one had ever sent her even a single flower before. Surprised, she opened the little envelope and read Alexander Andreos Scott's apology. She ran a finger across the petals. They were as soft as velvet and the true yellow of a Texas rose.

The stewardess arrived to unpack her two small suitcases, even though Honeychile told her she could easily do it herself. She watched, embarrassed, as the women silently folded away her blue sweater and a blouse and hung up the new heather-coloured 'novelty tweed' suit, bought from the Sears catalogue, as was everything she possessed. She knew the stewardess must be more used to handling luxurious silks and satins than her own inexpensive cotton underclothes and her single pair of silk stockings.

The stewardess hung her long black lace evening dress carefully on a satin hanger in a separate closet, then placed the high-heeled silver kidskin sandals the catalogue had promised would 'gleam as you dance', underneath it. She put Honeychile's battered old teddy on the bed, then smiled goodbye and hurried off to attend to her other passengers.

Honeychile looked at the evening dress. It was one of Sears' special 'Hollywood' models: '*As worn by movie-star Loretta Young.*' That's what it said on the label anyhow, and she believed them. The long, black rayon-lace dress, lined with pink taffeta, had cost the awful sum of nine dollars and ninety-five cents. More than she had ever paid for any garment in her entire life. She had been thrilled when she first saw it: but somehow, now, hanging on the luxurious padded white satin hanger, it looked cheap.

She had never owned an evening dress before, she never went any place to wear one. In fact, until now, she had not owned any kind of dress – at least not since the hated ruffled ones Rosie used to buy her when she was just a kid. Still, she knew from the movies that people on luxury liners always dressed for dinner, and she shrugged philosophically, telling herself that with all those gorgeous women on board, no one would even notice her anyway.

She remembered what Aliza had said to her, before she left. 'Beauty you ain't, girl; leastways not yet. But there's something about you, I don't know what it is. To tell you the truth, I'm still waiting for you to grow into your looks. One day, you'll get there.'

'Where?' Honeychile had demanded.

'To look like your father. He was a good-looking man, I can tell

you. *Real* good-looking. And he had that same thing you've got.'
Aliza had clamped her mouth firmly shut then, suddenly realising
what it was.

'*What*, Aliza? *What* was it he had?'

'Nothin' for your ears, Honeychile. Now just get on with that
packing,' Aliza had said, departing quickly for the kitchen.

Honeychile took a long bath, wallowing in the marble tub amid a
cloud of fragrant bubbles, feeling more and more like a movie-star.
Then she put on her new cotton underwear, the same kind she
had worn since she was a little girl, and, very carefully, the silk
stockings and the silver sandals.

She slithered into the black dress and tied her long blonde hair loosely
with a black satin ribbon, purchased at Elias's department store that
used to be Elias's Grain & Feed in San Antonio, where her mother had
once worked. She flicked a swansdown powderpuff over her freckled
nose and cautiously applied Tangee's new Cyclamen lipstick and
smacked her lips together the way you were supposed to, to get it even;
then she smiled to see how it looked. She licked the stray bits off her
teeth. It was okay, she thought doubtfully; it felt a bit sticky, but she
supposed she would get used to it. Then she added the final touch, a
dab of Woolworth's Malmaison Carnation scent, behind each ear.

She inspected herself in the long mirror, wondering uneasily if the
low neckline revealed too much of her bosom; whether cape sleeves
were correct for evening, and whether the bias-cut skirt that only
reached to her ankles was too short? And should it cling to her
quite so tightly? She tugged doubtfully at it. Worst of all, didn't
the pink taffeta under the black lace look a bit naked? As though
she had nothing on underneath?

She sighed, it was too late now. The black dress was all she had.
She wished she had some pearls but her only jewellery was the gold
ring with the Mountjoy crest, that had belonged originally to grandpa
Georgie, and then to her father. She always wore it. Like the teddy, it
was a talisman, a charm that bound her mysteriously to her father.

She set off nervously for the dining room, stumbling with the
motion of the ship and the unaccustomed heels.

The head waiter, standing at the top of the grand staircase, stared
at her, astonished. Honeychile gave him a tentative smile. She glanced

quickly at the crowded dining room; at the mirrored-walls and glittering jewel-like chandeliers; and the band playing the latest Jerome Kern melody in the shade of some potted palms. The tail-coated waiters were pouring magnums of champagne and the passengers were calling greetings and kissing each other on the cheek. It was like a movie dream come true. She stared harder at the passengers, and suddenly the dream turned into a nightmare. A hot wave of embarrassment burned her cheeks. *The movies had lied.* Nobody was wearing evening dress; every woman there was wearing a short little day dress. People were turning to look at her, smiling, and she felt herself blushing all the way from her toes to her hair. Mortified, she wished the floor would open up and swallow her.

Alex Scott watched her from the doorway. She looked as if she wanted to run away, but he knew she couldn't; she was frozen to the spot with embarrassment.

'Can I help you Miss,' the head waiter was asking.

'No need, Mario,' Alex took her elbow. 'Miss Mountjoy is with me. A table for two, Mario please, away from the crush.'

Honeychile glanced, agonised, at him. She saw he was not wearing white tie and tails. 'I'm dressed all wrong,' she whispered. 'I didn't realise. Everybody's staring. I can't go in there.'

'Your steward should have told you nobody dresses the first night out. It's a sort of tradition. Anyhow let them stare. They're only thinking how lovely you look.'

'Excuse me, sir,' the head waiter interrupted, anxiously, 'but Miss Molson said she was expecting you at her table, sir. She is with Lord and Lady Kinnon and the Biddles.'

'The hell with Miss Molson and the Biddles.' Alex glanced encouragingly at Honeychile. 'Just take a deep breath,' he whispered, 'and hold onto me.'

And then he swept her down the grand staircase, past the staring waiters, past the wild-eyed furious Viva and the curious Biddles, past all the other amused first-class passengers, to the haven of a table in the corner.

'I'm sorry,' Honeychile blurted, sinking thankfully into her chair. 'I seem to be causing you a helluva lot of trouble.' Tears trembled on her lashes as she looked at him.

He smiled. 'Not a helluva lot. In fact, no trouble at all.'

'I'm just plain mortified,' she said, still hot with shame. 'You must think I'm nothin' but a stupid country hick. And you're right. All I know is what I've learned from the movies and they don't tell you folks never dress fancy the first night. I guess I just don't know the rules.'

Alex looked at her thoughtfully. 'It's odd,' he said at last, 'but when I first met you, you gave me the impression you were the kind of woman who would not bend under adversity. You didn't weep or moan when that idiot photographer knocked you down, even though I could see you were hurt. "Ah, a strong woman," I thought. "One who can look after herself, young though she is." '

Honeychile lifted her eyes and looked at him, astonished. 'Did you really think that? Or are you just trying to make me feel better?'

'I never say anything I don't mean.'

She blushed again, this time with pleasure. 'I try to be strong. I've had to work hard, just to keep the ranch going, ever since Rosie spent all our money. And then there was the drought and the Depression and . . .'

'Why not begin at the beginning,' he suggested as the *sommelier* poured champagne. 'But first, what would you like to eat?'

She glanced helplessly at the vast menu. The Kitsville Diner was the extent of her restaurant experience, and their menu was a ketchup-smudged card listing meatloaf and chicken pot pie, and anyhow she rarely could afford to eat there.

He saw her dilemma and said quickly, 'Why don't I order for both of us.'

She agreed, relieved. 'By the way, thank you for the roses, Mr Scott.' Her face lit up with pleasure as she remembered. 'No one ever sent me flowers before. They're beautiful.'

'They were for a beautiful girl,' Alex lied gallantly. Still, he thought, dowdy and odd though she was, there was something about her that attracted him.

'I confess, I'm curious,' he admitted. 'Who are you? What are you doing, travelling alone on this ship?'

Honeychile told Alex about Lord Mountjoy's letter and that she was going to London because she knew her father would have wanted her to meet the last remaining member of his family. 'And because I really need the money,' she added honestly. 'I want Mountjoy Ranch to be the way it was when my father ran it. When I was a little girl and the land was green and our cattle among the finest in Texas.'

And then she told him the whole story, or most of it anyway. She left out the part about living in the rental park in San Antonio, with Rosie, and what happened afterwards, with Jack Delaney.

Watching as she spilled out her secrets and her soul to him, Alex thought how different she was from the sophisticated women he knew; so young and untouched by worldliness.

He thought regretfully that he had never possessed such innocence. He had never, even when he was young, made a move that was not planned and directed towards the next upward move, and then the one after that. Necessity and anger had been his driving forces, but obviously this girl had neither of those reasons. He'd bet she didn't know how to lie, or even how to flirt. He realised that for once, he was enjoying himself. Honeychile Mountjoy was like a tonic in his jaded world.

Looking into his calm grey eyes, Honeychile felt a bond of trust between them. Suddenly, she found herself telling him something she had never told anyone before.

'I was fifteen years old,' she said, 'when I saw Sheriff Wilkes' car coming down the lane. I thought it must be the dog causing trouble again, chasing cars down the highway. But he looked so solemn and strange I knew it had to be something worse.

'"Let me speak to Aliza," he said. "Alone."

'He walked into the house and a while later, I heard Aliza scream. I went running in there. She was sitting in the chair, rocking back and forth with her apron thrown over her face. I knew she was crying behind it.

'"Rosie wasn't really a bad woman," Aliza was saying to Sheriff Wilkes. "Just silly and misguided. She worshipped at the altar of Mammon, instead of worshipping our Lord. That woman thought everything that glittered was gold and she wanted it all. She wanted it so bad, she wasn't satisfied with her life here, nor with her child. Why, I doubt Honeychile has seen her mother for more than a couple of weeks in the last few years, ever since David Mountjoy died and left Rosie his money. The poor woman would've been better off if he didn't. Now look what's become of her."

'Sheriff Wilkes looked at me, standing in the doorway. "I'll leave you to break the sad news, to Honeychile," he said.

172

'She didn't need to. I already guessed Rosie was dead.'

Honeychile looked into Alex's eyes and added in a whisper, 'She was shot. Outside the Silver Dollar Saloon.'

Alex looked at her, shocked. 'You mean she was *murdered*?'

She nodded. 'They never found out who did it,' she said in a small tight voice. 'Aliza was right, though. Rosie didn't deserve to die like that. I understand her better, now. She was just different, she was restless, lonely . . . oh I don't know. All I know is I loved her, in a way. Sometimes I feel guilty, I think if I had been the kind of daughter she would have liked, maybe she would have stayed home on the ranch. And then she wouldn't have got shot.'

He said, 'But the only guilty person is the one who killed her. Did they ever try to find out who did it?'

She shook her head. 'It seems to me no one tried very hard; it was as though Rosie was worthless. Nobody even cared. Aliza said it was because the speakeasy was owned by gangsters; they wanted the murder hushed up so the customers wouldn't be afraid to go there. But I knew,' she said grimly, 'I always knew who did it. Jack Delaney killed her.'

'The new husband?'

She nodded. 'People said Jack was handsome, sort of like Clark Gable, but there was something mean and ruthless about him. Aliza thought he was the killer too. "Jack Delaney's the one done it," she said. "Sure as eggs is eggs, he shot Rosie." But Jack had the perfect alibi. He wasn't even in San Antonio that night. He was in a hotel in Houston, and the woman he was with came forward to prove it. *And* the hotel clerk, and . . . oh I don't know . . . other people. But I *know* Jack did it. He did it because he had always wanted the ranch, and he had heard they were digging for oil on our land. He told the police Rosie was a whore, that she was a tease, always running after other men, and that's why he'd left her. He said there were plenty of guys who would have shot her. She was that kind of woman.

'Anyhow, he came back to the ranch, driving a big black Cadillac, swaggering into the house like he owned the place. Because he thought he did. "I was Rosie's legal husband," he said to Aliza. "What was hers is mine. That's the law."

'"Not this time, mister," Aliza said.' Honeychile smiled, remembering the gleam of triumph in Aliza's dark eyes. 'This here ranch belongs to Miss Honeychile Mountjoy Hennessy, left to her in her grandfather's Trust. Rosie ain't never owned Mountjoy Ranch and nor will you."

'I thought he was going to kill Aliza, too. He lifted his hand to hit her and I shouted at the dog to set on him. It sank its teeth into Jack's hand, down to the bone, but I wished it had gone for his throat. I wanted it to hurt him the way he'd hurt my mother. I wanted the dog to *kill* him.'

Honeychile took a shaky breath. She glanced apologetically at Alex. 'I guess real ladies don't talk this way. They talk about the weather and music and stuff.' She blushed. 'I'm embarrassing you. Aliza always told me I run off at the mouth.'

'No you don't. And you're not embarrassing me. What happened to Delaney?'

'I guess he didn't want another dog bite. He left. He got as far as the door, then he turned round and looked at me. He said, "One day I'll be back, Honeychile. To get what's rightly mine. You can count on it, I'll be back."

'Aliza told me that, by law, Jack was my legal stepfather. "Let's hope he never tries to put claims on you, girl," she said. "Because if he does, this time we're sunk. Why, that man could whisk you out of here in no time flat, if he chose, and we might never see you again. Just the way we didn't see Rosie." '

Honeychile shivered, rubbing the goosebumps that had sprung up on her arms as she looked at Alex, and said with a little shrug. 'Anyhow, the oil wells didn't come through; so he just wasn't interested any more. But instead they found an underground spring. Can you just imagine how thrilled we were? We went crazy, jumpin' and hollerin' fit to bust.'

She laughed now, remembering. 'Oh, Alex Scott you can't imagine such happiness. But after that came all the hard work, struggling to put the ranch back on its feet again.'

Alex leaned across the table and took her rough hand in his. He looked admiringly at her; he knew only too well what she was talking about. He knew about having no money; about struggle and hard work, and ambition. 'I hope you're winning, Honeychile,' he said, encouragingly.

She shrugged, 'Just barely. But with Lord Mountjoy's help, I hope to be able to make a success of the ranch again. I want it to be exactly the way it was when my father was running it.'

Alex looked at her, enchanted. He had never met anyone like her. She was like a golden, innocent puppy falling over its own feet. She had an easy endearing intimacy that made you instantly her friend, and a sort of ingenuous charm. He wondered with a pang of regret, what would become of her in London, when she was suddenly showered with money and jewels and attention. He hoped it would not spoil her, because he liked her exactly the way she was. A breath of fresh air in his jaded world.

People glanced curiously at Alex Scott, holding hands across the table with the odd young woman in the cheap lace dress. 'Not Alex's usual type,' they whispered behind their hands. And 'A little *déclassée* for our Alex, don't you think?' And they laughed, amused, but Alex didn't notice and if he had he would not have cared.

After dinner, they wandered onto the Promenade Deck. They stood, leaning against the rail, watching the deep, dark waves slide by and the enormous wake foaming behind them. He said, softly to her, 'I love the ocean. If I'd had my way, I would have spent my life roaming the world, alone in a sailing ship, searching for unknown islands and hidden harbours.'

'Then why didn't you?'

He had asked himself the same question, many times. She made it sound so easy, as though he could have done whatever he wanted. 'It was just a small boy's dream,' he said, with a touch of bitterness as he remembered. 'In a way, though, I guess I am a kind of sailor.' And he told her about his fleet of freighters, about the new ship being built in Scotland, and about his true love: his yacht, the *Atalanta*.

His face looked weary in the light of the moon and she thought suddenly, he looked like a lonely man. Impulsively, she reached out and traced his profile with her finger. He turned and smiled at her, then took her hand and pressed it to his lips. She looked breathlessly at him.

He said, 'We have a lot in common, you and I, Honeychile. I had to fight for everything I got, too. And when I was a boy, living in Rome, I had to fight the other kids who called me "*batardo*", the bastard. But they were right, I had no father, so no matter how much I fought, I could never change the truth.'

'I had to fight in school too,' Honeychile said sympathetically. 'Rosie was always a scandal. I promise to keep your secret if you promise to keep mine,' she said. 'Cross my heart and hope to die.' And she made a cross with her finger over her heart.

He put his arm casually round her shoulders as they walked back to her cabin. At her door he turned her towards him, and said softly, 'Thank you for trusting me with your secrets.'

'I guess we're friends now,' she said, breathlessly, because all of a sudden she wanted him to kiss her so badly, her knees had gone weak.

'Friends,' Alex agreed. His lips touched hers for a brief instant. Then he was gone.

'Sleep well, Eloise Honeychile,' he called softly over his shoulder, as he walked away.

Honeychile did not see Alex Scott again on the voyage. When she asked the steward where he was, he told her Mr Scott was a busy man. He was a frequent passenger on the transatlantic route and usually he kept to his suite, working.

When the Queen Mary docked at Southampton, Alex Scott disembarked at dawn. From there he took the train direct to London where he had a meeting. He did not say goodbye to Honeychile and she did not know whether to be sad or pleased when an enormous basket of Parma violets arrived for her, glistening with dew and smelling divine.

'*The violets reminded me of your eyes,*' the accompanying note said. '*Good luck in London. Your friend, Alex Scott.*'

Honeychile buried her nose in the fragrant blossoms, remembering the feel of his lips on hers. She had dreamed of that kiss every night, and she was glad he had not forgotten her, after all.

The passengers lined the rails, waving and calling greetings to friends standing on the dock and the brass band played loudly. A porter placed Honeychile's flimsy suitcase into a first-class compartment on the train and soon she was on her way to London, where the luxurious maroon Rolls Royce with Bridges, the chauffeur, in a peaked cap and maroon uniform with gold buttons and epaulettes, was waiting to whisk her to her new life.

CHAPTER 21

Anjou d'Aranville leapt from the taxi at Paris's Gare du Nord. She paid off the driver, stuck her rail ticket between her teeth, slung her bag over her shoulder, grabbed a suitcase in each hand and sprinted on long spindly legs to where the Paris/London express was already steaming noisily away from the platform.

Harry Lockwood sprinted along behind her, praying for the train to wait and at the same time managing to appreciate Anjou's legs. He overtook her just as the train gave a final whistle. He grabbed a handle, wrenched open the door to a first-class compartment, threw in his case and leapt in after it.

'*Arrêtez, arrêtez un moment pour moi,*' Anjou screamed over the din. Shoving one suitcase under her arm, she made a wild grab at the door handle. '*Merde, oh merde,*' she half-sobbed, trotting alongside the moving train.

Harry grabbed her bag, then her arm and hauled her up and in, just as the train picked up speed. He staggered backwards, tripped over her suitcase and crashed to the floor with Anjou on top of him.

'Well,' he said, as their eyes met, 'that's one way to catch a train.'

'*Mon Dieu,*' she gasped, climbing off him and brushing down her skirt, 'I almost missed it.'

Harry Lockwood laughed at the scope of her understatement as he stood up and dusted his jacket. 'You did miss it. The train had already left.'

She said ruefully, 'Why am I always late? Can you explain that? I am twenty years old, intelligent, educated and with all my mental faculties. And I am always, invariably, chronically late.' She pushed her hair out of her eyes and looked appealingly at him. 'Is there something seriously wrong with me?'

Harry laughed again, taking her in appreciatively. She was very tall, five-ten or thereabouts, and slender to the point of breakability. She had an oval face, a wide-eyed gaze and a breathless way of talking, which might be due to racing down the platform but which he thought more than likely was her usual approach to life. Her eyes were a beautiful sea-green, her hair was the lustrous colour of bitter marmalade, and her full-lipped mouth curved in an optimistic anticipatory smile, as she regarded him, waiting for his answer.

'I doubt that very much,' he said. 'You look like a young woman in control of her life to me.'

'That's probably just the suit.' She waved deprecatingly at the little bronze tweed jacket and skirt she was wearing. It was last year's model; Suzette had spoken personally to Madame Chanel and managed to get it for a very good price. 'It's all my mother's doing,' Anjou said. 'She has made me over into her image of a smart society girl for my great uncle's benefit. Usually, I look like a student. You know, shirts and skirts and flat heels.' She stuck her long slender legs out in front of her, staring at her feet in their expensive brown suede shoes while Harry gazed admiringly at her.

'Silly, isn't it?' she said, smiling disarmingly at him. 'I told her I would not last long in London. "I shall be back *tout de suite, maman*," I said. "*Pouf*, just like that." I asked her, "If you cannot put up with me, then how can you expect anyone else to do so?" Anyhow, I plan to be back in Paris for the *rentrée*, in September. It will be my first semester at the Sorbonne,' she added with a big, breathless smile, knowing she was impressing him. 'I am to study maths and physics.'

The words had come out in one quick, unpunctuated flow and Harry shook his head in astonishment. 'And what do you intend to do once you have your degree?'

'Do?' Anjou frowned, genuinely puzzled. She had sufficient brains to get through school and the ability to cram the night before any exam and get good results. But college was only a means to an end: her freedom. Now, with the chance to get her hands on the Mountjoy money, she wouldn't need to go to the Sorbonne and live in a cheap room while she worked out how to become a successful courtesan. With Mountjoy's millions she would be richer than the men she had once hoped might keep her in the style both she and her grandmother Marie enjoyed.

'I never thought about what I might do,' she told Harry. 'Physics just seems too fascinating, doesn't it?'

'Not half as fascinating as you,' Harry Lockwood thought, 'and not nearly as naughty,' because there was definitely a hint of wickedness in her jewel-green glance and teasing smile.

Sir Harry Lockwood was forty years old and a very good-looking man, with smooth, thick blond hair, and hazel eyes with unusually dark lashes and eyebrows. He had a tall well-muscled body that looked good in the excellently tailored clothes he wore; and a perpetual tan from his frequent visits to glamorous and expensive resorts around the world. Harry spent a great deal of time in other people's smart summer villas in the South of France, and in grand villas in Barbados, or the Bahamas or Jamaica, in the winter months. He was always the welcome extra single man whose chief asset was his ability to entertain the ladies. And that was the reason he was invited; because, though Harry had a title, the unfortunate fact was he had no money.

Everyone knew Harry Lockwood had been looking for an heiress to marry for years. He had even been close to success a couple of times, but his tendency to be unfaithful before he even got them down the aisle had put a quick end to that. 'Harry Lockwood just can't keep his flies buttoned,' was what the men in his circle said about him, laughing as they added: 'And the other urge he can't control, is his gambling.' Still, on his jaunts abroad and at country houses in England, at least one of those failings had proven to be his asset. With the women, of course. And he could always somehow manage to come out the winner in the late night poker games, and pocket a couple of hundred quid.

Harry drew his eyes reluctantly away from Anjou's, as a steward knocked on the door and poked his head in. 'Dinner is about to be served, M'sieur,' he said.

Harry looked enquiringly at Anjou. 'Since you've had time to recover your breath, perhaps you would join me for dinner. You can tell me more about why you find physics so fascinating. And about becoming a smart society girl,' he added with a grin.

'I should be delighted, M'sieur,' Anjou smiled, giving him an assessing glance. 'But isn't that what is called "singing for my supper?" I know it's what my mother warned me about. "Do not speak to any strange men," was what she said. Of course what she really meant was, "Unless they have a title and money."' She laughed merrily as she leapt to her feet. She wriggled her toes in the new shoes, frowning resentfully. 'Ouch, they are pinching already,' she said, stepping from foot to foot.

'I think we should introduce ourselves,' Harry said, laughing at her. 'My name is Harry Lockwood.'

She shook his hand politely. 'And I am Anjou d'Aranville. Oh, no. I tell a little lie. From this moment I am no longer Anjou d'Aranville. I am Anjou Mountjoy.'

His eyebrows rose in astonishment. 'Mountjoy?' It was a name he knew well. Everyone did. Old Lord Mountjoy was one of the richest men in England.

'It's my great uncle's name. The one I'm going to stay with in London. He wanted me to use it. And because my *maman* wants to get her hands on the Mountjoy money, she said I must do so.' She looked at him and sighed. 'Oh, it's such a long story.'

'Tell me more, Anjou Mountjoy,' he said, taking her arm and walking her down the corridor to the dining car.

Over a lengthy dinner, Anjou told Harry all about Georgie Mountjoy and his affair with Marie.

'She was such a delight, my *grand-mère*,' she said wistfully. '*Maman* tried to keep me away from her, but of course she did not succeed. Marie could easily outmanoeuvre her and I spent the best times of my childhood at her apartment on the rue Bonaparte. She died a few months ago and I miss her terribly. She was my best friend, but *Maman* said she was a bad influence.'

She looked into Harry's eyes and said, 'My mother thought Marie was wicked, but I think she just enjoyed herself. What do you think, Monsieur Lockwood?' She batted her long eyelashes at him, pouting sexily, and he laughed out loud.

'I think you are an outrageous flirt, Anjou Mountjoy,' Harry said, enjoying himself. 'I don't flatter myself it's because a twenty year old girl finds an old man attractive, I think you probably flirt with any man who gets close enough.'

She sighed exaggeratedly, giving him that breathless wide-eyed look. 'Only the good-looking ones,' she replied innocently. 'And you are not old, Monsieur, merely "older".'

'Thank you, Mademoiselle Mountjoy,' Harry replied, amused. 'I think you have learned a lot from your *grand-mère*.'

'It's in my blood,' she admitted. 'My French blood, that is.' She shuddered delicately. 'My English blood must have been frozen at source in prehistoric times. Marie said that my father was a stuffed shirt, and not at all like great-grandfather Georgie. Now *he* was a rake,' she added with relish, as she demolished a plateful of steak-frites, then ordered crème brûlée.

She looked up at him, big-eyed. '*There are two others,*' she said in a loud stage-whisper. '*Two other bastards. Like myself.*'

Harry felt eyes swivelling their way as a sudden silence fell over the neighbouring tables. 'Well not quite bastards,' he said, smiling. 'That was your father, not you.'

She shrugged, spooning up the crème brûlée. 'It's the same thing. In France, anyhow. Our name is tainted, my mother says. Besides, we have no money, except what she earns. She's Madame Suzette, you know.' She looked expectantly at him.

'Is that so?' He wondered if Madame Suzette was a cabaret star, appearing at the Folies Bergères.

'Her hats are famous,' Anjou informed him. 'I'm supposed to be wearing one, but I think it fell off when I was running for the train.' She laughed, '*Maman* would kill me if she knew. She's setting me up to make a good marriage. But of course, I shall only marry for love.' She levelled her gaze at him. 'And sex, of course,' she added sweetly.

The silence at the tables around them deepened. 'Oh, you are not eating your floating island,' Anjou said merrily. 'May I?' And she scooped up his meringue hungrily.

Harry watched her in amazement. 'You look as though you live on lettuce leaves and birdseed. Wherever does it all go?'

She shrugged, looking astonished at her empty plate. 'I eat like a horse, but I've always been skinny like this. Perhaps I shall have some cheese,' she said eyeing the trolley as the steward came by.

'*Eh bien,*' she said over coffee, 'Lord Mountjoy is an old man. He has no heirs to leave his property and all his money to. So, what does he do? He sends a private detective to find Georgie's descendants.

181

C'est moi,' she pointed at her chest, 'and the other two. An English girl and an American from Texas. We are to meet in London. Lord Mountjoy will bring us out in Society and he will decide who gets first prize. The Mountjoy millions.'

'And who do you think it will be?'

'It's up to Lord Mountjoy's whim, I suppose.' Anjou shrugged her shoulder and gave him a careless little smile. 'As for me, I do not care.'

He thought she was lying, and he was right. Because Anjou wanted that money desperately. And she was determined not to let anyone stand in the way of her getting it.

'I am only doing it for my mother,' she lied again. 'She says I am a hopeless case, that no man will ever want such a frumpy bluestocking.' She sighed feelingly, 'Sometimes I think *Maman* does not understand me.'

'Somehow, I don't think she does,' Harry agreed, seeing through her little game; because he had recognised that Anjou was just like him. She was out for all she could get and she would use all her charms to get it.

The train was approaching Calais and they returned to their compartment. Harry summoned a steward and organised Anjou's luggage and her berth on the ferry, walking with her down the platform and onto the ship.

'Just to make sure you don't miss the boat,' he said with a grin.

She batted her eyelashes at him again, as she said, 'Oh no, Monsieur Lockwood. Make no mistake about that. I shall never "miss the boat".'

He escorted her to her cabin. At the door Anjou's eyes met his questioning ones. She was tempted, it's true, but she had grander ambitions than Harry Lockwood; and she was shrewd enough not to jeopardise them at this point.

'Goodnight, Harry,' she said, reaching up and giving him a quick kiss on either cheek. 'Thank you for a lovely dinner. I enjoyed myself.'

He grabbed her hand, pulling her closer, drinking her in with his eyes. 'Must you leave me so soon?'

Anjou gave a delicate little yawn. 'I'm so tired,' she said, sounding as sleepy as she could.

'Shall I see you again? In London?'

'But of course. I am certain our paths will cross again.' She withdrew her hand from his, opened the cabin door with the other and stepped quickly inside. 'Goodnight, Harry,' she said again, coolly.

The door closed in his face. Harry stood looking angrily at it for a moment. He could swear she had given him every reason to believe she was available for a night of passion; all that talk about sex, and those encouraging smiles and enticing glances. Then he smiled. Despite her sexy ways, Anjou was young; she was just a tease that's all and she had led him nicely up the garden path.

Harry grinned, remembering their conversation as he walked to the bar in search of a nightcap. He knew what Anjou had said was right, they would meet again. He would make a point of it. After all, wasn't she in line to inherit old Mountjoy's millions?

He saw her again the following morning, early. The sky over Dover was a dark gunmetal grey and rain slanted dismally down. Anjou was striding through the deluge towards the maroon Mountjoy Rolls. Her skirt was short and her legs long and a breathless smile of anticipation lit up her pretty face. She turned and saw him. She put her fingers to her lips and blew him a kiss, then she stepped into the Rolls, the chauffeur closed the door and she was gone.

Harry thought of the explosion when the three girls met. And of old Lord Mountjoy, like a spider at the centre of his web, luring them with his money, plotting his little game. He hoped Mountjoy knew what he was doing. Because one thing was certain: that one would be trouble.

CHAPTER 22

Laura Lavinia Swinburn did not want to become Laura Mountjoy. She hated the very idea of it. The ridiculous notion that she would suddenly become a débutante, dressed to kill and sprung on London Society like a rabbit from a conjuror's hat, filled her with horror.

'I've changed my mind. I'm not going,' she said rebelliously to Jeannie, even though she knew she must, because they needed the money. 'I hate it, and I hate Lord Mountjoy and I hate those two other girls.'

'How can you possibly hate them when you've never even met them?' Jeannie replied reasonably.

They were standing on the platform at Central Station in Leeds. The London express belched steam, enfolding them in a vaporous white cloud that was almost as bad as the dense fog that had delayed Laura's journey by a day.

'The fog was heaven-sent,' Laura told Jeannie. 'It's fate. Destiny, telling me not to go. It wasn't meant to be.'

'Forget destiny. Your father would have wanted you to go. So do I. And that's all there is to it.'

Jeannie did not add that, in her view, it would do Laura a world of good to get away from Swinburn and out into the real world. A small village and an isolated manor house were no place for a young woman. Laura needed to get away from the disaster of Haddon Fox and enjoy herself for a change.

Laura hung her head, staring at the sooty flagstones beneath her feet, delaying saying goodbye until the last possible minute.

'You are being ridiculous Laura,' Jeannie said, exasperated. 'It's a marvellous opportunity. Other girls would be green with envy and here you are acting as though you are going to jail, instead of to a wonderful house, with dances and parties to look forward to. *And* meeting your own relatives. Stop being so silly and get on the train.'

The guard was walking down the platform, slamming doors when Billy Saxton, carrying an armload of newspapers, hurried past them and into the first-class compartment. Because of the dense fog, he had almost missed the train.

He glanced out of the window at the frail old lady in her out-dated clothes and the sullen girl in the horsy plaid suit and green sweater. The old lady was letting her have it and, from her lowered head and stiff posture, he'd bet she wasn't used to being told off. And, from the grandmother's sweet expression, he didn't think she was much good at it, anyhow.

The guard yelled 'all aboard', and the old lady gave the girl a little push towards the open carriage door.

'I don't ever want to leave you,' Laura wailed suddenly, flinging her arms round her. 'I hate leaving Swinburn. Oh, I wish I didn't have to go.'

Jeannie hugged her tightly. 'Don't cry, Laura. It's for the best, you'll see. You will have the time of your life, I guarantee it. And when it's all over, I shall still be here at Swinburn, waiting for you to tell me all about it.' She held Laura at arm's length, looking tenderly at her. She tidied a few strands of tear-wet hair from her face, then kissed her soundly. 'Now, be off with you. And remember, your father would expect you to behave like a lady. And so do I.'

The guard was already swinging his green lantern. He blew his whistle, the train clanked and groaned in readiness, and still Laura stood reluctantly on the bottom step leading into the first-class compartment. She threw a last pleading glance over her shoulder but Jeannie set her face in a determined smile.

'Hurry, Laura,' she called. 'You're holding up the train.'

Laura climbed unwillingly aboard, the guard slammed the door after her and the train steamed steadily away from the platform.

Watching the grandmother, still waving, still smiling, Billy could have sworn he caught the glitter of tears in her eyes.

The door to his compartment slid open with a woosh. The girl was standing there, glaring at him.

'Oh, damn,' she said tersely, 'I didn't expect there would be anyone in here.' She checked her ticket reservation against the number on the seat opposite him, then glanced at her luggage, already stacked

186

in the overhead rack by the porter. It was her seat all right. 'Well, you're just going to have to put up with me,' she said, slumping into the blue velvet seat. And then she burst into tears.

Billy sighed, irritated. He had planned on reading the newspapers; perhaps a bite of lunch later; a quiet journey. He watched her, saying nothing. Better just to let her cry it out. Meanwhile, she was a damned nuisance, and noisy with it. He had a lot on his mind and he could have lived without her interrupting his thoughts.

Billy Saxton was one of the biggest racehorse owners in Europe, though these days he spent more of his time in America overseeing the business he had inherited from his wealthy American mother, than he did at his magnificent estate in Wiltshire.

Billy's wonderful Jacobean house, Saxton Mowbrey and its surrounding thousand or so acres, including the village of Mowbrey, had been in the family for only three generations. His grandfather had bought it from the impoverished owners when their fortunes had just gone down in the world, and his had just gone up – thanks to his chance discovery of a chemical bleaching agent that he packaged and marketed astutely as 'Saxton's A-One All Purpose Cleaner, suitable for all your laundry requirements.'

Grandfather Saxton had cleaned up on his A-One All Purpose Cleaner, becoming one of the giants of the industrial nineteenth century. Then Billy's father had inherited the lot and married the American breakfast cereal heiress, Gianna Lombardi, and when they died, Billy inherited the double fortune.

He was thirty-six years old, educated at Harrow and Cambridge, with a Masters degree in business from Harvard University and a lifetime's degree in horses and racing, which were the great pleasures of his life. He was a quiet, self-effacing man with a booming voice and a slight stammer when he was excited, which happened whenever one of his horses was winning.

Billy Saxton booming, 'C-c-c-c-come o-n g-g-g-g-giddy up why d-d-don't you,' was one of the favourite jokes of the racing world. They said by the time he got it out, the damned horse was already past the post.

Billy was a modest man who hated publicity and the only time he had his picture in the newspapers was when one of his horses won an important race. To him, the horses were the stars of the show and he directed all the praise to his trainers. 'I only buy the horses,' he would say. 'These chaps are the men who made them winners.'

He glanced at the girl opposite. She was still crying noisily and he wondered what to do. He sighed, irritated. He had some important decisions to make and he had hoped to be alone to be able to think things out. He had spent the past couple of days looking over Foxton Yard with the idea of transferring a couple of his horses there to be trained. Everything had seemed orderly: there was some good-looking horseflesh there and the place was immaculate. But there was just something about it, something he couldn't quite put his finger on. It was too quiet, *too* orderly, with stable lads creeping round avoiding his eyes instead of running around yelling at each other, as they normally did, slinging hay and dropping tin buckets with a terrible crash. Even the horses seemed subdued and he suspected Haddon Fox was the reason.

After a while the girl sat up. She straightened her shoulders, took a handkerchief from her bag, mopped up her tears and blew her nose. She threw him an angry glare.

Her eyes were red-rimmed and swollen under level dark brows, but he noticed they were also a beautiful amber colour, and her long lashes were clumped together with tears, forming little star points around them. Her hair was a glossy brown, the colour of his favourite bay horse, and it fell in a heavy silken bob to her shoulders. Her skin was light-olive, matt as thick cream. Her nose was straight, her cheekbones wide and her mouth stubborn. In fact, she did not look English at all. With that colouring and those dark eyes, she reminded him of his Italian mother.

He said coolly, 'Are you g-g-g-going to tell me what's wrong? Perhaps I can help.'

'You can't,' she said flatly. 'Nobody can help me. I'm doomed to a fate worse than death, or . . . or anything.' Her eyes flashed with anger.

'D-d-d-d-death *or* anything?'

'You know what I mean,' she gave him another sullen stare. 'Anyhow, I don't know why you are so concerned. You don't even know me. You're just a stranger.'

'True. But I'm a s-s-stranger whose peace was interrupted when another s-s-s-stranger hurled herself into his train compartment and burst into tears. It's normal, I think, to express concern.'

She had the grace to look ashamed. 'Oh dear, grandmother would hate me for that. She can't abide rudeness. I'm sorry.' She looked close to tears again. 'I mean, I do apologise, sincerely.'

He nodded, understanding. 'I accept your apology in the spirit in which it was g-g-g-given.'

She smiled, suddenly impish. 'Oh, poof,' she said, 'you don't look like a stuffed shirt, so why talk like one?'

When Billy was interested, he forgot about his stammer. 'How do you know I'm not a stuffed shirt?'

She looked him over, consideringly. He was a tall, solidly-built man with thick sandy hair, stuck down with water to stop it from curling. He had a long face, a bit like a horse, really; nice blue eyes, a longish nose, a strong chin and an unexpectedly firm mouth.

'It's something about the mouth,' she teased. 'That sardonic little twist. Perhaps it means you're cruel. That would be much more exciting. Like Mr Rochester. You know, in Jane Eyre?'

'I am aware of the Brontës,' he said, amused. 'Despite the fact that I am not a Yorkshireman.'

'Then what are you?' Laura stared curiously at him, momentarily forgetting her grief and the fate worse than death.

He shrugged. 'Scottish, Italian, American. Perhaps even English. But definitely not a Yorkshireman.'

'Well, of course, anybody could see that,' she retorted spiritedly. 'Yorkshiremen are the best men in the world.' There was a far away look in her eyes and he guessed she was thinking of one young man in particular.

'You can't possibly be all those nationalities,' she said, suddenly coming back to earth. 'Two are permitted, anything more is excessive.'

'And under the rules of this game, am I permitted to choose my two?'

She laughed, her face lighting up with interest. 'Go ahead,' she said. 'You first. Then it's my turn.'

'Let me see.' He stroked his chin thoughtfully. 'I guess I'll take Italian/American – that counts as one, and Scottish.'

'Hah,' she said triumphantly, 'I knew you were foreign. Me too, but not so extravagantly as you. Three quarters Italian, one quarter English.' She met his eyes eagerly. 'Do you know Florence? My mother came from there and I've never had the opportunity to visit it. My parents were both killed when I was just one year old, drowned when the ferry capsized. They were on their way to see my Grandfather Fioraldi in Tuscany, but of course, they never got there.'

She sighed deeply, as if the oft-repeated story still pained her. 'I never knew any of them; I have never even been to Italy. I've never been anywhere much, except away to boarding school in Harrogate, and that wasn't so far from Swinburn. My grandmother Jeannie brought me up and I couldn't have wished for anyone more wonderful. She's everything to me. Even my own mother could not have loved me more.'

Tears trembled again on her lashes. Billy took a white linen handkerchief from his jacket pocket and handed it to her, silently.

'She's so old now, you see,' Laura said tremulously. 'I hate to leave her alone at Swinburn. She's not exactly *alone*, of course. But without *me*. Oh, if only old Mountjoy hadn't written offering this huge bribe, I would still be at Swinburn, where I belong. I would not have to go through with this silly débutante thing.'

'Lord Mountjoy?' Billy repeated astonished. Mountjoy was a country neighbour in Wiltshire and as far as he knew he saw no one except a few old cronies. 'You are going to London to see *Lord Mountjoy*?'

She nodded. 'Unfortunately, that seems to be my fate.'

'Hardly "*worse than death*", I should have thought.'

'If you compare it with Swinburn, and grandmother and Haddon Fox, it is,' she retorted, 'even if Haddon *is* a traitor. I hate London, and Society, and all that silly dressing-up.'

'Haddon Fox?' he asked surprised. Suddenly he was intrigued. He could satisfy his curiosity about this girl and about Haddon Fox at the same time.

He said, 'I'll tell you what, you must be hungry after all that crying. Why don't we have a bite of lunch and you can tell me all about Haddon Fox and Lord Mountjoy and your grandmother. And Swinburn, of course.'

'Don't forget my racehorse,' she cried, leaping to her feet and smoothing her creased tweed skirt.

He thought she was built like a racehorse herself, all coltish legs and big long-lashed eyes. But her stockings had a run in them, her feet looked enormous in the clumsy lace-up shoes; and the dreadful tweed suit looked as though it came from a jumble sale. Which it had, though he did not know it.

'I can't wait to hear about it,' he replied, taking her arm as they walked down the corridor to the restaurant car.

'So,' he commanded, when they were seated and had ordered, 'begin at the beginning.'

Laura levelled a wary look at him. 'Do you think grandmother would approve? After all, you are a total stranger.'

He hesitated. Obviously she did not know who he was, and he didn't want to tell her because he wanted to hear her unbiased view of Haddon Fox. 'You're absolutely right. Perhaps it's better that way. Two strangers on a train, telling each other their stories. Just like in the movies.'

'But you haven't told me anything about yourself,' she said suspiciously.

'That's because you're doing all the talking, as well as wasting time crying,' he pointed out. 'But I will tell you my first name is b-b-b-b-Billy.'

'Laura.' She shook his hand.

'Right then, you go first. And begin at the beginning. Let's start with Lord Mountjoy.'

When she had finished her story, he said, 'So now you are on your way to become a débutante.' He lifted a sceptical eyebrow. 'The fate worse than death?' Laura scowled miserably at him, and he laughed and changed the subject. 'Tell me about Haddon Fox.'

'Haddon was, I mean he *is*, a little older than I. Twenty-six next August to be exact. He is tall. He has blond hair, the silky kind that slips over his eyes all the time. His eyes are blue. *Marine blue*, he always says proudly, because his father was an admiral. All the Foxes have been naval men, right from Nelson's days, except for Haddon. They live in a very grand house, Foxton Hall, and Haddon trains racehorses. I helped out at the Foxton Yard for a couple of summers when I was still at school. That's how we met. And fell in love,' she added glumly.

'And that's why you don't want to go to London. You want to stay at Swinburn and marry him?'

She bit her lip, staring dispiritedly at the Brown Windsor soup sloshing round her plate as the train raced over the track. She said, 'Haddon's family is very aristocratic. They thought I was not good enough to marry their son. They wanted a title for him, someone with money and property. Haddon said they wanted an "alliance" not a love match.'

'And what did Haddon say?'

She shrugged, defeatedly. 'He got engaged to Lady Diana Gilmore. Just like that, without even telling me first.'

Her eyes brimmed with tears again. 'You mentioned your horse,' he said hastily as the steward removed their soup plates, and served rare roast beef and Yorkshire pudding. 'The other reason you wanted to stay at Swinburn.'

'Ah, my lovely Sasha,' she said, brightening instantly. 'She's a chestnut mare. She was Haddon's horse. He thought she had a weakness in her foreleg and wanted to get rid of her, but nobody would buy her. He said she was worthless and had better be put down. She was only a two year old, and three is when they start to really show their worth. I just couldn't bear it, she had such a noble head. I swear when Haddon said that about putting her down, that mare turned and looked straight at me. She gazed at me just like this.'

Laura gazed soulfully at Billy. He thought her eyes were exactly the colour of good malt whisky.

Laura said, 'I *swear* Sasha knew she was going to die. So of course I told Haddon I would buy her, even though I had no money. "How much?" I asked, thinking he would just say, "Take her, she's no good anyway."

'"Twenty pounds and she's yours," he told me, slapping her on the neck and pointing out all her good qualities, her breeding, her youth. "Who knows she might be a winner after all," he said.'

Laura frowned, looking unhappy. 'I didn't think it was quite fair of him to ask so much when he knew I didn't have any money. And anyway if he'd had her put down, he wouldn't have made a penny. Still, I telephoned grandmother and told her the problem; about how Sasha had looked at me, and how beautiful she was and that I would just die too if she were put down.'

Billy smiled. There were no half measures about Laura. It was black or white, life or death. He said, 'So of course, grandmother paid up.'

'She certainly did. She said it was my birthday present, but as I had already had one birthday present that year, this would have to do for the next.' Laura sighed happily, remembering. 'I've looked after that horse like a baby. And you know what? Haddon was wrong. I massaged her and walked her and trained her, and there's nothing wrong with her foreleg after all. It was just a temporary thing.'

She laughed, gaily. 'I don't think Haddon has ever forgiven me for beating him out and getting a valuable racehorse for just twenty pounds. I entered her in three novice races at Ripon last season: she won two and came third in another. I have high hopes for her, I think she's going to make my fortune and then I intend to start my own training stables, at Swinburn.

'So you see,' she added earnestly, 'that's why I need to go to London and get involved in all this stupid social stuff. In order to get the Mountjoy money for my own Yard. I shall train winners and make a fortune and look after grandmother Jeannie the way she's always looked after me.'

'And beat Haddon Fox at his own game,' Billy said shrewdly, seeing through her.

Laura smiled wickedly in anticipation of her revenge. 'I vowed I would show him, and I will. When I have the Mountjoy money, I shall be richer than Haddon. It will be nothing but the best for my stables. I shall lure away his clients with my success and they will bring their horses to me, instead of him.'

'Then you think you are as good a trainer as Haddon Fox?'

'Better,' she retorted, scornfully. 'Haddon is lazy, he lets other people do the work. Worse, he lets them do the thinking.' She frowned, analysing what she had just said. 'Haddon is not too clever,' she said honestly, 'though I never would have admitted that, had you asked me a few weeks ago. And yes, I am a good trainer. I've had horses all my life and I've worked with them since I was thirteen. At least I did during the school holidays. But mostly it's an instinct, a feeling for things; you *know* when a horse is good. The rest is just hard work. And besides, I love it. I never want to do anything else.'

'Not even get married? Have children?' he suggested, smiling.

'Certainly not. Not after Haddon. I shall never trust a man again.'

'But Haddon's not your real reason for wanting the Mountjoy

money?' It was a shrewd guess because, despite her bravado, he could tell there was more to the story.

Laura's eyes met his across the table. 'You're too clever, Mr Billy whoever-you-are. How do you know so much about me? You're right of course. Money's tight at Swinburn and grandmother is really worried. She tries to hide it, but I know her too well.'

Laura brushed her smooth brown hair from her eyes impatiently, as she said, 'You see, Billy, I had it all planned. I was going to marry Haddon. We were going to run Foxton Yard together. We would train a lot of winners and then I could take care of my grandmother the way she has always taken care of me. I had my life all planned. And . . . well, you know the rest. I tried desperately to think of ways to earn enough money to keep up Swinburn. I even thought of becoming a jump-jockey – I'm good over the hurdles and I could lose weight, but damn it, I'm too tall. Then Lord Mountjoy's letter came and I knew I had a chance to do something about it.

'I'm not going begging though,' she added fiercely. 'By rights, grandfather should have inherited the family fortune. Then my father, and then me. But, instead, old Lord Mountjoy has it and he's dangling it over our heads like bait. So now I have to go and jump for it. Before the others do.'

'And that is the reason your grandmother wants you to go.'

Laura glared furiously at him. 'Of course not. My grandmother is the least mercenary person I know. She just wants me to go and have a good time. Be introduced to Society, meet other young people. Young men I expect she really means. She thinks it will take my mind off Haddon and my problems.'

'I suspect your grandmother may be right,' Billy said, amused.

Laura waved away the apple pie and cream offered by the steward. 'I hate London,' she said scornfully. 'I hate débutantes and I hate those other two girls, even before I meet them. They'll just be snobs and I'll bet they are only after the Mountjoy millions. Why else would they come running? All the way from America and France?'

'Perhaps they also need the money?'

She considered the possibility, then shook her head. 'Not as much as I do. Anyhow, all I want is enough for grandmother, and my stable. As far as I'm concerned, they can have the rest. The Mountjoys didn't offer to help before, and it's only now the old man has no one left, that he's even interested.'

She tossed her head, her eyes flashing dramatically, 'Well, I for one am not prepared to play his game. I shall sabotage him every chance I get.'

'I imagine you will,' Billy agreed, impressed.

'I feel quite worn out,' she said, when they were back in their compartment. 'All that talking. And crying.' She yawned, covering her mouth politely with a chapped red hand. 'Grandmother would be so ashamed of me, talking about myself all the time. And I never got to ask about you. I had so many questions.'

Laura was asleep within minutes and she was still sleeping when the express pulled into King's Cross station. He watched her, thinking how honest and unpretentious she was. She was the most real girl he had spoken to in ages. *And* she didn't even know about his racehorses and his money.

Billy leaned across and took her hand. It was rough and the nails were bitten. 'Wake up, Laura,' he said. 'We're here.'

'Oh nooo,' she wailed, instantly awake. 'This is it. My fate worse than death.' But she had the grace to smile, shamefacedly, at him as she said it.

He called a porter for her, watching as he loaded a shabby old school suitcase with 'L. Swinburn, Queen Ethelburga's' stamped on it, and a couple of brown carrier bags. He looked at her, smiling. 'I guess this is goodbye, Laura.'

'You were right,' she said. 'About our game, I mean. You *are* more than two nationalities. You pronounced my name the Italian way, and you preface it with the American "I guess". So with the Scottish and English, that makes at least three.'

He laughed, 'And maybe more. I'm a very truthful man.'

She looked levelly at him. 'I still don't know anything about you. Perhaps I shouldn't have told you all my secrets.'

'They're safe with me,' he promised. 'Safe as death.'

She shuddered at the word, then leaned forward and dropped a sudden kiss on his cheek. 'Thank you for the lovely lunch. Thank you for understanding.' She hesitated, looking into his nice blue eyes. 'I hope I shall see you again, some day,' she added. And then she was off, loping down the platform after the porter. She did not look back as the chauffeur in the maroon livery greeted her, and they disappeared towards the Mountjoy Rolls, waiting at the exit.

Billy stood, with hands stuffed in the pockets of his dark blue overcoat, watching until she was out of sight. One thing he knew for certain, old Lord Mountjoy would have his hands full with Laura. His life would never be the same again. And, somehow, he suspected, nor would his own.

He decided he would make a point of calling on Lord Mountjoy and getting himself invited to that ball. He grinned, thinking of the surprise on Laura's face when she saw him. He would have to confess who he was, of course, and they could talk about horses and racing. Maybe he could help her. In fact, in a way, he had already helped her: thanks to her astute assessment of Haddon Fox, he had definitely decided not to use Foxton Yard. Laura was already getting her revenge.

He was smiling as he hailed a taxi and was driven to Claridge's, where he lived in an enormous suite, when he was in London.

CHAPTER 23

Mountjoy House took up an entire city block on Curzon Street. It was built of pale French limestone, with dozens of tall windows, and topped by a grey mansard-roof. There was a cobbled entrance courtyard with massive iron gates and a top-hatted porter in a little lodge. Ornamental trees in green wooden tubs were spaced around its perimeter and were changed regularly with the season. A pair of tall bay trees, clipped into pyramid shapes, stood at the top of the broad marble steps leading to the carved oak double-doors, where the silver-haired butler, Johnson, was waiting as Anjou stepped out of the Rolls.

'Good afternoon, Miss Mountjoy,' he said. 'My name is Johnson.'

'Good afternoon, Johnson,' Anjou replied, glancing round the lofty hall. A magnificent staircase swept from the centre to a columned upper gallery; the floor was patterned marble and the elaborate plaster cornices were picked out in gold leaf. The walls were covered in massive tapestries and paintings, and a dozen or so spindly gilt Louis IV sofas were arranged between marble consoles with elaborate flower arrangements. It looked like a palace and she thought, pleased, that Lord Mountjoy must be even richer than she had expected.

Johnson led the way up the grand staircase. 'Miss Honeychile arrived yesterday,' he told her. 'And we expect Miss Laura on the afternoon train.'

'Miss *Honeychile*?' She raised an amazed eyebrow.

'She is from Texas, Miss. She is in the yellow room, at the end of the hall.' Johnson threw open a door and stepped to one side to let her pass. 'Lord Mountjoy thought you might care for the blue room, Miss.'

'Well, it's certainly blue,' Anjou said, taking in the blue-patterned Persian rugs, blue-patterned wallpaper and heavy blue brocade curtains. It was enormous, with a high ceiling, a huge four-poster bed, a writing desk under one of the three windows looking out onto Curzon Street, and various other small tables, chairs and sofas, and a scattering of standard lamps with fringed shades. There was a dressing room and a bathroom with a tub encased in mahogany panelling and a complicated assortment of brass taps.

'It's perfect, thank you, Johnson,' she said, smiling. 'I think I am going to be very happy here.'

'Your personal maid, Agnes, will be up shortly, Miss, to unpack for you. And tea will be served in the small drawing room downstairs, at four o'clock.'

Anjou's eyes sparkled at the thought of her own maid. She thought life was looking up, and if she were clever, she might never have to be poor again; she might not have to become a courtesan after all; or heaven forbid, be forced to marry for money.

Leaving Agnes unpacking her things, she walked slowly down the stairs. The banister was made of carved onyx and the sumptuous burgundy carpet felt soft beneath her feet; she loved the luxury of it all, the richness of it. She wanted it so badly. She wanted to be mistress of this house, to entertain in style, to spend money as lavishly as if there were no end; and with the Mountjoy millions, she was sure there would not be.

She peeked into an enormous drawing room; and a smaller drawing room; a library; a study; a morning room; a vast dining room and a smaller dining room. And at the back of the house, a beautiful ballroom, with a glossy parquet floor and magnificent Waterford chandeliers. A dozen tall French windows led from it onto a flagstone terrace, with steps leading into a formal garden.

'*Mon Dieu*,' she said, impressed, 'so this is where our ball will take place.'

She walked back into the hall and stood looking confidently around, just as Honeychile appeared, loping down the beautiful staircase, towards her.

Honeychile had spent the night alone at Mountjoy House, except for the dozens of servants. She had dined alone, served by a liveried footman and supervised by the cool, silver-haired butler, and she had been too intimidated to eat. She had been lonesome, in the massive old four-poster in the cavernous bedroom, crowded with antiques and

198

gloomy paintings of Mountjoy ancestors. When she had turned out the lights, the shadows seemed suddenly to creep closer; the glowing red embers of the coal fire in the grate, hissed and sparked, and the streetlamps flickered ominously outside the long windows. Wondering about ghosts, she had closed her eyes and tried to sleep, but she could not. Now, she was just happy someone else had arrived.

'Lordy, am I glad to see you,' she cried, leaping down the last few stairs. She held out her hand, 'Hi, I'm Honeychile. Oh no, I'm not, I guess I'm Eloise.'

Anjou looked her up and down, taking in the badly-cut tweed suit and clumsy shoes. She said, amused, 'So, this is what a Texan looks like.'

'What d'you mean?' Honeychile said, taken aback. 'Texans look like everybody else, don't they? One head, two arms, two legs. Kind of normal, I should have said.'

Anjou smiled wickedly, 'About as normal as your name.'

'Well now, you've got no call to say a thing like that,' Honeychile retorted, stung. 'Anjou is not exactly a regular sort of name. It's a case of the pot calling the kettle black, if you ask me.'

'No one is asking you.' Anjou frowned. '*Eh bien*, and where is Lord Mountjoy? He is expecting me.'

'He was expecting me too, but he hasn't shown up yet. The butler told me he was delayed by fog. We were supposed to "make ourselves at home" and not set foot out of this door until he gets here.'

Anjou laughed merrily at the idea. She said, 'Obviously Lord Mountjoy is an optimist. Do you not realise, Honeychile Mountjoy, that outside this door all London awaits us? Shops, cafés, night-clubs?' Her eyes sparkled with anticipation. 'And I, for one, cannot wait.'

'You mean you're going to disobey him?' Honeychile asked, awed by her confidence.

'Well of course I am. If Lord Mountjoy is ill-mannered enough not to be here to greet his guests, then he can hardly expect us to sit around and mope. What do you say, Honeychile, are you game for an adventure?' Honeychile hesitated, and Anjou added, provocatively, 'Go on. *I dare you.*'

Honeychile was never one to turn down a dare, but still she hesitated. She said, 'I don't have any money.'

'We don't need money. We shall go for a stroll in the park, feed the ducks, observe the English in their natural habitat. We shall ride on one of those big red buses and browse through Harrods and Fortnum & Mason.'

Honeychile laughed and Anjou added, inspired, 'I shall bribe you with tea at the Ritz. What do you say to that, Honeychile Mountjoy?'

'It's a deal. I've never had "tea" and I've never been to the Ritz.'

Anjou winked, as they strode to the door. 'Well, you know what they say,' she smiled demurely, 'there's always a first time.

'Johnson,' she called, 'we are going out for tea. We shall be back later.'

'Excuse me, Miss Anjou,' he said looking shocked, 'but Lord Mountjoy said you were to wait here for him.'

'And when Lord Mountjoy arrives, that's exactly where we shall be. Right here, waiting for him,' she replied coolly.

At the end of Curzon Street Anjou asked a policeman how to get to the Ritz; then they strolled through Mayfair and down Burlington Arcade into Piccadilly. She swept through the doors of the grand hotel as though she owned it. The dazzling marble, gilt and crystal-chandeliered Ritz could not compete with Mountjoy House for grandeur, but she thought, pleased, that it was certainly livelier. A string quartet was playing softly in the background and it was crowded with young people, having a good time.

The head waiter showed them to a quiet table near the wall, half-hidden by a potted palm, but Anjou tilted her chin haughtily and said she certainly was not going to sit where no one could see her. Then she marched to a table in the centre of the room, next to one where a couple of attractive young men were seated. She threw them a calculating glance from beneath her lashes as she took a seat. She thought, satisfied, that they were perfect.

As she ordered tea, Anjou gave them a seductive little smile. '*Mon Dieu, mais il fait très chaud, ici,*' she said, wafting the menu in front of her face like a fan.

Honeychile didn't speak French but she guessed what she meant by the fan. 'You don't know what hot is until you've ridden the range at noon on a summer day in Texas,' she said with a grin. 'A hundred and ten in the shade, only you're not in the shade because there is none.

Boy, do you sweat. You just can't wait to get back home and stand under the pump in the backyard and wash all that dust off you.'

Anjou glared at her. She sighed and shook her head exasperatedly, glancing at the young men. They smiled back at her and she looked casually away. She knew all it would take was an encouraging word, and they would join them. She decided not to give it to them, at least, not yet.

Their tea arrived and they devoured the tiny cucumber and smoked salmon sandwiches, the scones piled with strawberry jam and thick fresh cream, and delicious little French pastries, while Anjou kept up a stream of inconsequential chatter, glancing every now and again at their attentive neighbours.

When she had finished, she licked the cream from her lips with a pointed pink tongue. Then she looked directly at the two young men. She smiled and they smiled eagerly back.

The waiter gave her the bill and she studied the amount, then opened her handbag and rummaged ostentatiously through its contents. 'Oh, *mon Dieu*,' she cried clutching a hand dramatically to her heart.

'Whatever's the matter?' Honeychile asked, puzzled.

Anjou stared innocently back at her. 'I seem to have left my purse at home. I do not have a single *sou* with which to pay this bill.' And then she turned and threw a helpless glance at their neighbours.

Honeychile gave a horrified gasp: visions of being marched through the Ritz hand-cuffed to a policeman, and of months spent washing dishes in the hotel kitchens, flashed through her mind. 'What shall we do?' she whispered, agonised.

And then, just as Anjou had known he would, the fair-haired young man at the next table leapt to his feet.

He said, 'Excuse me, but I couldn't help overhearing. I know how embarrassing this must be for you, but won't you please allow me to help?'

Honeychile stared at Anjou, smiling up at the young man. She suddenly realised that Anjou had known all along she had no money. That this was all a plot, and it was working.

'A saviour,' Anjou said, admiringly, giving him her full attention. 'You see, Honeychile, it is true, after all, what they say about the English. They are perfect gentlemen. Just look how he is offering to

201

help two poor damsels in distress. I must thank you, Monsieur . . . ?'

'Rollo Furness, and Archie Brightwell,' they said promptly.

'I am Anjou d'Aranville Mountjoy, and this is Honeychile.' She waved a casual hand at Honeychile who was watching in horrified amazement as Rollo laid a five pound note on top of the bill.

'Mountjoy?' Archie said, interestedly. 'Any relation to the old Earl?'

'Our great uncle,' Anjou said grandly. '*Eh bien*, now we were thinking of going to Fortnum & Mason.' She stood up, smoothing her skirt, not looking at them.

And again, just as she had known they would, Rollo and Archie offered to escort them to the store. When they emerged an hour later, she was laden with boxes of chocolates and flowers.

'How do you do it?' Honeychile demanded, mortified as the young men dropped them off at Mountjoy House in a taxi and they waved goodbye.

Anjou shrugged, 'It's easy when you know how,' she replied with that wicked laugh. 'And somehow, Honeychile, I don't think you ever will.'

Laura sank back against the luxurious soft leather cushions as Bridges manoeuvred the Mountjoy Rolls through the London traffic. She noticed people turning their heads to stare at the expensive car, and she thought how much Haddon would have enjoyed being wafted through London in a magnificent Rolls Royce Silver Ghost, driven by his own liveried chauffeur.

That was the trouble with Haddon, she realised now. He didn't want the love of a good and faithful woman; Haddon wanted expensive houses and cars and clothes. He wanted yachts and villas in Barbados. And what's more, he knew he was never going to *earn* them, because he was lazy. With a rich wife, he could employ someone to run Foxton Yard; then he could dress up in expensive tweeds and play at being the 'well-known trainer', while somebody else did all the work. Just the way she had.

She decided, for the hundredth time, that she was better off without him. Then why, she asked herself again, did it hurt so much?

'Damaged pride,' was what her grandmother Jeannie had said.

'That's what you are suffering from, my girl. And there's no better cure for that than another man.'

Laura hoped, wistfully, that she was right. After all, she told herself, when she was talking with Billy on the train, she had hardly thought about Haddon at all. She decided Billy was really nice. Interesting too. She had kissed him, impulsively, simply because he *was* so nice, but now she thought about it, she had done all the talking and she hardly knew a thing about him.

It was a pity because she would probably never see him again, she thought as the big car turned down Park Lane and edged slowly through the evening traffic.

Bridges made a left turn into Curzon Street and then another left into a large cobbled courtyard. Laura peered interestedly through the window at the enormous house. 'My goodness,' she said, impressed, as a footman opened the door and she stepped out. 'I should certainly like grandmother to see this.'

Johnson was waiting at the top of the marble steps and the footman retrieved her old school suitcase and her brown carrier bags.

'Not quite what you're used to, I'll bet,' Laura grinned cheerfully.

He threw her an amused glance, but it was more than his job was worth to laugh, not with Johnson watching him like a hawk.

'Good evening, Miss Mountjoy,' Johnson greeted her at the top of the steps. 'I trust you had a pleasant journey?'

'Very pleasant, thank you,' Laura said, thinking of Billy again.

'My name is Johnson, Miss.'

'How d'you do,' Laura said with a polite smile.

'The footman will take your luggage up to your room, Miss. If you would care to follow me, I shall show you the way.'

Laura followed him up the magnificent staircase, wide-eyed at the grandeur of her surroundings. 'My goodness,' she said, staring down the long burgundy-carpeted corridor, 'this is as long as a lacrosse pitch.'

She glanced right and left at the life-sized marble statues of Roman emperors and Greek nymphs that she had no doubt were the genuine article; at the gorgeous flowers on the marble consoles, and the little gilt and satin Louis-something French sofas that she was sure no one ever sat on, they looked so hard.

'Miss Honeychile is in the yellow room at the end of the hall,'

Johnson told her, 'and Miss Anjou is opposite in the blue room. Lord Mountjoy suggested that you might like the rose room, next to Miss Honeychile's.'

He opened the double doors with a flourish and stood back to allow her to enter.

Laura stepped inside and looked at the dizzying bower of rose-patterned wallpaper, rose-coloured swagged curtains and rose-sprigged carpet. Even the enormous bed had a rose chintz headboard and coverlet, and there were enough rosy-patterned china bowls and whatnots to stock a shop. Plus all the other silver and gilt objects scattered on the dressing-table and the numerous other little tables.

She thought of her room at Swinburn Manor, with its simple striped cream wallpaper, the plain dresser and the old brass bed where they said her mother had given birth to her. 'It's certainly different from home,' she said.

The footman placed her suitcase on the luggage stand as carefully as if it were an expensive Vuitton trunk, and a young maid appeared in the doorway.

'This is Josie,' Johnson said. 'She will be your personal maid, Miss Laura. She will help you in any way she can.'

'My personal maid?' Laura looked, astonished, at the pretty blonde girl in her black dress and organza cap and apron. She laughed, thinking how ridiculous it all was. 'Well, who knows, Josie, this might be fun after all,' she said.

'Yes, Miss,' Josie replied primly, but when Johnson wasn't looking, she smiled.

'Lord Mountjoy was delayed by the fog, Miss. He will be here as soon as possible,' Johnson said. 'Meanwhile, the other young ladies have already arrived, and dinner is planned for seven-thirty. Drinks, if you care for them, are at seven, Miss, in the small drawing room.'

'The small drawing room,' she repeated. 'Thank you, Johnson. I shall certainly be there.'

Laura wandered round her room, picking up one exquisite object after another, marvelling at the workmanship, and the antiquity, and the possible value. She tested the bed and found it firm but comfortable, which was better than most English houses where new mattresses were not considered a priority, and mostly you slept on old horsehair-stuffed Victorian ones that sagged in the middle and whose broken springs played havoc with your back.

She sat at the dressing table and looked at herself in the ornate silver mirror, wondering if she looked any different in this expensive looking-glass than she did in her own plain one at home. Then she wandered into the bathroom where Josie was running her bath. She took the stopper off the crystal container of bathsalts, sniffing appreciatively.

'Rose, of course,' she said.

'What else, Miss?' Josie agreed. Their eyes met and they laughed. Laura perched on the edge of the pink-marble encased tub, looking at her.

'Tell me, what's it like working here, Josie?' she asked.

'Like, Miss? Well, it's a good job I suppose.' She arranged a pink towelling bathrobe and slippers on a rose-chintz *chaise-longue*, near the tub. 'To tell you the truth, Miss, I've only just been promoted from parlourmaid. There hasn't been much call for ladies' maids in this house, you see. Not since the Countess died, and that's more'n forty years ago.'

'You mean Lord Mountjoy has lived here alone, all these years?' Laura imagined the old man rattling around in his big grand house, with just his memories for company.

'That's right, Miss. He gives a dinner party once a month, to repay hospitality, he says, but there has been no real entertaining here for years. I must say, Miss, we are all looking forward to it. The ball, and all that. It'll bring a bit of life to the old place again.'

Laura knew it wasn't done to question a servant about her employer, but curiosity overcame her scruples. 'Lord Mountjoy?' she said, 'what's he like? Really?'

'Why, I'm not sure, Miss, I hardly see him. His Lordship is a bit irascible, I suppose, quick-tempered, you know. I don't think he is long on patience, anyway. But he's a fair employer, Miss. Very fair.'

Laura thought about Lord Mountjoy, as she lay in the bath, smelling of roses. She wondered how fair he would be when he heard her reason for wanting his money. Well, not all of it. Just enough to buy her stables and set herself up as a trainer. She thought he could probably just sell off the contents of her room and have enough for that. It would be a drop in the ocean of his seemingly boundless wealth.

Josie told her they would not be dressing for dinner, since Lord Mountjoy was not expected. 'It will be just the three young ladies,' she said, helping Laura into her second-best dress; an amber-coloured silk that her grandmother had cut down from an old one of hers. She wore her grandmother's amber earrings and a plain gold bracelet that she had received on her eighteenth birthday, and sensible brown court shoes.

Josie brushed her hair until it shone and asked her if she wanted her to put it up, but she said no, it was fine as it was. And then she was ready.

'Here we go, Josie,' she said with a grin. 'I'm ready to meet my fate.'

She laughed, thinking of Billy, and how she had told him it was 'a fate worse than death'. As she ran down the grand staircase, she hoped it wasn't true.

Johnson was in the hallway to show her to the drawing room. 'The other young ladies are waiting for you, Miss,' he said, throwing open the door.

'Miss Laura Swinburn Mountjoy,' he announced grandly.

A tall blonde girl leapt to her feet and walked towards her, smiling. The other, a red-head and a beauty, leaned sullenly against the marble mantel. She made no move to greet her, and Laura guessed she was assessing the competition.

'I'm glad to meet you,' Honeychile said, shaking her hand. 'And this is Anjou.' Anjou held out her hand reluctantly. 'I think it's real nice we can all be friends,' Honeychile beamed. 'And I confess I've never had a real girl friend before.'

'Does that mean you've never had a boyfriend either?' Anjou asked, with a supercilious smile.

Honeychile looked startled. 'Why sure I do. Tom Jefferson is my very dearest friend. There's nothing Tom doesn't know about me. Well, almost nothing,' she amended quickly.

Anjou raised a sceptical eyebrow. 'Is that so?'

Honeychile said angrily, 'Listen-up, Anjou d'Aranville Mountjoy. Where I come from folks don't try and twist your words round until they're something you don't mean. They speak their minds and they speak straight.'

'Bravo,' Laura clapped her hands delightedly. 'But you had better get used to it, Honeychile. The English are experts at *not* saying what they mean. They'll snub you so cleverly you won't even know you've been snubbed. Then they'll say it's because you're so thick-skinned.' She sighed, feelingly. 'I know, from experience.'

'I'll bet you've never had a boyfriend, Honeychile, have you?' Anjou baited her again.

Honeychile blushed. 'I've never had time to think about it, I'm too busy.' She thought about Alex and how her heart had leapt when he'd kissed her, and the flowers he had sent her. 'Why, yes I do,' she blurted, suddenly. 'I surely do have a boyfriend.'

'What's his name?' Laura asked, fascinated by the game.

'His name is Alex. Alex Scott.'

'Not Alex *Andreos* Scott,' Laura said, astonished.

Honeychile looked at them, bewildered. 'I met him on the ship. We had dinner. He kissed me,' she added defiantly.

Anjou hooted with laughter. 'The richest man in the world kissed *you*? Ah, now I remember,' she added, mockingly. 'The famous, rich, mystery man, Alex Andreos Scott. I had dinner with him too, just the other night in Paris, at this intimate little bistro he knows.' She sighed dreamily, rolling up her eyes. 'He's such a man of the world, *mon amour*, Alex. And so *sexy*, he kisses so well . . .'

'Stop it,' Laura warned, looking sympathetically at Honeychile. Tears of humiliation were welling in her eyes.

'You . . . you *bitch*,' Honeychile cried, turning and storming to the door.

But Anjou and Laura were not looking at her any more. They were staring beyond her at the man standing silently in the doorway, watching them.

Honeychile ran right into him. She dashed the tears from her eyes and looked up. 'Oh,' she gasped.

Anjou hastily put down her gin and vermouth, and Laura stood up straight. Honeychile took two paces backwards, speechless with fright.

Lord Mountjoy's eyes were frigid as he looked them over, silently. A minute passed, and then he said icily, 'I trust that little encounter is not your usual form of polite conversation, young ladies. If it is, then I shall certainly need to retract that phrase *ladies* and replace it with *kitchen maids*. It seems to me the conversation I overheard was about on that level. I am sure you will agree?'

Honeychile hung her head miserably; she knew she would never learn to behave like a lady.

Laura knew they had been caught red-handed. 'I apologise, Lord Mountjoy,' she said, feeling as though she were up in front of the headmaster for her transgressions.

Anjou hesitated for a moment, then she ran towards him. 'Oh, *poof*, Uncle Mountjoy,' she said gaily, 'it was just girls' talk, that's all.' She deposited a kiss on his cold cheek.

'Now, we shall attempt to create a better impression for you. We shall introduce ourselves. I, of course, am Anjou, and I am thrilled to meet my only English relative, at long last.' Looking into his eyes, she gave him her sincerest smile. As she had thought he would, he smiled back. A touch begrudgingly, to be sure, but the danger was over.

'This is Laura Swinburn,' she said, not giving her a chance to speak for herself. 'Laura is from Yorkshire, I believe. And this,' she waved a careless hand at tall, blonde Honeychile, whose head still drooped in embarrassment. 'This is Miss Honeychile, all the way from little old Texas.'

'How d'y'do,' Lord Mountjoy said gruffly. Now they were here, he had no idea of what to say to them. He hadn't spoken to a young woman in years, and certainly not to any foreign ones. He thought longingly of Sophie Mountjoy. She had been married to a distant cousin, also killed in the war. She had promised to look after them like a mother hen, though privately, he knew better. Sophie Mountjoy had never been a 'mother' and what she would do, was watch them like a hawk. With Sophie in charge, 'his girls' would not even be able to think of putting a foot wrong. Yes, he told himself thankfully, Sophie would whip them into shape in no time.

He took the gold half-hunter from his waistcoat pocket and checked the time. 'Yes, well then,' he said, putting it back again. 'I'm off to my club. Report to me tomorrow morning, in the library, at nine sharp. We shall discuss your futures then.' And he turned and left them, staring wonderingly after him.

CHAPTER 24

At a few minutes before nine the following morning, Lord Mountjoy was prowling the tartan carpet, hands behind his back, thumbs twitching agitatedly, glaring at the clock on the mantel as the minute hand ticked slowly closer. It rumbled and whirred, then the little gold cherub struck a tiny gong nine times.

'They are late,' he said out loud. 'Damn it all, I knew they would be. Women always are.'

There was a knock on the door and he barked, 'Come in.'

The French filly was first; somehow he knew that one was not the sort to be at the end of any queue. Then the Yorkshire lass, and lastly the American.

'Good morning, Lord Mountjoy,' they chorused, as though they had rehearsed it.

'I hope you slept well, Uncle,' Anjou added with a sweet smile.

'Humph, thank you. Yes, yes . . .' he replied, taken aback.

He walked silently round them, inspecting them as critically as he might a troop of cadets on the parade ground, at Sandhurst, and then he tallied up the results. He had one tall, gangling, outrageously blonde Texan farmer; one sullen, horsy, tomboy Yorkshire gel, and one French bluestocking with far too short a skirt and a skittish look about her. His heart sank as he wondered how the dickens Aunt Sophie Mountjoy could turn them into débutantes. They looked a hopeless case to him.

He glanced at the clock again, thinking that Sophie was late too. What was wrong with women that they couldn't be on time? There was a knock at the door and Johnson announced, 'The Lady Sophie Mountjoy, sir.'

The girls' heads swung round as she swept into the room. She was tall and regal, and very much the grand dame, with immaculately coiffed white hair and a prominent bosom, liberally adorned with diamond brooches.

'Morning, William,' she said, in a booming voice that could have been heard a mile away, kissing the air next to his cheek. 'Not that it is a good morning. The rain is enough to drown a duck and the traffic is abominable.' She turned and looked at the girls and they stared apprehensively back at her.

'Well, well, and what have we here,' she said, holding a gold lorgnette to her eyes and inspecting them carefully.

She looked up at Mountjoy and said, scathingly, 'The Mountjoy girls, indeed. More like the Mountjoy ugly ducklings. This is going to be expensive,' she warned him, 'it's going to cost you a great deal of money to turn these creatures into Cinderellas and find them a Prince Charming.' She put her lorgnette to her eye again, looking at their feet. '*And* to find a glass slipper big enough.'

'I shall put them in your capable hands, Sophie,' he said worriedly. 'Do what you can with them. As long as they don't disgrace the Mountjoy name,' he added, anxiously.

'Leave it to me, William,' she said, 'If anyone can do it, I can.'

As Lord Mountjoy hurried from the room, heading for the familiar safety of his club, she said to them, 'You had better introduce yourselves.'

Anjou was first, of course. 'Anjou d'Aranville, Aunt Sophie,' she said, swooping forward and planting kisses on both her well-powdered cheeks.

Aunt Sophie waved her away, horrified. 'The first thing you must learn is not to kiss English people, especially on a first acquaintance,' she said, 'it's simply not done.'

'Sorry, Aunt Sophie,' Anjou smiled winningly at her.

Laura offered her chapped, nail-bitten hand. 'How do you do,' she said, 'I'm Laura Swinburn.'

Aunt Sophie sniffed delicately, holding a handkerchief to her nose. 'And still with a whiff of the stables about you,' she said, holding a handkerchief to her nose.

Laura blushed, 'Oh dear,' she said, 'I usually wear this jersey when I muck out the yard. It's clean, but somehow the horsy scent just lingers.'

'Lesson one: you will not wear stableyard jumpers in the drawing

210

room,' Aunt Sophie warned. 'Kindly remember that, my girl.'

Honeychile stuck her chin in the air; she was who she was and the hell with what Aunt Sophie thought. 'Honeychile Mountjoy Hennessy,' she said, 'from Texas.'

'Texas, humm?' Aunt Sophie studied her through the lorgnette again. 'That's where Georgie ended up, isn't it, at the ranch?'

'Yes, ma'am, he did. I never met him though. He died before I was born.'

'Wasn't your mother an actress?'

Honeychile smiled, thinking how pleased Rosie would have been with that description. 'Yes, ma'am, she was Rarin' Rosie, the Sexiest Stripper on the Circuit, when my pa met her.' She felt their astonished eyes on her.

'Goodness me,' Aunt Sophie said, taken aback. 'I don't think we should go broadcasting that fact around the drawing rooms of Mayfair. Perhaps if you just said she was in the theatre, that would be quite enough.'

When she had recovered from the shock, she said in her booming voice, 'Well now, young ladies, we have our work cut out for us. We have a lot to accomplish in a very short period of time if we are to make you presentable to Society. It is a challenge, I admit, but one that I think Lord Mountjoy and I can rise up to, and we certainly expect you to do the same.' She glared at them, then added warningly, 'There will be no slacking, no slovenliness and no laziness. I simply will not tolerate it. The Mountjoys have always been known for their spirit and their pride. I shall expect nothing less from you girls.

'You will need to learn how to be agreeable,' Aunt Sophie said, looking at Laura. 'And not to be a show-off,' she added warningly to Anjou. 'And how to listen instead of talking too much,' she told Honeychile.

'I can see that you are all completely lacking in any dress sense and in dire need of good clothes,' she said. 'Personally, I cannot abide French designers; in my view they simply do not understand English taste. I have, therefore, made an appointment with a new young designer, Norman Hartnell. He will make your ball dresses and your Presentation gowns. We shall also go to Victor Steibel, and to Beta, in Knightsbridge, for day dresses and suits.'

She sighed as she looked at them and thought of the enormity of her task, and said, 'Meanwhile, I am taking you to Swan & Edgars this very minute, because I cannot abide looking at you one moment longer, in those ghastly garments.

'And as for you, my dear,' she added frostily to Anjou. 'You are showing far more leg than is decent. I shall personally tell the dressmakers to lower your hems to a more seemly level.'

Anjou sighed, thinking regretfully of Paris, and Schiaparelli and Chanel and Worth, whose clothes she would have died for.

They spent the rest of the morning sitting in a private dressing room at Swan & Edgars while relays of salesladies wafted in and out, presenting skirts and blouses and woollen jumpers, shoes and dresses for Aunt Sophie's approval.

They returned to Mountjoy House for a quick lunch, and then on to Hartnell's where they were measured, and Aunt Sophie told him exactly what they would need. Bolts of sumptuous fabrics were brought from the workrooms and draped on them and the final choices were made.

After that, they visited Madame Vacani at her studio in Kensington, and made appointments for private lessons in dancing and the art of the Court curtsy.

Then Aunt Sophie looked at her wilting charges and said, 'It's time for tea. But as you are not yet presentable enough to be taken to Gunters, I shall pack you off home.' And they piled wearily into her chauffeured Daimler and were dropped off back at Mountjoy House.

After that, their days were crammed with lessons. They had lessons in deportment, in etiquette, elocution and dancing, in how to make a proper Court curtsy and how to be 'agreeable' at dinner or with a dance partner. Aunt Sophie said they must learn country pursuits in order to take part in house party weekends, and they spent hours running round a tennis court in an attempt to become suitably proficient. But nobody had to teach Laura and Honeychile to ride.

'Aunt Sophie I promise I shall be amusing and agreeable,' Anjou said mutinously, watching Laura and Honeychile gallop off down Rotton Row, looking as though they had been born in the saddle, 'but I shall never go near those nasty smelly creatures.'

She won a reprieve from the riding, but she did not win the battle of the short skirt. Aunt Sophie's eagle eye behind that gold lorgnette did not miss a thing, and Anjou knew it. London waited temptingly outside the door of Mountjoy House, but regretfully she decided to bide her time.

Aunt Sophie saw to it they were outfitted for every possible occasion, and endless fittings were necessary, as they were equipped with suits and day dresses; evening gowns and velvet capes with satin linings; shoes, hats, kid gloves, alligator handbags and silk underclothes. Lord Mountjoy was not sparing a penny; the Mountjoy girls would look the part. Meanwhile, they were kept under wraps, virtual prisoners at Mountjoy House, until their launch at their own grand ball.

Somehow, the newspapers had got hold of the story of Lord Mountjoy's long-lost great-nieces, and everybody knew about them; they were London's best-kept secret, and competition for an invitation was keen. Besides, there hadn't been a ball at Mountjoy House in forty years, and everyone was excited at the prospect of seeing the wonderful house again. Lord Mountjoy retreated to the safety of his country house in Wiltshire, out of their way, but to Anjou's chagrin, Aunt Sophie moved in for the duration. Until they were safely 'launched', as she put it.

'Like a ship,' Laura laughed. 'All they have to do is crack a bottle of champagne over us, and we shall set sail on the turbulent sea of Society, ready to be rescued by the first handsome man who fancies us.'

'Not me,' Honeychile said, with a shudder.

They were lounging exhaustedly in Laura's room after a hard day of dress fittings and running round a tennis court, which Honeychile thought was harder work than roping heifers.

Honeychile was wearing a pink bathrobe, and she had just washed her hair. She was drying it in front of the fire, and her cheeks were pink from the heat and her blue eyes sparkled like sapphires. Anjou realised, surprised, that she looked different. She supposed they all did, even Laura looked pretty and feminine, wrapped in a blue silk kimono, painting her newly grown nails a bright pink.

'Aunt Sophie's not going to like them,' she said with a grin of satisfaction, waving her hand round to show them. 'Too disgracefully bright, my girl,' she said in an exact imitation of Aunt Sophie's booming contralto, and they all laughed.

'If you don't want to get married, then what do you want, Honeychile?' she asked, wafting her hands in the air to dry the polish.

'I want Uncle Mountjoy's money,' Honeychile replied.

'Well, that's honest,' Anjou said.

Laura looked scathingly at her, 'Let's face it, that's what we are all here for. I know I am.'

'And why do *you* want the money?' Anjou asked, lazily, stretching out on the pink sofa with her feet up.

'Two reasons,' Laura said. And she told them about her grandmother, who had no money left, and the treacherous Haddon Fox. 'I thought I would be able to take care of grandmother, the way she's always cared for me. I know how difficult things are for her now; money is really tight. She tries to hide it, but I know her too well. I saw how her hands trembled when the post came and she opened the bills. Sometimes I would catch her, just sitting, staring into the fire, as though she expected to find an answer to our financial problems in the flames. It's just not fair that she has to worry about money, at her time of life,' she added sadly. 'She's always given everything to other people, a lifetime of caring and devotion. Now it's up to me. All I need is enough to start my own training yard so that I can look after her and Swinburn. Then I shall be happy,' she added.

'I wonder,' Anjou said sceptically.

'Well what about you, *Mamzelle* Anjou?' Laura snapped. 'What's your reason? Besides clothes and jewels and men?'

Anjou laughed. 'I have my reasons,' she said, 'but they are private. And what about Miss Texas? The girl who does not want to get married and probably doesn't even want the money. She's just too good to be true.'

Honeychile was glad she was sitting by the fire so they wouldn't notice her blush. Anjou was always baiting her; she guessed she just liked to get her riled and then see her explode in anger. Well, this time, she promised herself, she would not.

'It's simple,' she said quietly. 'I need the money to replant the land, and re-stock it with the finest cattle. I want Mountjoy Ranch to be the way it was in my father's day. I've let him down, and now the ranch is almost worthless. After he died my mother spent all the money. Then she got married again. She just showed up at the ranch

214

one day and said, "This is my new husband, Jack Delaney." A few years later, he shot her,' she said.

Anjou sat up, startled, staring at her, and Laura said, shocked, 'You mean he *murdered* your mother?'

Honeychile nodded. 'I'm sure he did.' And she told them the story of Rosie's death outside the speakeasy and Jack Delaney's alibi.

'And did he ever come back to claim the ranch?' Anjou asked, fascinated.

She nodded, 'But you see the ranch belonged to me. It was left in trust and he couldn't get his hands on it. At least, not then, not until he figured out a way.' She looked at them, watching her, their eyes wide with sympathy. Even Anjou looked concerned. But still, she couldn't tell them about it. She had never talked about what happened, but she had dreamed about it all the time, at first; until it had faded into a blur. She thought she had put the bad memories behind her, but that night, she dreamed about it again, and all her fears returned.

Jack Delaney had always known he was a smart guy. That's how he had gotten rich in the years since he had left Rosie. He 'owned' automobile dealerships in six counties, though in reality they were a front for laundering Mafia money. He also had a big house in Houston, and drove a large customised black Cadillac with red-leather upholstery.

He was rich because he was ruthless; he knew all the right business moves and how to make them. But he was still 'owned' by the Mob. They were the bosses and he was the underling. What they said, he did. So, when he read in the newspaper about the company prospecting for oil on Mountjoy Ranch and that they expected to find a major strike, he realised how rich Rosie was going to be. And then he wondered how he could turn it to his advantage.

He told himself, that, after all, he was still legally married to Rosie. She had never sued for divorce, and he had just kind of let it slide. There was no reason he couldn't get back with her. He knew she'd go for it. She would think he was after her money, but he would bring her here, show her his big house, his fancy lifestyle and tell her, 'Baby, I've got more money than you do, right now. Hell, if I was after your money, I would have *waited* until that oil came in.' He would remind her that there was always a chance Mountjoy Ranch might never gush oil, and that he hadn't waited to find out. 'I'm asking you now, Rosie, to come back to me,' he would say. 'I'm sorry for what happened girl. I've missed you like hell, but I couldn't just come crawling on my hands and knees. A man has his pride, after all. Come home, Rosie, and be the wife of a rich man, then you needn't ever worry in case the oil doesn't come in.'

He knew Rosie was a romantic at heart and she would be overwhelmed by the flowers and the diamond ring and sweet talk he would give her. She would come back to him, and if they never found oil, he would throw her right out again.

'Nothing ventured, nothing gained,' he told himself that night when he telephoned her at the Silver Dollar Saloon.

But Rosie just laughed when he asked her to meet him, and she laughed even harder when he told her why.

'You must think I was born yesterday, Jack,' she told him, still laughing. 'I'm gonna be richer than you ever dreamed of, baby. And you ain't gettin' your hands on a single cent of it.' And she put the phone down on him.

It had taken Jack a while to figure out what to do. He knew Honeychile owned the ranch, and that it hadn't been worth two cents until the oil was mentioned. As Rosie's husband he was legally Honeychile's stepfather. And, with Rosie out of the way, he would *still* be her legal stepfather. Only now, *he* would be in charge.

It was a pity about Rosie, he thought, as he planned what to do, but he had given her her chance and she had turned him down.

He didn't plan on doing the job himself. Not that he was squeamish, and it would not be the first time, but he needed a water-tight alibi. He called a hit-man he knew, made the arrangements, paid his money, and on the planned date, he took a woman to the Warwick Hotel in Houston. They had drinks in the bar, dined in the restaurant, and said goodnight ostentatiously to the concierge, well after midnight, when they took the elevator upstairs to their room. Later that night, Rosie was shot in the alley miles away in San Antonio.

Jack had decided the best plan was simply to go to Mountjoy Ranch and tell them it was his. He hadn't banked on Aliza being so smart, nor Honeychile's hatred. Still, when they told him to get out and set the dog on him, he knew what to do next.

He went to see Andersen, the Mountjoy attorney, and told him he was Rosie's grieving husband. He admitted they had lived apart, but

216

said it was Rosie's choice and that she was an independent lady, and that he had tried many times to get her to return to him.

'Rosie had no need to end up in a cheap rental park,' he said, 'I would have kept her in style. She and Honeychile could have lived with me, in a fine house in Houston.

'I'll be honest with you, Andersen,' he said. 'I always loved that child, I've known her since she was just a kid. Even though she's not my own flesh and blood, it doesn't take away that bond. As a matter of fact, one of the hardest things, when Rosie left, was giving up Honeychile. I just doted on that little girl.'

He threw up his hands resignedly. 'And now, with poor Rosie gone, and the girl still so young and no one to look out for her, I said, Jack, this is your chance to make amends. To Rosie, to Honeychile. And to yourself.'

He looked Andersen straight in the eye and said, man to man, 'Hey, you know what I mean, you probably have kids of your own. When I read about the terrible thing that happened to Rosie, I said to myself, Gosh darn, I'm just gonna have to do something to help that poor motherless child. After all, I am her step-daddy.

'So, Mr Andersen, I would like to give Honeychile the kind of home she never had. See that she gets good schooling, even college if she wants it. Honeychile will have a proper father now. Someone who cares. Someone who will always be there for her.'

Andersen was impressed with the articulate, good-looking, smartly dressed man sitting opposite him. With Rosie dead, he was in a dilemma about Honeychile anyway. She had no other relatives. Jack Delaney was the only one. And the fact was that, legally, he was her stepfather. The proof of it was right here in his hand: Rosie and Jack's marriage certificate.

Still, he hesitated. There might be a lot of money at stake. Who knew if Delaney was not just another confidence trickster out to get his hands on the Mountjoy oil.

Andersen checked on Delaney and found that in fact he did own an expensive house in Houston, as well as several other properties, and that he had thriving automobile dealerships in six counties, and a substantial investment portfolio, picked up cleverly from the leavings of the stock market crash, and already flourishing again. Where Delaney got the money to buy his properties and his dealerships and his investment portfolio seemed shrouded in mystery, but he was a pillar of the Democratic community, and well thought of by the local politicians, where Delaney's generous contributions to their campaign coffers were welcome.

In a couple of days the deed was done: Jack Delaney was appointed Honeychile's legal guardian and trustee of the Mountjoy Ranch and estate, until she turned twenty-one.

Delaney returned triumphantly to Mountjoy Ranch. Only this time he took a couple of heavies with him, and a woman dressed as a nurse, as well as the Court Order stating that Honeychile must go to live with him.

He tried to be nice about it, for appearances' sake, but Honeychile wasn't having any of it.

She stood on the porch, glaring at him, holding the snarling dog back by the collar, flanked by the black woman and her son.

She said, 'I'm warning you now to get off my property before I set the dog on you again.'

'Honeychile, Honeychile,' he said, holding up his hands, pleadingly. 'I'm here to talk to you. To tell you what's happened. I only want to help you, girl. Now, don't set that dog on me, just hear me out, why don't you?'

'Get out,' she said, contemptuously.

Jack sighed, 'Now why d'ya have to go spoilin' things? Your ma always said you went out of your way to be difficult, and I guess she was right. But the fact is, I have a Court Order here, signed by the Judge of San Antonio county, and by your attorney, Andersen, giving me legal custody over you until you reach the age of twenty-one.

'Show her the Court Order, Vinnie,' he said to one of the henchmen.

Vinnie looked warily at the dog. 'Here you are,' he said, walking towards her.

The dog growled but she held onto it. She took the legal paper with the official red seal and read it. Her face turned pale and her voice shook as she thrust it back at him.

'You'll have to kill me to get me out of here,' she said. 'Just like you killed my mother.'

Jack turned to the nurse. 'Y'see what I mean,' he said, pointing a finger to his head and twisting it round. 'The girl's nuts, her brain's been turned by what's happened. She just doesn't know what's right any more.'

Then he said, 'Honeychile, you have your option. You come with me now and we work this out. Or I go to the Sheriff and get him to make you come.' He looked at her. 'What d'ya say? You come willingly, or by force? It's all the same to me.'

Honeychile looked defeatedly at Aliza. She knew he wasn't fooling and she had no choice.

'I'll go,' she said to them. 'But I'll be back soon enough, you'll see. I'll go see Mr Andersen and tell him it's all a mistake. He'll soon cancel that Court Order.'

She handed the dog's lead to Tom and climbed into the back of the Cadillac. The nurse got in one side of her and Vinnie the other. She turned her head away as they drove off and the tears came, leaving stains all over Jack's custom red-leather upholstery and a bitter salt taste in her mouth.

The nurse made no move to comfort her and Jack did not take the road to Houston. Instead, he drove north.

'Where are we going?' she asked, realising. 'I thought you said Houston.'

'Better calm her down, like we planned,' Jack said to the 'nurse'. She had the syringe ready and before Honeychile had time to notice, she pushed it deep into her arm.

It was a long drive, but Honeychile did not know that. And when she finally woke up she was in the Valley View Sanitarium, committed by two doctors whose signatures were on the admittance form, 'Until such time they considered her of sound mind and responsible for her actions.'

The Valley View Sanitarium was a three-storey Gothic mansion embellished with towers and turrets and black-beamed gables, set in the middle of the Texas Hill Country. It had been the country retreat of an eccentric Victorian entrepreneur, and he had built it in an ugly ochre brick that must have cost a fortune to transport out into the wilderness. The old man's dream house now played host to fifty or so patients with varying degrees of mental instability, whose families were willing to pay the price to get their relatives out of their lives.

Narrow gravel paths circled the house, cutting across lawns and past the flower beds to a high perimeter wall, topped with jagged shards of glass. Electric gates were guarded by uniformed men and at night the grounds were patrolled by dogs. It was said that few who entered Valley View ever came out again.

Honeychile awoke to a room full of white light. It was small and brightly lit. It had a brown linoleum floor and stark white walls with a dark green dado. The single window was set high and there were iron bars across it.

She raised her head, gasping as the pain jagged through it. She tried to put up her hands to touch it, but she could not. She tried to sit up, but she could not do that either. Lifting her head, cautiously this time, she saw thick leather straps crossing her chest, pinning her arms to her sides. And there were more straps across her thighs and ankles.

Terrified, she lay back on the thin pillow. She wanted to shout for help, for someone – anyone – to come and help her, to tell her what had happened and where she was. But when she opened her mouth to scream, nothing came out. Trembling with the effort, she tried to remember how she had got here. Her mind was a blank. It was as though she had no past.

She closed her eyes, listening to the oppressive silence, counting off the seconds, the minutes, the half hour. An hour passed and still no one came. She struggled against the leather straps, but she was trussed tight as a dead chicken. She stopped counting and stared at the ceiling, waiting in the terrible silence for what would happen.

The door burst open with a crash and a big, red-headed woman in a white uniform poked her head in. 'So. You're awake at last.' She strode purposefully to the bed and grasped Honeychile's wrist in her massive hand, checking the watch pinned to her chest as she took her pulse. 'Mmmm, racing again,' she said finally. 'I guess we shall just have to give you something to calm you down.'

She strode out of the door and reappeared moments later pushing a white-enamelled trolley containing shiny surgical steel dishes and vials and syringes. Honeychile's eyes widened with horror as she realised the woman intended to give her an injection that would put her to sleep again. She would never find out where she was and why she was here, and when she could leave. *If* they would ever let her go.

Her voice finally pushed its way into her throat. 'No,' she screamed, 'no, no, no. Don't do that, please don't.'

The woman stared at her, the syringe poised in mid-air. 'My, my, I guess that's the temper they warned us about.' She came closer, smiling grimly. 'No wonder they had to put you in here. They said you were violent, and I can see it in your eyes. Such a rage. My, oh my.' And lifting the sheet, she plunged the needle deep into Honeychile's buttock.

Honeychile cried out in pain and fear. 'Tell me where I am,' she whispered, 'please . . .'

The nurse stood with her arms folded, watching her. 'Where are you? Why, you're in the Valley View Private Sanitarium, young lady. And you can thank your lucky stars you have a stepfather who cares enough about you to put you in here. Otherwise you'd be in the state asylum, locked up in a public ward with all the other psychos.'

But Honeychile was already receding down that dark tunnel of emptiness where nothing existed and there was no past and no present and no future. Only blackness.

She did not know if hours or days or weeks had passed when she finally returned to the land of the living. A crack of light came from the slightly open door and in its faint glow, she saw someone sitting next to the bed. A nurse, a younger woman this time. She had fair hair and her skin was so pale she seemed to glimmer in the darkness. And she was sleeping.

Honeychile lay quietly, watching her. She remembered the big nurse vividly and what had happened and she desperately did not want it to happen again. She told herself she must appear calm; she must speak quietly and reasonably. She had to find out why she was in the Sanitarium.

Still strapped to the bed, she lay silently, waiting for the pale nurse to wake.

The night had changed to grey when the nurse finally stretched her arms over her head and sighed deeply. She checked her watch, yawning, and said, 'Lord, is that the time.' Then she glanced at her patient.

Their eyes met and the nurse looked surprised, as Honeychile said quietly, 'I've been waiting for you to wake up.'

She smiled. 'That was mighty considerate of you, young lady. And how are you feeling this morning?'

'Why am I tied down?'

'So you get a good rest, my dear. And so you don't go roaming round the halls, creating havoc.'

'Did I do that?' Honeychile looked astonished.

The nurse laughed. 'Not as far as I know. You've been quiet as a mouse ever since you came in. Round about a week ago.'

'A week? You mean I've been strapped to this bed for a whole week? But why? Why am I here? What did I do?'

The nurse began briskly straightening the sheets. 'That's for Doctor Lester to discuss with you. He'll be doing his early morning rounds soon, so you won't have long to wait. Then we shall see what to do about these straps.'

A minute later the doctor poked his head around the door. He looked enquiringly at the nurse and then at Honeychile. 'How's she doing this morning?' he asked.

'Better, sir. She seems calm.'

He strode into the room and stood looking down at Honeychile. He was a tall man with an untidy mop of grey hair, bushy black eyebrows and an expressionless face. 'Feel like sitting up?' he asked.

Honeychile nodded. The nurse hurried to unfasten the straps and she sighed with relief, stretching her cramped limbs.

'Sorry we had to do that,' Doctor Lester said briskly, 'but at the time it was for your own good.'

'You mean you thought I might run away? Or that I might hurt someone?'

He studied his notes and said, 'We thought you might harm *yourself*. You had gone through a difficult time. Do you remember what happened?'

'My mother was killed. And Jack Delaney did it,' she said, her voice agonised, as she remembered.

The doctor sighed and shook his head. 'Your stepfather was right; you were irrational. And you are still behaving irrationally. He thought, after all you had just gone through, you needed complete peace and quiet. Valley View is just the place for that kind of care, Honeychile.'

'This is a place for crazy people, isn't it?' she cried. 'Jack Delaney told you I was mad and had me locked up in here. Why can't you see the truth? He only married my mother because he thought she

222

was rich. And he only wanted to become my guardian so he could finally get his hands on the oil money. He's a murderer, and now he's got me out of his way, he can do whatever he likes with the Mountjoy Ranch.'

The doctor glanced meaningfully at the nurse and shook his head. He said briskly, 'Nurse Grenowski is going to help you take a bath, then you will have breakfast. After that, maybe you'll take a little walk around the house; sit in the day room with the other patients. It will do you good to have a little company. Perhaps tomorrow you will take a stroll in the gardens. I'm here to help you, Honeychile. All you have to do is trust me.'

Honeychile wanted to scream at him to let her out of here, but she had seen that meaningful look pass between him and the nurse. She knew screaming wouldn't help her. They would just shake their heads again and say, 'See, Delaney was right.' She would need to act as sane and rational as possible, and not fight and cause a scene; or they would sedate her again.

The doctor patted her drooping head as he stood up to leave. 'Just be a good girl, Honeychile, and do as you are told,' he said. 'You'll get to like it here, after a while.'

That afternoon, Nurse Grenowski took her for a walk along the gravel paths that bisected the lawn into neat triangles. Honeychile saw the high walls and the guards with the dogs. Her heart sank. She knew now there was no way out and she burst into tears.

'This is just a hospital, like any other,' Nurse Grenowski said, soothingly. 'Many of our patients are frightened by the outside world. It represents danger to them. The walls and the guards are not so much to keep you in, but to keep that other, frightening world, out.'

It sounded so plausible, Honeychile almost believed her. Except she wasn't frightened of the world, she was frightened of being in here.

She saw the doctor the next day. 'I want to go home,' she said, looking pleadingly at him. 'Please, I'm really not crazy. You must be able to see that.'

He smiled distantly. 'The past few months have been very traumatic for you. You are disturbed. Mr Delaney is very concerned about you. He only wants the best for you. You must stay here until you are better.'

She was trapped. Jack had got her where he wanted her, out of the way, like Rosie. Now he even had control over the ranch. And if the oil ever came through, it would all be his. She guessed Jack was paying off the doctor to keep her there. All hope left her as she realised that he could keep her there for ever.

The days at Valley View were all the same, with the exception of Sundays, when all those who were able, attended morning services in the cold little wooden chapel, built on a grassy knoll several hundred yards from the main building.

Weeks passed. Every morning, Honeychile asked when she could go home. She begged the doctors to let her out, telling them she was not crazy, but they just sighed and gave her another tranquillizer, or a shot that made her woozy and blurred the edges of reality.

Months passed in a blur of routine and apathy. Honeychile became like all the other women; sitting silently in the day room, staring for hours on end at the rain-spattered window, or into the flames of the well-guarded fire. She ceased even to notice the violent patients who were strapped into their chairs; and those who drooled from slack, lolling mouths, laughing wildly at nothing; and others who held long conversations with people only they could see.

She spoke to no one. What was the use, she asked herself in the endless dark nights, locked in her narrow room with the barred window, where she had to stretch on her tip toes just to catch a glimpse of the leafless chestnut tree. Rosie was dead and they had put *her* in prison instead of Jack. She was never going to get out.

It was snowing the day Mr Andersen came to see her, six months later. It was the week before Christmas. Coloured paper chains made by the listless patients, most of whom could not remember what Christmas meant, were strung around the walls, and a tall blue spruce stood in the hallway, its lovely spicy-sweet scent overlaying the hospital smell of disinfectant.

Honeychile was sitting by herself in the window-seat of the day room. An unopened book lay in her lap. She had taken it from the shelf weeks ago and had yet to read a single word. Books had once transported her to other worlds; now she knew they could not. She was separated from reality, and also from her dreams.

224

It was bitterly cold and the ancient steam-heating clanked and roared, sending gusts of hot air swirling round, leaving icy stretches in-between. Huddled in a baggy grey sweater, Honeychile watched her breath forming patterns on the icy window-pane. Tentatively, she put out a finger and wrote a name on it. *Fisher*. She thought about her dog and the tug of pain at her heart reminded her she was still alive.

'Honeychile, you have a visitor,' the nurse said to her. 'Come along girl, hurry up. We don't want to keep him waiting, do we?'

Honeychile's heart did a double flip of fear. She knew it must be Jack. She stared frozen with terror at the nurse.

'Mr Andersen has driven all the way from San Antonio to see you,' the nurse said. 'He's waiting in the office. Come on, Honeychile. Whatever is the matter with you?'

Hope sent her pulse racing, then she remembered that Andersen had signed the Court Order giving her to Jack. He was not coming here to help her.

Andersen turned from the window as he heard them enter. He stared at her, taking in her emaciated looks, her sunken eyes, her apathy.

'Dear God, Honeychile, whatever have they done to you?' He swallowed hard to keep the tremor of shock from his voice. 'Come here, child. Sit down, why don't you.' He did not add that he was afraid her scrawny legs might buckle under her at any second.

Andersen took a seat opposite her. He cleared his throat nervously. He said, 'I am here to apologise to you. I made a very grave error of judgement. I was wrong to place you in Jack Delaney's care.'

Honeychile looked warily at him, but she said nothing.

'Delaney is the subject of an FBI investigation into organised crime,' Andersen said. He coughed and mopped his brow, avoiding her eyes. 'Not that I expect you to know about things like that, Honeychile. The first I knew about it was when the FBI contacted me, asking about the Mountjoy Ranch and the oil.'

He cleared his throat, nervously, again and said, 'Unfortunately there is no oil. The company sank a dozen wells and came up with nothing. They have decided to abandon the field. I'm sorry, Honeychile. But at least there are a couple of thousand in the bank, so you are better off than if they didn't drill.'

He leaned forward, his hands on his knees, looking sorrowfully at her. 'I'm just so sick about what Delaney did to you, putting you away in this Sanitarium. I came up here right away, as soon as I heard about it. I've come to take you out of here, my dear.'

He patted her hand, anxiously. 'Obviously, Delaney is no longer your guardian. And no longer in charge of the Mountjoy Trust. It all reverts to you, and I am at your service to help you administrate it.'

Honeychile looked round the colourless, institutional room with the barred windows and the view of the high wall with its lethal glass shards. She did not care any more about Jack Delaney or Dr Lester or the Mountjoy Trust and the oil money. She was getting out of here. She was going home to Mountjoy Ranch, at last.

Sometimes the dream ended there, but on the good nights, she lived again the relief of her homecoming; of being wrapped in Aliza's arms; of seeing the clear blue sky above her, and knowing she was free. It was something she would never forget.

When she awoke the next morning at Mountjoy House, still with the image of the Sanitarium imprinted on her mind, she glanced round her sumptuous room, at the tall silk-framed windows, and at Ellen, the maid, carrying in her breakfast tray, and for a moment, she was not sure which was the dream. And then she heard Laura's voice in the hall, and Aunt Sophie complaining they were going to be late, and she remembered that Jack Delaney belonged to the past. And this was her real life now.

CHAPTER 25

Looking quite handsome and distinguished in white tie and tails, Lord Mountjoy descended the stairs of Mountjoy House at exactly six p.m. on the evening of the ball. He stood in the grand hall, glancing approvingly round at the elaborate flower arrangements and the burgundy carpet that rolled all the way out of the door, down the steps to the courtyard. He had a word with Swayne, standing in the hall looking like a waiter in his rented black tie and tails and, thank heavens, without those ghastly creaking boots. Mountjoy knew he could trust him to keep an eye on security; the man had eyes like a hawk, he didn't miss a thing.

He went outside and inspected the weather: it was a bit overcast but warm and pleasant, and with a bit of luck there would be no rain. He went back inside and poked his head into the dining room where the enormous table was set for the sixty dinner guests.

'My goodness,' he exclaimed, eyeing the display of silver and vermeil, the magnificent Spode dinner-ware; the heavy, cut-crystal glasses glittering under the chandeliers, and the gold epergnes, tumbling with frosted bunches of grapes and rose-gold peaches and walnuts; and the dozen heirloom silver candelabra, waiting to be lit. Ivy trailed the length of the stiff white damask linen cloth, scattered with white camellias; and white roses and lilies with glossy green leaves were arranged in a dozen silver bowls down the centre.

He inspected the dozens of footmen in the maroon and gold Mountjoy livery and white gloves, and, for this special occasion, powdered wigs. He discussed the wines with Johnson, checked the labels and asked anxiously if he was sure the champagne was cold enough.

Then he walked through the house to the ballroom where Ambrose and his band were already setting up their instruments. He said good evening and that he had heard they were the best, and that he didn't expect them to let him down tonight.

Swags of greenery were draped everywhere and dozens of little gold tables and chairs were scattered round the edge of the floor. The walls were lined with hundreds of little gardenia trees clipped into a circular shape and all in full bloom. Their delicious scent was overpowering and brought back nostalgic memories of the parties he had attended in his youth.

He looked into the small drawing room where the famous photographer, young Cecil Beaton, was preparing to take pictures of the Mountjoy girls in all their finery, and found it transformed. Bolts of heavy white satin were draped over screens and Beaton was busy arranging a silk *chaise-longue* and a couple of little rose-coloured chairs in front of them. Mountjoy looked uncertainly at him, and said that he hadn't known that taking a girl's picture involved such a lot of fuss, and then he wandered back through the house to the safety of his library.

He looked at the gilt cherub clock on the mantel. Six forty-five. He had told the girls to be here at seven on the dot. First they had to be photographed, then the guests were expected at eight for dinner, and the ball would begin at ten.

'William, are you there?' Aunt Sophie swept through the door, looking like Queen Mary with her high-piled Edwardian hairdo, a choker of pearls and diamonds, and an old-fashioned dress of coffee-coloured lace over cream satin with a little train that swished round her heels as she walked. 'Ah,' she said, spotting him. 'You'll be glad to know all the arrangements are in place. I checked, just to make sure. But who on earth is that peculiar man in the hallway? He looks like a policeman.'

'Ex-policeman,' Mountjoy said. 'He's the one who found the girls for me. I put him in charge of security.'

'Security?' she looked astonished. 'I hardly think any of our guests are going to steal the silver, William.' She glanced at the old-fashioned diamond watch pinned to her lace bosom. 'The girls should be down any minute,' she said.

He looked apprehensively at her, hoping it was going to be all right. There was a tap at the door. Clearing his throat nervously, he called, 'Enter.'

Anjou was first, of course. She paused theatrically in the doorway, then she glided elegantly towards them. She stopped in front of Lord Mountjoy, smiling into his eyes, giving him time to admire her.

Her dress was of the palest lily-of-the-valley leaf-green satin, with tiny straps that left her shoulders almost bare; it was draped smoothly over the bosom and flared from her tiny waist in heavy folds. Her beautiful red hair was swept up at the sides and hung in fat curls down her back. She looked, Mountjoy thought, with a pang of nostalgia, like the Winterhalter portrait of her ancestress, the Countess Caroline, hanging in the hall at Mountjoy Park.

Laura was right behind her. She smiled at her uncle and at Lady Sophie as she walked towards them. Her burnished brown hair shone like silk, curling under like a pageboy's. Her white dress had a silk bodice held up by narrow straps, and the flouncy tulle skirt was embroidered with pearl and crystal beads; and she reminded Mountjoy of the wedding pictures of his own great-grandmother.

Honeychile was last. She walked towards them with that long-legged stride that used to be so clumsy, only now, somehow, it looked elegant. Her corn-gold hair had been cut to shoulder-length and it curled softly round her face. Her dress was pale butter-yellow taffeta that rustled richly as she walked; cut tight to the waist with a wide fichu neckline that framed her shoulders, and a flowing skirt, puffed out with taffeta petticoats, that rustled enticingly beneath.

Looking at her, Lord Mountjoy thought of all of them, she was a true Mountjoy. She had the arrogant nose and the brilliantly blue eyes, though hers were surely the bluest he had ever seen. And somehow, dammit, she had the character.

They stood in front of him and then quite suddenly, with a rustle of silk skirts, they swept down in a deep curtsy.

Mountjoy stared at them and a lump came into his throat. 'Beautiful,' he muttered, and again, 'quite beautiful,' as they rose gracefully to their feet. He thought of the first day he had seen them and saw how they were transformed: their complexions were porcelain under a light touch of powder; their hair immaculate and their dresses perfect. The Mountjoy girls were tall, graceful, and lovely. At last, they looked the part.

'Well done, Sophie,' he murmured, 'jolly well done.'

He opened the long blue suede box waiting on the library table and took out a fabulous string of perfectly-matched South Sea pearls, the size of marbles. He looked, consideringly, at his girls. 'For you, I think, my dear,' he said, clasping them round Honeychile's slender neck.

'Are they real?' she gasped, awed.

'Dammit girl, of course they are real,' he snapped back, indignantly. 'I've never given a woman a jewel in my life that was not genuine.'

Next he took out a necklace of emeralds, set in diamonds. It gleamed and glittered in the light and Anjou held her breath longingly, as he looked first at her and then at Laura, undecided.

'For you, my dear,' he said finally with a smile, and Anjou breathed a sigh of satisfaction as the emeralds were clasped round her neck.

'And for Laura,' he took out the final treasure. A necklace of pink Burmese rubies, centred with a single enormous pendant, surrounded by diamonds. He fastened it for her, and she put her hand up to touch it, smiling nervously at him. 'It's beautiful,' she said.

Mountjoy regarded the three of them: they were flushed with excitement and breathless with nerves. He was suddenly overwhelmed by their new young beauty and innocence, and by a feeling, rare to him, that he thought, surprisingly, might be called 'love'. These were the last of the Mountjoys, his own flesh and blood. They were, after all, the Mountjoy girls. He stiffened his upper lip, blinking back the threatened emotion.

'They were my mother's jewels,' he said gruffly, 'your great-grandmother. I think she would have liked you to have them. Tonight you are a credit to her.'

Three pairs of scared eyes smiled back at him; they were drooping with nerves now and he could detect a glint of panic in their eyes.

'Attention,' he barked, and they straightened up quickly. He marched up and down, hands behind his back, thumbs twiddling.

'As an old soldier, this is how I prepared myself for battle,' he said. 'First a shot of whisky, then a prayer. Then it was up and out of the trenches and into battle. May I suggest you do the same thing. Only in your case we shall substitute a sip of champagne for the whisky. And always remember,' his eyes drilled into them, 'you are *Mountjoys*.'

He poured the waiting champagne and said, 'First we shall drink to Aunt Sophie, without whom none of this would be possible.'

'To dear Aunt Sophie,' they said, raising their glasses, and then impulsively Laura ran over and kissed her, and the others followed suit.

'And I wish to propose a toast to Uncle Mountjoy,' Laura said, smiling at him, 'for being the nicest, dearest uncle any girl ever had.'

And, to his embarrassment, they all came over and kissed his cheek too. He was really quite relieved when Johnson said, 'Excuse me, sir, but Mr Beaton is waiting to photograph the young ladies,' and Aunt Sophie whisked them off to the small drawing room.

He smiled at Johnson, 'Like old times tonight, isn't it, Johnson,' he said.

'Indeed, it is, sir. Mountjoy House looks just the way it did in your father's day.'

'Yes, it's been a long time,' Mountjoy said, pleased. 'A long time. But I think we are back on course again now, Johnson.' And he sipped his usual evening glass of malt whisky, which he preferred to champagne, glancing every now and then at the clock, waiting impatiently for his guests to arrive.

At ten minutes to eight, he was standing by the front door, peering anxiously into the courtyard. Footmen in their powdered wigs and Mountjoy livery lined the steps and Jerome Swayne was watching the scene carefully, from a position in the shadows.

'Dammit, I hope they are not going to be late,' Mountjoy muttered. 'The invitation said eight o'clock.' He walked back inside just as Aunt Sophie appeared with his girls. 'There you are,' he said, relieved. 'I hoped you weren't going to be late as well as the guests. I should have felt foolish, standing here receiving them alone.'

'Oh don't fuss, William,' Aunt Sophie said crisply, arranging his girls in a line next to their uncle, then taking up her position next to him. 'Now remember,' she said to them, 'first you smile, then you shake hands and repeat the person's name. "Good evening, Lady so and so, I'm so glad you could come." Remember?'

'Yes, Aunt Sophie,' they chorused.

Anjou's eyes met Laura's, and she winked, and Laura had to suppress an urge to laugh. She pictured herself mucking out stables at Foxton Yard while Haddon strode round in his perfect tweeds, criticising; and she thought of her simple life at Swinburn, and it all seemed so far away. She wished her grandmother could be there, but Jeannie had refused the invitation; she said it was very kind of Lord Mountjoy to invite her, but at her age she felt the need to go to bed early, and besides, she was sure Laura would enjoy herself more without having to look after her grandmother. It wasn't true, Laura had told her, but Jeannie had said this was an event for the young; it was Laura's night and she would be thinking about her, and that was that.

Madame Suzette had, of course been invited too, but to her chagrin, she had slipped on some wet leaves in the rain on the Champs Elysees and broken her leg, just the week before, so she was unable to travel. And a good thing, too, Anjou thought, feeling the excitement rising in her veins, sending her blood coursing and her heart pounding. She didn't need her mother's eagle eye on her; it was bad enough with Aunt Sophie. Tonight was the beginning of a whole new life and she meant to have fun. At last.

Honeychile smoothed the folds of her beautiful yellow taffeta dress, wondering what Aliza would say if she could see her now. Would she finally think she had 'grown into her looks'? Would she think that now she looked like her father and had that mysterious quality she said he possessed? She thought her father would have been proud of her tonight; finally, she was a Mountjoy.

Standing in his corner by the door, Swayne looked admiringly at Georgie Mountjoy's granddaughters, thinking of the search that had led him through Europe and America. He thought that if Georgie were here now, he would be proud of them; he could see Lord Mountjoy certainly was, though he'd bet the old boy would never admit it. There was the sound of a car arriving in the courtyard and he squared his shoulders, placing his hands behind his back, standing in the 'at ease' position of a soldier or a policeman, mindful of his important position as chief security officer. As the first bejewelled and lavishly-gowned guests walked up the steps and were announced by Johnson, he thought it was a pity his wife couldn't be here tonight, to see all this. And the spaniel too, though for once, he had thought it better to leave him at home.

Lord Mountjoy introduced his great-nieces to his guests as they arrived. They shook hands and smiled and, as he said afterwards to Aunt Sophie, did beautifully. 'Never know they weren't to the manner born,' he said. 'It has to be in the blood, you see, Sophie, it's in the Mountjoy genes.'

Laura shook hands enthusiastically, repeating the names, just as Aunt Sophie had told her. 'Good evening, Lady Harcroft, so glad you could come. Lord Harcroft,' she smiled. 'Good evening, Mrs Winter, Mr Winter. I'm so glad you could come. Good evening, Mr Saxton, I'm so glad . . . Good Lord,' she said, opening her eyes wide in surprise, 'it's Billy.'

He grinned at her, 'How are you, L-l-l-laura?'

'Saxton,' she gasped, and her eyes opened even wider, 'you mean you are the racehorse owner?'

He shook her hand, 'The very same,' he said modestly. 'May I ask you for a dance later?'

'I should like that.' She let go of his hand reluctantly, smiling as she watched him walk away. 'Imagine seeing him again,' she thought, pleased.

Anjou was already bored with shaking hands; she noticed Laura had met someone she knew. 'Who was that?' she whispered, smiling at the next guest.

'Oh, just a friend,' Laura whispered back.

Anjou glared jealously at her, wondering who Billy Saxton was. She knew his name from somewhere, she was sure. 'Good evening, Lady Devlin, Lord Devlin,' she said, but she was already eyeing the couple next in line behind them.

Now there was an attractive man, she thought, with a familiar little flutter of excitement. *And* she knew who he was. Throwing Honeychile a glance from the corner of her eye, she saw she had not noticed. She held out her hand and said, 'Good evening, *Signorina* Matteo, Good evening Mr Scott.' She gave him a deep look, holding his hand for a second too long. 'I'm really so very glad you could come,' she murmured directly to him.

If Alex Scott noticed her interest, he did not show it. He had eyes only for Honeychile, standing at the end of the line. He remembered the frightened girl almost in tears, standing at the head of the staircase on the liner, and he thought Honeychile Mountjoy had come a long way. He saw how elegant and graceful and charming she was, greeting everyone with a genuinely warm smile, shaking their hands firmly, curtsying to the Princess Matilda. He felt a little thrill of pride for her, a warm feeling in his heart; and he thought that without doubt she would be the loveliest girl there tonight.

'Good evening *Signorina* Matteo, how very nice of you to come,' Honeychile smiled at her. 'Good evening . . .' her eyes met Alex's and she stopped in mid-sentence. She closed her eyes and then opened them again, as if not believing what she saw. 'Oh, Alex,' she said in a soft little voice that caught at his heart.

'How are you, Honeychile?' He took her outstretched hand in his.

'I'm just so glad to see you,' she blurted, then she blushed, she could never keep her feelings secret.

'And I am glad to see you looking so . . . so well,' he finished, aware of the couple behind him, waiting to be introduced to her.

'Shall I see you later?' she asked, hopefully.

'Of course.'

She watched as he took the Italian woman's arm, noticing that she was pretty. Jealousy flickered in her eyes and she forced herself back to her job, shaking hands and greeting people. But her heart was soaring; Alex was here and she would see him later.

The guests were in the large drawing room drinking the champagne cocktails Aunt Sophie had insisted on serving, over Lord Mountjoy's protests. 'You simply have to move with the times, William,' she had said grandly. 'I have drunk them at the Savoy and jolly nice they are too. Besides, this is a young people's party, not for old fogies like us.'

The last guest arrived and Mountjoy checked his watch. It was eight twenty-seven. He glanced at Johnson, waiting in the hallway. 'Are we ready, Johnson?' he demanded worriedly.

'As you instructed, sir, dinner will be announced precisely at eight-thirty.'

'Good, good. Now, Sophie, you organise the girls, make sure they are sitting with someone amusing. I don't want them to be bored at their own party.'

Aunt Sophie sighed. 'Do stop fussing, it's all arranged.'

Johnson walked to the door of the drawing room. 'Ladies and gentlemen, dinner is served,' he announced grandly.

The cavernous dining room had become intimate with candlelight. Laura caught her breath, admiring the magnificent table setting, and the flowers and the footmen standing behind each chair. 'I've never seen anything like this,' she whispered to Honeychile.

'I have,' Honeychile whispered back, 'in the movies, sitting in the front row of the Kitsville Roxy,' and she laughed.

'Oh, my goodness,' Laura said, stopping at her place and finding Billy Saxton standing next to her. 'Are you my dinner partner?'

'It certainly looks like it,' he replied, and they grinned at each other, pleased.

Anjou drifted elegantly along the table; she knew she was sitting near the top, but she didn't know who her dinner partners would be; Aunt Sophie had refused to tell her. She sighed deeply, seeing that the man on her right was the French Ambassador, who was seventy if he was a day, but the man on her left was an unknown. She glanced at his name on the place card: Lord James Mattrington. She saw him, walking towards her, and she smiled; he was young, and good-looking and he had an appreciative glint in his eye. She thought, relieved, that Aunt Sophie hadn't let her down after all.

Honeychile scanned the table hopefully, searching for Alex. Her heart sank as she noticed him on the opposite side of the table and a couple of places down; she had so hoped he would be sitting next to her for dinner. She thought despondently, he was so busy speaking, in Italian, to the lovely *Signorina* Matteo, he didn't have eyes for her anyway. She looked at the names of her dinner partners: a Mr Michael Davenport and Sir Charles Woodman. She remembered her manners and smiled as they took their places. They were young and attractive, and very interested in her.

'I have to tell you, Miss Mountjoy, that all London has been talking about the three Mountjoy girls,' Michael Davenport said, smiling at her as the footman served the first course. 'You were London's biggest secret.'

Honeychile laughed at the idea that anyone might be curious about her. 'Well, here's the answer to your secret,' she said. 'And please, why don't you call me Eloise.'

He grinned and said, 'But I heard your name was Honeychile. Everybody knows it already. Why can't I call you that?'

'My father always did, so why not?' she agreed.

'I don't think anyone expected Lord Mountjoy to be presenting quite such a dazzling array of grand-nieces,' Sir Charles said.

Honeychile blushed, but she replied the way Aunt Sophie had told her she should when she received a compliment. 'Thank you,' she said, with a polite smile.

She could see Alex, talking to the woman on his left and she thought how distinguished he looked, and how handsome. He glanced up and caught her eye; he smiled encouragingly at her, and she smiled back, wishing she were sitting next to him.

The French Ambassador's wife was a customer at Madame Suzette's, and Anjou already had him enchanted: and she had James Mattrington intrigued. 'Who are you?' he asked, amazed. 'Where did you come from? Lord Mountjoy has sprung you on waiting London like rabbits from a hat. Only he never warned us you were beautiful.'

She gave him that knowing glance from beneath her lashes. 'Shouldn't we be talking about the weather? Or the theatre, or the opera? Aunt Sophie told me that was what the English talked about at dinner.'

He laughed, 'Touché, mademoiselle, but it is permitted for a man to pay a girl a compliment.'

'Then I accept your compliment, monsieur,' she said gravely, but she smiled promisingly at him.

Laura threw a grateful glance at Aunt Sophie, sitting at the foot of the table; she had known how much she loved horses and racing, and she had given her Billy Saxton as a dinner partner. 'Of course, she didn't know we had already met,' she told him, smiling eagerly. 'And anyhow, I do think you are a bit of a fraud, letting me go on like that about how good I was with horses and about Haddon Fox.'

He laughed, 'Don't you wish Haddon could see you now? Gorgeous and glamorous. And lovelier than the famous fiancée, I'll bet.'

She sighed, and said thoughtfully, 'You know, I don't. Besides, I'm awfully glad he's not here, because I would rather be sitting next to you.'

Their eyes met. 'M-m-my w-w-word,' he said, impressed. 'I can see you're a girl who says what she means.'

'Always,' she replied firmly.

'I'll let you in on a secret,' he said, bending closer to her, 'I got myself invited tonight, specially to see you.'

She looked at him, delighted. 'You did?'

236

'I dropped in on the old boy when he was at Mountjoy Park, soon after I'd met you. I said I'd heard he was throwing a big party and I hoped I was invited. I knew, since we were neighbours and I was quite respectable, that good manners would prevail and Mountjoy would not be able to say no.'

'And I suppose when Aunt Sophie saw your name on the list, she thought, "Ah, I'll put him next to Laura at dinner. They can talk about horses all night."'

She laughed and he thought how very pretty she was. 'Lucky me,' he said.

Lord Mountjoy had a Princess on his right, and a Duchess on his left, but he wasn't paying them as much attention as he should. He was too busy keeping a worried eye on his girls. 'They seem to be doing all right, don't you think, Caroline?' he asked the Duchess.

'My dear William, they are delightful,' she said, looking at them. 'Each one a beauty. However did you do it?'

'Thank Sophie,' he said, thinking of how they looked when he first saw them. 'She waved her magic wand and somehow, there they were.'

'Mountjoy, this food is excellent,' the plump Princess said. 'You'll have to watch out someone doesn't steal your chef.'

'If that means you, Matilda, then I warn you now, I shall fight tooth and claw to keep him.' He grinned at her, enjoying himself; they had known each other for more than fifty years and were old friends. 'What do you think of my girls?' he asked, proudly.

She glanced up from her plate of diced quail in a raisin sauce, and looked carefully at them. 'The brown-haired one will marry Billy Saxton,' she predicted. 'The blonde will cause a scandal, and the red-head will give you trouble.'

Mountjoy stared at her, impressed and a little concerned. The Princess was known for her prognostications. And she was always right.

237

CHAPTER 26

When the footmen began to remove the last plates, Lord Mountjoy checked his watch, rang the little silver bell, and got to his feet.

'Ladies and gentlemen, my old friends and some new ones,' he said, glancing down the table, smiling. 'I have asked you here tonight because I have the honour to present to you my great-nieces, gathered here after a great search – and at no little expense I might add,' he said as an after-thought and everybody laughed. 'After a great search, perhaps not quite to the four corners of the globe, but certainly far enough. Anyhow, here they are, and I ask you to raise your glasses in a toast. To Anjou,' he lifted his glass and bowed to her; 'to Laura,' he bowed again; 'and to Honeychile, who I now know no one will ever call by her proper name of Eloise.'

Everybody laughed again as they raised their glasses. 'And now,' he cried in ringing tones, because he was quite enjoying himself, 'let the dancing begin.'

Billy grabbed Laura's hand as they spilled out into the hall. 'Give me your dance card,' he said. She handed it to him gladly, and he scrawled his name across most of the dances. 'Have to leave a few for the other fellows,' he said regretfully.

The sound of music came from the ballroom and the great hall was already filling with people arriving for the dance. Laura hurried to join her uncle and Aunt Sophie and the other two girls, in the receiving line. 'Another two hundred and fifty people, oh Lord,' she groaned. But Anjou's eyes were sparkling; she liked nothing better than a party and this promised to be a good one. Honeychile looked wistfully after Alex, disappearing into the ballroom with the Italian Ambassador's daughter; she hoped he would ask her to dance.

Swayne patrolled the courtyard, keeping an eye on the waiting chauffeurs; in his experience chauffeurs were not to be trusted. They had access to the house through the kitchen, and it was an easy thing for them to slip away and pick up a nice bit of silver without anyone so much as noticing. And then there were all the extra staff, hired for the night: the footmen, looking like the Queen's guards in their powdered wigs that shed kitchen flour all over the place, because that was what they used to get them so white. Any one of them could be a villain: nobody really knew where they had all come from, except, perhaps, the employment agency. Then, of course, there were the guests; it was not unknown for society folk to be a little light-fingered when temptation, or lack of money, overtook them.

Yes, he certainly had his job cut out for him tonight. And he was not going to let Lord Mountjoy down.

When enough hands had been shaken, Aunt Sophie reprieved the girls. 'Go get your dance cards filled up,' she commanded. 'Enjoy yourselves my dears.' She smiled fondly as they hurried eagerly away. 'How lovely they look, Mountjoy,' she said with a pleased sigh. 'And how young and innocent.'

Honeychile stood on the edge of the dance floor looking for Alex; she noticed a purposeful young man approaching and smiled politely as he filled in her card for a waltz; then, avoiding the other eager would-be partners, she worked her way through the crowd to Alex. She stopped, shocked, when she saw Anjou with him. He was writing his name on her card and she was giving him that secret little smile that she always gave to attractive men, whether they were waiters or dress designers or Lords of the Realm. Alex returned Anjou's card, smiled politely and turned away.

He saw her looking at him and their eyes locked. 'Honeychile,' he said, and she could have sworn the crowded room emptied of all its party people and they were alone, because that's how intimate his voice made her name sound. He took her hands in his and kissed her lightly on the cheek. Still holding onto her hands, he stepped back and looked at her. He shook his head, marvelling at how lovely she was. 'You are truly beautiful,' he said softly.

'Whoever would have thought it?' she asked, remembering herself on the ship when they met.

'I knew when I saw you, you were different. And now look at you.' He smiled, 'I was right.'

She blushed, then remembering Aunt Sophie's etiquette lessons, said, 'Thank you.'

'How many dances can you promise me?' he asked lightly.

She held out her card, 'All of them,' she said simply, looking at him with her heart in her eyes.

Alex Scott was not usually at a loss for words, especially with a woman, but he was now. He saw what her eyes were telling him and he knew that at that moment he had a choice. He could allow himself to fall in love with her; or he could step away, as he should do, and let her get on with her life. She was too young, too unworldly for a man like himself. And yet she lured him far more than any of the sensual, sophisticated sirens he usually spent time with. But then, he never gave any of them his heart.

'Perhaps two?' he suggested, remembering his companion, Gina Matteo, whom he had escorted to the ball.

'The supper dance?' she asked eagerly, knowing that it would mean she could keep him with her for the longest time, and it would give them a chance to be alone together.

He hesitated, thinking of Gina; but she was an old friend, she would understand. He quickly wrote his name and handed her back the card. 'I shall look forward to our dances, Honeychile,' he said, stepping back to allow the other, younger, men to claim her.

As he walked away, he wondered why he had done it. The answer was very simple, he couldn't help himself. He told himself she was too young, too naïve, too good for him; but it didn't stop him wanting her. There was something about the way she looked at him, so trustingly with those fathomless blue eyes. Eyes like that could lure a man, entice him with their innocence, enrapture him. If he were not careful.

Lord Mountjoy surveyed the dancers; he knew he should be doing his duty and dancing with the Princess, but she had unnerved him with her silly predictions for the future. He glanced keenly around the dance floor, searching for his girls: he spotted Laura at once, whirling by in the arms of Billy Saxton. Just as she had been ten minutes ago, he realised suddenly. Good Lord, was the girl going to dance with no one else? He must find Sophie and have a word.

There was Honeychile, dancing with young Michael Davenport, and very charming she looked too. He nodded, satisfied; Honeychile caught his eyes on her and she smiled and waved. Dammit, he thought, if she didn't look exactly like her grandfather Georgie when she smiled like that.

He searched the floor anxiously, for Anjou, then at last he saw her. He wondered who on earth she was dancing with? Good Lord, could it be that bounder, Harry Lockwood? He certainly didn't remember inviting him, and nor would Sophie. If she had anything to do with it, a chap like Lockwood wouldn't get within a hundred yards of her girls. Frowning, he made his way over to where Sophie was sitting at one of the little tables, talking with the other dowagers.

Anjou gazed into Harry's eyes, not because she fancied him particularly, but just for practice. It had been a long time since she had felt a man's arms round her, and somehow Harry's felt good.

'I didn't expect to see you here,' she said, insinuating herself just a little closer.

He moved his white-gloved hand further across her back, holding her tighter. 'I don't usually attend débutante balls,' he confessed. 'It's not my style. But tonight, Camilla Staunton was left in the lurch by her husband. He's an army man and he was called away suddenly to supervise a Royal inspection of something or other, and she asked me to deputise.' He grinned, 'I doubt that Lord Mountjoy would have thought of inviting me personally.'

'And why not?' She looked enquiringly at him and he laughed.

'Because, my dear Anjou, I am not the sort of man fathers and great-uncles allow near their daughters.'

'Oh? And why is that?' she asked, so innocently that they both laughed.

'I have a feeling you know the answer to that one,' he said, holding her so close her breasts pressed against him. 'And I also have the feeling,' he whispered, 'that you and I are two of a kind.'

She pushed him away suddenly. 'Perhaps,' she replied coolly. 'And there again, Harry, perhaps not.'

The music finished and she turned her back on him and walked away. He smiled regretfully, but he had that feeling that things were not over between him and Anjou. In fact, they hadn't even begun.

He strode through the crowd to Honeychile. 'Miss Mountjoy, our dance, I believe?' he said, holding his hand out to her.

She glanced up at him. 'Oh, please, call me Honeychile,' she said with a polite little smile. 'Everybody does.'

242

'Honeychile it is, then.' He led her onto the floor and put his arms round her, holding her at a respectable distance. 'Are you enjoying your ball, Honeychile?' he asked, amused by her shyness.

'It's wonderful. I've never seen anything like this; the beautiful dinner with the table looking so magnificent, the music, the gardenia trees.' She gave him a radiant smile that took him by surprise; he thought she really was quite lovely. But she was not his style; she was too naïve, too straightforward. There were no underlying sexual nuances with her, the way there were with her cousin. Honeychile Mountjoy was just too good and virginal for a man of his tastes. Nevertheless, he put himself out to be charming to her, the way he did with every woman, and at the end of their dance he left her smiling and thinking what a nice man he was. So gentle and polite, so kind really.

Anjou found Alex standing alone, watching the dancers. There was a brooding expression on his face, and she thought he looked like a man with dark secrets. There was something definitely intriguing about a man like that. She went over to him and tapped him on the shoulder. 'Mr Scott?'

He swung round, startled. He had been lost in his thoughts. 'Miss Mountjoy.'

'Isn't this our dance?' She held out her card for him to inspect.

'I believe it's the next one,' he said, looking at it.

She heaved a resigned little sigh, 'Oh, then I must wait.' She gave him that special intimate smile and said, 'But, since you are not dancing, and I seem to have lost my partner, then why do we not dance this one together anyway?'

He laughed as he took her hand and led her onto the floor. He put his arm round her and Anjou caught her breath as a little frisson of excitement ran down her spine. She thought he was the only man there tonight she really wanted; he was older, he was rich, he was mysterious, and he was sexy. As he held her in his arms and they danced to the slow, 'Begin the Beguine', she asked herself, what more could any girl ask for?

Laura said to Billy, 'Don't you think I should make an effort and dance with somebody else?'

'Certainly, of course you should,' he said, holding her tighter, and she laughed.

'People will talk,' she protested, weakly.

'They will only be talking about how I asked you to m-m-m-marry me.'

She stumbled and he caught her expertly. 'What did you say?' she asked, astonished.

'I just said that one day, I shall ask you to marry me.'

'Oh,' Laura said, thinking about it. 'And I suppose you know what my answer will be?'

He shook his head and said, 'No, but you can't blame a man for hoping.'

'Is this love at first sight, then?'

'Second. The first time your eyes were all red and your nose was running. Let's face it, you hardly looked your best. Still, it was good enough to intrigue me. I haven't been able to get you out of my mind since.'

'Oh, Billy,' she said, feeling suddenly weak at the knees because she thought she was falling in love too, and she liked him so much it made her glad.

Sitting with Aunt Sophie, Lord Mountjoy waved to Laura and she waved happily back, blowing him a kiss.

'Little minx,' he said, watching her fondly. He said to Sophie, 'Princess Matilda told me she's going to marry Billy Saxton.'

Aunt Sophie looked at the pair, gliding slowly round the ballroom floor, gazing into each other's eyes. 'I don't know where Matilda gets her information from, unless it's directly from God,' she said tartly. 'But this time I shouldn't be in the least surprised if she's right.'

Mountjoy thought that he had better not tell her what the Princess had said about the other two; instead he said, 'What's that bounder Lockwood doing in my house? Did you invite him, Sophie?'

'No, I did not. Camilla Staunton had the nerve to bring him because her husband had to drop out at the last minute. I don't know why she bothered, it's not as though they were invited to dine and then the numbers would have been wrong. I have a feeling she's no better than she ought to be, anyhow.'

'Is that so?' Lord Mountjoy thought, astonished, how little he knew about the women of his acquaintance. 'And what about that fellow, Scott?' he asked.

'Well of course I invited him. He's one of the richest men in the world, and it's quite a coup to have him attend. He's not very social, you know, and any London hostess would die to get him to their dinner table. He's Italian, and that's why he brought the Ambassador's girl; apparently they are old friends.'

'He's too old for her,' Mountjoy said, looking at them.

'He's not marrying the girl, William, he's simply dancing with her,' Sophie said, exasperated. She got to her feet, sweeping her little satin train gracefully to one side and said, 'This next one is the supper dance. I'd better talk to Johnson and make sure everything is ready.'

Alex released his partner, Gina Matteo. He said, 'You're sure you don't mind? About the supper dance?'

She shook her head. 'I have plans of my own, dear Alex. You don't imagine you were the real reason I came to the ball with you, do you?' And laughing, she hurried away.

He looked around the room for Honeychile and caught a glimpse of her yellow dress near the door. The music had already started as he pushed his way through the crowd towards her. She was looking anxiously round, then her eye caught his and she heaved a sigh of relief.

'I thought you had forgotten me,' she said, walking into his arms as though she belonged there.

'Of course not,' he said politely, but what he meant was he would never forget her.

The band was playing a favourite song of the moment, 'A Nightingale Sang in Berkeley Square'. He thought she was as light as a feather, as she danced with him. 'I feel this song was meant for me,' he said, 'as a resident of Berkeley Square. Though I've yet to hear the nightingale.'

'You live there?' she asked, surprised, because it was in Mayfair and not too far from Mountjoy House. She thought she must have walked past it a dozen times and not known.

'Amongst other places; Rome, Manhattan. And on the *Atalanta* whenever I get the chance.'

'I remember,' she said, because he had told her on the liner how much he loved his yacht.

'I shall miss you, when you go away on your yacht,' she said. 'Or to those other places.'

'How can you miss me?' he said, laughing at her, but he knew exactly what she meant. 'We barely know each other.'

'Oh yes we do.' She looked hurt. 'You know more about me than any other man in the world. Even though I didn't tell you quite everything.'

'Oh? And why not?'

'Because it hurts too much to talk about it,' she said simply, shivering as she thought of Jack and what had happened. 'One day, I shall tell you,' she added, 'and one day you will tell me about yourself. All your secrets.'

He nodded, 'Perhaps I will,' he agreed, but he knew he never could.

'Ladies and gentlemen, supper is served,' Johnson announced from the doorway as the song ended.

Anjou spotted them, walking to the supper room. Honeychile had linked her arm in Alex's and she was smiling up at him. She thought, jealously, that surely he could not be interested in little Miss goody goody Texas. Then Michael Davenport took her arm and she sighed regretfully, as she followed them in.

One of the things everyone remembered afterwards about the Mountjoy girls' ball, was the exquisite food served at the supper, as well as the absolute rivers of champagne, and the magnificent floral arrangements and the heady scent of the gardenias in full bloom in the ballroom. It was, they said, one of those special summer evenings that would go down in history, as they remembered the midnight supper of lobster and champagne, and the tiny fresh strawberries brought specially from the Perigord, piled high with thick fresh Devon cream. They would remember Ambrose playing 'A Nightingale Sang in Berkeley Square', and sitting out on the wide marble staircase, laughing and talking with each other, and wandering on the terrace in the moonlight that seemed to have been switched on specially for their benefit. And some of them would remember, it was the night they fell in love.

Alex Scott knew he would, because falling in love was not something he did any more. He had hardened his heart against any such emotion. But when Honeychile Mountjoy came into his life, he had no defences against her, because she was not playing a game he knew and understood. She was not playing a game at all; she was simply

246

offering him her heart and though he knew he was not allowed to accept it, he was weak against the new emotion he was feeling.

They strolled, side by side, along the moonlit terrace, while she told him more about her life, because he seemed to have an insatiable curiosity about her. He said he wanted to know everything. And she laughed, and told him about her real world, that was so different from this London one, and, she knew, from his.

'I feel so safe, here in the darkness, with you,' she said, leaning her arms on the balustrade, and looking out at the couples strolling in the garden beneath the trees, all lit with tiny Chinese lanterns so it looked like a garden in a fairy story.

The music struck up again, in the ballroom. He put his arm round her shoulders and said, 'It's time for our last dance.'

'That sounds so final.'

Impulsively, he dropped a kiss on her hair; he thought she smelled wonderful, like fresh-cut grass; a clear, clean scent.

'Shall we see each other again?' she asked as they danced their last dance together.

He sighed at her ingenuousness; it allowed him none of the usual leeway of excuses. 'I hope so,' he replied, 'though I doubt your uncle would approve.'

'I shall make him approve,' she said, suddenly determined, and he laughed and said, 'I think you have a queue waiting for you,' and he stood back, as she was whisked away by the nice handsome young man, who was exactly the sort he knew she would marry.

Anjou saw her opportunity again and she grabbed it. '*Je m'excuse*,' she said to the man waiting patiently for her to dance with him, and picking up her long satin skirts, she ran through the crowd to where Alex was standing alone.

'Our dance, I believe,' she said, breathlessly.

'Again?' he asked astonished, as he took her in his arms.

'No one else seems to want to dance with me, except you,' she said, pouting at him. He laughed. Anjou gave off a sexual message that was hard to ignore. 'Anyhow, I'd prefer to dance all night with you,' she said, insinuating herself closer to him.

'Don't you ever stop to think what people would say if we danced all night together?' he asked, amused.

'Of course I do.' She snuggled dreamily closer, resting her head on his shoulder.

He stepped back, holding her away from him, looking severely at her. 'Anjou, try to behave,' he said.

'But I am. Believe me, Alex, if I were misbehaving you would know it.' Throwing back her head she gazed meaningfully into his eyes. 'Don't let all this virginal satin mislead you, Alex darling,' she whispered. 'I would do anything for you.' Leaning closer, she whispered again, 'Anything.'

Alex sighed with exasperation, then he began to laugh. He thought Anjou must have been born a *femme fatale*. She was a little vamp; she was trouble in the making and he hoped, for Lord Mountjoy's sake, that she married quickly. The dance ended and he escorted her firmly back to Aunt Sophie. Then he collected his partner, Gina, said goodnight to his host and hostess, and left without seeing Honeychile again.

She looked anxiously for him, but Laura told her she had seen him leave. 'Billy wants to give a house party, next weekend at Saxton Mowbrey,' she said, conspiratorially. 'I shall ask him to invite Alex, specially for you.'

Breakfast was being served on the terrace; it was three a.m., and the hungry young people devoured scrambled eggs and bacon and kedgeree, then danced until the dawn came up and the weary band finally packed up to leave.

Lord Mountjoy said to Sophie, after the last guest had left and he watched his girls walking tiredly upstairs to bed, that it was the best party Mountjoy House had seen in fifty years.

When they had all gone, Swayne patrolled the ballroom, finding a lost diamond earring and a pearl bracelet. He put them in his pocket, along with the other items of expensive jewellery he had found earlier, thinking the rich were a careless lot. He made a list of what he had found and where, and then he handed it to Johnson to put in Lord Mountjoy's safe until the following day – or today really, since it was already five o'clock – when the earrings and bracelets would be returned to their owners.

It had been a long night, he thought, lighting up a Woodbine, but an amusing one. It was interesting, seeing how the other half lived, and it had been quite a party. He felt some sort of pride as he thought of the part he had played in it; if it were not for his successful search, there would have been no Miss Mountjoys to give a grand ball for. And he would have lost out on a very lucrative job, and a very interesting evening.

He couldn't wait to get home and get his shoes off, though, because his feet were killing him. He would put his boots on the minute he got back and take the spaniel for a walk. Then he would sit down and have a nice cup of tea and tell his wife all about it.

CHAPTER 27

Lord Mountjoy was the only one to appear the next morning, promptly at eight-thirty, for breakfast in the small dining room. The servants had been hard at work and the house looked immaculate again. He helped himself to devilled kidneys from the silver dish on the sideboard and sat at the head of the table, sipping coffee and glancing through the newspapers. 'By jove, it's my girls,' he said, astonished, looking at the large photograph featured prominently on the social pages of *The Times*, and the *Express*. '*The Mountjoy cousins, at the ball given for them by their great-uncle, the Earl of Mountjoy, at his Mayfair residence last evening*,' the caption said, above Cecil Beaton's picture.

The lump came into Mountjoy's throat again, as he looked at it. Each girl was posed theatrically in her billowing ballgown. Each looked reed-slender and seemed almost to tremble with suppressed energy and youth; one blonde, one red-haired, and the other dark, and each of them lovely. Honeychile was reclining on the pale silk *chaise-longue*, her elegant hawk-like profile half-turned to the camera. Her mane of blonde hair tumbled round her shoulders and she was twisting the long rope of fat pearls around one finger and gazing into space. Laura, looking delicately lovely, gazed at her; while beautiful Anjou faced the camera boldly, head-on, wide-eyed and breathless-looking, ready for what the world might offer.

'*The Toast of London*,' the *Express* trumpeted, over the picture, and '*The Girls Everybody Wants To Know*'.

'My goodness,' Mountjoy exclaimed, 'they're famous.' He thought of Princess Matilda's warning and he hoped worriedly, she wasn't right. The Mountjoys had never been famous for anything; they were of the opinion that the only mentions in the press should be

251

announcements of engagements, marriages, births and deaths; and perhaps the odd mention in the Court Circular.

Still, he thought, pleased, it had been a good party, and all of the newspapers said so. By ten o'clock, the doorbell was ringing with deliveries of flowers for his girls; and soon after that the telephone started, and it seemed to him, it simply never stopped.

Everybody wanted to know them; and the public wanted to know *about* them, via the press. 'As if we were movie stars,' Honeychile said, astonished by all the attention, and the sight of her glamorous photograph in the newspaper. She cut it out immediately and sent it to Aliza with a long letter, telling her all about the ball, and that she was in love 'with a wonderful man'. She said she knew Aliza would think it was a bit soon to go falling in love, and so did she, but she just couldn't help herself.

Jeannie Swinburn saw it in the *Express*, and she telephoned her granddaughter excitedly. 'I looked at it and I thought to myself, can that be our Laura? But of course, I knew it was, because you've always been a lovely girl. I just never saw you in anything pretty, only those old things you wore to the stables.'

'Prepare yourself for the worst, grandma,' Laura said cheerfully, 'I found a man with even bigger and better stables than Haddon's. And I have the feeling I'm going to be spending an awful lot of time there.'

'Where?' Jeannie demanded. 'Remember, you are supposed to be in London having a good time, and finding yourself a nice young man to take your mind off Haddon.'

'Oh, I have, grandma, I have,' Laura reassured her. 'He's the one who owns the stables.'

Jeannie sighed, 'Well, I only hope he's a better man than Haddon.'

'I promise he is,' Laura replied, and there was something in her voice that made Jeannie believe it.

Anjou read every word that had been written about them ten times, re-reading the mentions of, '*The beautiful Mademoiselle Anjou d'Aranville Mountjoy, daughter of the comtesse d'Aranville, who looked outstanding in a pale green satin Hartnell gown.*'

She lay back on her pillows, smiling happily as Agnes brought her breakfast tray, thinking about all the men she had met and danced with. She decided James Mattrington was interesting; he

252

had taken her in to supper and had told her all about his country house in Gloucestershire, where he rode with the hunt as often as he possibly could. She thought, disappointed, that the English passion for horses was too much of a good thing. Just look at Laura, it was all she thought about; and now she had met Billy, she would probably just add him to the string of horses that populated her mind. She thought about Harry: she knew he was a rogue, but he was an amusing rogue, and that always interested her. But not as much as Alex Scott, the Mystery Man, did.

Now there was a man worthy of a woman's interest: and she knew plenty of women were *very* interested in him. Beautiful women, many of them rich and well-known. He was reported as escorting them to dinner, taking them to parties and on his yacht. But none of them had succeeded in capturing him, and that only made him more intriguing.

The bouquets of flowers had started arriving at the house at ten o'clock. By noon, it was awash with them, but for Laura the only one that mattered, was the bunch of roses from Billy, sent by rail to London from the Saxton Mowbrey garden. '*You have come into my life as fresh and lovely as a garden rose*,' his card said. She had not thought Billy would be so poetic and she pressed it to her lips, touched.

Honeychile was in the morning room, going through the newspapers with Aunt Sophie when the basket of Parma violets arrived from Alex, with a little card that said simply, '*I shall never forget last night.*'

Her face lit up with happiness, and she buried her nose in their fragrance, hiding her pleased blushes.

Aunt Sophie never missed a thing like a girl's blush: there was usually a story behind it. 'Who on earth are the violets from?' she demanded, suspiciously.

'Oh, from Alex Scott,' Honeychile replied, as casually as she could.

'Alex Scott sent you flowers?' Aunt Sophie said, astonished. 'I didn't know you even knew the man.'

'We met on the ship, coming over,' Honeychile explained quickly, hoping to put her off the scent. 'We became friends, and I had supper with him last night.'

'How extraordinary.' Aunt Sophie wondered how she had missed that, but the house had been so crowded it was difficult to keep an eye on three girls at once. 'He seems a nice enough fellow,' she said, 'despite what they say about him.'

Honeychile wondered exactly what *they* said about him, but she decided against asking. She was just so happy with his flowers and the message, that he 'would never forget', she wanted to be alone and re-live every moment with him.

The telephone rang and the parlourmaid arrived to say it was for Lady Sophie, and she disappeared into the study to answer it. When she returned, a few minutes later, there was a pleased smile on her face. 'Laura, dear,' she said, 'that was Billy on the telephone. He is having a large house party at Saxton Mowbrey this weekend, and he has invited us to attend. He says he's celebrating his birthday and promises it will be a lot of fun.'

Laura heaved a sigh of relief: she had not been sure Aunt Sophie would allow them to go, but it seemed she approved of Billy. 'He has some wonderful horses there,' she said eagerly, 'Lucky Dancer, and Eagle Ridge, were both Derby winners, years ago. Now they're retired, and at pasture, at Saxton Mowbrey. He promised I could ride them.'

'How exciting for you, my dear,' Aunt Sophie smiled her approval. 'But it won't be all horses, you know; there's to be a grand birthday dinner on Saturday night, and more dancing I expect.' She sighed, thinking she wasn't as young as she used to be and she only hoped, as chaperone to three young women, she could keep up the pace.

Alex was surprised when Billy called, and asked if he would care to join his house party that weekend. 'It's sort of a c-c-c-celebration of m-m-my b-b-birthday,' Billy explained, 'I've bought myself a birthday present, a new colt. I thought you might be interested to see him; I think he's going to be a winner. And b-b-by the way, all the M-m-m-mountjoy girls will be there.'

'Of course I'll come Billy,' Alex said, warmly. 'And I can't wait to see the new horse.' But as he put down the phone both he and Billy knew he meant he couldn't wait to see Honeychile again.

Saxton Mowbrey was a beautiful Queen Anne house built of red brick, faded with the years to a pale coral pink. Two wings of honey-coloured Cotswold stone had been added, incongruously, at a later date, but somehow they added rather than detracted from its beauty. It was a cosier, more intimate house than the cavernous Mountjoy Park, with its state rooms and galleried halls, and Laura fell in love with it as quickly as she had fallen for Billy.

'Quicker,' she said to him, 'because this is love at first sight, and ours was second.'

It was set in lovely rolling parkland, dotted with clumps of magnificent oaks and elms, and copses of silver birch. A stone-balustraded terrace ran along the rear of the house, facing onto a croquet lawn, and a grass tennis court, rose gardens and fountains and herbaceous borders. A long table with a white cloth had been set up under the shade of an enormous chestnut tree and maids in blue cotton dresses and white aprons were busy carrying out trays of sandwiches and crumpets and cakes, jugs of lemonade and a great Russian silver samovar of tea.

The Mountjoys were almost the last to arrive, and people were already sprawled lazily on plaid wool rugs on the lawns, or seated in groups at the table, and the sound of laughter and cheerful conversation drifted in the summer air. It was, Laura thought, quite perfect.

Billy thought Laura looked perfect too: in her full-skirted pink piqué cotton dress, with her glossy brown hair and shining whisky-coloured eyes, she was even prettier than she had been the other night in her ballgown and ruby necklace.

'Oh, Billy, I just love it here,' she cried, 'it's as lovely as Swinburn.'

'Would you marry me just for my house?' he whispered.

She thought for a minute and then said mischievously, 'No, but I might for your new racehorse.'

'I'll show you him later,' he promised. 'Do you realise I haven't kissed you yet?' he whispered, as Aunt Sophie turned and looked pointedly at them.

She looked demurely at him. 'The stables would be an appropriate place for a first kiss, don't you think?' she whispered back, and he squeezed her hand; then they hurried to catch up with the others.

Honeychile glanced quickly round, searching for Alex. Her heart plummeted, when she saw he was not there; she hoped he had not changed his mind.

Anjou glanced round too, taking in the cast of characters for her weekend and finding some of them more than acceptable.

Billy introduced them all and to Honeychile's surprise, people seemed interested in her life. She sat on the lawn with Billy and Laura and a group of his friends, telling them about her ranch in Texas; about riding the range and the cattle round-ups.

'You must try some of my horses tomorrow, Honeychile,' Billy said. 'You can take your pick, though I imagine you and Laura will both want to try my old Derby winners. They'll still give you a terrific ride for your money.'

Honeychile thought of the sedate little gallops down Rotton Row, and she was thrilled at the idea of riding a racehorse. She told them about her Appaloosa, and the fine quarter horses her father used to keep, before he died; and all about Aliza and Tom, and how they had almost discovered oil on the land a few years back.

Watching her, Aunt Sophie remembered with an exasperated sigh, her warning words, to talk less and listen more. She recalled that Honeychile had told her that Aliza always said she 'ran off at the mouth' and now she knew what she meant. The girl simply did not hold anything back, but oddly, it didn't seem to matter; they were listening raptly to her, and seemed quite enchanted that she was so different.

Anjou drifted off along the terrace, aware of the charming picture she made in a shady straw hat and a green and white cotton dress; and of the men's eyes on her, as she leaned on the balustrade, looking over the lawns and the flower gardens, to the rolling vista of the parkland beyond.

She thought jealously that Laura was lucky to have hooked Billy so casually, without even trying. He was a catch, there was no doubt about that. She remembered that Alex was supposed to be here; she was sure that with just the tiniest sign of encouragement he would come running; men always did. And he was a bigger and better catch than Billy.

Alex drove the Bentley Sport Touring car too fast down the winding country lanes leading to Saxton Mowbrey. It had a two hundred horsepower engine, two carburettors, and a top speed of a hundred and thirty-five miles an hour; and he loved it. But for once his mind was not totally on it; and he was driving fast because if he did not, he might turn round and go back again. Which is exactly what he knew he should do.

He thought of Honeychile, just minutes away now, and he knew he had to see her. What was it about her, he wondered, half-angrily, that drew him so strongly. It was as if fate and the gods had recognised that they were meant for each other; even though his destiny meant they were not. He was obsessed with her: he could not get her out of his mind. And that was why he had leapt at Billy's offer. The idea of spending a long weekend in the country with her, was just too tempting.

'The hell with it,' he told himself as he swung the car through the gates of Saxton Mowbrey. 'For once, I shall enjoy myself and not even think of tomorrow.'

Dinner that evening was an easy informal affair: the women wore simple long dresses and the men wore dinner jackets, instead of white tie and tails. Honeychile and Laura were sharing a room and they inspected each other, critically, before they went downstairs.

'You look wonderful,' Laura said. 'Blue is definitely your colour, and I love the softness of the chiffon. It makes you look like Titania, a "faerie queen", with your long blonde hair and mysterious deep blue eyes.' She laughed, 'Alex is simply going to fall at your feet and worship you, when he sees you tonight.'

'The way Billy worships you?' Honeychile asked, wistfully.

'Is it that obvious? That we are in love?' Laura asked, squirting *Je Reviens* on her wrists and throat. She thought for a moment then lifted her skirt and dabbed some behind her knees. 'I read somewhere you're supposed to do that,' she told Honeychile. 'They say the scent comes out when you walk.' She fluffed Yardley's powder on her nose and added a hint of blue eyeshadow and just a touch of pink lipstick. 'There, how do I look?' She turned to Honeychile for inspection.

Honeychile thought she looked delicious. 'Good enough to eat,' she said. She threw her arms round her, impulsively. 'I'm so glad I met you, cousin Laura,' she said, as they hugged each other.

They walked hand in hand down the wide, creaking oak staircase and out onto the terrace where drinks were being served. 'Now all we have to do is to get Alex Scott to propose to you this weekend, and we shall all be happy,' Laura said. 'Well, all except Anjou,' she added, 'and I'm sure I don't know exactly what would make that girl happy.'

They stood at the french doors leading onto the terrace, looking out at the scene. Watching them, Alex thought they looked like happy little girls, waiting for the party to begin. Then Honeychile looked at him; she walked towards him, with her eyes fixed on his face, seeing only him in the crowd of people, and he felt he must be the luckiest man in the world.

'How are you?' He dropped a kiss on her cheek, smelling that faint lovely scent of her skin again. They strolled along the length of the terrace, away from the crowd.

'I thought you weren't coming,' she said, breathlessly.

'But I promised I would. I was looking forward to it all week.'

'Really? Truly?'

He laughed, there was no guile about her and he loved her for it. 'Truly.'

'Dinner, everyone,' Billy called, 'come along now, or Cook will be angry with us for spoiling her soufflées.' And laughing, the party surged indoors.

'I've put you next to Alex,' Billy whispered in Honeychile's ear as they passed by, and she smiled her thanks.

'It's like old times,' Alex said, sitting next to her at the long Jacobean oak table. 'You and I having dinner together. Only now we know each other better.'

'Do we?' She raised her eyebrows, questioningly. 'I've just realised I know you, but I don't really know who you are.'

'Perhaps one day, I might tell you,' he said, thoughtfully. 'But not now. Let's not spoil things.'

Sitting further down the table, Anjou watched them from beneath her lashes, wondering what they were talking about, and why Alex seemed so pleased to see Honeychile. Then she turned her attention and the full battery of her charm on the very attractive and very interested man next to her.

Dinner went with a swing. They ate delicious cheese soufflées with an anchovy sauce, then fillet of beef Wellington; an ambrosial summer pudding with cream, and then celery with Stilton and a good Wensleydale which Billy told everyone was a Yorkshire cheese and had been bought specially for Laura. The women left the men to their port with the warning that it should only be one glass, otherwise they would all just go off to bed and leave them to it.

They drank coffee and gossiped in the drawing room and when the men came in, fifteen minutes later, a game of Charades was proposed.

After that, they played Sardines for a while, racing round the big old house, finding hiding places, which was a good excuse for the girls to find a dark place to be with a man and sneak a kiss or two. Honeychile was no exception; she found herself in a linen room with Alex, and he took her in his arms and held her close for a moment. 'What a place finally to kiss you,' he said, and then he did just that.

She trembled in his arms with the shock of it; it wasn't just her lips that were involved, it was her whole being, and it was wonderful.

'Caught you,' Anjou's triumphant voice said, as she flung open the door. She glanced knowingly at them as they drew apart, but just then Laura came running down the hall. 'Caught you all at one go,' she said, and they returned, reluctantly, to the drawing room.

They rolled up the rugs and put on some records, and danced, and more than one couple was observed to slip quietly out onto the terrace for a stroll in the garden.

'I must be getting old,' Aunt Sophie said wearily to Anjou. 'It's way past my bedtime and you young people want to dance all night. And so did I, I suppose, in my day,' she admitted.

'Please, Aunt Sophie, why don't you go to bed,' Anjou said. 'We know how to behave ourselves properly and I promise you we shan't disgrace you.'

'Perhaps I will,' she agreed, getting to her feet with the aid of her cane, because her arthritis was bothering her this week. 'Now, don't stay up too late,' she warned, kissing Anjou goodnight. 'Remember, it's not just an old saying, a girl really does need her beauty sleep.'

Anjou watched, satisfied as Aunt Sophie limped off to say goodnight to Laura and her host. She stopped for a word with Alex, who was sitting with Honeychile. Gallantly, he took her arm and escorted her upstairs to her room. When he came down again, Honeychile, Laura and Billy were making plans to go to the stables early in the morning, before breakfast.

'Dawn is always the best time for a ride,' Laura was saying. 'Especially for a racehorse, and I want desperately to ride Lucky Dancer.'

'Meanwhile, I propose a backgammon tournament,' Billy said, and he soon had everyone organised in teams who would play in relays at four boards. They were all surprised, later, when Alex came out the winner. 'Just luck,' he said modestly, but Honeychile saw he was a skilful player. 'I learned it in my youth,' he told her, 'whiling away the long hours at sea on a freighter.'

It was the first time she had ever heard him say anything about his past, and she waited for him to tell her more, but he changed the subject. 'I'm even better at poker,' he said.

She grinned confidently at him, 'Bet I can beat you,' she challenged. 'Where on earth did you learn to play poker?'

'The cowhands taught me when I was a kid. I used to hang out with them in the longhouse, after supper. They would be sitting around playing, I'd look over their shoulders, and I guess I just picked it up. And when I got bigger, they let me play. Tom was the only one who could ever beat me,' she warned, 'so be prepared.'

They wandered onto the terrace, along with the others, holding hands and strolling the little paths leading through the rose gardens. 'It's late,' he said regretfully. 'I should let you go to bed.'

'But I don't want to leave you.'

'There's always tomorrow,' he said, and he was happy, because he knew that, for once, it was true. He kissed her then, properly, holding her as though he never wanted to let her go, which he didn't.

They walked back to the house and she said anxiously, 'Do I look as though I've just been kissed?'

'I certainly hope so,' he said with a smile. But he smoothed back her hair and gave her his handkerchief so she could wipe her smudged lipstick, and then he kissed her on the tip of her nose and walked with her to the foot of the stairs. 'Goodnight, Honeychile,' he called. And he told himself that, tonight, he was a very happy man: that he would take his happiness exactly one day at a time, and be content with that.

Laura was already in her nightdress when Honeychile returned to their bedroom. 'Well?' she asked eagerly. 'Did he kiss you?'

Honeychile blushed, admitting he had. 'I knew it,' Laura said triumphantly. 'He couldn't take his eyes off you all night.' She laughed as she said, 'Billy is saving our first kiss for the stables tomorrow. He said it would be appropriate; sort of sealing our fate and the horses too, because soon I shall be looking after them.'

'Has he asked you to marry him?' Honeychile asked, astonished.

'As good as, several times.' Laura stretched luxuriously, then climbed into bed. 'Aren't we just the luckiest girls,' she said sleepily. 'And it's all thanks to Uncle Mountjoy.'

As Honeychile prepared for bed, she hoped sincerely that she would be as lucky as Laura.

Billy was waiting at the stables for Laura, long before sun-up. His own horse, a massive, coal-black hunter, eighteen hands and with a wary look in its eyes, by the name of Monster, was already pawing the ground, eager to be off. Billy brushed him down, then gave him a hearty slap on the neck that the horse knew meant affection, and went to take a look at his new colt, as yet untried and un-named, but for whom he had high hopes.

The colt was a beauty, no doubt about it; a high-stepping chestnut, quivering with energy, responsive and competitive. He took the brush and began to groom it in long smooth strokes, and the young horse shivered with pleasure. They liked each other already, Billy thought, pleased.

'There you are,' Laura was standing in the doorway, looking at him and then at the young horse. 'Oh, Billy,' she said, quite forgetting that she had run all the way to the stables to kiss him, 'he's a beauty.'

'Isn't he, though?' He stood back, proudly, as they both admired the colt. 'Take a look at those legs on him, see the strength?'

She ran her hand over the colt's flanks, feeling the smooth muscles underneath. She patted his neck and gave him a quick kiss on the nose. 'Beauty,' she said, 'that's exactly what you are.'

'That's no name for a colt,' Billy laughed. 'You'll have to do better than that.'

'I just gave him his first kiss,' she said, suddenly remembering why she was here, at the crack of dawn.

'So you did.' Billy moved closer, circling her waist with his arms. 'Am I destined always to come second to a horse?'

'Not always,' she admitted. And, finally, he kissed her. When he took his mouth reluctantly from hers, she opened her eyes and smiled at him. 'That's what we shall call him,' she said, pleased, 'Crack Of Dawn. Oh no, Dawn Cracker, that's it. Then when he's winning we shall look at each other and remember our first kiss, here at the stables before dawn.'

'And the second,' he agreed, kissing her again.

'Good morning, anyone around?' Alex called from the yard, and they drew apart, smiling and pleased with each other.

'Here we are, Alex,' Billy called. 'Come and tell us what you think of the new colt. Laura just named him Dawn Cracker.'

Alex admired him, while the grooms tacked up the horses, and then Honeychile came running down the path and across the yard towards them. Like Laura she was wearing a yellow sweater and jodhpurs and riding boots, and Alex thought she looked so easy and natural and lovely, and as though she belonged here.

They looked at each other and said good morning, and admired the colt and drank cups of coffee.

Honeychile rode Eagle Ridge and the sheer exhilaration of galloping such a magnificent animal along the Saxton Mowbrey bridle paths in the misty early morning, made her laugh out loud. 'If only Tom could see me now,' she yelled to Alex, galloping beside her. Then she and Laura set their horses to a race, crouching low over the horses' necks.

'Like a pair of jockeys,' Billy said proudly. 'Just look at those girls go.'

Later, they had breakfast on the terrace; then they lazed away the morning, playing croquet and reading the newspapers. Billy had organised a tennis tournament in the afternoon, and to Laura and Honeychile's surprise, Anjou, looking wonderful in a very short white skirt, gave a dazzling performance, leaping at the net with ferocity, determined to annihilate her opponent and win.

After they were beaten in the doubles, Alex and Honeychile wandered away, walking along the riverbank hand in hand. And, because they seemed so close now, and so much in tune with each other, and she knew he would understand, she told him about what happened when Jack Delaney came back to get her, just the way Aliza had said he would.

262

She felt the reassuring closeness of him, as they sat together on the bank of the little river, watching the mallards, and the moorhens paddling by, as she said, 'There was a time when I thought I would not live to see another blue sky, or ride another horse, or even grow up and fall in love.'

Alex wished he could remove the burden permanently from her memory. He knew how hard it was to live with such pain; he had lived with it himself for many years now.

'One day you will forget all that,' he said comfortingly, holding her hand. 'One day, I promise, you will remind yourself that you haven't thought about Delaney in years, and after that he will disappear from your memory entirely. He won't exist any more, and you will. You will be the strong one and Delaney will be gone.'

She looked hopefully at him, wanting to believe, but the old fear was still there. 'So, now you really know the worst about me,' she said, with a sigh. 'There's absolutely nothing more to tell.'

Aunt Sophie was pleased with the way her girls looked that evening, for the dinner and dance to celebrate Billy's birthday; very young and pretty in long silk dresses from Jacqmar. It was not a grand ball, it was just a country party and very nice too, she thought approvingly. The food was excellent, the wines were good and the local band played very well, for dancing. She decided that Honeychile was spending far too much time with that Scott man; and that Billy was so suitable she herself could not have picked anyone better for Laura. And wasn't that Harry Lockwood that Anjou was dancing with again? Good Lord, how was it that man seemed able to get himself invited everywhere, she wondered?

'How did you get invited?' Anjou asked.

'I didn't,' Harry replied. 'I'm here as escort to Camilla Staunton.'

'Ah, you're the deputy husband again,' she said maliciously.

He grinned, 'Perhaps.' He held her away from him, inspecting her. 'You look bored,' he said.

She glanced moodily at him. 'Is it that obvious?'

'To a close observer, yes.'

'You would be bored too, cooped up in here with all these men who act like children, playing silly games,' she said spitefully. 'I'm beginning to think the English never grow up.'

'I expect they're just enjoying themselves. It's just not your style.' He caught her looking over his shoulder at Alex, dancing with Honeychile, and he said, 'And I suppose the Italian is.'

Anjou looked him in the eyes, 'Let's get out of here,' she whispered urgently. She glanced round and saw everyone was busy, dancing or talking. 'Wait here for a few minutes, then follow me,' she instructed. 'I'll be out on the terrace, waiting for you.' And she drifted away from him.

He looked for her outside, a few moments later, as she had instructed. She appeared from the shadows and took his hand. 'Come with me,' she whispered, gliding down the steps into the garden. She took him to the gazebo in the rose garden, then she put her arms round him and said, 'Now, you can kiss me.'

Harry enjoyed kissing Anjou; she was willing and eager and she knew how to kiss a man. He was sure she knew more than that, but tonight she was not going to let him prove it, though he tried: he put his hand on her breast and felt her respond as she thrust herself closer to him. And then quite suddenly, she shrugged herself out of his arms and said, coolly, 'That's enough, Harry.' She tidied her hair and straightened her dress, and said they would go back to the dance now.

He thought she was a little tease, but by now he recognised Anjou's style, and he promised himself that one day she would be his. And he was so hot for her that that day couldn't come soon enough for him.

Honeychile not only beat Alex at seven card stud that night: she beat all the other men too, and she promised to teach the women the fine art of stud poker the following day. It was five in the morning when she finally said goodnight to Alex, and then he couldn't kiss her because other guests were still around.

He watched her go, regretfully. His lost weekend was almost finished. He knew he had behaved badly, kissing her, allowing her to believe he cared. When he knew there was no future for them. His life was different. Its path had been set many years before, and he could not change it. Not even for Honeychile Mountjoy.

When Honeychile awoke on Sunday morning, the maid brought an envelope with her name on it, along with the breakfast tray. She recognised Alex's writing and opened it eagerly.

My dear Honeychile, it said, *I'm afraid I must be in Rome for a meeting tomorrow, and I shall leave before you even wake. I have enjoyed being with you this weekend, and I thank you for trusting me with your secrets. I shall be travelling a great deal over the next few months, and shall not have an opportunity to see you, but I hope you enjoy yourself and all the parties, and that you will be happy. With my good wishes, Alex.*

The smile disappeared from her face. She didn't know what to make of it; was it goodbye? She read it again, and somehow, she knew it was. Alex was stepping out of her life and encouraging her to be happy, with someone else, not him. 'But why?' she asked herself, a thousand times that day.

'Why?' she asked Laura, when she returned from her early morning ride with Billy. 'I thought last night, he really cared. He was so understanding, so loving. Oh, dammit, I swear he loves me.'

'Did he tell you that?' Laura asked shrewdly. Honeychile shook her head, miserably. 'No.'

'Well, there you are then. Sometimes men can be such beasts,' she said with a sigh, hugging her tearful cousin.

The rest of that Sunday passed in a sort of haze for Honeychile. After tea, when they were driving back to London in the Daimler, Aunt Sophie said that her face looked as cloudy as the skies, which were threatening rain.

'There goes our wonderful summer,' she complained, as the first drops plopped against the windows. And Honeychile thought sadly, that she was right.

CHAPTER 28

A few weeks later, Lord Mountjoy was sitting in his library, taking his evening glass of the Macallan and listening to the racket going on around him. The latest dance tune blasted from a record player; a girl was singing along with it; two others were arguing, a door slammed, the telephone rang, as it seemed to do endlessly these days, and it was always for one of his girls. Mountjoy House was alive again, with laughter – and sometimes tears; with comings and goings, and impromptu parties after the theatre. Young men appeared constantly on his doorstep and he gave them the once over before they took his girls to the theatre, always in a group of course; they were never allowed out with a man on their own. Except, perhaps for lunch, as long as it was someone Sophie was sure about. Occasionally, they were permitted to go to a nightclub, again always in the company of others, and he would telephone ahead first and make sure that the head waiter at the Café de Paris or Cyranos, or whatever silly names these places called themselves, knew to tap his girls' escorts on the shoulder come midnight, and remind them it was time to go home.

Tonight was the big occasion, the presentation at Court. Lord Mountjoy looked at the invitation on the mantel: *The Lord Chamberlain is commanded by Their Majesties to summon the Lady Sophie Mountjoy and the Misses Anjou, Laura and Eloise Mountjoy to a Court at Buckingham Palace. Ladies: Court Dress with feathers and trains; Gentlemen: Full Court Dress*, it said grandly. He was a bit concerned about it, but Sophie said everything was in hand and the girls had been practising their curtsys and how to manage their gowns with the long trains, all day.

It was eight o'clock and Lord Mountjoy was already dressed. He was wearing full-dress Guards' uniform, with unconscionably tight, white buckskin breeches that had taken him and his valet a long time to pull on; high leather boots, polished to a mirror gloss; a scarlet fitted jacket with a high collar, gold epaulettes and gold buttons, covered with gold braid and his military decorations. His white gauntlet gloves and tasselled gilt helmet were waiting in the hall, and damned uncomfortable he felt too, he thought, but he supposed it was worth it, for his girls' sake.

He knew he was too early, the presentation began at nine-thirty, but he was enjoying listening to the sounds of excitement coming from upstairs as the girls got themselves ready. Unlike before the ball, this time he was certain they would be a credit to him.

Sipping his whisky, he thought, contentedly, that the Mountjoy girls were the toast of London: they were invited to dinners and dances, and weekend parties at country houses, where, he had heard, Honeychile had achieved fame for teaching the other guests how to play seven card stud; and she and Laura had also stunned everyone with their prowess on horseback; and that flirtatious Anjou always looked absolutely gorgeous. The Mountjoy girls were written about in the social columns of the *Daily Express* and the *Mail*, and featured in *Tatler* and *The Bystander*. They seemed, to him, to run from one social activity to the next, dashing home in-between to change their clothes, while he sat, slightly bewilderedly on the sidelines, enjoying the action vicariously.

Anyhow, he thought, happily, Mountjoy House was certainly alive again in a way he couldn't remember it being for years; not since he was a boy and his parents constantly filled all their houses with guests and gave grand dances and dinners, where tiaras were worn and the dozens of footmen belonged to the house and were not hired merely for the night, the way he had hired some for his ball. Times were changing, he recognised that, and thank God, with the advent of his girls, he had been given the opportunity to change with them, and not just fade away; a lonely, crusty old man, until it was time to pop him in the family tomb, along with the others.

Aunt Sophie bustled into the room, looking even more like the old Queen in an ecru lace dress, carrying her gold embroidered train over her arm.

'You look well, William,' she said approvingly, 'I always like to see a man in Court Dress. It sets off a good figure, you know, and you have kept your shape well for your age.'

'Thank you, Sophie,' he said, 'but a chap can't help feeling he's a bit over the hill for these tight breeches. I remember when I was a young man, the endless fittings to get them just right. I suppose I was a bit of a peacock then, like the young ones taking my girls out now, are.' He looked her over and said admiringly, 'Anyhow, old girl, you're looking jolly good yourself. Yes, very nice, very nice indeed.'

'Thank you, William,' Lady Sophie adjusted her diamond tiara then bent her head to inspect the array of jewels on her large bosom, and said, 'The girls should be here any minute.'

Lord Mountjoy glanced at the gilt cherub clock, as always, but they were not late tonight. In fact they were early. 'There you are,' he said, pleased, as they trooped slowly through the door, lovely in pale satin dresses carrying their long trains over their arms. They wore long kid gloves, with Prince of Wales feathers in their hair. They each wore the single short strand of pearls and matching earrings he had bought them to mark the event, because ostentatious jewellery was frowned upon for young girls at such an occasion; and they carried small bouquets of lilies of the valley and tiny golden roses.

A smile lit Lord Mountjoy's face as he looked at them, 'Oh, I say, well done,' he beamed. 'You look,' he searched for exactly the right word, 'dazzling. Yes, that's it, dazzling.'

'I hope we don't disgrace ourselves and trip over our trains or fall down when we curtsy,' Laura said, laughing at the very idea. 'Everyone we know is so nervous.'

'No need to be nervous,' he boomed, 'they say the new young Queen is very nice, and the King's a good enough fellow, kind-hearted. I've known him for years.'

'It's time we were leaving,' Aunt Sophie stood up. 'Come along, girls.'

The servants lined up in the hall to see them leave, and they smiled admiringly, waving as they stepped into the waiting Rolls and were driven away, out into Curzon Street, through Mayfair into St James's and the Mall.

Traffic was almost at a standstill with the cars full of débutantes heading for the Palace. The pavements were jammed with spectators, peering eagerly into the windows, 'as though we were the Queen herself,' Laura said, astonished and a bit embarrassed by all the attention. But Anjou loved it; she smiled back and even waved, until

269

Aunt Sophie told her sternly not to; and finally they were there.

The Rolls pulled under the *porte-cochère* in the palace court-yard where Beefeaters in their picturesque red costumes stood on guard. As they walked through the great doors into Buckingham Palace, Honeychile thought if only Aliza could see her now. Somehow she was sure her father could, up in heaven, and she knew that he would be proud of her.

They took their seats in the Throne Room, looking around and smiling at familiar faces. A military band was playing loudly and at the far end of the room the two thrones, surmounted by a red canopy, waited for the King and his Queen. As well as the girls to be presented and their families, the room was crammed with the Diplomatic Corps, and the military and naval personnel in full-dress uniforms and their wives, all beautifully dressed and wearing tiaras.

There was a roll of drums and everyone stood as the National Anthem was played and Laura nudged Honeychile excitedly as the young King George and Queen Elizabeth entered, followed by other members of the Royal family and the Ladies-in-Waiting. 'Here we go,' she whispered, excitedly, as they walked nervously down the long corridor. When it was their turn, their names were announced, and, led by Aunt Sophie, they walked in front of the two thrones, turned to face their Majesties, kicked back their trains as gracefully as possible, and made their deep curtsies. There was just time to catch a glimpse of the Queen's lovely smile and her beautiful cream lace dress, and to think how kind the King looked, and how smart in the red and gold uniform of a field marshall, and then it was time to move on.

When the presentations were over, canapés and drinks were served and Lord Mountjoy took great pleasure in introducing his great-nieces to his old friends and colleagues, who told him he was a lucky fellow and they were the prettiest gels there. Like everyone else, they wandered through the great rooms of Buckingham Palace, admiring the art objects and the paintings, though Anjou was mostly admiring the men who she thought looked very sexy in their buckskin breeches.

They waited until their car arrived, and drove them to the Court Photographers in Piccadilly, where a crowd of other excited young women were already waiting to have their pictures taken. They drank coffee and talked about how exciting it was, and about how they were sure they were going to fall when they curtsied, and some almost had; until it was their turn. Then they were photographed separately, and then together; then each of them with Aunt Sophie and then all of them with Aunt Sophie, until they were exhausted.

When the ordeal was finally over, they drove back to Mountjoy House and a champagne supper, which Lord Mountjoy said they certainly deserved.

Anjou was pleased with the prestige of the Court presentation, but she was bored with the social whirl. She craved excitement and she had found out exactly how to get it: she had taken up her old ways, and her 'escapes'.

Sometimes, when she returned home from a dance or the theatre, she would say goodnight to Lord Mountjoy, who always waited up. She would climb the magnificent staircase, turn at the top, blow a kiss to her uncle watching indulgently from below, and call 'Goodnight'. Then she would speed along the corridor, down the servants staircase at the back of the house, out of the servants' door, into the alley where a young man would be waiting. Then on to the 400 in Leicester Square, where René, the head waiter, knew her well by now; or the Café de Paris in New Coventry Street, The Blue Lagoon, or Quaglinos; Anjou knew them all.

Laura warned her she was getting a reputation for being fast, but Anjou merely shrugged and said it was just talk. She said she wasn't the only deb at the nightclubs and if they had half her spirit they would come and see for themselves instead of grumbling at her.

Laura shook her head, exasperated; she knew by now it was no use arguing with Anjou. She could not fathom the extent of Anjou's boredom and restlessness that made her seek that extra charge of excitement the illicit act brought her. If it was forbidden, Anjou wanted it.

Anjou enjoyed the country house parties now, because they gave her ample opportunity for misbehaviour; she was wise enough to stay away from the eager young men who would have loved to get her into bed; sleeping with a married man was safer because he would never tell, and more exciting because it was doubly forbidden; and also because they were more experienced, and Anjou loved to make love. She was a tease, too: she set out to be as alluring as she could to other girls' boyfriends; laughing when they succumbed to her wiles

271

and dropped their girls, and came running after her instead, only to be given the cold shoulder.

'Why do you do it?' Laura demanded angrily. 'What's wrong with you? You just go round breaking people's hearts for no good reason.'

'Oh, *pouf*, it's just a game,' Anjou replied, airily. 'And besides, no harm was done.' But Laura, who had comforted several of the heartbroken girls who had been cast aside in favour of Anjou, knew better.

'Anjou always wants what she can't have,' she said to Honeychile, one afternoon at Saxton Mowbrey. They were riding a couple of Billy's fine horses, ambling their way back along the lane to the stables, to the east of the house. 'I swear I don't know what's wrong with her, but it's a good thing Uncle Mountjoy and Aunt Sophie don't know the truth about what's going on. Uncle thinks she is just perfect, "so beautiful, so charming, so sweet," he says. Huh,' she snorted angrily, 'little does he know. It wouldn't surprise me at all, if she went after Billy, just to make me mad.'

She stared, surprised as they came round the corner and saw Anjou emerging from the stables, with Billy behind her. 'Good Lord,' she exclaimed, 'what's she doing in there? Anjou hates horses, she never usually goes near the stables.'

Anjou gave Laura a sly little smile as she rode up, smoothing down her cotton skirt ostentatiously. Laura looked suspiciously at her, and then at Billy. He shrugged his shoulders and held the reins while she dismounted.

'I just thought I would come and see what you all got up to, here at the stables away from Aunt Sophie's eagle eyes,' Anjou said, sweetly; then she sauntered serenely away.

She may have looked serene but inside she was seething. She didn't really find Billy attractive, but she had made a pass at him anyway, just to test her power over Laura, so to speak. She had crept up on him in the stall where he was grooming his new colt.

'Is this the true love of your life?' she had said teasingly, and when he had swung round, surprised to see her, she had put her arms round him and kissed him. 'Or perhaps *I* might be?' she had whispered. Billy had laughed at her. 'Not my sort of f-f-f-filly, I'm afraid,' he had said, and she had retreated, pouting.

She was not used to rejection, especially by men she considered un-attractive. She told herself, angrily, that she had half a dozen men who wanted to marry her if she gave them the slightest encouragement. It wasn't quite true, but there were four, and two of them had titles. She promised herself she would get her own back on Billy, one day. Meanwhile, Camilla Staunton was arriving this afternoon, without her husband again, and, surprise, surprise, so was that 'husband deputy', Harry. Perhaps she would have some fun tonight after all.

'What was Anjou up to?' Laura asked Billy, suspiciously.

'Nothing to worry about, she came to look at Dawn Cracker,' he said easily. 'Anjou is harmless, you know, just a bit of a tease, that's all. She knows how to get you girls riled up.'

'She certainly does,' Laura agreed.

Honeychile left them alone together, and Laura watched her walking down the lane, back to the house. Her head drooped and she looked so sad and lonely; she said worriedly, 'Billy, whatever's happened to Alex Scott? Honeychile never hears from him, and I know he's back in London because I've seen him: at the theatre the other night, and once walking through St James's. She swears she thought he loved her, but he seems to be going out of his way to avoid her.'

He shook his head, 'They say Alex is like that; love them and leave them, seems to be his motto. Though why he picked on Honeychile I don't know. He usually goes for older, more experienced women. Poor girl,' he added sympathetically. 'I shall have to think who I can introduce her to to take her mind off him.'

'You can try,' Laura said doubtfully, giving him a quick kiss and thinking what a nice man he was. 'But somehow I don't think she's ever going to forget him.'

Nevertheless, Billy sat Honeychile next to an old friend of his at dinner that night. Charles Marshall was American; he was different and he was interesting and amusing, and though Honeychile did not forget Alex, because she never would, he kept her entertained, and he beat her at backgammon later. 'Just the way Alex did,' she said sadly, wondering if she would ever see him again.

Camilla Staunton kept a keen eye on Anjou, immersed in a back-gammon game with Harry; she knew a predator when she saw one. Instead of paying attention to her, when after all she had been the one who had brought him to Saxton Mowbrey, because certainly he would not have got through the door of Billy Saxton's house without her, Harry was with Anjou.

Camilla was thirty-seven years old, blonde and attractive. Her husband was fifty, a military man, immersed in his soldierly activities and often away for weeks on end. She had learned early in her marriage to look for amusement, and passion, elsewhere, and Harry was certainly not her first lover. But he was the current one, and she was damned if she was going to give him up to Anjou Mountjoy.

The two of them were sitting by the window, sipping champagne and it looked to her like they were doing more talking than playing backgammon. She walked over and said, meaningfully, 'Goodnight Anjou, goodnight, Harry darling. It's getting late and I'm quite sleepy. I shall go up to bed now.'

Harry got to his feet, 'Goodnight, Camilla, sweet dreams,' he said, and he gave her a quick peck on the cheek.

Anjou smiled as Camilla gazed meaningfully at him again: she got the message and she knew Harry did too. They watched her stroll towards the door; she paused and looked back at them, over her shoulder, and Anjou laughed.

'Night-night time, Harry,' she teased. Then she yawned, covering her pretty pouting mouth with a beautifully manicured hand. 'I believe I am quite tired too. Perhaps I should also wish you goodnight. I shall go to bed, like Camilla.'

He leaned closer and whispered, 'But Camilla will be waiting for me, and you will not.'

'How do you know?' she murmured, giving him her wickedest smile. 'Unless you try to find out, of course,' she added as she walked away.

Anjou was attracted to Harry, despite the fact that she knew he was no good and had no money. A little fling was all she wanted, and she made that clear to him when he tapped at her door, half an hour later. He walked right in and put his arms round her. She was wearing a satin nightdress that had certainly not been Aunt Sophie's choice; slit at the sides all the way to the waist and at the front, almost down to her navel. Not that it stayed on long because Harry was an impatient lover.

'I've been waiting for this moment since I first met you,' he murmured in her ear as they sank together onto the bed. 'I knew it was only a matter of time, because we are alike you and I, Anjou. We are both wicked and opportunistic. And that's why I could even fall in love with you, if you'd give me half a chance.'

Anjou covered his mouth with her hand, 'No love,' she said, knowing full well that Harry had the Mountjoy money on his mind, just as she did herself. 'Let's just make love instead.'

Harry was an expert lover; after all, he had had years of practice. And he was as expert as Anjou at effecting a quick disappearance afterwards. No one even suspected that he had been in her room; except for Camilla, of course, and she never spoke to Harry again. But she mentioned around London that she knew for a fact that young Anjou Mountjoy took after her dissolute grandfather, and that she was no better than she should be.

Back in town the following week, Anjou went to the theatre with Honeychile and Laura. Billy and his American friend, Charles Marshall escorted them, and Laurie Foster, who was the younger son of a Duke, was Anjou's escort. Actually, she was quite enjoying herself: he was attractive and fun and they were going onto the Café de Paris afterwards. But then she spotted Alex Scott sitting in the stalls, a few rows away.

She glanced at Honeychile and saw that she had seen him too; she thought, impatiently, that Honeychile had no defences; she simply sat there looking as if her world had come to an end because the man she had fallen for was with someone else, and he hadn't even so much as telephoned her since Billy's party.

'Isn't that Alex Scott, over there, Honeychile?' she asked, innocently. 'I wonder who he's with? She looks very beautiful, don't you think?'

Laura glared warningly at her, but it was too late.

'He's with Gina Matteo,' Billy said. 'They are old friends, from Italy.'

Honeychile wondered sadly, what she had done? What she had said, that Alex didn't want to see her any more? One moment he was loving and attentive; the next he just disappeared from her life as though she didn't exist. She kept her eyes averted from him and Gina as they filed slowly from their seats after the show, and she did her best to be light-hearted and have fun at the Café de Paris, but she was glad when the night was over, and she could retreat to her room and spend another sleepless night, asking herself what had gone wrong.

At least now she knew Alex was back in town. She thought hopefully he would call her, but the week passed and he did not. Laura took Billy up to Swinburn for the weekend, to meet her grandmother, and she asked Honeychile to go with them. Anjou was going to a dance in Gloucestershire, and she knew she would stay at home alone and just think about Alex, who was probably out with Gina, or one of a dozen women who she was sure were only too willing and eager to spend an evening with him.

'You can be our chaperone,' she said, encouragingly, 'And besides, there's no point in moping around here alone, waiting to see if Alex is going to call. He's probably going away for the weekend too, everybody does,' she added.

Honeychile was glad she said yes because she got to meet Jeannie Swinburn, and to fall in love with Swinburn Manor.

'It's not really a Manor,' Laura explained to them on the train, 'it's nothing like Saxton Mowbrey or Mountjoy Park. It's really quite small, a Bradford wool-merchant's house. It's very old-fashioned, and sort of falling to pieces here and there, but I love it.' She looked anxiously at them, because she wanted them to love it too.

She wasn't really surprised when they did: 'How can you not?' she asked proudly. The weather was balmy, the sky was blue, the sun shone on the grey stone Manor; and Jeannie was waiting at the door to greet them.

'Honeychile, my dear,' she said, hugging her immediately. 'I feel I know you already, from everything Laura has told me about you.'

She looked searchingly at Billy with her faded blue eyes, then she said warmly, 'I can see Laura has chosen well. She always was a sensible girl. At least,' she corrected herself, thinking of the disaster with Haddon Fox, 'most times she was.'

Laura rolled her eyes to heaven, then looked at Billy and laughed. 'I think Billy is quite pleased I chose him, grandma,' she said, 'but he did a bit of the choosing too, you know.'

'Then I'm glad he did,' Jeannie said smartly, 'and he's most welcome to my home.'

'She'll be kissing you too, Billy, before you know it,' Laura warned him. 'She's a great one for kissing, my grandmother.'

'So that's where you get it from,' he said, amused, and they all laughed.

It grew cool that evening, as it often did in the Yorkshire Dales, and they had supper by the fire with the three black and white border collies sprawled at their feet, looking hopefully for scraps. Honeychile thought it was the most comforting and homely place she had ever been, and she told Jeannie so.

'I know you're a long way from your own home, so you must think of this as yours too,' she replied warmly.

Laura showed them the stables the next morning, and the mare that she had bought from Haddon for twenty pounds. Billy inspected the mare closely, running his hands over her flanks and walking round her, looking at her feet. 'You got yourself a bargain,' he said, impressed. 'We might have to stable her with Dawn Cracker, bring the pair along together. See whose horse wins,' he added with a grin.

Laura patted Sasha on the neck and the horse whinnied with delight as she gave her an apple. 'I'll train them both, if you'll let me,' she offered.

'I wouldn't dream of allowing anyone else near them. We shall have to extend the stables and create a proper training yard for you.'

'Really?' she gasped, astonished. 'But when?'

'Soon,' he promised. 'When you marry me.'

'But you haven't asked me yet,' she said, laughing.

'Don't worry, I will,' he replied. 'First I have to ask your uncle's permission, and Aunt Sophie told me it's better to wait for a while, because he might think we haven't known each other long enough.'

'My grandmother doesn't think that,' she said.

He grinned at her again. 'I know. I already asked her and she said of course I could marry you, get you off her hands at last.'

Laura sighed, happily. 'Why am I the last to be asked,' she marvelled. 'The engaged-to-be, the object of your desire, the one you love.'

'I have to get up my courage first, buy a ring then go down on one knee. I'm a m-m-m-man who b-believes in doing things p-p-properly,' he added.

She sighed and said, 'Then kiss me properly, Billy, before you forget you love me, you're so busy doing everything else properly.'

* * *

277

Later that afternoon, they drove into Harrogate to pick up some pills Jeannie needed from Boots, and to show Billy the gardens and poke round the antique shops. They had a wonderful tea at Betty's and were just coming out when they bumped right into Haddon, coming in.

'Good Lord, Saxton, it's you,' he said, heartily, offering him his hand. 'What are you doing back up here? Come for another look at my stables, have you?'

'How are you, Haddon?' Billy said easily. 'No, no, I'm not looking round for a trainer any more. I already found one.'

'How are you, Haddon?' Laura said, smiling broadly.

'Good Lord, Laura.' He looked at her, astonished and then at Billy. 'You mean Laura is going to train for you?'

'That's right,' Billy replied, smiling. 'And I couldn't think of anyone better.'

'Goodbye, Haddon,' Laura called over her shoulder, as they strolled away down the street.

'Thank you,' she said to Billy, 'but it's not really true. I'm not really your trainer, I'm only going to train Cracker and Sasha.'

'That's only the beginning,' he promised, squeezing her hand.

Jeannie was sad when it was time for them to leave the next day. 'Remember, don't be a stranger,' she said to Billy, and he promised he would not. 'And Honeychile my dear, come and stay any time you like,' she said.

The weather was hot and sultry in London the following week. It made Anjou even more restless. She was thinking about Alex, in fact she found herself thinking about him constantly, but unlike Honeychile, she was prepared to do something about it. She looked through the telephone directory and found the address of the Scott Shipping Lines, in St James's.

She smiled at herself in the mirror, then she put on a cool sleeveless silk dress, fixed her hair so it fell sexily over one eye, sprayed herself with her favourite scent, Jicky, and took a taxi to St James's.

'Mr Scott, please,' she told the receptionist. The woman looked at her a little strangely, and Anjou guessed that Alex's girlfriends did not usually show up at his office.

'Tell him that Miss Mountjoy is here to see him,' she ordered. She paced the hall of the beautiful Regency house, wondering mischievously what Alex would say when he saw her.

'If you would come this way, Miss,' the receptionist said, leading her up the blue-carpeted stairs to Alex's office. He was waiting at the door, and he stared, astonished at Anjou. She rushed past him before he could say anything, and said, 'I know you were expecting Honeychile, but it's just me, Alex, instead. I thought we might have lunch, and talk about her. You know she's been quite sad that you haven't called her.'

'Anjou, what are you doing here?' he said, exasperatedly. 'And thank you for the invitation, but no I cannot have lunch. I am a very busy man. And no I do not want to discuss Honeychile with you or anyone else. Now, will you please leave, before I get very angry with you?'

She knew he was going to open the door and she leaned her back against it. 'Please, Alex, don't throw me out,' she said softly. 'I'm not like Honeychile, naïve and easily hurt. I understand a man like you.'

Despite his anger, Alex had to laugh. 'You are a very silly young woman,' he said severely, 'and if your Uncle Mountjoy knew you were here, he would be very angry with you.'

'But he doesn't know, and he never will,' she persisted. '*Please* Alex? All I ask is lunch.'

He walked to his desk and pressed a button, summoning his assistant. Anjou was forced to move as the door opened behind her. 'Please show Miss Mountjoy out, Stavros,' he said, coldly. 'I think she is on her way to lunch.'

Anjou scowled at him. 'I haven't finished with you yet, Alex,' she promised. 'You'll have lunch with me one day.' And with one last smouldering glance at him, she flounced from the room and back down the blue-carpeted stairs.

It seemed to Alex that everywhere he went after that, Anjou was there too; he didn't know how she managed it, but she made a point of attending the same events. And each time, she came sidling up to him, whispering in his ear, inviting him to lunch, to cocktails and dinners. He thought she was amusing, but she was reckless and dangerous. Beside, he wasn't interested. She was the wrong Mountjoy girl.

CHAPTER 29

Alex Scott could not get Honeychile out of his mind. She was there last thing at night, before he finally slept, and again first thing in the morning, when he was shaving, seeing her lovely young face in the mirror instead of his own. Now, in his office in St James's, he was staring out of the window, still thinking of her.

The day was beautiful, with a hard-blue, early-summer sky. The bright sunlight seemed to throw everything into sharper focus. Except his mind. He was supposed to be thinking about whether he should make an offer on the Greek's tanker fleet, and for the first time in his life he simply could not concentrate.

Turning impatiently from the window, he told himself not to be so ridiculous. He sat at his desk, forcing himself to look at the papers neatly arranged in front of him by his assistant, Stavros.

He ran his hand absently across the smooth patina of the desk, remembering how he had bought it twenty years ago, when the man he had hated all his life was finally ruined. They had auctioned off the contents of his grand offices and his homes, and Alex could still recall the bitter-sweet pleasure he had taken in bidding low and taking home the spoils of his revenge.

Now, except for the aesthetic one of the finely crafted wood under his hand and the patina that gave it a soft amber glow, there was no more pleasure.

He got up, and began to pace the large, beautiful room, examining the spoils of his own personal war: the Isfahan silk rug; the Chippendale tulipwood bureau; the Italian renaissance carved mirror. All were trophies of a long battle which, for a short, sweet while, he had thought he had won. He had sought to replicate the older man's office, using his things, taking over his life. And it had brought him no joy. In this entire room, the only things he had bought with love in his heart and not hate, were the paintings.

He looked closely at his art works: at the treasured Canaletto; the Giotto study painted on wood; a trio of Leonardo drawings. And the newest acquisition: a small Monet of a summery flower-filled garden that he had seen in the window of a Left Bank art dealers, and which he had fallen in love with on the spot, and known he could not live without.

There had been an easy answer to that. He had simply gone into the dealer's and paid the asking price without a quibble, because he felt an artist who could reach his soul was worth more than a man who merely dealt in commodities and ships. But there was no such easy answer about falling in love with Honeychile Mountjoy. In fact, there was no answer at all.

He sat at his desk again, looking through the figures Stavros had carefully prepared, but his eyes kept turning to the little Monet garden in the golden easel sitting on his desk, and his mind kept turning to the past and things he did not wish to think about. At least, not now.

He sighed as he sat back in his leather wing-chair. He stretched wearily, clasping his hands behind his head, swivelling his chair round until he was looking out of the large window at the tops of the sun-dappled plane trees, and the blue sky. It was no good, he couldn't think straight. He would go for a walk, clear his head; maybe take a look at what the art dealers had to offer in Bond Street. That should focus his mind nicely.

He summoned Stavros, told him he was going out for an hour or two, straightened his striped Italian silk tie, put on his jacket and ran lightly down the wide, blue-carpeted staircase of the beautiful Regency house that was now the palatial offices of the Scott Lines.

He strolled across Piccadilly into Old Bond Street, pausing here and there to inspect the displays in the expensive shop windows. He had reached Clarges Street when a blonde young woman hurtled round the corner and ran right into him. Her silly little hat flew off the top of her head and straight under the wheels of a passing taxi, and her handbag crashed to the ground, spilling lipsticks and powder compact, address book, pens, combs and coins across the pavement.

'Honeychile,' he said, laughing. He felt as though his dream had come true; he was holding her in his arms.

'Oh,' she said, startled, looking into his eyes. And then, 'Oh, Alex,' in that soft breathy way that turned his heart over.

'Where are you off to in such a hurry?'

She looked bewildered for a minute, as though she had quite forgotten. 'The hairdresser. I'm late, that's why I was running. I guess I'm just lucky it was you I ran into, and not some stranger.'

'I'm afraid your hat wasn't so lucky.' They looked at the straw hat, squashed flat by the taxi's wheels, laughing as they bent to retrieve the contents of her bag from the pavement.

Alex picked up the hat and handed it to her. 'Do you think it can be resuscitated? Or has all life been permanently crushed out of it?'

She laughed again, a joyous rippling laugh that made him smile. 'I'm afraid it's "a goner", as Laura would say. It doesn't matter. I hate wearing hats. I only do it because Aunt Sophie Mountjoy says it's "proper" and I should.'

They stood looking at each other, smiling. She was wearing a hyacinth blue summer dress the exact colour of her eyes, with white strappy sandals and little white gloves. Her shoulder-length corn-gold hair gleamed in the sunlight and in his view, it did not look in the least bit in need of a hairdresser's attention. She was absolutely perfect, just as she was.

'I would ask you to lunch,' he said, though he knew he should not, 'but you're on your way to the hairdressers.'

'I'd rather be with you,' she said honestly, still looking at him with those fathomless blue eyes.

'Then you shall.' He took her arm and flagged down a taxi, with the feeling of a man burning his bridges behind him. He held open the door for her, said, 'The Berkeley, please,' to the cabbie, and climbed in beside her.

They sat, looking at each other, still smiling. 'Look how pleased with ourselves we are,' he said. 'Like two schoolchildren playing truant. I should be at work and you should be getting your hair done. The sun must have gone to our heads.'

'It's fate, that's all.' She looked at him, her head tilted to one side, and the smile still on her face. 'Don't you believe in fate, Alex?'

His eyes met hers. 'Only on days like this.'

The taxi whizzed through the traffic and pulled up in front of the Berkeley. The top-hatted doorman hurried to open the door. 'Good afternoon, Miss Mountjoy,' he said, with a cheery smile at her.

'Afternoon, Joseph. How's your wife? Feeling better, I hope?'

A smile crossed Alex's face, as he thought of the gauche, embarrassed girl he had met just a few months ago on the liner. Now she was an accomplished and very beautiful young woman who doormen at smart London hotels greeted by name – instead of greeting him. He waited patiently until Honeychile found out the details of Joseph's wife's recovery.

'I'm so glad she's better,' she said finally. 'It must have been worrying for you.' And Alex could tell she meant it.

'Did anyone ever tell you you are a very nice young woman?' he asked, in the restaurant, as they took a seat at a table by the corner window.

'Only you,' she smiled. Then she added, 'And Uncle Mountjoy.'

'You seem very fond of him?'

'Of course I am. Oh, he puts up this prickly front to keep you at a distance, but it's only to cover up his loneliness. I think he has been lonely for so long, he didn't know how to behave with people any more.'

He looked at her, amazed. 'And how is it you're so wise, for one so young?'

'Not wise,' she said gently. 'Just experienced in loneliness.'

Their eyes met across the table. 'You too,' she said. 'I can tell you know about loneliness, Alex. Why? A man like you who has everything?'

'Appearances can be deceptive,' he said abruptly. And then the waiter came and they had to break off their conversation and order poached salmon and salad, and a bottle of the white Bordeaux that was his favourite and which he promised she would like.

He sat looking at her, still not able to believe how she had changed. She was so grown-up, so sure of herself, yet she still had that same, direct, tell-all ingenuous charm. He listened while she told him about Laura's romance with Billy and how happy she was; about the parties she had been to, and how her tennis game was coming along. They had talked about nothing important at all, he thought, regretfully, and lunch was almost over.

They lingered over strawberries and cream and the last drop of wine. 'And you, Honeychile?' he said, taking her hand across the table, the way he had that first night on the ship. 'Tell me, are you happy?'

Tension crackled between them. 'Today, I am,' she said softly, 'Right this very minute, I know I am happy.'

It was time to go, and still he was loathe to leave her. He suggested a walk in the park, anything to delay the moment of leaving. Just for these few hours, he would allow himself the luxury of being with her.

People were sprawled out on the grass and in striped canvas deckchairs, enjoying the sun and listening to the silver band playing show-tunes and regimental marches. He took off his jacket and they sat under a shady chestnut tree, lazily watching the passing scene. The ice cream vendors were doing a roaring trade and children raced excitedly past, on their way to feed the ducks on the Serpentine, or sail toy yachts on Round Pond.

'Whenever I see all this English greenness, I think of my poor ranch,' Honeychile said, wistfully. 'The land is so worn and tired it just blows away on the wind. But when my father was alive it was as verdant as this park.'

'And one day it will be again,' Alex said. 'When Mountjoy gives you the money.'

She plucked a blade of grass and bit on the end, tasting the sweetness. 'Somehow that doesn't seem to be my priority any more,' she said. 'I admit, I came to London because I needed the money. And I still need it, but now it's different. I really care about Uncle Mountjoy, and Laura. And I guess Anjou too, even though she drives me crazy. Of course, I would like Uncle Mountjoy to give me some money to save the ranch, but somehow, now, I just can't bring myself to ask for it. He's been so generous already, and I think he really cares about all of us.'

She lay back on the grass, pillowing her head on her arms. Alex folded his jacket under her head to make her more comfortable. She looked at him and said, 'You know all about me. Well, almost all. And I know nothing about you. Except for the gossip. Do you think that's fair?'

'My business enemies say that I am not a fair man.'

She smiled. 'That's business. And besides, I'm not your enemy. You're like d'Artagnan in the Three Musketeers,' she said. 'That "*strange elusive Pimpernel*." Nobody knows exactly who you are, or where you come from. *Who* are you, Alex?'

'Sometimes I wonder that myself,' he said, and there was an edge of bitterness to his voice. 'But if you really want to know, then I shall tell you.'

Honeychile sat up, she wrapped her arms round her knees, watching him, interestedly.

'I was born in Rome,' Alex said, 'In a little charity hospital tended by the Brothers of St John of God, on the Isola Tiberina, a tiny island in the middle of the River Tiber.

'My mother was Greek. She was on holiday in Italy with her family when she met the man who was to become my father. He was handsome, aristocratic and older than she was. Old enough to have known better, because she was young and naïve and in love, and he took advantage of that. Of course, she got pregnant, but when she told the man he said he was not responsible. He said he wasn't her first, nor her *only* lover; that a woman like her obviously had a dozen men in her bed, and the child had nothing to do with him.

'He abandoned her and she had no option but to tell her father and ask for his forgiveness and mercy. He did not give it to her. His good name meant more to him than his daughter. He disowned her and left her, alone in Rome, to fend for herself.'

Alex fell silent. He had never spoken of these things. The wounds had been salted with enough anger in his youth to cauterise them, and he had shut them out of his mind. Now he felt them burn once again as he told Honeychile the story of how with typical courage, his mother had picked herself up and got on with living.

'Her name was Cristina Andreos,' Alex continued, 'but she added Scott, choosing an English name in the hope that it would give her respectability and to disassociate herself from her father. She found work in a café. It was only a working-men's place, but the food was good and she learned how to cook pasta and sauces, and she worked until she was too far pregnant to go on.

'She saved every cent, living in a tiny, dark room in an old house on a dark, narrow street in Trastevere. A week after she gave birth, she took her baby with her and sold flowers in the Campo dei Fiori in the mornings, and on the corners of the affluent streets near the grand hotels at night. The immaculate white apron and black shawl she wore were a symbol of her poverty, not her peasant standing, because Cristina was no peasant. Her father was a Professor at the University in Athens. She spoke three languages and was well versed in classic Greek and Latin, the language of emperors and kings. She named me, her son after one, Alexander, hoping that one day something of the illustrious greatness of the original might rub off on me.

'When I was old enough to be left in the care of a neighbour, my mother went back to work in the café at night, and in the daytime she continued to sell flowers in the streets. She worked eighteen hours a day, six days a week. The free day, a Sunday, she spent with me. She taught me Latin and Greek, and to speak English and French; she encouraged me to believe I could be anything I wanted. But meanwhile, everyone in the neighbourhood knew she had no husband and her son was the lowest on even their low scale. "*Il batardo*," the bastard.

'As a child,' Alex said, 'I hung around *Il Sorrentino*, the restaurant where my mother worked, helping in the kitchen. When I was nine, I was given a proper job, clearing the tables. I felt the sweetness of earning money, of those coins jingling in my pocket at the end of the week. And I knew that for me, money was the only road to freedom and independence.

'I observed everything: the rich patrons, their fine manners, how they ate delicately. I noticed their clothes and the elegantly casual way they wore them. I listened to the way they spoke and practised their superior accent at home, alone. I observed the way the men behaved with the women, treating them like precious ornaments, instead of roughly and coarsely, the way they did in my poor neighbourhood. All the while I was pouring water into fine glasses at *Il Sorrentino*, I was learning how to improve myself. But no one had to teach me about business. It was an instinct with me.

'"The Greeks always knew how to trade," my mother told me, when I was older and lured by the sea. She borrowed money from a couple of the regular customers at the café: they knew her well and had been coming there for years. And I became the owner of a small fishing boat.'

Alex shrugged, 'And that's how the Scott Line began,' he said, still marvelling at his unprepossessing beginnings. 'With a sixteen year old boy and a rusting old boat in a little fishing village outside Rome; to where it is today, with vessels traversing the globe, registered in Panama and Gibraltar and Japan.

'Within a couple of months, I had sold the fishing boat for a profit and bought a larger one. I employed two men to fish for me and then I rented a second boat, taking it out myself, and thereby almost doubling my profits. For two years, I did this; buying and selling boats and renting others, until I had my own fishing fleet of a dozen boats and thirty men working for me. Then I sold the lot, and with that money, I bought myself a junky old freighter and began shipping sulphur from Cartagena in Spain.

'I never forgot the smell of that first ship: it will live in my memory for ever,' he said bitterly. 'I reeked of the filthy rotten-egg stink, it was in my clothes, in my hair, embedded, it seemed, in my very skin. But I was making money. I bought my second freighter a year later.

'With my profits from the sulphur cargoes, I bought my mother a tiny restaurant in the Piazza Navona, with a little apartment above. At last she had a home of her own, small though it was. She was a fabulous cook and soon "Tina's" was patronised by the wealthy and successful.

'Still, I hated her to work so hard, and the following year, with three vessels now shipping iron ore and steel from Germany, I was able to buy her a pretty villa in the Tuscan countryside, a place where she could rest, away from the hot Roman summers. But she could not be idle for long. She tended her vineyard there and served her good, full-bodied Montalcino wines in her restaurant, where they gradually began to gain some fame. I invested more money in the vineyard, planting new vines, employing a man to oversee the production. And it flourished.'

Alex looked at Honeychile. He smiled; 'It seemed I could do no wrong,' he said.

'My mother loved her little café; the customers were faithful to her and her fine food and wines, but she always resisted the temptation to expand. "Tina's" stayed small and exclusive and the rich and famous and ordinary alike, stood in line for a table.

'Now, my mother is retired,' Alex said. 'She lives between her vineyard in Tuscany and an apartment in Rome. Finally, she is able to rest, and be the "serene and gentle lady" I always dreamed she would be.

'So, now we know all about each other,' he said, getting to his feet. He took Honeychile's hand and pulled her up, holding her close to him for the space of a second. So close he could smell the faint perfume of her skin, as fresh and green as new grass.

'Thank you for telling me,' Honeychile whispered, thrilled that he had trusted her with his story. 'Now I feel I really know you. We have no secrets.'

But Alex knew he had not told her *all* his secrets.

They strolled back through the summery streets of Mayfair. Trees cast pools of shade on the hot pavements, and the scent of wallflowers and stocks and snapdragons wafted from the gardens in the Squares.

Alex was silent and Honeychile eyed him anxiously from the corner of her eye; she wondered if he was regretting telling her about his past. She had felt so included in his life, so close to him, and now he was remote again. Sometimes she thought he was deliberately putting a great distance between them.

They stopped outside Mountjoy House. 'Won't you come in?' she smiled, hopefully. 'I'll give you tea to refresh you for the long walk back to St James's?'

He said coolly, 'I must say goodbye, Honeychile. I enjoyed being with you today.'

She looked expectantly at him, half-smiling, waiting for him to ask her out to dinner, or the theatre; anything, just so they could be together. 'No tea?' she asked, with a teasing laugh.

Alex sighed; what he was doing was not easy. 'It's better if we do not see each other again,' he said abruptly. 'You're young. Go enjoy your life, meet some charming young man who can offer you everything I cannot. Forget about me,' he said, regretfully. And he turned and walked away.

'Alex, Alex . . .' she ran after him. She grabbed his arm, oblivious to the passers-by staring curiously at them. Her great blue eyes stared imploringly into his. 'Why? *Why*, Alex?'

'I'm sorry, if I misled you,' he said quietly. 'I'm truly sorry.'

She saw the finality in his face and she let go of his arm, watching as he strode away from her. 'I'll never forget you, Alex,' she whispered. 'I'll always love you.'

They were the same words she had said to her father at his funeral, when she was just a little girl, hoping that he would come back for her. But he never had, and somehow she knew, neither would Alex Scott. It was over before it even really began.

PART III

CHAPTER 30

'Laura and Billy are thick as thieves, these days,' Anjou said, jealously. 'I can't understand what she sees in him. With that stammer, it's impossible even to hold a conversation with the man. It must be his money that she finds so attractive.'

They were at Mountjoy Park for the weekend. She was standing sullenly by the drawing room window, with her arms folded and a bored look on her face, watching as Laura climbed into Billy's sporty little red Triumph and they sped down the driveway, off on some expedition to the stables, no doubt. She had not forgotten that Billy Saxton had turned her down that day and she took every opportunity to undermine him.

Honeychile sighed, sometimes she simply did not understand Anjou. She could be nice-as-pie one minute, and the next she was the bitch she had called her that first day.

'Really, Anjou, why do you have to be so downright mean?' she asked. 'You know Laura is in love with Billy, and he is with her. I'll bet anything he asks her to marry him this weekend. Besides,' she added, 'Billy only stammers when he's with strangers, or watching his racehorses run. *Or* when he's with people he doesn't like, so I guess that must include you,' she added.

Honeychile was sitting on the big blue Knole sofa. She was wearing immaculately cut jodhpurs and hand-made riding boots, a bright yellow turtle-neck sweater and a tweed jacket. Her bowler hat lay on the sofa next to her. She looked a lot different from the blue-overalled dusty girl at the ranch. She was waiting for Uncle Mountjoy; they were going riding together, and he had promised she could try out the new mare Billy had found for him and assured him was going to be a winner.

She tapped her riding crop absently against her polished leather boots. She loved these weekends in the country; they gave her an opportunity to ride wonderful horses and at least that was *one* thing she did not have to learn. Even the critical Laura could not fault her on horseback. Besides, it got her out of London and away from Alex.

After the day they had spent together, she seemed to see him constantly, but always at a distance: in the audience in the theatre; in a crowd at a dance; or a few tables away in the same restaurant. London was like a small town, everybody gossiped, especially in the powder rooms at the dances where wallflowers went to hide their shame and over-enthusiastic dancers went to pin up a broken strap, or have their hems stitched. All the girls claimed to be in love with him. And wherever Alex Scott went, gossip followed.

Everybody knew where he had been seen and with whom, and they all secretly envied the woman he was with. 'He's the catch of the decade,' they said, 'now the Prince of Wales has gone.' But their fathers did not think so. They thought Alex Scott was a foreigner and a scoundrel; how else did he get so rich so young?

'*Mon Dieu*, I am so *bored*,' Anjou cried, exasperated. 'Tell me, why am I here? Stuck in this mausoleum of a house in the middle of the deserted countryside with only horses for company. I *hate* horses, I *hate* the countryside, I never want to see another blade of grass again.'

Honeychile stared curiously at her, striding angrily up and down the length of the fifty foot drawing room. She really did not understand what made Anjou tick. 'You're just jealous, that's all,' she said. It was a shot in the dark, but it seemed to hit home.

Anjou stood in front of the sofa, confronting her. '*Eh bien*, and what have *you* got to be so smug about, Miss Texas?' she demanded furiously. 'Dear Alex . . . "*my boyfriend*" you called him, the one who kissed you. Where is *he*, huh? I'll tell you where? He's at Blenheim for the weekend with the Italian Ambassador's daughter, that's where. He's dumped you, little Miss Texas, because he probably finds you as boring as I do.'

Honeychile did not know whether to laugh or cry; Anjou looked so ridiculous, red-faced with anger and frustration. She knew Anjou didn't mean it. Later, she would come repentantly and apologise. She always did. But it didn't lessen the hurt of what she said.

'I'm off.' She stood up and pushed past Anjou.

'Oh *merde*, go ride your stupid horses, why don't you,' Anjou yelled after her. 'You know what I said was true.'

Honeychile knew Anjou loathed all animals, especially horses. She shuddered at the mere mention of them. 'Only the mad English adore them,' she said scornfully. 'They would probably take them to bed, if they could.'

But of course Anjou never said things like that in Lord Mountjoy's presence. She was too clever for that. Anjou had one face for when she wanted to make an impression on people, and one face for the truth. Sometimes she behaved so outrageously, she was so selfish Honeychile thought she could never forgive her. But then she would be so sweet, so apologetic, so *sincerely* sorry, that of course, Honeychile always did.

Maybe that was part of the trouble with Anjou, she thought later, as she cantered along the bridle path with her uncle. No matter how bad she was, everybody always forgave her.

'Put the young 'un flat out,' Mountjoy shouted instructions behind her. 'Let's see what she's made of.'

She dug in her heels and galloped the beautiful bay mare for more than a mile, forgetting Anjou in the sheer delight of the speeding animal beneath her.

'That gel has a fine seat,' Mountjoy murmured admiringly to himself, cantering along behind her. 'Georgie always rode like that. She's a chip off the old block all right, no doubt about it.'

He thought about Laura, who also rode as well as any man, and better than most, and pride swelled in his chest. He could be damned proud of '*his girls*', he told himself, smiling as he remembered Anjou, who knew how to twist a fellow round her little finger, even an old chap like himself.

Anjou might not ride a horse, but she had more charm than most other girls. She would make a brilliant marriage, he was sure. And now young Laura was getting engaged to Billy Saxton. Billy had asked his permission just last night, after dinner at Saxton Mowbrey, when they were sipping a damned fine 1894 Taylors Port and enjoying a fair bit of Stilton. Kept a good table, Billy Saxton. His family may have made their pile in trade, but he was a good chap.

Now the other fellow, Alex Scott, who Anjou had told him Honeychile was keen on, had to be a bit of a bounder. They said he had made millions before he was even twenty-one, and now he was one of the richest men in the world. 'You couldn't trust a fellow like that,' he said to himself. Something had to be wrong, but nobody seemed to know exactly what. Still, he could see Honeychile was unhappy, and it bothered him.

Mountjoy sighed, looking at Honeychile cantering the mare back towards him, along the bridle-path. He felt sorry for her, falling in love with a wrong 'un. He would have to see if he couldn't drum up some kind of entertainment to divert her. Cheer the poor girl up. Women were funny about these things; falling in love and all that rot. He had never fallen in love in his life and nor had any of the fellows he knew. They married who they were supposed to and did their duty and that was that.

He sighed again. Times had changed and he supposed things were different in his day. He would call Sophie, when he got back, and ask her to organise an engagement celebration, here at Mountjoy Park. They would have a big house party, and he would tell Sophie to be sure to invite some nice eligible fellows for Honeychile and Anjou. All the neighbours would have house parties for the dance, and everyone would come. What was the name of that band leader the young ones were all so crazy about? Ambrose, was it? Or Carroll Gibbons? Sophie would know. And they would have fireworks, a grand pyrotechnic display over the lake.

Lord Mountjoy recalled that cold January day, just a few months back, sitting on the train from Bath to London. It had been his seventieth birthday and he had told himself he was lonely and old.

He laughed out loud as he set his horse to a gallop, racing Honeychile back down the bridle-path. He was lonely no longer, and what's more he did not even feel old. He felt like a new man.

Billy never did ask Laura to marry him. They were in his red Triumph, driving from Mountjoy Park to Saxton Mowbrey; he had stopped to allow a slow-moving herd of Friesians to plod past them into a field, when she turned to him and said, 'You don't have to go down on one knee Billy. I intend to marry you, whether you ask me or not.'

He laughed and kissed her and said, 'Well, that's a relief.' Then he took a blue suede box from his pocket and showed her the beautiful ring with a flawless round diamond. 'For you, my lovely Laura,' he said, solemnly, as he placed it on her finger. Then he looked at her and added, 'with all my love.'

'Oh, Billy,' she cried, kissing him, 'it's beautiful, wonderful.' They looked at each other, smiling, and she said, 'Just imagine if I hadn't met you on the train that day. I might never have known you. Whatever would I have done, without you.'

'I would have found you,' he said, kissing her again. 'I would have seen you in some London ballroom and our eyes would have met across the room and we would have known instantly we were made for each other.'

She laughed, 'Instead, you had to lend me your handkerchief to dry my eyes and listen to my moaning about poor old Haddon.'

'He'll never know what a fool he was,' Billy agreed, as the last of the cows sauntered into the field and the farmhand closed the gate, and they drove on, dismissing Haddon from their minds and their lives as though he had never existed.

Laura and Billy's engagement was announced in *The Times* the following week. Laura read it at breakfast at Mountjoy Park, nibbling toast and drinking hot coffee, and she thought, pleased, that at last it was official. She looked at the large round diamond Billy had given her. He had lots of his mother's jewellery in the bank vault, including her engagement ring, but he had wanted to give her something that would belong to her alone, a special ring that bound them together always, and so he had gone to Bond Street and chosen this ring himself.

Laura ran her eye down the column of engagements, stopping to read the very last one again. It was short and curt and it said that the wedding arranged between Lady Diana Gilmore and Mr Haddon Fox would not now take place.

'Good Lord,' she said, startled. Then, 'Poor Haddon.' And she meant it. She was so happy she wanted everyone else to be happy too. But she forgot all about him, as she drove over to Saxton Mowbrey to inspect the stables and make plans for the new training yard Billy was going to build for her. And she didn't even remember her vow to get her revenge on Haddon; it was simply not important.

The engagement party took place at Mountjoy Park a few weeks later. Aunt Sophie and Laura had arranged it. Laura didn't want it to be too formal, just jolly good fun, and they invited a houseful of friends to stay, and there were more at Saxton Mowbrey; and all the big houses locally had house parties too. The Mountjoy gardeners were busy bringing in great sheaves of flowers and hundreds of little orange trees from the hothouses, and electricians swarmed over the place for a week, setting up the special wiring. An enormous marquee with a special wooden floor for dancing was erected on the back lawns, and jugglers and conjurors and fortune tellers and magicians and strolling musicians were hired to entertain the guests.

Mountjoy Park was floodlit for the occasion and so was the lake; thousands of tiny lights were strung in the trees and along the terraces. Looking at it before their guests arrived, Laura told her uncle she had never seen anything so beautiful, so majestic, so enduring.

'The last time it was floodlit was for my own engagement to Penelope,' Mountjoy said, 'but I don't recall it looking quite so lovely.'

Jeannie Swinburn came to stay and she was the star of the show. She looked charming in a new dress made specially by Rachel in Harrogate, that was rather nice even though it had been a bit of a rush job to get it ready in time. It was a lovely violet-blue velvet, with long tight sleeves and a slender skirt that flared out a bit at the hem. With it she wore the diamond necklace that Adriana Fioraldi had given Laura's mother on her wedding day. The colour brought out the blue of her eyes and her pink cheeks, and with her silver hair upswept, Laura told her she looked like a queen. 'Elinor of Aquitaine, or somebody,' she decided. 'Regal anyway.'

Madame Suzette was by far the smartest woman there in a grand gown of amber satin embroidered with bronze beads, with a matching organza stole that swept all the way to the floor. At dinner Aunt Sophie had made sure to place her between a member of the French diplomatic corps and the Italian Ambassador, in whom she seemed to have found a soul mate.

Anjou was probably the most beautiful girl there, though not the happiest. She wore a green chiffon gown that was daringly almost backless and exactly matched the colour of her eyes, and the emerald necklace Lord Mountjoy had given her. There was a queue of men waiting to dance with her and competition for the supper dance was intense until Anjou resolved it by saying she was going in to supper with a young Scotsman, whom she had never met before that night, but who she definitely found intriguing. He was tall and lusty-looking and spoke with a fascinating burr, and he promised to teach her the reel after supper.

Honeychile wore blue, soft and silken with a flowing skirt and a low-cut neckline that Aunt Sophie had pronounced quite shocking, though not nearly as shocking as Anjou's backless frock. But the huge rope of Mountjoy pearls filled in the bosom part quite well, when they were properly arranged. She wore a gardenia in her hair and danced every dance with a different young man, wishing they could be Alex.

Laura wore a flowery dress of cream silk patterned with roses, and she looked like the perfect English rose herself, radiant with happiness. Her eyes sparkled as brightly as her new engagement ring, and everyone noticed how Billy just couldn't take his eyes off her.

They were, Lord Mountjoy said, contentedly to Sophie, the perfect couple.

CHAPTER 31

It was a Thursday night and Honeychile was alone at Mountjoy House. She had stayed home with a summer cold, and was feeling sorry for herself and very lonely. Anjou had gone to a dance at Claridge's with a group of young people; and Laura was at the country house for a long weekend, though really she was spending all her time with Billy. Or at least as much as Aunt Sophie would permit. And Lord Mountjoy was up in Scotland, inspecting his moors for the grouse shoot that would take place in August.

A warm wind wafted the curtains at the open window, bringing the London sounds of traffic and the scent of the massed flowers in the courtyard and in the window-boxes. If she closed her eyes, Honeychile could remember the different night sounds of the ranch: the hot searching wind sighing through the parched grass, the whistle of the train, the bellowing of thirsty, dying cattle.

It seemed so far away; another lifetime lived by another person. And yet it was locked in her heart for ever. With her eyes closed, she conjured up a picture of Aliza, standing at the stove, fixing flapjacks for breakfast; of Fisher lurking under the table where she could sneak him forbidden morsels; and Tom hurriedly draining his coffee-cup so he could get to the stables and begin his day's work. She was just thinking, longingly, of how much she missed them and the ranch, when Johnson knocked on her door with the cablegram on a silver salver.

She looked astonished at him. 'Why would anybody be sending me a cable from Texas?' she asked, worriedly, ripping it open. She read it quickly and then again.

'I trust it is not bad news, Miss,' Johnson said, waiting to see if there was a reply.

'Bad news?' She looked at him, stunned. 'Oh no. No, it's not bad news.'

'Do you wish to send a reply, Miss?'

She read the cablegram again, still not quite believing it. 'No,' she said, 'not now. I have to think.'

Johnson departed and she sank into a chair, reading the cable again and again until what it said finally sank in: BIG OIL STRIKE MOUNTJOY RANCH NOW YOU CAN COME HOME AGAIN LOVE TOM ALIZA.

How could they have struck oil, she wondered. They had stopped drilling years ago when they had found nothing.

The telephone rang. It was Andersen, the lawyer from San Antonio.

'It's taken me a day to get through,' Andersen explained, 'but I guess you've got Tom's cable by now?'

'I have,' Honeychile said, shocked at hearing his voice again. She had never seen him since the day he came to the Sanitarium to apologise for giving custody of her to Jack Delaney.

'Well, I can tell you this time, Honeychile, it's true. And if it hadn't been for Tom messing around, searching for water we might never have come across it. Those smart-alec wildcatters surely didn't. They must have been digging in the wrong place, when all the time, not a hundred yards away was a mother-lode of oil.

'Tom was just drilling wherever he got the hunch, but instead of water, all that was coming out of the ground was thick grey ooze. So he telephoned me and I took a little trip out there to inspect the scene. "Darn me, if that don't look like oil, young feller," I said. The very next day I had a team over there with a proper drill. They put in a rig and drilled for maybe a week, then rich black oil just spurted out of that dead barren ground as though there was no end. And apparently, Honeychile, there isn't. The experts tell me that Mountjoy is potentially one of the biggest fields in Texas. And you are gonna be a very rich young woman.'

Honeychile thought of the familiar pastures dotted with ugly oil derricks, spitting out money. She thought of Tom, who had discovered it, and Aliza, and how, if she were going to be rich, then they would be rich too. And she thought of Andersen and how close he had come to ruining her life. She knew she could not trust him.

'I have it all planned out,' Andersen was saying, and she could

302

hear the satisfaction in his voice. 'We shall make a favourable deal with an oil company to exploit the field, just the way we did before. And you won't have to worry about a thing, Honeychile. All you have to do is give me your power of attorney, and let me handle everything for you.

'Don't you wait too long now, Honeychile,' he warned, when she said she had to think about it. 'These oil fellers are hot to go. The sooner you sign on the dotted line, the sooner the money is in the bank.'

Honeychile stood at the window, staring into the lamplit street, thinking about what to do. Andersen was dealing with a different person from the frightened, ignorant child she had been last time they had signed over the rights to prospect for the oil. She was older and wiser, and Rosie was no longer around, ready to sell out to the first offer so she could get her hands on the money and spend it.

She knew Andersen would be out to line his own pockets. If she gave him power of attorney, he would be able to do whatever he liked, and she would never know.

She wished Uncle Mountjoy was here to advise her. She considered telephoning him in Scotland, but it was too late, and anyhow she knew he would tell her to wait until he got back to London and then they would see what to do.

She paced the floor; she couldn't wait, she was too excited, too nervous. She ran to the phone and called Saxton Mowbrey, but they said Billy and Laura were at a dinner-dance near Bath, and not expected back until late.

Honeychile knew there was only one other person who could help her. The best person of all. The expert businessman who would know exactly what she should do about Mountjoy oil.

She glanced at her watch. It was almost midnight. She picked up the phone, thought a minute, then put it back down again. She had not spoken to Alex since the day they had lunch, a month ago. It was late, he might be with someone. But she had to see him. She would get a taxi to Berkeley Square; then she could walk past his house, see if the lights were on. If they were, she would ring the bell and ask the manservant if Alex were alone. If he was with someone, she would just leave; he would never even know she had been there.

She knew she should really wait until tomorrow. But she told herself that tomorrow she would have to tell Andersen what to do.

Even as she talked herself into it, she knew it was only half true. It was an excuse to see Alex again. Smiling, she changed into a pretty dress, brushed her hair and dabbed on a touch of Chanel No. 5.

Anjou was at the Florida Club in Berkeley Square; she had sneaked out from the dance at Claridge's with Archie Reynolds. She glanced impatiently at Archie, her escort and partner in crime. She thought how unattractive he was, with his pink cheeks and fair hair and round blue eyes. And how boring.

She had talked Archie into taking her to Ciro's, in Soho. It was very glamorous with a dance floor lit from beneath and it had been packed to the rafters; from there they had gone onto the Café de Paris, and then here, to the Florida in Berkeley Square, which was a mistake because there was hardly anyone there that night, just a few older-looking couples dancing on the revolving floor. Suddenly this did not seem like the good idea it had at the beginning of the evening.

She thought of all the men she had met, and how easy it was to get them under her spell, promising them everything with her eyes until they were ready to do anything for her. But they were all so dull and cautious. Anjou had always preferred things that were forbidden: people, nightclubs, sex. There was a perversity in her nature that enjoyed the secret thrill of forbidden knowledge.

She thought about the elusive Alex Scott. Somehow that man was always on her mind. Alex Scott played the field. No one could catch him, though heaven knows, many had tried.

She glanced at hot young Archie, sweating in the candlelight and looking more and more unappealing and younger every minute. And she thought about man-of-the-world Alex and how much more desirable he was, and how she always enjoyed a challenge, especially one with daring and the thrill of danger to it.

Anjou got up from the table. 'Goodbye, Archie,' she said, and she walked away, leaving him staring after her, goggle-eyed with shock.

Anjou collected her black velvet cape with the satin lining, then she went to the Powder Room. She emerged ten minutes later, freshly lipsticked and powdered and smelling of her favourite perfume, Guerlain's sharp, sophisticated *Jicky*.

It was foggy out and she wrapped her cape closely about her.

Refusing the doorman's offer to get her a taxi, she strode purposefully across Berkeley Square.

Alex was in his study, working late. He had just showered and was in his bathrobe, when the doorbell rang. He glanced, astonished at his watch. It was after midnight and the staff had gone to bed long ago.

He sighed impatiently, wondering who it could be at this time of night. He walked through the hall and opened the door.

'Anjou,' he exclaimed, looking shocked. 'What on earth are you doing here?'

'I was at the Florida Club, just across the Square,' she said, looking as desperate as she could. 'Something happened. I . . . I must talk to you, Alex. You're the only one who can help me.'

'But it's late,' he said concerned. 'You should go home, Anjou. I'll call you a taxi and speak to you in the morning.'

'No, no, it can't wait.' She pushed past him into the hall. She stood there, looking beautiful in her black velvet cape with her red hair tumbling about her shoulders and her narrow green eyes, watching him. Then she turned quickly and, before he could stop her, strode into his study.

Anjou stared curiously around the spare, masculine room, at the large desk and walls of shelves, and the comfortable sofa in front of the fire. On the table beside it was an open book, and a plain silver tray with a decanter of scotch and a half-filled glass.

'So this is the lion's den. I wondered what it would be like,' she said, with that little cat-smile. 'Well? Aren't you going to offer me a drink?'

'Anjou, this is a very compromising situation, I shall call you a cab right away,' Alex picked up the phone. 'Whatever it is you need to talk about will have to wait.'

'*No.*' She came over to him. '*Please, Alex.* Just hear what I have to say.' She put her hand on his arm, staring urgently into his eyes. 'Alex, I love you. Oh, I know you'll say I'm just a foolish young woman, but I can't get you out of my mind. I stayed away from you because I thought you wanted Honeychile, but now I know you don't.'

'Anjou, for God's sake,' he said, exasperated. 'You mean you came here at this time of night just to make this ridiculous statement of love?

305

It is simply not true.' He turned back to the telephone and dialled the number of the taxi rank on the corner.

She said softly, behind him. 'I've come here to prove my love to you. Just look, Alex, how much I love you.' The black velvet cape with the lining of palest green satin, slid to the floor with a faint silken rustle as he turned round and looked at her.

'My God,' he said, slamming down the phone. 'Are you crazy?'

'I'm not crazy, Alex, you are.' Smiling seductively, she stepped forward and wrapped her arms round him.

Honeychile paid off the taxi at the corner of Berkeley Square. Now that she was here, she wasn't so sure she was doing the right thing. After all, it was very late. Alex would probably be in bed, or he might be entertaining. She walked down the street, slowing as she approached the house. Her heart lifted; there was a single light downstairs. He must be in there, working, and at this time of night, he would certainly be alone. She told herself that after all, she had a legitimate reason for needing to speak to him urgently. But, as she walked up to the steps, her heart was beating faster, and she knew it was because she was going to see him.

The front door stood open. Surprised, she knocked and after a minute, went in. She walked down the carpeted hall; there was a familiar perfume in the air, spicy and sophisticated. There was a light on in the room to the left and the door was ajar. She knew she should not, but she pushed it open and peeked in.

She stared, shocked, at the woman in Alex's arms. She was wrapped around him so tightly they might have been one. And apart from her high-heeled gold sandals, she was as naked as on the day she was born.

Alex's eyes met her horrified ones over the woman's naked white shoulder.

'Honeychile,' he called, despairingly. 'My God, Honeychile.'

Astonished, Anjou untangled herself and turned to look. '*Mon Dieu*,' she said with a triumphant smile. 'If it isn't little Miss Texas herself.'

Honeychile turned and fled. She heard Alex call after her, but she did not look back. She ran out of the house and down the street, the tears flowing unheeded down her face. '*How could he*,' she said to herself, '*how could he, oh how could he, how could he . . . ?*'

Across the square, the revellers were leaving the Florida, hailing taxis and laughing and talking. Harry Lockwood told the two men he was with that he preferred to walk, and said goodnight.

It was a warm night, though a bit foggy, and he was feeling particularly good because earlier in the evening he had won the princely sum of five thousand pounds from a man he was sure he could no longer call his friend, even though he had won fair and square. He never cheated at cards. He might be poor but he was still a gentleman about these things; he was just a damned good poker player, that's all. And a true gambler.

As he walked across the square, Harry thought to himself that if he ever got really lucky and married a rich woman, he could happily spend the rest of his days at the tables in Monte Carlo, wearing perfectly cut tails and diamond studs. They might be considered a bit flashy but he wouldn't be averse to showing how rich he was, after being poor for so many years. He could almost *feel* the thrill of risking thousands on the turn of a card. That, he thought wistfully, was the true pinnacle of experience. To risk all and not to care whether you won or lost. To play for the sheer excitement of the game, and not just because you needed to pay your damned bills.

He glanced up, as he heard footsteps. A young woman was running towards him. Her blonde hair was flying and tears were running down her face. She stumbled and he caught her in his arms.

'Why, Honeychile Mountjoy,' he said, astonished. 'Whatever is the matter?'

He quickly flagged down a passing taxi. He put Honeychile into it, instructed the cabbie to just drive around until he told him different, and then got in next to her.

'Put your head on my shoulder, Honeychile,' he said. 'Cry your eyes out, if you must. Then afterwards, you can tell me what it's all about.'

While she proceeded to do just that, he asked himself exactly what Honeychile Mountjoy was doing alone and in tears in Berkeley Square after midnight? He did not know the answer, but it promised to be interesting.

After a while, Honeychile sat up. He gave her his handkerchief and she mopped her eyes and then looked miserably at him.

He thought she looked terrible, as though her world had come to an end. He told the cab driver to take them to Lyons Corner House on Coventry Street, then he said to Honeychile, 'Powder your nose, darling. I'm taking you for the English remedy for all that ails you. A nice cup of tea.'

Harry handled the situation terrifically well: he whisked her through the busy all-night tearooms to a quiet corner table and ordered tea and sticky buns. He told her just to take her time, then she could tell him what was wrong. And then he waited for her to come to her senses, because she seemed to be in a daze.

The tea was exactly the right antidote. She sipped it cautiously, the colour gradually came back into her face and she ceased to look as though she might go and faint on him at any minute.

He munched on a sticky currant bun, and said conversationally, 'When I was a child, my mother used to bring me here during school exeats, as a special treat. I've loved these buns ever since.'

Honeychile said nothing. She just watched as he poured more tea and then ate another bun. 'Not exactly a grand sort of place to bring a girl,' he said, 'but just right under the circumstances, I thought.'

'You're so kind, Harry,' she said impulsively. 'I can't think what I would have done, if I hadn't run into you.'

'Well then, I'm jolly glad you did,' he said gallantly. He hesitated, looking at her. Honeychile was not his type. She was too straight-ahead for him. He preferred women with a bit more mystery, and by that, he thought with a reminiscent grin, he meant sexy. Like her cousin, Anjou. Now *there* was a woman.

'More tea?' He re-filled her cup, summoned the waitress and ordered a couple more buns. Then he looked expectantly at Honeychile.

'So?' he said. 'Care to tell me what all that was about?'

Honeychile looked doubtfully at him. 'Can I trust you?' she asked in a tremulous voice that he knew was not the least bit like her normal one.

Harry was just relieved she had finally spoken. He had thought he might have to sit here all night until she came to her senses, and that would have put him – and Honeychile – in trouble with old Lord Mountjoy. The old boy might disinherit her before she was even made an heiress.

'Honeychile,' he said, looking sincerely into her swollen eyes. 'Of all the men in London, I am the one you can trust. You have no idea,' he added with a smile, 'how many women have confided their most personal secrets to me, and not once have I so much as breathed a word.' He did not tell her that the confidences had usually been told to him in bed, and part of his success was due to his discretion. And that he was only discreet because if he were not, he would never be invited to another Mediterranean villa or country weekend house party again.

'Come on, darling,' he said gently, 'why not just begin at the beginning, and tell me everything. Then we'll see what to do about it.'

Honeychile took a sip of tea, then she took a deep breath and began to tell him about the mother-lode of oil under the Mountjoy Ranch, and that she was going to be rich.

Harry looked at her with new respect; she was a millionaire in her own right; she didn't even need old Mountjoy's money. In fact, from what she was telling him, it sounded as though she would probably be much richer even than Mountjoy. Suddenly, Honeychile was looking very much more attractive.

She told him how she didn't trust Andersen and had needed Alex Scott's advice, and so she had gone to see him.

Harry raised a sceptical eyebrow. 'Now, darling,' he said, 'wasn't it rather late to go paying a call on a man?' He shook his head, 'Naughty, Honeychile.'

She blushed with shame. 'I wish I had never gone,' she whispered. 'If only I hadn't.'

Harry looked alarmed. 'Nothing happened did it? I mean, Alex didn't make a pass at you . . . or anything? Did he?'

She shook her head, miserably. 'He was with . . .'

Harry leaned across the table to catch the whispered name; he thought it might pay to have something on a man like Alex Scott, you never knew when it might come in useful.

But he was astonished when she blurted in an anguished whisper, 'He was with Anjou.'

Harry remembered his own little fling with Anjou; she was a sexy little kitten and she knew her way around. He knew Anjou had only slept with him because she was bored; the opportunity had been there and she had taken it. Besides, she had recognised that they were alike: they both lived on their wits and their nerve. He admired her but she despised him because he was so poor. He had called her several times, afterwards, with the Mountjoy money very much on his mind, but Anjou had been too clever for that. She had not returned his calls and he had got the message. She was after bigger fish, a grander title and more money than he could offer.

He thought about Honeychile and her new fortune and how he might end up in the Saville Row white tie and tails and diamond studs in Monte Carlo, after all.

'I never want to see Alex again,' Honeychile said tremulously. 'And I just can't bear to face Anjou in the morning. Oh Harry, what shall I do?' She looked imploringly at him.

There were two subjects Harry was expert on: one was gambling and the other was women. He thought about the oil wells on Mountjoy Ranch and he knew if he played his cards cleverly, that money could be his. Honeychile was weak and vulnerable, and he knew exactly how to play her.

He was gentle, charming, the knight in shining armour. The helpful serf to her maiden in distress. 'I'll do anything I can to help you,' he told her earnestly. 'And I think I know how. I have a friend in New York. He heads an important law practice on Park Avenue and he is very well respected; he's no fly-by-night out to take advantage like Andersen. Jock Lamont is just the man you need to advise you.'

He looked triumphantly at her, 'It just so happens he's in Paris right now.' He glanced at his watch, 'It's two o'clock. We could catch the boat train at seven and be there late this afternoon.'

Honeychile stared at him, half-astonished, half-wary, and then he added his trump card. 'The best thing is, it gets you out of here. It gives you a breathing space. You won't have to face Anjou, or Alex.'

He saw her doubts change to relief as she thought about it. Then she said worriedly, 'But I don't have any money.'

Harry thanked God for the five thousand pounds in winnings that he knew would be in his bank account that morning. He said, 'I hope you will allow me the privilege of taking care of everything.'

She looked wary again and he smiled sincerely at her. 'Don't worry, darling,' he said, 'I'll book separate hotels, and you can be back the next morning, if you wish. Unlike your friend Alex, I wouldn't dream of compromising a woman.'

She looked trustingly at him. 'How can I ever thank you for rescuing me?'

Let me count the ways, Harry thought, smiling.

'You're a true friend,' she said, gratefully. 'I shall never forget this.'

'Just pack your bag quickly and all your troubles will be over,' he promised.

He knew exactly how to play this game, when to be gentle and helpful and when to turn on the charm. He was an accomplished actor and this was a role he had been playing all his life. He'd bet good odds that Honeychile Mountjoy would be Lady Lockwood before she knew what had happened.

Lord Mountjoy was not pleased when he stepped off the overnight Edinburgh to London express, two days later, and heard the newsboys shouting his name. He looked at the headlines, MOUNTJOY HEIRESS ELOPES TO PARIS, and his face turned pale.

He sat in the Rolls reading about Honeychile running off with the well-known gambler and ladies' man, Harry Lockwood, and for the first time since his wife died, he felt like crying.

'Why?' he asked himself, sadly, over and over again. 'Why did she do it?'

He asked Anjou and Laura the same thing when he got to Mountjoy House and summoned them, at once, to the library.

'Tell me what happened,' he commanded. 'I go away for a few days, everything seems fine and the next thing I know Honeychile has run off with that scoundrel Lockwood. Why, I ask you?'

'She certainly kept it a secret from me,' Anjou said quickly. 'I suppose she fell in love.'

Laura looked sceptically at her. 'I know who she was in love with and so do you, Anjou. And it certainly wasn't Harry.'

'Then who was it?' Mountjoy demanded, wondering how so much intrigue could go on under his own roof and he not know a thing about it.

'She was in love with Alex Scott,' Laura said. 'Of course she knew it would never come to anything, and I don't think she even saw him any more.'

She stared at Anjou. 'But you probably know more about that than I do.'

Anjou said hurriedly, 'All I know is I spoke to her before I left for the dance at Claridge's on Thursday night. She had a cold and didn't want to go. I got home late and I slept late the next morning. I never even saw her and I have no idea why she ran off with Harry.'

She avoided Laura's eyes; she knew Laura suspected she was involved in some way, but she certainly wasn't about to tell her what had happened. And besides, she thought vindictively, if Honeychile was stupid enough to run away with Harry, she deserved all she got.

Mountjoy looked sadly at the cable announcing their marriage. He sighed deeply, thinking of Harry's bad reputation as a gambler. He told himself he would never understand women. Of all the girls, Honeychile was the last one he would have expected to behave so irresponsibly. He only hoped Harry would not break her heart. Why, oh why, he asked himself sorrowfully, did she do it?

CHAPTER 32

Three months later, in their grand Manhattan townhouse, Honeychile was asking herself exactly the same thing.

It was nine o'clock on an unexpectedly hot Saturday morning and she was in their bedroom, sipping coffee and staring out of the window at leafy Central Park. She could not bear to look at the empty bed. The sheets were neatly turned back and the pillows were undented, just the way the maid had left them, because Harry had not come home last night, and the bed had not been slept in.

She asked herself, what had gone wrong? Harry had been so wonderful at first. He had taken her to Paris and installed her at the Bristol, and he had taken a suite for himself at the Ritz. The lawyer, Jock Lamont, had met them there that evening. They had had drinks and dinner at *Vefour* while they discussed the new Mountjoy Ranch oil-strike. Jock had agreed to look after her interests and he said she wasn't to worry, he would see that this time, she was not cheated.

Afterwards, she and Harry had strolled hand-in-hand along the banks of the River Seine, marvelling at the beauty of the city. Suddenly he had surprised her by telling her that he was in love with her; that he had been from the moment he first saw her at the ball at Mountjoy House, but he had thought he didn't stand a chance.

'You were the Mountjoy girls,' he said, sadly. 'The heiresses-to-be. I know old Mountjoy wanted at least a Duke for you – I'm sure he would have liked a prince, but there were none left. What chance did I stand, with a lowly title and not much money. At least not yet, though I am working hard to make my own fortune.'

He put his hands on Honeychile's shoulders, looking deep into her eyes. 'I know I shouldn't say this, Honeychile, but I'm crazy about you. And at least I've behaved like a gentleman, which is more than can be said for Alex.'

He put a finger under her chin, tilting her face up to him. 'Forget him, darling, and marry me,' he said, his voice husky with emotion. 'I promise on my honour I will look after you, and I shall love you always.'

Honeychile felt the knife twist once again as she thought of Alex with Anjou. She thought Harry might not be a richer man but he was certainly a better one. With Harry, she would be safe. And she couldn't help hoping it would hurt Alex when he heard she was engaged to him.

'I'll marry you, Harry,' she said.

A look of intense pleasure came over his face. He closed his eyes hardly believing his luck, and Honeychile smiled too, touched by how obviously he cared. She told herself that Alex had never loved her like this. He had kept her at arm's length because he'd been seeing Anjou secretly all the time. She was wounded and the need for revenge burned in her heart. So, when Harry said why wait? Let's get married right away? She agreed.

Harry arranged everything: he booked a suite on the French liner, the *Normandie*, sailing from Cherbourg to New York that evening. He whirled her into the shops on the rue de la Paix and bought her a beautiful cream chiffon dress and a matching picture hat trimmed with pink silk roses. He took her into Chaumet and bought her a gold wedding band and had it inscribed inside with their initials and the date, and he promised her a diamond 'as big as his love for her', later.

That same evening, as the liner sailed through the choppy Atlantic waters off the coast of Brittany, Honeychile became Lady Lockwood. She wore her blonde hair upswept so she would look older and the large cartwheel hat hid the tears glittering in her eyes as the Captain gave them his blessing. She was already wishing she had not done it, but it was too late to back out.

Their first night was not the love-filled emotional experience she had always imagined it would be. But that was when she had thought she would be with Alex.

Harry went tactfully out onto the deck for a cigarette, while she prepared for bed. She brushed her hair and put on the pink silk nightdress trimmed with thick ecru lace that Aunt Sophie had chosen for her, ages ago it seemed, at the White House on Bond Street. It was modestly high-necked and expensive enough, Aunt Sophie had said, so she needn't be ashamed when the maids at the grand houses where she spent weekends, unpacked for her.

'Never skimp on good underthings,' Aunt Sophie had warned, 'because that's what servants notice, and they always gossip.'

Honeychile was looking at herself in the dressing table mirror, big-eyed with apprehension and wishing she were anywhere else but there, when Harry knocked on the door.

He looked admiringly at her. 'You really are lovely,' he said. He put his hands on her shoulders, smiling at their reflection in the mirror. 'Did I remember to tell you tonight, Lady Lockwood, that I love you?' he asked.

Relief had surged through her. She told herself it was going to be all right after all.

'You get into bed, darling,' he said, going into his dressing room. 'I'll be with you in a minute.'

Lying in bed, waiting, she could hear him singing a tune from the latest musical in the shower. He reappeared a few minutes later, wearing expensive blue silk pyjamas and she wondered if his mother had told him the same thing Aunt Sophie had told her. Anyway, there they were, the two of them in their expensive nightclothes, strangers in the same bed.

Harry kissed her, then he turned out the lamp and said, 'Darling, I can't wait,' and he kissed her some more in the darkness.

Harry caressed her breasts, he kissed her neck, and then her shoulders. She waited for the great emotion to happen, for that surge of love and passion she knew was missing in both of them. Harry was gentle: there was a sharp pain when he finally penetrated her, and she gasped, but that was the most emotion she felt. Long after Harry had kissed her goodnight and retreated to his side of the bed and fallen asleep, she lay there, with her eyes open, gazing into the darkness, thinking of Alex and what a terrible mistake she had made.

She reminded herself that Harry was the knight in shining armour who had come to her rescue. Harry loved her and he deserved the best. Marriage was for ever and she vowed she would be a good wife to him.

And that was why, a few days later in Jock Lamont's palatial Park Avenue law offices, she had not thought twice about signing away half her new fortune to her husband.

As soon as the deed was signed, Harry went on a shopping spree. Admittedly, the first thing he bought was for her: the diamond 'as big as his love' that he had promised her – a fifteen-carat, emerald-cut, pure white, flawless solitaire set in platinum, from Van Cleef & Arpels. She had gasped nervously at the cost but he had said, a touch impatiently, 'For God's sake, darling, we're rich. Let's at least enjoy it.'

He had telephoned his tailors, in Saville Row, and ordered several suits and three sets of tails. Then he had ordered hand-made shoes from Lobb and two dozen hand-made shirts from Charvet in Paris. After that, he had gone shopping in New York, buying white dinner jackets for Palm Beach, where he planned to take her, and more shirts and ties and anything that took his fancy. Including a set of large diamond studs that made the single pearl ones she had bought him as a surprise gift, look insignificant. She had not realised Harry was such a peacock.

He complained she was looking dowdy and sent her to the Paris couture room at Bergdorf Goodman to buy a new wardrobe of expensive clothes. After all, she told herself, when the dozens of packages were delivered to their suite at the Plaza, she had to look the role, now she was Lady Lockwood. But the new things did not bring her much pleasure; she thought longingly of that other shopping expedition with Aunt Sophie, and she found herself wishing sadly that she could put the clock back.

Later, Harry had telephoned Lord Mountjoy and apologised for his outrageous behaviour in running off with his great-niece. 'All I can say, sir,' he had said sounding very sincere, 'is that I love Honeychile and she wanted to elope as much as I did.'

Mountjoy had doubted that, but he had reluctantly wished them well. He had told Harry to take care of Honeychile and then he had asked to speak to his niece.

He did not ask Honeychile why she had done it, he merely said he assumed she had her own good reasons, and that anyhow, now the deed was done, he was sure she would be a good wife and not let down the Mountjoy name. He did not say 'any further' but Honeychile thought that was what he was thinking.

Then he said, surprisingly, 'I miss you, Honeychile. We all do.' She had the feeling he wanted to say he loved her, but he had rung off before she had time to tell him she loved him too, and that she missed him and Laura and even the old dragon, Aunt Sophie, more than anyone in the world. Except Alex, who haunted her dreams, waking and sleeping.

After that, Harry had insisted they buy the expensive townhouse and had spent a fortune on doing it up. Harry simply could not stop spending; he was like a child in a candy store with money jingling in his pocket and plenty more where that came from. His money was as bottomless as the oil wells it came from, and he had begun to gamble again.

Now, Honeychile was sitting in their room, waiting for him to come home and tell her where he had been all night.

She re-ran the previous night's events in her head, trying to think where she had gone wrong. They had gone out to dinner and the restaurant was half empty, something Harry hated because he always needed to be where the action was. He said he liked to see and be seen, and what the hell was wrong with that?

'Everybody with half a brain and enough money is out of town for the weekend,' he complained, 'they're at their country place, or by the sea.' And then the idea occurred to him. 'That's exactly what we need, Honeychile. A country estate. Perhaps Newport,' he added. 'I hear the right sort of people go there and the sailing's good. We could buy a sail boat, maybe even a yacht.' He looked at her with a smile that was not a smile, and added, 'Of course, it would have to be a decent size. Larger than Alex Scott's.'

Honeychile looked at the delicious food on her plate, wondering why it suddenly looked so unappetising. 'Why must you always bring up his name?' she asked.

Spearing a piece of roast duck, he said, 'Perhaps because I often wonder exactly how far my wife's relationship really went with him.' He chewed the duck, enjoying both its flavour and the pained expression on her face.

'Not again, Harry, please,' she said quietly.

'Why not?' He speared another piece of duck. 'After all a man is entitled to know the truth about his wife.' He looked mockingly at her. 'And I wonder, Honeychile, whether, in fact, the truth was *exactly* what you told me that night. When you came tumbling out of Alex Scott's house and into my arms?'

317

She simmered with anger. 'Let's change the subject,' she said abruptly, as the waiter poured more wine into his empty glass. She had hardly touched hers. 'I don't think we should buy a country estate, especially in Newport. I just wouldn't fit in there.'

He looked her speculatively up and down, 'You're right. But *I* would, Honeychile. In fact, *I will.* And you will just have to put up with not feeling good enough for Newport society, even though we shall be as rich, if not richer than they are.'

'Aren't you forgetting, Harry, that *I* am the one who is rich?'

She didn't say *'and not you'* but he knew what she meant. He put down his knife and fork, aligning them carefully on his plate. He said coldly, 'Perhaps you should read the documents you signed at Jock Lamont's office a little more carefully, darling. It seems to have slipped your mind that we signed a marriage agreement: fifty-fifty was the score. You own fifty per cent of me and I own fifty per cent of you. For life. So you see, darling, we are *both* rich.'

Then he called for his bill, flung some money on the table and walked out on her. Burning with shame and embarrassment, Honeychile took a cab back to the Beekman Place house Harry had insisted on buying the first week they were in New York.

It had twenty rooms and Honeychile knew it was far too big for them, but Harry had said he was sick of living in a suite at the Plaza; he was a man who needed space. He had summoned a well-known interior decorator and told him he had exactly one month to fix it up, with a princely bonus if he completed on time, and daily fines if he went past the deadline. The decorator had given them an instant mix of expensive antiques and starkly modern white carpets and sofas, complete with expensive paintings and knick-knacks. He collected his bonus and Harry was satisfied, but Honeychile thought the expensive house was cold and soul-less.

There wasn't one thing in it that she had chosen herself, not even the colour scheme in their bedroom; black and white with red accents. The carpet was black, the curtains and bed were covered in expensive heavy white silk, and the sole ornament was a giant red Venetian glass vase, filled with tall Arum lilies, whose scent she had come to hate. She thought the room would have suited Rosie perfectly.

Harry had not been home when she returned from the restaurant. She had showered and put on a robe, then she had sat in their bedroom, waiting for him to come back. She wondered how a man could change so much in such a short space of time. He had been so understanding at first. Now, he often stayed out until all hours of the morning, but this was the first time he had not come home.

She picked up the letter from Tom that had arrived with the morning post, and read it again. She had made Tom manager of the Mountjoy oilfield, and he said he thought she should come out and see for herself how things were. She was surely not going to believe how everything had changed. He hoped she was happy in New York with her new husband and he and Aliza would surely love to meet him.

Harry arrived an hour later. His dinner jacket looked rumpled, he had lost his tie somewhere *en route* and he badly needed a shave.

He flung his jacket onto the bed and glanced at her without speaking. He slid his black silk braces over his shoulders and ran his hands through his blond hair, yawning.

'Harry?' she said, standing by the window, watching him. He threw her a glance out of the corner of his eye and Honeychile bit her lip, holding back her anger. After all it was Harry who had behaved abominably last night, humiliating her by walking out of the restaurant. It was Harry who had stayed out all night doing . . . God knows what. Gambling away her money, she supposed. And now she was going to have to be the good wife and apologise. It was her own fault, she thought, wearily. She should have insisted on an engagement instead of running away with him. She should have listened to her head and not her wounded heart. Now it was up to her to try and make a go of things.

She said, 'I'm sorry, Harry. I don't remember what I said, but if I hurt you, then I am truly sorry.'

Harry peeled off his shirt and flung it next to the jacket on the bed. He turned and looked at her, surprised. He had expected a tirade of accusations.

He shrugged, 'Oh well,' he said, relieved there wasn't going to be a row; after the night he'd just spent, he didn't have the energy for a fight with Honeychile. 'I suppose things did get a bit out of hand.' And he walked into the bathroom and closed the door.

Honeychile heard the sound of the water running and Harry singing in the shower. She wasn't sure whether he had accepted her apology, or whether he had even apologised himself, but she was just relieved that things seemed fairly normal again.

She took his dinner jacket and shirt from the bed and carried them into his dressing room. She noticed the perfume lingering on the lapels of his jacket. It was not hers. She put the shirt in the laundry basket and left the jacket to be sent to the dry cleaners.

Biting her trembling lip to stop from crying, she dressed quickly and then went back into the bedroom to wait for him. She knew Harry must have been with another woman and she didn't know what to do about it. No one had told her about this; no one had warned her; she had no idea how to deal with an erring husband. She thought about all the other nights Harry had stayed out late. 'Playing a friendly game of cards with the other fellows,' he said, and she wondered if it were true. Somehow, she doubted it. She had only been married three months and already her husband was being unfaithful. She wondered desolately what she was doing wrong.

Fifteen minutes later, Harry came back into the bedroom. He was immaculately dressed in a grey Prince of Wales check suit, his neatly combed blond hair was still wet from the shower, and he looked as fresh and innocent as a forty year old schoolboy. Honeychile said, 'Harry, I've been thinking, we need to get away for a while.'

He stared at her, surprised. 'Sounds like a decent idea,' he said, cautiously.

'I would like to go to Texas. After all, we've never even seen our oil wells yet, and besides, I would like to show you my home, and introduce you to Aliza and Tom.'

Harry knew all about Aliza and Tom; she had gone on endlessly about them and how wonderful they were until he had finally told her she was a sentimental fool and he had heard enough. But it was true he hadn't seen what was going on at the oilfield. It was time he paid a little visit, just to let them know who was boss-man around there and to make sure they didn't forget it.

Harry never waited for anything. He looked at his watch and said, 'We shall go today.'

Honeychile leapt to her feet, looking as pleased as if he had given her a wonderful present. 'Really? Today?' she repeated, thrilled. 'We shall have to find out about trains . . .'

'Forget trains,' he said, picking up the telephone and dialling. 'I'll hire a plane; the pilot will have us there in less than half the time.'

Honeychile rushed to get ready; she sent Aliza a telegram saying they were coming and she couldn't wait to see her, and two hours later they were in the air. As it turned out it would probably have been quicker to have gone by train after all, since they ran into a thunderstorm over Carolina and had to land at a tiny airstrip miles from anywhere.

Harry paced the tiny control room like a caged tiger, smoking cigarette after cigarette and running his hands through his rumpled blond hair in that habitual gesture that Honeychile now knew meant he was very angry. The hours passed and eventually, so did the storm and they took off again in the twin-engined executive model Cessna aircraft, flying low over the coastal plains, heading for Texas.

The chauffeured Cadillac limousine Harry had hired was waiting for them at the little airfield outside San Antonio. As they drove along the familiar highway towards Kitsville, Honeychile told Harry excitedly about how she used to spend her Saturday afternoons in the Roxy, dreaming her life away; she pointed out the fence that marked the boundary of their land; and then on the horizon she saw the steel towers of the oil derricks sticking into the sky, and she knew that like her, Mountjoy Ranch was not going to be the same as when she left.

The big car bounced over the ruts in the lane, just the way Rosie's old Dodge used to. And Fisher came bounding to greet them, barking madly until she leaned out of the window and said, 'Hey, Fisher, remember me?' Then he sat down at the side of the road, with his head cocked to one side and one ear pricked up, as if he were wondering if he heard correctly and it really was her.

Aliza was on the porch, waiting for them. She held out her arms and Honeychile ran right into them. 'Oh, Aliza,' she said, half-crying.

After a while, Aliza pushed her away and looked at her for a long moment. 'You've finally gone and done it,' she said, wonderingly.

Honeychile looked anxious, afraid she seemed too different. 'What have I gone and done?'

'You've finally grown into your daddy's good looks,' Aliza said with a grin. 'Didn't I tell you you would?'

Honeychile laughed. Then she remembered Harry, waiting behind her. She looked apprehensively at Aliza: she knew her better than she knew herself; she could always sense when something was not right. She said, 'Aliza, this is my husband.'

Aliza held out her hand and said, 'Glad to meet you, Harry. Welcome to Mountjoy Ranch.'

Harry shook her hand, distantly, taking in the shabby wooden house, set in a sea of brown dust.

Honeychile looked too: it looked pretty much the way it always had. The old recliner where Rosie used to sit, smoking sulkily and staring into space, was still on the porch, and she thought how sad it was that her mother had not lived to enjoy these new years of plenty. And how terrible it was that Jack Delaney had never been named as her murderer.

They went indoors and Harry's lip curled with contempt as he stared round the simple living room, at the old catalogue furniture, scarred from being tossed around in the tornado, that Rosie had been so proud of; at the black pot-bellied stove, and the cook-pots simmering fragrantly on the ancient cast-iron range with the special supper Aliza was preparing.

Harry carried the suitcases into the bedroom. He said, disbelievingly to Honeychile, 'This is where you lived?'

'All my life,' she said simply. 'I was born in the bedroom over there. And I probably would never have left if Lord Mountjoy hadn't sent Edgar Smallbone looking for me. I would have just stayed here, working the ranch. Or now, I guess, overseeing the oil production, for the rest of my days.'

'Then you should thank providence Mountjoy did send for you,' he said coldly. 'For God's sake, Honeychile, you can't expect us to stay here in this hovel.'

She tilted her chin, angrily. 'Whether you like it or not, this is my home,' she said, quietly so Aliza would not hear. 'And yes, I do expect you to stay here. And while we're here, might I remind you that it's my home and my land that are currently keeping you in a luxury house in Manhattan, as well as in Saville Row suits and diamond studs. So, while you are here, I expect you to act like the good husband, even if you are not.'

Harry flung the suitcases onto the bed. He said angrily, 'I'm not a man who washes his dirty linen in public, but I'm warning you,

I shall stay here one night and that's it.' He took off his jacket and looked around with the eyes of a man used to suites at the Ritz. 'Where's the bathroom?'

She took him down the hall and showed him. It was small and spotlessly clean, even if the tiles were old and cracked. He gave a disparaging snort and Honeychile's cheeks burned with anger, and she closed the door. She went to find Aliza. She was at the stove, frying chicken for supper. Honeychile's favourite.

'Seems nice, your new husband,' she said, glancing speculatively at her. 'Handsome too,' she added.

Honeychile stood with her arms folded, watching the oil spitting and spluttering as Aliza added the chicken, sniffing the familiar aroma that always made her mouth water.

'Things have changed some, since you left,' Aliza went on. 'There's oil derricks all over the place, way to the north, beyond ten acre pasture. I'm surely glad they didn't find oil right next to the house, else we'd have been listening to those things whirring day and night. And they ain't pretty, no ma'am, they surely ain't pretty.'

'They're making us rich, though,' Honeychile said, dipping her finger in the chocolate cake batter and licking it.

'Rich maybe, but your manners ain't improved none,' Aliza said, smacking her hand away with the wooden spoon. 'I thought you would be all grown up by now. Sophisticated, like that Ginger Rogers you so admired.'

Honeychile laughed, wistfully. 'Somehow, Aliza, I don't think I'm ever going to be as sophisticated as Ginger. I haven't changed. Under this smart dress beats the same old heart.'

'Looks to me like you're different,' Aliza said, turning to look at her. 'Looks to me like you've lost those old rose-coloured glasses you used to wear and come down to earth with a bump. Is that what the high-life does for a girl? Takes her illusions away?'

'Sometimes, I guess,' Honeychile admitted sadly.

'*Honeychile.*' Tom was standing in the doorway. His handsome face was almost split in two with a smile as she ran to him. He wrapped his arms round her. 'Oh, baby, baby,' he murmured, 'you've no idea how good it is to see you.'

She buried her face against his shoulder, content. She knew now she had come home.

Harry came into the room. He stood with his arms folded, watching them broodingly.

'Well now,' Tom said, smiling, 'here's your husband lookin' for you.'

Honeychile noticed the icy expression on Harry's face as Tom strode across the room. He grasped Harry's unwilling hand in his, pumping it up and down. 'Glad to meet ya, Harry,' he said.

'How do you do,' Harry said, patronisingly. Honeychile was reminded of the kids at school and their snobbish mothers, and she suddenly wanted to haul off and hit him for being rude to her family, just the way she did back then.

'You will forgive me if I don't dine with you,' Harry added, 'The journey was a long one, and it's very hot.' And then he turned and walked back into their room.

Aliza looked at Tom and then at Honeychile, but she said nothing. They ate their fried chicken out on the porch, the way they always had done and Honeychile told them all about Laura and Anjou, glossing over the bad part. And about the Ball, and the Court Presentation, and Aunt Sophie, and how kind and lonesome she thought her Uncle Mountjoy was. But she did not once mention Harry.

They sat outside until late, Aliza on the porch swing, Tom and Honeychile on the steps. Fisher came to rest his head against her knee and they listened to the whistle of the train speeding across the plains in the distance, and the occasional whinnying of the horses in the stables.

Later, she walked over there with Tom and said hello to Lucky. The Appaloosa nuzzled her hand as it took the apple she gave her, and she patted its neck and told her she hadn't forgotten, and that they would go for a ride in the morning, early.

On the way back to the house, Tom asked her if she was happy. They looked at each other in the glimmering dark, as she thought about it. She knew she was not happy, and with Harry, she never would be. She thought of how much she loved Alex and what a fool she had been. Aliza was right: she had lost the rose-coloured glasses of youth and innocence. She saw life clearly now. Harry had married her for her money. He was a gambler and a womaniser. And she had made a terrible mistake.

She said, 'It's different Tom. I thought I knew what happiness was, but now . . . I'm not so sure.'

'Happiness is simple, girl,' he replied. 'When you've got it, you recognise it all right. Just remember this, Honeychile, if that man don't make you happy, you can always come home again.'

Honeychile smiled as she kissed him. But she knew it was too late and she could never come home again. At least, not in the same way he meant. She was different now.

Harry was sleeping when she went to their room. There was a half-empty bottle by the bed and the room stank of whisky. She thought it was just like when Rosie was home.

She undressed and climbed into bed, careful not to touch him. She couldn't bear to feel his hot skin against hers, his whisky breath in her face, his cheating hands on her body. She closed her eyes and listened to the sounds of the ranch: the sigh of the wind in the grass, the call of a nightbird, the sheer empty silence. And she felt that old loneliness creep up on her again.

She was up before dawn, riding the range with Tom, and for a short while she was happy again. When they got back, Harry was sitting at the table on the porch, eating pancakes and bacon and eggs.

'Better hurry, Honeychile,' he said. 'We're meeting with the production men in half an hour for a little business talk, and a tour of the oilfield. We shall be leaving immediately after that, for New York.'

He was so arrogantly insensitive, Honeychile wanted to throw his coffee in his face. Instead, she said, 'I'll be ready,' and went indoors to pack her things.

Aliza was tidying up the kitchen. 'Y'all want breakfast?' she asked.

Honeychile shook her head. 'I've got to go, Aliza.'

'I know that. But you will come back?' She looked anxiously at her.

'I'll be back,' Honeychile promised. 'And I shall be alone.'

Aliza shook her head and said, 'I'm sorry, baby.'

'Me too,' she said, finally admitting the truth. 'It's just a mistake, that's all. A great big mistake.'

CHAPTER 33

Congressman Jack Delaney knew he looked like Clark Gable. Enough people had told him so for him to believe it. 'The only thing different is the ears,' he would say, sleeking back his dark hair and admiring his own flat well-shaped ears in the mirror. 'And maybe it's not the only thing better than Clark's,' he always added, laughing coarsely.

It was true: he did resemble the movie star, and it was a resemblance he cultivated. The little moustache, the lop-sided grin, the easy slouch. It knocked women out, soon as they saw him. They were all over him, especially now that he was a 'somebody'.

Being a 'somebody' was something he had to work at, because the truth was that without his powerful backers behind him, he would be a 'nobody' again, real fast. And he was still not high enough, on the upwardly mobile political scale of those that counted, for his own satisfaction.

He was owned by his powerful money-no-object backers, the gangsters who had put him in Congress to look out for their interests, and obstruct such matters as lobbying against gambling, or the meat-packing industry, and the Transport unions. With their money and power behind him, it had been easy to bury the past, and the unproven allegations of corruption from which he had emerged clean as a whistle. And it had taken a lot of work on his part, as well as a lot of anguish and danger, to get that kind of support.

It was the lavish campaign parties he threw with their money at his big white-porticoed house in Houston; his generous donations with their money over the years to the Party coffers; plus his good looks, his sincere smile and firm, manly handshake, and an expensive propaganda campaign, that had clinched the election for him.

He was sitting in his large, comfortable office in the Senate building. His feet were propped on the broad desk, empty of any urgent documents needing his attention; a small pungent cigar was clamped between his teeth, and his arms were behind his head. He was thinking about what to do next.

He knew he had the looks, the professional charm, and the know-how to go further. He could become a Candidate for the Presidency, but that might take years and he was an impatient man, and besides, Roosevelt was still firmly entrenched in the White House, despite the New Deal. No, Delaney thought, the man in the wheelchair was in there for a good long while yet. All he could do would be to work his way slowly up to Senator, being noticed, making his mark.

The slowness of it all, filled him with gloom. The Washington lifestyle limited a man of his needs. There were times when he longed for the good old Prohibition days of rum-running and numbers-rackets and women.

Swinging his legs from the desk, he stubbed out his cigar with a deep sigh. Those were the days all right. But his past had been carefully edited by his backers. Now he was known as a widower who had cared so deeply for his wife, Rosemary, that he had not yet found a woman good enough to replace her. That scenario went down well with all the grass roots voters out on the campaign trail: the housewives adored him for his loyal sentiments; the younger women fell for him; and the men admired the fact that, in true Texan fashion, he was a self-made man; a 'man's man'. In the depths of the Depression, Jack had known how to give them hope.

'Luck doesn't come out looking for you, my friends,' he had said in a thousand speeches in a thousand dusty halls in small anonymous towns he hoped sincerely he would never see again. 'You have to go and find that old lady. Yes sir. And I am just the guy to help you. Vote for me, and the luck that I found will turn into yours.'

The local band had played loudly. Beer and soft drinks and hot dogs, all paid for by the gangster backers, were served to the crowd; women were given rosettes, and babies red, white and blue bonnets and a smacking kiss.

'Even the damned dogs had been patted,' Jack thought morosely, because more often than not he had felt like kicking their asses. He hated dogs, always had; and they seemed to hate him right back. Dogs were not attracted to him; they growled and showed their teeth when he patted them, making their owners look suspiciously at him, as though the creatures were a good judge of character.

The whole trouble with his upward reaching ambitions always came back to the fact that he was owned by the mob. They had paid to put him in Congress, and now they paid him to look after their interests. And it was just not enough. Jack felt like a poor man. There were guys with their own family fortunes in the Senate House; men who did not think twice about spending half a million or even more on a campaign. Men with homes in New York and Saratoga and Palm Beach. Men with private camps in the Adirondacks and big white yachts moored in Bermuda. His rival in Texas was just such a man. Richer than he was, and just as corrupt. He was after Jack's place in Congress, and he was prepared to do anything to get it.

Jack had the feeling his backers were cooling towards him. The phone calls were not so frequent, nor so friendly. He was no longer summoned to the top men's parties, the way he used to be. In fact, he thought uneasily, he was sure he was being pushed out in favour of the newcomer, who had a stronger position and offered more than he could. Loyalty, he knew, was not a word much used by the mob. At least, not in this connection, where a man's worth had outrun its usefulness.

He had read in the Houston press, about the oil strike on Mountjoy Ranch, and he was wondering, as he had done before with Rosie, how to turn it to his advantage. And, just like Rosie, he knew what to do. Only this time he decided he would take care of little Miss Honeychile, once and for all. Unfortunately, now he would have to get rid of the new husband too; he couldn't afford any problems there. He anticipated a bit of a fight with the Mountjoy Trust, afterwards, but he would use the credibility of his position to push the legality of his claim to her estate. He had no doubt he would win. And all it would take was a good lunch and a phone call.

Jack liked the Mayflower Hotel. It had a dark, discreet bar where he could down a couple of Irish whiskies and have a quiet business conversation, and the restaurant served his steak exactly the way he liked it: no frills, medium rare with a baked potato, a couple of beers and no dessert.

'Save all that sweet stuff for the women-folks,' he said, playing his role as the genial southern Congressman to the hilt. 'I'm a Texan.

We like our steaks, and y'all know how to cook 'em. That's good enough for me.' The fact that he had been born and raised in Boston's North End had been buried many moons ago and he was now a southerner, born and bred.

The bartender smiled hello and gave him his usual double whisky without being asked, and the bowl of hard pretzels Jack was addicted to. Jack downed the drink, signalled for one more, then made his way to the telephone booth in the hallway. He dialled the operator and asked for a New York number, waiting impatiently, fingers drumming on the shelf. Finally, a man answered.

'Vito,' he barked. 'Where the hell were ya? Yeah, well it must have been a helluva late night. Or else a helluva woman. Listen fella, I have a little problem that needs taking care of. Know what I mean? Yeah, it's personal, in a way, but it pays the same.'

He took the piece of paper with the address from his pocket. 'Listen boy,' he said softly, 'this is kid gloves time. No mistakes, y'understand? Okay, here's the information.' He glanced over his shoulder, making sure no one was within earshot, then quietly he gave Vito Harry Lockwood and Honeychile's name and address, adding her description: tall, blonde; you couldn't miss her.

'The cheque's in the mail,' he said grinning at his own joke, because of course the money would be sent to the hit-man through a network of couriers so it could never be traced back to him. 'Half now, final payment on completion of the job.'

He smiled, satisfied as he walked back to the bar that afternoon, sipping his whisky and chatting with the barman about the weekend's Notre Dame game. He waved a cheery goodbye, had an amiable few words with an acquaintance *en route* to the dining room, and passed the time of day with a colleague in the hall. Then he sat down and ate his steak with more gusto than he had in the last six months.

CHAPTER 34

Alex Scott had his usual suite on the Queen Mary for his trip to New York. And, as usual, he kept to himself for most of the voyage, so it wasn't until the third night out, when he went to a cocktail party given by an old acquaintance, that he met Anjou.

He was standing in the doorway of the verandah suite, surveying the crush of smartly-dressed people and wishing he had not felt the need to be polite and make an appearance, when a familiar voice said from behind him, '*Bon soir, chèr* Alex. I wondered when you would emerge from your lair.'

He turned and their eyes met. He had not spoken to Anjou since that night at his house when he had wrapped her in her cloak and driven her home. She had begged and pleaded with him all the way, saying she had not meant any harm; she was sorry; it was all just a bit of fun, and she really did love him.

He had listened in stony silence until they reached Mountjoy House, then he had said, icily, 'Anjou, you do not know the meaning of the word love. You are a selfish, scheming woman. You have hurt Honeychile more than you can ever know, because you simply do not have those kind of feelings. Women like you float over the surface of life, cushioned by your looks and your charm, taking exactly what you want when you want it.'

He had held open the car door for her and she had slithered out, clutching her cape around her and looking at him with frightened eyes.

'I don't think I'm *that* bad,' she pleaded. 'Naughty maybe, but not *bad*. Oh, Alex, please don't reject me. I came to you because I loved you. I wanted you so much, and you never even noticed me. I just had to do something to get your attention.'

'Goodbye, Anjou,' he had said coldly, getting back into the car and slamming the door. He leaned out of the window and added, 'And if I hear one *whisper* about this from anyone, I shall come to Lord Mountjoy and tell him the truth about what happened, and what a little bitch you really are.'

He had driven away, watching Anjou in the driving mirror, staring after him with tears streaming down her shocked face.

Looking into her beautiful green eyes now, smiling so innocently at him, he thought, with pain, about Honeychile married to Harry Lockwood, and he knew it was all Anjou's fault.

'Oh, come on, Alex,' she put her hand on his arm, gazing penitently at him, 'let's let bygones be bygones. I promise to behave.'

'We have nothing to say to each other,' he said icily, pushing away from her through the crowd. He could feel her angry eyes on him and he thought she was a woman who didn't know when to leave well alone.

He wondered why she was going to New York, and if she had known he would be on board. Later, he asked the purser who Miss Mountjoy was travelling with and was told she had boarded with the Lord and Lady Malvett and their daughter.

Alex managed to avoid her for the rest of the voyage, but he was aware of her sulky presence a few tables away in the dining saloon. A couple of times he passed her on deck with the Malvett daughter and he nodded briefly and strode on.

Late at night, he allowed himself to think about Honeychile, and how hurt she must have been to run off and marry someone else. The thought of her in Harry's arms made him groan out loud. He knew he should have told her the truth about himself, but loyalty had kept his secret. He wanted no one, not even her, to know.

Honeychile was home alone when the telephone rang the next afternoon. She looked dispiritedly at it, guessing it was Harry explaining, once again why he had not come home last night. There was a sigh in her voice as she answered it.

'Honeychile, it's Alex,' he said, and her heart turned over. She should have put down the receiver, cut him off without speaking. But she could not.

'I need to see you,' he said. 'I can't let you go through life thinking that what you saw was my doing. Honeychile let me at least explain. That's all I ask.' He hesitated and then said, 'No, that's not true. I can't be in the same city and not see you. I need to know how you are, if you are . . . busy in your new life?'

'No,' she whispered, 'I'm not busy. I'm not busy at all.'

'Then will you meet me?'

'Where?' She wanted to see him so badly she could hardly wait.

'In the Oak Room, at the Plaza? At five?'

She nodded. 'I'll be there.'

He was too early, like an anxious swain, with his eyes fixed on the door for the first glimpse of his love. He had told himself a hundred times that he did not love her, he could not love her. But when he finally saw her he knew he had lied.

She looked thinner, sleek and sophisticated and very New York, in a black linen dress with a wide-brimmed black straw hat, and the Mountjoy pearls. Her corn-gold hair hung in a shining pageboy and there was an anxious look in her sapphire eyes as they met his across the room.

'Thank God you came,' he said relieved, 'I was afraid you wouldn't.' He looked round the busy room, then said, 'Let's get out of here.' He took her arm, feeling the silky warmth of her skin like an electric current under his fingers, as they walked across from the hotel and into Central Park.

The park was crowded, but they did not notice; it was as if they were the only two people in the world. He told her she had been on his mind, ever since that night. Then he held her hand and they sat on a park bench while he told her the truth about Anjou.

Children pedalled past them on tricycles; sedate city dogs trotted by on the end of leads; lovers held hands as they walked past, but he had eyes only for Honeychile.

She thought of the mess her life had become and she said sadly, 'How could she do such a thing? She was like a sister to me.'

He shook his head and said, with a sigh, 'It's difficult for us to understand women like Anjou. She may care about you, but nothing stands between her and what she wants. Anjou would sacrifice her own mother and then not understand the destruction she caused – after all, to her it was only a bit of fun. In Anjou's world, Anjou comes first.'

He took her hand, 'But what about you, Honeychile?'

She shrugged, 'I believe Harry is happy. He's out gambling every night. I just don't know where he is most of the time, and the truth is I don't care. You know I love you, Alex, so I guess in a way I'm cheating on him just as much as he's cheating on me.' She sighed, wearily. 'It doesn't matter any more. I was a stupid young fool. I made a terrible mistake and now I'm living with the consequences.'

'There is an alternative.'

'Divorce? Oh, yes, I've thought about it. Every time he comes home, half drunk, and starts telling me about his triumphs, I think about it.' She looked honestly at him. 'Why didn't you ask me to marry you, Alex?'

'There is a reason. I can't talk about it. Let's just say, it's my punishment.' He put his arm round her shoulders, pulling her closer. 'It's not because I don't love you, Honeychile. You know I do. And if you ever need me, all you have to do is call.' And he kissed her.

It was a kiss, she knew, that sealed her fate. She would always love Alex Scott, even though he did not want to marry her.

They held hands in the cab on their way back home, but he did not kiss her again as he said goodbye, and he did not ask to see her again. She stood on the steps of her smart house, watching as the yellow taxi nosed its way through the traffic and down the street, taking Alex away from her. She looked at the card he had given her, with his address on Fifth Avenue, and his telephone number, wondering how she would be able to resist calling him.

The telephone was ringing as she opened the door. She ran to answer it, catching her breath in shock as Anjou said, 'Honeychile, *chérie*, it is your most repentant cousin calling to apologise. Oh, Honeychile, I know I hurt you,' she said sincerely, 'I didn't mean to. It was just a silly mistake. I didn't know you and Alex were seeing each other. He means nothing to me, honestly. Please, *please*, say you will forgive me.'

Honeychile could almost see her mischievous little-cat smile, her green eyes narrowed with amusement and her head tilted pleadingly to one side, so sure she would be forgiven.

'*Chérie, speak* to me,' Anjou sounded upset. 'Let me come to see you, to apologise in person then you will see how sincere I am. Please, *please*,' she coaxed. 'I really miss you. And besides, Uncle Mountjoy asked me to be sure to visit you and find out how you are. He will be so hurt if I go back and say my lovely cousin refused to see me.'

Honeychile thought of what Alex had said and for once she resisted Anjou's charm; this time she was not going to be beguiled. All her troubles were because of her. She said, 'Go away. I don't want to see you ever again,' and she put down the phone.

She shivered as she walked upstairs to her room. She turned off the air conditioning and flung open the windows, letting in the warm evening air, rubbing her arms to get rid of the goosebumps. She didn't know if they were caused by the frigid air or by Anjou's call; both had turned her blood to ice.

She took a shower, then dressed reluctantly for the dinner she and Harry were going to that night. She didn't want to go but she knew there was no way of getting out of it. It was easier just to do as he wished and save another confrontation that always ended up with her in tears, and him storming out the door and not coming back until the next morning, or even later.

She put on a pretty taupe-coloured chiffon dress, and her favourite earrings, antique-drops from Russia in palest amber scrolled with gold, and the enormous diamond 'trophy' ring that Harry liked her to wear, because it showed everyone how rich he was that he could buy his wife such a fabulous jewel. She thought bitterly how he had said it was 'a diamond as big as his love', more like as big as his monumental ego.

She sprayed a touch of Chanel No.5 at her throat and sat looking at herself in the mirror, wishing it were Alex she was dressing for; Alex who would look at her and tell her she was beautiful tonight; Alex whose bed she would sleep in.

'Honeychile? Where the hell are you?' Harry called from the foot of the stairs.

She wondered what the servants thought of their constant fighting, but tonight she didn't even care. Anyhow, she remembered, it was the maid's night off.

'Here I am, Harry,' she said, walking down the stairs towards him.

He looked her up and down, 'Where are *you* going, all dressed up?' he demanded truculently.

She saw at once he had been drinking. His tie was askew and his blond hair had that familiar rumpled look it got when he had been running his hands through it, which usually meant he was angry.

335

'You said we were dining with the Jamiesons,' she said calmly.

He winced, clapping a hand to his forehead as he remembered. 'Oh, Christ, so we are.' He strode into the drawing room heading for the drinks table. 'Where the hell's the ice,' he grumbled loudly, pouring himself a hefty scotch. 'I told the maid to have a fresh bucket here at six prompt every evening.'

Honeychile looked at her watch. 'It's eight o'clock, Harry. I guess it melted and she removed it before she went off duty.'

He sipped his drink, watching her broodingly. He said, 'You're the one who's supposed to be in charge of the servants. Why didn't you order her to refill it?' He gave a short bark of laughter. 'I suppose it's asking too much of a girl brought up in a slum to understand servants. After all, yours call you "family". And I'll tell you something, Honeychile, if they weren't black I might be inclined to believe they were, the way you behave.'

She sank into a chair, watching him warily. It was hard to tell exactly how drunk Harry was; he never staggered, he just became more and more aggressive depending on how much he'd had. He circled her, spilling scotch onto the white carpet from the brimming glass, eyeing her critically.

'Is this the outfit you consider good enough to have dinner with my friends in?' he demanded truculently. 'It looks more suitable for dinner on the famous ranch.'

'It's from Mainbocher,' she said quietly. 'One of the best American designers.'

'Hah, Americans, what do they know about style. All they think about is money.'

'Which is why I'm wearing your ring, Harry. So they'll know how rich you are. *And that's the only reason you bought it.*'

He thrust his face close to hers. 'Sometimes I wonder if I married the wrong Mountjoy girl,' he murmured. 'Sometimes I wonder why I didn't marry Anjou. After all she was in line to inherit the old man's money, *and* she was beautiful, and so *available*.'

'So why didn't you?' she demanded angrily.

He stood up and took a mouthful of scotch. He said with an exaggerated sigh, 'Because, my darling, I had already sampled the goods. And I was a little concerned as to exactly how many other men had been as lucky in taking the fair Anjou to bed.' He smiled

336

nastily, eyeing her up and down, 'At least with you I could be certain I was getting a virgin.'

Honeychile stared at him, horrified. 'Anjou . . . ?' she stammered.

'Exactly, darling. Sexy little Anjou.' He laughed. 'One more Mountjoy girl to go and then I shall have had them all. I imagine young Laura would be splendid on top after all that experience in the saddle. And anyhow, either of them would be better than you, darling Honeychile.'

She stood up, smoothing down her chiffon skirt, looking murderously at him. 'I should kill you, Harry,' she said, contemptuously. 'Everybody said you were no good and they were right. How I ever thought you were my knight in shining armour, coming to my rescue, I don't know.'

She pulled the fabulous diamond from her finger and tossed it on the floor between them. 'That's what I think of your so-called "*heart full of love*", Harry. And of you. You are not worth the dirt beneath the feet of men like Tom and Lord Mountjoy and Billy Saxton and Alex Scott. As they say where I come from, Harry, "You ain't worth a plugged nickel." '

He stared, astonished, at the ring, glittering under the lamplight on the white rug, then at her. 'Where are you going?' he demanded, as she walked away.

She did not reply. She ran upstairs to their room, pulled off the lovely chiffon dress and tossed it on the floor. She dressed hastily in a shirt and skirt and grabbed a jacket and her purse, ready to flee. Realising she didn't know where to go, she sank dejected onto the bed. She didn't even know where to run away to.

She leaned her face against the pillow, wondering desolately what to do. The old teddy her father had given her lay next to her, and she reached out to stroke his face. One ear was missing and he had been patched lovingly by Aliza over the years, but he was still that link to her father, the man she had never really known and whom she wished with all her heart was here to help now.

Sighing, she got up and walked down the stairs. Harry was waiting in the hall, glass in hand. He stared moodily at her.

'What about dinner at the Jamiesons?' he demanded.

'You go, Harry,' she said, walking past him to the door.

'I can't go on my own. They are expecting both of us.'

'Then cancel, tell them I'm sick.'

He grabbed her shoulder roughly. 'Where are you going?'

'Out.' She opened the door quickly and ran down the steps.

'Don't bother to come back,' he yelled after her.

'I won't, Harry,' she promised through gritted teeth, as she strode down the street.

She walked for what seemed miles, telling herself she would not call Alex. She had got herself into this marriage; now it was up to her to get herself out. She thought about Harry sleeping with Anjou, and she knew it was true. She thought about where she would go, what she would do. She knew there was no future for her with Alex. She was on her own.

It was late when she turned into an automat. She took a cup of coffee from the machine and sat at a small table in the corner, looking round at the other patrons. They were grey and tired, eating their cheap solitary meals silently. She looked out of place in her smart jacket and skirt and for the first time since she heard about the oil, she felt rich.

She thought back to her life; remembering the daily grind of poverty; the drabness of it all. She remembered facing each day with hope, and the despair each time that small hope was obliterated, and how hard she had worked to keep the ranch. And then she thought about Harry spending that hard-won money, gambling it carelessly away.

She gritted her teeth in anger: she decided she would divorce Harry; she would bribe him with a generous settlement. If he refused, she would fight him all the way to the Supreme Court to get her inheritance back.

Finally, she understood the power of money. Now she could do what her father would have expected of her. She would create the Mountjoy Foundation to give scholarships to children who, like herself, had dreams and ideas and no means of achieving them; and to build hospitals, and to help women in need. There was so much that could be done with all that money, and now she had a purpose in life and she was determined to work hard to achieve it.

As always, Alex came into her mind. The card with his telephone number and address seemed to burn a hole in her purse. She eyed the public telephone in the corner; all she had to do was dial his number.

But it was no good. Alex had made it clear to her that afternoon: there was no future for them.

She went to the machine and got another cup of coffee, sitting quietly at her table, watching the other customers come and go, thinking about how to deal with Harry, and about her new idea.

Anjou was bored, as usual. She was in her room at the St Regis, on 58th Street. Lord and Lady Malvett and their daughter had departed for a weekend in the country; it had been easy to convince them that she was meeting an old friend of her mother's, and that she would be perfectly safe on her own. But now she had managed one of her famous 'escapes', everything had gone wrong.

The man she had met on the boat and arranged to see, had called to say his fiancée had arrived unexpectedly and their assignation was off. She hadn't even known he had a fiancée, just that he was rich and eligible and that she had been very attracted to him. She thought wistfully that if she ever decided to marry, it would be to a man like that. Or like the elusive Alex.

On an impulse, she picked up the phone and dialled Alex's number; she let it ring for ages but there was no reply. She banged the receiver down, sulkily, thinking of him out on the town with some gorgeous woman.

'*Merde, oh merde*,' she said, pacing the floor angrily. Here she was, alone and free in New York and she was stuck in her room like a wallflower at the ball.

She glanced at the time, almost ten-thirty. She thought about Honeychile and Harry. If they had been out to dinner, they should be on their way back by now. She couldn't call first, because Honeychile would slam the phone down on her again. Instead, she would go over there; then they would have to let her in. She would tell Honeychile she was sincerely sorry, and remind her that after all, they were cousins and shouldn't bygones be bygones by now? And then maybe she could talk them into taking her to a nightclub.

She changed quickly into a jade-green silk-jersey evening dress that hung in a straight line from narrow shoulder straps, barely skimming her body. She brushed her red hair into a smooth cascade, letting it fall sexily over one eye; then she sprayed herself lavishly with Jicky and put on the emerald necklace Uncle Mountjoy had given her. She collected her cape and her gold mesh evening purse, and gave herself one last satisfied glance in the mirror. Downstairs, the doorman called a cab for her, and within minutes she was on her way to Beekman Place.

Harry was lying on the sofa in the drawing room when the doorbell rang. He waited for the maid to answer it, then he remembered that she was off duty tonight. Grumbling, he hauled himself up, put on his shoes and went to the door.

'Good Lord,' he said, staring at Anjou. 'What are you doing here?'

She smiled at him. 'I've come to pay you and Honeychile a little visit, Harry. Aren't you going to ask me in?'

'Come to atone for your sins, have you?' he asked maliciously.

Anjou laughed. She put her gold mesh evening bag on the hall table and flung off her cape. 'I suppose Honeychile told you? About Alex?'

'Well of course she did, the silly girl. If she hadn't I wouldn't be here now.' He added thoughtfully, 'In a way, I suppose I have you to thank for my good fortune.'

'Indeed you do, Harry. And in return, I need to ask you a little favour.'

He raised his eyebrows, disbelievingly. 'Only a *little* favour, Anjou. My, how times must have changed.'

'Lord Mountjoy doesn't know anything is wrong between us. He thought I would be spending time with Honeychile. He asked, specifically, that I bring back all her news.'

'You've spoken to her?'

'This afternoon. She put the phone down on me.'

Harry laughed, that short sharp bark that was a sarcastic comment rather than amusement. 'I wonder why?'

'I told her I was here to apologise to her. And I meant it. Of course I wasn't sorry at the time; I thought she was silly not to have gone after Alex when she wanted him so badly. I thought she was too goody-goody and full of girlish ideals. Much good it did her. Anyhow, *where is* Honeychile?' She looked expectantly at him.

Harry poured gin and vermouth into an expensive crystal glass. He

340

added an olive and handed it to her. He knew Anjou's tipple from old.

'Gone,' he said, shrugging his shoulders. 'She walked out on me. Into the night without so much as a goodbye.'

Anjou's eyes widened with astonishment. 'You mean *she's left you*?'

'That's it in a nutshell, darling. Apparently, *for better or worse* – even if it was in French on the *Normandie* – means nothing to her. My guess is she'll go back to that ghastly ranch in Texas.'

Anjou glanced round the luxurious room with its important paintings and expensive little objects arranged on tables and shelves. 'The same ranch that is keeping you in style, *n'est ce pas, mon chèr* Harry? Isn't there an old saying, "*do not bite the hand that feeds you*"?'

'If there is, I don't want to hear about it,' he said with a grin. 'And anyhow, I'm rich now. "In my own right," as they say. Fifty-fifty was the deal I struck with little ole Honeychile. And that, my darling Anjou makes me a very rich man indeed.'

Anjou closed her eyes, shocked. Then she opened them and looked incredulously at him. 'Honeychile gave you *fifty per cent* of Mountjoy oil? My dear Harry, surely you owe me more than just *one little* favour? You owe me a hell of a lot. Why, if it were not for me, you would still be sleeping with women for a living, and gambling to pay your debts. Not that I imagine things have changed much,' she added maliciously, 'otherwise why would poor Honeychile have left?'

Harry shrugged, 'Who cares. And you can have whatever your little heart desires.' He walked across the room and picked up the diamond ring from the rug where Honeychile had flung it. 'Here,' he said, dangling it in front of her. 'How about this?'

She snatched it from him, examining it critically under the light. 'It's magnificent,' she said, awed.

'Keep it,' he said carelessly. 'Honeychile doesn't want it any more.'

Anjou smiled as she slipped the ring onto her finger. She knew it was worth a fortune. She went over and put a record on the victrola. It was a Jerome Kern medley and they were playing 'Smoke Gets In Your Eyes'. She walked over to Harry and insinuated herself into his arms, swaying against him. 'Dance with me, Harry darling,' she said, giving him that smile.

He held her close as they danced smoochily, barely moving from

341

the spot, just holding each other. He ran his hand up and down her naked back. 'So smooth,' he whispered, 'so *sexy*.' He bent his head, kissing her neck, breathing in her perfume. 'Mmmmm, soooo . . . *Anjou*,' he murmured.

She lifted her head and kissed him on the lips, thrusting her tongue into his eager mouth. 'Mmmm,' he said again, 'Am I to believe that you are going to be grateful, Anjou?'

She smiled wickedly at him. 'I'm a well brought up young lady,' she said, 'I was taught always to say thank you properly when I was given a present.' Laughing, she linked her hand in his and they walked slowly upstairs, stopping every now and then for more lengthy kisses, on the way.

It was in the early hours of the morning, when Honeychile returned. She had sat in the automat, thinking out her life and her future, and then she had walked, all the way home.

She was exhausted and her feet hurt as she put the key in the lock to let herself in. She sighed as she closed the door behind her. There was a light on in the drawing room and she wondered if Harry were home. Then she saw the gold mesh evening bag on the hall table.

She took a step closer and looked at it. She smelled the perfume. A sharp, sophisticated heady scent she knew only too well. With a feeling of *déjà vu*, she stood in the hall, listening, but the house was silent. Her heart sank to her shoes as she slowly climbed the stairs and opened the bedroom door.

She took a step backwards. She stood there, too horrified even to scream. At her feet lay the remains of her old teddy bear, covered in blood. And where Harry's head should have been was a gaping red hole. His blood and brains were everywhere: on the white silk bed, the walls, the carpet.

Shock and terror hit her with the impact of a bomb. She turned and ran down the stairs, out of the house and into the street. She ran as though she had wings on her feet, sobbing hysterically. She slowed down when she saw the telephone on the corner. Frantically, she fumbled in her purse for a coin and Alex's number.

He answered at once. 'Harry's dead,' she wailed. 'Alex, please, oh please, you've got to help me.'

CHAPTER 35

Alex's penthouse on Fifth Avenue overlooked Central Park. It was light and airy and, with its simple Italian country antiques and tiled floors, felt more like a farmhouse in Tuscany, than a Manhattan apartment.

Honeychile lay crumpled on the sofa in a terrified daze. Alex gave her brandy, and then he held her in his arms until she was finally able to tell him what had happened. She sat in a devastated heap amongst the toast-coloured linen cushions on the big pine sofa, looking up at him, waiting for him to tell her what to do.

He said, 'Obviously, the police are going to suspect you. I doubt they will believe you were walking round the streets for hours, or drinking coffee in an automat while Harry was being killed. So as an alibi it's not much use.'

She stared at him, big-eyed with horror. 'But I didn't kill Harry,' she cried, 'they *have* to believe me.'

'Unfortunately, the truth is rarely that easy. It needs to be proven. You are going to need an alibi, Honeychile, one with a witness to corroborate it.'

He sat beside her and took her hands. 'I know you did not kill Harry, *carissima*.' He stroked back her tumbled hair and kissed her hot forehead tenderly. 'There is a way out,' he promised, 'but you must trust me.'

The news hit the early morning headlines: MOUNTJOY HEIRESS HELD FOR QUESTIONING IN MURDER OF HUSBAND. CLAIMS SHE SPENT NIGHT WITH TYCOON.

Anjou read it locked in her room at the St Regis. Cold and shivering with terror, she clasped her arms round herself, as though for protection, pacing the floor like a trapped cat.

343

She remembered, with total recall, climbing angrily out of Honey-chile's bed. She had looked disgustedly at Harry, already snoring on the other side. He had had too much to drink to be any good; he had fumbled around for ever it seemed, until she had lost her temper and said, 'Oh the hell with it Harry, if you can't make love to me then just leave me alone.'

'Sorry, old girl,' he had muttered, and then he had turned his back on her and fallen asleep.

She had picked up Honeychile's old teddy bear from the floor and flung it at him. It landed on the pillow next to him and he murmured something, pulling the sheet up around his ears.

'Take your teddy to bed with you, you silly Englishman,' she had said, angrily, 'it's about all you're good for.'

Then she had picked up her clothes and marched disgustedly into the bathroom. She had slammed the door and turned on the shower. She had stepped inside the marble cabin and closed the glass door, then stood under the flow of hot water, letting it wash the memory of Harry's fumbling hands from her body. She had looked at the diamond ring on her finger, turning it this way and that to catch the light and thought maybe she hadn't made such a bad deal, after all. And she hadn't finished with Harry yet. He owed her, and she meant to collect.

She had stepped out of the shower and dried herself on the lux-uriously thick towel with 'H' embroidered on it, wondering if it were Honeychile's or Harry's.

She had dressed carefully, then looked for her purse with her powder compact and lipstick. She remembered she had left it in the hall. She sighed, and quickly dusted Honeychile's powder puff over her nose. She examined the lipsticks but they were the wrong colour so she decided against using one. She put on her cape and opened the door. She put her hand to her mouth, shocked, and the diamond glinted in the lamplight, but this time she didn't notice. She stood for a terrified moment, taking in the bloody scene.

The thought crossed her mind quickly, that if she had been in bed with Harry, that might have been her. Her flesh crawled with horror and, picking up her long dress, she ran from the room, down the stairs, through the hall and out into the street, slamming the door behind her.

She ran as far as she could from the terrible house on Beekman Place, then flagged down a cab and in a trembling voice, told the driver to take her back to the St Regis.

Anjou went to the window and stared blindly out at the traffic rushing past; at the people hurrying along the sidewalks, everybody doing the normal things they did every day. Only for her this day was different. 'What have I done?' she whispered. '*Mon Dieu*, what have I done now?'

Back at Alex's apartment, Honeychile sat on the terrace, going over and over the events of the past night. The vivid picture of Harry, with his brains splattered across the white silk bedspread, stuck in her mind. Even with her eyes open, that was what she saw. She remembered Anjou's purse on the hall table, and she knew she must have shot him, even though Alex didn't think so.

Alex had come to her rescue. He had told the police she had spent the night with him. His lawyer had proven that she did not possess a gun, and that no guns were kept in the house. She had been with Mr Scott at the time Sir Harry was killed. The police had no evidence against her, and they had let her go, reluctantly.

The doorbell rang and Alex answered it. Anjou glanced quickly at him, then rushed past him into the living room. 'Where is she?' she cried, 'Where's Honeychile?'

Honeychile stared, unbelieving, at her. 'How dare you come here,' she cried. 'How can you, after what you did.'

Anjou grasped her arm. 'No, it's not true.'

'I *know* you were there,' she cried. 'This time you went too far. *You* shot Harry. Why? *Why* did you do it? Did he reject you this time? Was that the reason?'

'It's not true, I *swear* it's not. I admit I was there. I went to the house to apologise to you. I wanted us to be friends again. I swear I didn't go there deliberately to see Harry.' Watching them, Alex shook his head wearily. Anjou was seeking redemption, again. And this time he'd bet she would be successful.

Anjou sank to her knees, sobbing wildly, clutching at Honeychile's skirt. 'Things just sort of happened. We went to bed . . . afterwards, I was in the shower. Harry was sleeping. I thought I heard a noise, but the water was running and it was difficult to hear things properly. And besides, they say a gun with a silencer makes almost no sound, just the tiniest plop.

'Oh, Honeychile, it was awful, terrible. I came out of the shower . . . there was blood everywhere and bits of Harry's shattered head and your teddy spread across the bed, the floor. I looked at Harry and I thought, If I had been in bed next to him, that might have been me, splashed across the walls.

'All this passed through my mind in the space of a second,' Anjou went on. 'Then I realised the murderer might still be in the house. I just ran out of there. I ran and I ran . . .'

She gazed beseechingly up at Honeychile, 'I didn't mean to sleep with Harry, it just sort of happened. Oh, Honeychile, you know I'm no good,' she cried remorsefully. 'Why, oh *why*, do I do these things.'

Honeychile sighed deeply; she wished she knew the answer.

Anjou was on her knees, still clutching at her, weeping. '*Please* believe me. For once I am speaking the truth. I know I am bad. I lie and I cheat and I steal other women's husbands. But I am not a murderer.'

Honeychile felt herself melting. Sighing, she placed a soothing hand on Anjou's head, stroking back her beautiful red hair. She was in such despair, she could not find it in her heart to hate her. 'It's all right, Anjou,' she said wearily, 'I believe you.' And they sat together on the sofa, holding each other, crying for Harry, and for themselves.

Alex took care of everything. He put the subdued Anjou on the Pan Am Clipper leaving for London that afternoon. Then he called Lord Mountjoy and told him about the tragedy. He told him that his own lawyer was representing Honeychile and he was certain she would not be implicated. He apologised for the indiscretion they had committed and which he had been forced to reveal to prove her innocence. He said he took entire responsibility for that. Honeychile was not to blame for anything.

On the other end of the transatlantic line, Mountjoy was stunned by the turn of events.

'Of course she hasn't done it,' he said angrily. 'We Mountjoys don't kill, unless it's the enemy, in battle. You can tell those New York bobbies that our family motto is, "Valour with Honour", and

346

if they want me to come over there and demonstrate it to them, I will,' he added. 'And now that you have compromised my girl, Scott, I expect you to do the right thing by her.'

The police were baffled: there seemed to be no motive for Harry's murder. Alex thought about what Anjou had said: that if she had been in bed next to Harry, it might have been she who was shot.

He remembered Harry's hair was almost as blond as Honeychile's, and that he was in a darkened bedroom. The police had said the sheet was covering Harry's face, and that his back was towards his assailant. Was it a case of mistaken identity? Or had the murderer meant to kill them both?

But *why* would anybody want to kill Honeychile? Alex knew that money was the usual answer, and the person who stood to gain by her death was Jack Delaney. Delaney was still Honeychile's legal stepfather. With her dead, he could finally get his hands on the Mountjoy Ranch and the oil money. It might involve a legal battle, but he would have a strong claim.

He called his lawyer. He told him what he suspected, gave them all the information he had, and asked them to track down Delaney. He told him Honeychile was staying in his apartment, while he took a suite at the Pierre. Then he hired round-the-clock bodyguards to keep watch outside her door.

Abrams got back to him the next day. Jack Delaney was still living at the big house in Houston. Only now he was Congressman Delaney. The FBI investigation had failed to implicate him with the Mob. He had been a generous contributor to the local Democratic coffers for many years, and had been elected Congressman four years ago. He lived like a rich man, though nobody knew where he got his money from. He was said to have his sights set on becoming a Senator and a Presidential candidate.

'Delaney thinks big,' Abrams said. 'He has powerful backers, and looks like a man on his way up. It seems he is a man without a motive. He also has a water-tight alibi for the night Harry was killed.'

Just like he did for Rosie, Alex remembered. But he still believed Delaney was guilty.

The next day, the police informed them that they had found footprints leading to the basement area, and evidence that the lock had been tampered with. They now believed the killer was a man, probably a robber who had thought the house was empty and had shot in panic when he saw Harry. Alex hoped for Honeychile's sake, they were right.

He knew that if there was to be anything between Honeychile and himself, it was time for the truth. They had already burned their bridges so publicly, there was no more need for discretion. All the world thought they were lovers anyhow.

He sent someone to pack Honeychile's things and ordered his private plane to be ready and waiting at the airport. That night, they were winging over the Atlantic, to Rome.

CHAPTER 36

Lord Mountjoy summoned Swayne to Mountjoy house. 'You're an ex-Scotland Yard man,' he said, 'What do you think about Harry's murder? Of course my girl did not do it, there is no question about that,' he added. 'The point is, who *did* shoot Harry Lockwood? And why? Obviously the man was a scoundrel, but people don't go shooting other people just because of that.'

Swayne had studied the evidence. He said, 'It seems to me, your Lordship, from what I can read into the case, that New York's finest are on the wrong track. They think a robber shot Sir Harry, when it's my belief the real target was Miss Honeychile. In my experience, it's always either money or sex at the bottom of a murder case. And she's a very rich young woman.'

'Well, in this case it was obviously her money they were after. But who would inherit if she died? Certainly not I. Perhaps those people she lived with, at the ranch?' He shook his head. 'No, that can't be it. They brought her up, the girl thought the world of them.'

'It's my belief sir, that we will find it is a person from her past; someone involved with her mother, perhaps. From what I've heard, she was an extraordinary woman. There was a second husband, Miss Honeychile's stepfather. And I happen to know he was a man she hated. Miss Laura gave me that information, sir.'

'Indeed?' Lord Mountjoy looked surprised. He asked himself why it was he never knew what was going on under his own roof.

'Well, keep an eye on things for me, would you?' he said wearily. 'I don't like this idea that someone is out to get my girl. No, no, I don't like it one little bit. It's not something we bargained for when we began our search. I want her protected, you understand me?'

'I understand she is in Italy with Mr Scott,' Swayne said, phrasing it as delicately as he could. 'I feel sure he has her well protected, your Lordship.'

'I dare say you're right,' Mountjoy admitted, gloomily, thinking that his girl went from one bounder to the next. What was wrong with women that they couldn't just find a decent chap and settle down. When she returned he would see Scott made an honest woman of her. They could hardly have the wedding at St Margaret's, not now that everybody knew about them. Perhaps a small service in the chapel at Mountjoy Park, and a nice reception afterwards. Give them a good send-off, and all would be well.

He thought about Laura's wedding to Billy next month. The girl could have had St Margaret's, but no, she had insisted on St Swithen's in Swinburn, that could hardly hold more than fifty at a push. Still, they would have a big reception, afterwards, and everybody would come to that. She and Billy were so popular, they had made so many friends. He was a good fellow, and they were ideally suited. Yes, he was very pleased with Laura.

That left Anjou. The poor girl had returned from New York, down in the dumps and terrified by what had happened. It was his fault, of course, for allowing her to go to New York with the Malvetts in the first place. The poor child simply had not known how to handle things. It was just sheer bad luck she was there when it happened. He would have to get together with Sophie and see what they could do about fixing her up; she needed to settle down, marry a nice strong chap who would keep her in line. Give her a few children to take care of; that would take that skittish edge off her soon enough. Besides, she was a beauty; he had high hopes for his girl, Anjou.

'Will that be all, sir?' Swayne was waiting patiently, his hands clasped behind his back, feet, in their solid black boots, firmly apart in the 'at ease' position.

'What? Oh, let's not forget Laura's wedding, up at Swinburn. The wedding presents will be on display at Swinburn Manor and I want you to be in charge of the security. And to arrange with the local constabulary about holding up the traffic and such like, for the wedding procession.'

'Of course, sir, I should be delighted.' Swayne beamed; Laura was by way of being a favourite. 'I assume Miss Honeychile will be attending, sir, so I shall be able to kill two birds with one stone, so to speak.'

'So you will, so you will,' Mountjoy said pleased. 'Lady Sophie and Mrs Swinburn will finalise the arrangements with you, later.'

'Thank you, your Lordship.' There was a pleased smile on Swayne's face as he departed. The Mountjoy case had proven very lucrative, and now there was Laura's wedding, plus the added interest of the murder of Sir Harry Lockwood. As he hopped on the bus back to the Strand, he thought he would take the dog up to Swinburn for the wedding. He knew it would like that. And he also thought what a feather in his cap it would be if he beat out the famous New York Police Department, and solved the mystery of who had killed Sir Harry Lockwood.

CHAPTER 37

Alex drove the little red Bugatti convertible along the last mile of the winding coast road leading to the tiny fishing village of Positano. He glanced at Honeychile, beside him. She was lying back with her eyes closed and her hair blowing in the wind. She looked pale and exhausted, but there was a little smile on her face.

'Almost there,' he said, swinging the car round the last bend in the road.

'Oh,' she said, and 'Oh, Alex.' She sat up, pushing the hair out of her eyes, looking at the wonderful view.

The village tumbled down the cliff, its tiny pastel-coloured houses covered in bougainvillea and geraniums and lines of colourful washing. Far below them, the *Atalanta* swung at anchor on the smooth azure water of the crescent-shaped bay; seabirds hovered above in the flawless blue sky, buffeted by a slight breeze; and the air smelled of wild thyme and rosemary and of the sea.

'I never imagined any place so beautiful,' she said, thinking of all the books she had devoured as a child, dreaming of seeing the world. She gave a happy little sigh. 'It's perfect.'

He laughed, pleased. 'Wait until you see the *Atalanta*. Then you'll see perfection.'

Two young sailors in striped blue T-shirts and white pants were waiting at the top of the steps, leading down through the village to the harbour. They greeted Alex enthusiastically, and wished Honeychile a smiling *buon giorno*.

Leaving them to take care of their luggage, they walked hand-in hand, down the steps and the steep cobbled paths through the village, stopping to admire a balcony tumbling with geraniums; and peering curiously at the shadowy, bead-curtained doorways, and tiny shops.

Small children ran after them, shouting *buon giorno*, and laughing; followed by a chorus of barking dogs.

In the tiny harbour the *Atalanta*'s smart white dinghy, was waiting to take them to the yacht.

'My pride and joy,' Alex said, looking at his sleek ship, out in the bay. 'I've had her for ten years and she's given me more pleasure than anything else I've ever owned in my entire life.'

The *Atalanta* was built like a clipper, teak-hulled, long and lean with three masts and trimly furled sails; and the crew of ten were lined up on deck to greet them. Alex knew them all by name. He shook their hands and introduced Honeychile, then he showed her around.

It was a man's ship, a vessel to be sailed, not a showplace for rich people to drink and party. The decor was crisp and simple, with no frills and everything immaculately shipshape. The teak decks were smooth as silk, the brasswork polished until it glittered, and the ropes were coiled into neat white snakes. The bridge was a model of what a bridge on a fine yacht should be, with charts stacked neatly in wide drawers and the latest navigational instruments. On the bow was a polished brass plate with the ship's name, and the owner's flag fluttered from the topmost mast.

The main saloon was enormous, with simple cream wool carpeting, taupe linen chairs and sofas, and a marble fireplace, filled, in the warm summer months, with a great bouquet of field flowers: giant daisies and cornflowers and ferns. The dining saloon had an antique pine table that would seat twelve, with black linen-covered chairs; and on the afterdeck was another table with blue canvas chairs under a blue awning, for outdoor dining. It was, Honeychile said, 'simply perfect'.

'We sail as soon as the dinghy returns with the luggage,' Alex said.

She looked happily at him. 'Where are we going?'

'We shall follow the path of the moon, wherever it takes us,' he told her, smiling.

A steward showed Honeychile to her state-room. It was large and simply decorated, with a nautical navy and white colour scheme. The specially made carpet was white with a navy striped border, the crisp little curtains at the brass-ringed portholes were navy, held back with white cords, and the bed was covered in a simple

354

white linen spread, piled with sumptuous pillows. It was exactly right for a boat, Honeychile thought, pleased that there were no Persian rugs and gilded headboards.

Her bathroom was large and luxurious, and the maid was already hanging up her things in the roomy walk-in closet. She smiled, remembering the voyage on the Queen Mary, and her meagre wardrobe. Now she had more than enough to satisfy any woman. And now, she thought, dreamily, as she slept off the exhaustion of the long journey in the beautiful bed, she also had Alex.

She awoke at six, feeling refreshed. She showered and put on a long navy chiffon slip of a dress that left her arms and her back bare. She brushed her long blonde hair until it hung smooth and straight round her shoulders. Then she walked, barefoot, out onto the afterdeck.

The setting sun had turned the sea a rich magenta; the lights of Positano twinkled across the bay and the sound of music and voices wafted across the still water. Over the cliffs, a full moon was already rising. Honeychile thought it could not have been a more perfect setting.

'Sunsets become you,' Alex said lightly, looking admiringly at her. Then he smiled, 'But I suspect moonlight will also. We are lucky tonight, Honeychile. We have been favoured with the beauty of the sun, the moon and the stars, all at once.'

'Yes, we're lucky,' she agreed. Then she walked towards him and into his arms.

Alex held her close; the soft pressure of her breasts was against his chest, the scent of her hair in his nostrils. He kissed her, a lingering gentle kiss, filled with love.

He held her face in his hands, looking longingly at her. 'I can't believe you are really here,' he murmured. 'That we have each other, at least for a short while.'

'I can stay for ever, Alex,' she promised. 'All you need do, is ask.'

He sighed as he let her go. He walked to the table where champagne was chilling in a crystal bucket, and poured two glasses. 'We shall drink to you, Honeychile,' he said. 'Now you can put the past behind you. You must forget what happened to Harry, and be happy.'

They ate dinner under the blue canopy on the afterdeck, listening to the slap of the incoming tide against the hull. Afterwards, they took the dinghy back to the village and strolled hand-in-hand again, through the narrow cobbled streets. They found a café and sat outside on little metal chairs, sipping grappa and watching a group of old men playing a noisy, argumentative game of dominoes. Women sat outside their doors, gossiping, children shouted and played and dogs ran underfoot.

It grew late. The proprietor began noisily to pile chairs onto the tables and put up his shutters. 'Tomorrow is another day, *signori*,' he said, surveying them. '*Ecco*, now is time for bed.' And he burst into a snatch of romantic song as he whisked away their empty glasses and wiped the table clean.

'*Buona sera, Capitano*,' he called, jovially, eyeing the lavish tip Alex had left. '*Buona sera, Signora. Molte grazie. A più tarde.*'

Back on the ship they stretched out on cushioned chairs on the afterdeck, looking up at the starry sky.

Alex turned his head to look at her. 'I remember when I saw you on the deck of the Queen Mary, you had stars in your eyes, just as bright as these.'

She sighed, regretfully. 'I think I've grown up since then.'

The boat rocked slightly as the anchor was pulled in and the engines started up. Alex looked at his watch. It was midnight.

'Where are we going?' she asked lazily.

'I told you, we shall follow the path of the moon. When we get out of the bay there should be enough wind to put up some sail. Then you'll see what my *Atalanta* can really do. She cuts through the waves as smoothly as a dolphin.'

'You really love this ship, don't you?' she said.

He nodded. 'I found her, half derelict in a boatyard near Marseilles and bought her for a song. I spent months re-designing her; I chose the deck timbers, I supervised the building of the new hull, and the installing of the new masts. I feel she is my creation, a part of me.'

He pulled her to her feet and walked, with his arm around her bare shoulders to the rail. 'Watch,' he commanded. She looked at the sailors climbing the rigging; and then first one sail, then another, unfurled. Then the wind caught them and they were speeding through the starry night, heading for the moon.

She could see the happiness in Alex's eyes. She said, 'Why don't you just give it all up, Alex? You're a rich man. You could spend all your time on your boat and be happy?'

He shrugged, 'If only it were that easy. The *Atalanta* makes me happy because she is one of the few things I bought for love, and not as the spoils of my own private vendetta. A war against the man who was my father.'

He put his arm round her, pulling her closer. He never talked about the past, not even to his mother. He lived every day as it came, moving quickly on, not sparing time to think because remembering was too painful, and because it made him hate himself even more for what he had done. It was not easy telling the woman he loved that he was a cruel and vindictive enemy, but if there was to be anything between them, first she must know the truth, and the story of his revenge that had haunted him all his life.

'I was eleven years old,' Alex said, 'when I first saw my father. It was late when he came into *Il Sorrentino*, but I knew it must be him from my mother's reaction. Her face turned pale and her eyes grew dark with shock. The man had not even remembered her; he looked right through her as though she did not exist. She was just another servant to him. She turned and fled into the kitchen, but I stayed to watch.

'He was tall, handsome, arrogant. An aristocrat with an important name and the owner of a shipping line. Everyone knew his ships, the freighters and especially the liner, the *Excelsior*, that had made him rich. And the café owner and the waiters fawned over him, delighted to have such an important man patronise their place.

'There was a boy with him, his son. He was younger than I, but so confident, so sure of his rightful place in the world as the son of a rich aristocrat. And I was just a poor boy, filling their glasses with water. And my mother, tight-lipped and trembling in the kitchen, was the long-forgotten lover; merely the woman putting food on their plates. To them, we were less than nothing, not even worthy of their notice.

'I thought how it should have been my mother on that man's arm; with pearls at her throat and wearing a fine dress; being waited on and treated like the lady she was. And I should have been the son, walking proudly beside my arrogant, assured father, who had never acknowledged my existence and who I knew now, never would.

'I remember staring at the boy. He was like a young prince, so sure of himself and his heritage and his place in the world. At that moment, I vowed I would get my revenge.

357

' "One day," I said to my tearful mother, "one day, I shall get even with him for what he did to you. *To us.* I promise you, I will." '

Alex paused. He was leaning on the rail, his hands clasped loosely in front of him, staring at the silver path the moon had left on the ocean. But Honeychile knew he wasn't seeing it. He was seeing the face of his father, and of the son who should have been him.

'Years later,' Alex said, at last, 'when I became successful and rich and had power, I went in search of them, and my revenge. I found my enemy weak. They had lost money in imprudent business ventures. Their properties were heavily mortgaged: the palazzo in Rome, the country villa, the townhouse in Paris. The liner had been sold to try to repay some of the debts. Everything they owned was in jeopardy.

'Acting in secret, I bought their ships. I went to the bank and bought the mortgages on their properties, until I owned them all. Then I sent a representative to demand immediate payment on everything.'

Alex shrugged. 'Of course, they did not have the money. I foreclosed on the mortgages and evicted them from their properties. Now, I had their ships, their lands and their homes. I had my victory.

'I did not tell my mother what I had done; she was a gentle woman and would have been shocked by my callousness. All I said was that I had had my revenge.

'I thought to myself, now at last, I will be happy. Now *I* was "*the young prince*," and the other, legitimate son, was reduced to poverty. Of course, they did not know it was I who had foreclosed on them, I who had finally ruined them.

'Ironically, one day a while later, the son came to my office asking for a job. I sat behind my desk, looking at my rival, and I knew I had him in my power. He was tall, blond, handsome; young and polite, still with the confidence of his breeding, his education, his privileged upbringing. *His name.*

'The son smiled confidently at me; how could he possibly be turned down for a position. He was experienced in shipping, he was who he was. He had so much to offer.

'I refused him the job.

'His confidence disappeared; he was desperate. "You don't understand, sir," he pleaded. "I *need* this job. My family have fallen on hard times. My father is ill from worry. Please, sir. I'm begging you." '

Alex could still see himself, and the little ruthless shrug of the shoulders as he walked away from him. 'They say charity begins at home,' he called carelessly, over his shoulder. 'You have a title, a family. See if they will give you a job.'

Alex looked sombrely at Honeychile. 'My revenge was complete. I thought I would be happy. After all, I had everything, didn't I? I was successful, rich. I had bought my mother a palatial apartment in Rome, and a place in the country. But somehow, my half-brother's pleading eyes haunted my dreams.

'Eventually, there came a time when I was happy as well as successful. I had finally put the past out of my mind. Then, one day, I read about the suicide of the man who was my father. I was troubled, deeply ashamed. I couldn't bear to think about it.'

Alex straightened up. He put his hands in his pockets and began to pace the deck. He looked so alone, so desperate all of a sudden, Honeychile wanted to run to him, to hold him, to tell him it was all in the past and he must forget. Then he stopped his pacing and turned to face her.

'Now *I* was the one who was weak,' he said. 'And in my weakness I went to the son and told him who I was and what I had done. I told him it was *I* who had bought up their mortgages and foreclosed on them, that it was *I* who had taken their ships and bankrupted them. That *I* had ruined them. Then I returned all their properties and their ships, and I paid a large sum to compensate them for what I had done.

'And that, I thought, was that,' he said to Honeychile, his voice flat and unemotional. 'I admitted my mistake. I gave the son power again. *And his revenge was even worse than mine.* I have been punished for what I did every day of my life since.'

He saw the tears in her eyes and the sympathy on her lovely young face. 'Don't feel sorry for me,' he said harshly. 'I am not worthy of it. And that's the reason we are going on this little voyage. Because I need you to know the truth about me, to see it with your own eyes. Tomorrow, you will understand.'

He glanced at his watch. He was as aloof as if the magical evening they had just spent together had never been.

'It's late,' he said abruptly. 'You must get some sleep.'

'But Alex,' she protested, and he covered her lips with his fingers.

'Goodnight, sweet Honeychile,' he said. 'As the café owner said, "tomorrow is another day". And we shall both need some sleep.'

He took her hand and escorted her to her cabin. 'Sleep well, *cara mia*,' he said. And then with the lightest kiss on her lips, he turned and walked away, back onto the deck where he could be alone with his thoughts.

CHAPTER 38

Alex did not sleep that night. He was used to it, there had been many nights over the past years when he had not slept; many nights when he had prowled his wonderful apartment in Rome, his magnificent house in London, or the Manhattan penthouse; asking himself if it had all been worth it. If the price was not, after all, too much to pay. And the answer was always the same.

He would have given everything he had simply to turn the clock back and begin again. But life did not offer those options. Your choices were presented at the moment: you made them and you lived with the results. Or at least you looked as though you were still living.

The ship's sails had been furled and the *Atalanta*'s powerful engines purred in the background as she surged steadily through the night. He leaned against the rail, staring into the depths of the indigo sea, and into the depths of his own soul.

He had not meant to fall in love with Honeychile. He had fought against it, God knows. But there was no turning back the clock; his choice had been offered that very first night on the liner, when he had seen her standing at the top of the dining saloon steps, looking frightened and vulnerable. And so innocent.

He should have recognised that men like him had no right to such innocence. It had no place in a life like his. The women he chose were never innocent; they knew what he was offering: a temporary affair, a few moments companionship that allowed him to believe he was living in the real world. Honeychile was too good for that.

The trouble was they had burned their bridges so publicly in New York, everyone thought they were lovers anyway. He had compromised Honeychile to save her; but he still could not marry her. Now he was about to show her the truth, and then life would present its choice to her. And he knew, in his heart, that he would lose her. It would all be over between them.

He glanced up as four bells sounded the change of watch. He stretched his arms over his head, trying to loosen the tense neck muscles, then he walked along the deck and up the companionway to the bridge.

The first mate was on duty. He saluted and said, '*Buona notte, Capitano.*'

Alex told him he would take the watch, and he could go and get some sleep. He studied the chart for a moment, then took the wheel. He always loved this night watch. Being alone in the darkness, feeling the power of the speeding ship beneath him, cutting smooth as a shark through the water. He had guided his ship through storms where the wind whipped the sea into a fury. The yacht had rolled and pitched under the force of the waves, but he had had no fear. He had known death was one decision that was not his to make. Still, he was not a man to go down without a fight, and he had fought the elements and won. He was, it seemed, a man who could never lose. Except when it came to his heart.

As the cool, misty dawn broke, the *Atalanta* was sailing north, hugging the coastline, nearing her destination. Alex handed over control to the duty officer and went below in search of coffee.

Honeychile was there before him. She was wearing a white shirt and skirt and her hair was tied back with a blue ribbon that matched her eyes. She was sipping a cup of coffee, staring at the mist hovering over the sea. She turned to look at him and he smiled.

'You look about fourteen years old,' he said, lightly. 'How's the coffee?'

'Strong, but good.'

He went to the buffet and poured himself a cup. 'Did you sleep well?'

'Did you expect me to?'

Their eyes met. He thought hers were sad; she thought his were weary. He shrugged, 'It's a nice time to be up, at dawn, on a ship.' He held out his hand. 'Come, bring your coffee on deck with you, and I'll show you.'

They stood on the afterdeck as the sky took on a pearly glow. Suddenly it was shot through with rose, then gold, then the sun's warmth sent the mist spiralling from the still surface of the water. The silence was total, not a voice, nor the cry of a bird; even the sea was quiet.

'Every time I see it, I think it must have been like this at the dawn of creation,' Alex marvelled.

Honeychile was remembering all those lonely dawns on the ranch, where the hot sun struck like a blow the moment it rose over the horizon, and the wind searched like a predator through the shrivelled grasses. Dawn there was over in minutes, and the flat landscape shimmered exhaustedly again in its daily battle with the never-ending dry heat.

'Paradise must be like this,' she said, wonderingly, as the mist dispersed: the calm sea sparkled blue again in the sunlight; the rugged green cliffs hung like a theatre backdrop in the distance, and the air was so fresh and clean she felt she was drinking it along with the coffee.

She felt the ship's speed and looked enquiringly at him. 'Where are we going so fast?'

'To a place I know.' He checked his watch, 'We should be there sometime this afternoon. Meanwhile, how about some breakfast? Mario is already setting it up on deck. You can dine on fresh fruits from Positano, coffee from Rome, bread baked by our own chef and preserves from Fauchon in Paris. Or if you wish, American-style hot cakes, and eggs and bacon, though I cannot claim to know where they come from.'

She laughed, and his heart lifted. If he was going to hurt her, again, he would rather it were just the one swift blow later. Then they would see what would happen.

He went off to take a shower and she thought, relieved, he seemed his old self again. She had never thought of Alex as vulnerable; he only ever showed his invincible side to the world. Now she knew different.

When he returned, they breakfasted on the fresh bread and Fauchon preserves and fruit, talking of how lovely the landscape looked, how serene the morning was, of this and that and nothing at all. Nothing important, anyway, like what was to become of them, Honeychile thought, sadly.

Afterwards, he said he had some work to take care of, and she changed into a bathing suit and lay in the pale sunlight, half-dozing over a book.

Alex did not appear for lunch and she picked, half-heartedly at a salad, alone.

At two-thirty, he sent the steward to tell her they would be arriving at their destination in about twenty-five minutes, and then they were going for a drive. Honeychile hurried to get ready, wondering apprehensively what all the secrecy was about.

She dressed quickly in a simple blue cotton dress and sandals. She flipped a comb through her wet hair, added a touch of lipstick and went up on deck.

Alex was waiting for her. He looked weary, like a man who had not slept. 'There you are,' he said, 'Just in time.'

The *Atalanta* was already at anchor and the dinghy was waiting. He held her hand as she stepped in, and he kept hold of it as they chugged across the bay to a pretty little port, dreaming under the hot afternoon sun.

A car was waiting for them, a fast expensive Mercedes. Honeychile looked at Alex as he took the wheel. 'Where are we going?'

'To the most beautiful house I know,' he said quietly. 'To show you the reason I can never ask you to share my life.'

'Alex don't,' she said, suddenly afraid. 'There is no need. You know I love you. I don't care what secrets you have. Please, let's not go.' She put her hand urgently on his arm as if to hold him to her.

'We must,' he said, gently. 'I will let you see for yourself, the result of my victory.'

They drove in silence along the meandering road, through the hill country dotted with vineyards and ancient villages, until finally he slowed the car down and turned into a sandy white lane, leading upwards, through an avenue of poplars. Vineyards spread like a symmetrically patterned carpet thrown over the slopes of the hillside, and at the top, lost behind a grove of ancient olives and cypresses, was a wonderful, sprawling, terracotta-coloured house.

'The Villa d'Ombrusco,' Alex said. ' "The house of the shadows." It used to be my home, the place I loved best in the world. I thought, when I bought it, that God could have given me no more beautiful a setting to spend the rest of my life.'

The housekeeper, an older, smiling woman dressed in black, flung open the door and greeted them. 'Ah *Signor*,' she said, 'it is good to see you again. *Buon giorno, Signorina.*'

'How are things, Assunta?' he asked, stepping into the cool, tiled hall.

'The same as always, *Signor*,' she replied. 'One cannot grumble. Perhaps the *Signorina* would care for some refreshment,' she smiled at Honeychile. 'The drive is a long one and it is hot today. I have prepared fresh lemonade, and there are the little *biscotti* you like so much, *Signor*.'

She escorted them into a beautiful salon furnished with fine antiques and comfortable sofas. French windows led onto a flagged terrace, overhung with vines and dotted with tables and cushioned metal chairs. An old olive tree cast shade over the courtyard beyond, and in one corner, a stone Bacchus head spilled water into a stone bowl with a pretty tinkling sound.

Honeychile said, 'I can see why you love it so.'

'Loved,' Alex corrected her. 'Now it is just the monument to my destructive power.'

'I have told the *Signora* you are here,' Assunta said, carrying in a tray with a jug of lemonade and tall glasses clinking with ice. She glanced at Honeychile as she put it down on the table. 'We do not have many visitors,' she said regretfully, 'apart from the *Signor*.'

There was the sound of footsteps on the tiled floor and Alex got up quickly. He hurried to the door to greet the woman as she entered. He held her close, kissed her on either cheek, then he took her arm and led her towards them.

She was painfully thin, a beautiful woman with flowing dark hair and a pale, ageless, sculpted face. She leaned on Alex's arm, walking slowly with the aid of a cane as though her limbs were too frail to support even her meagre weight. Honeychile saw she was beautifully dressed; and that her fingers gleamed with diamonds and there were pearls at her throat. As they came closer, she did not greet her, or acknowledge she was there. She saw that her big dark eyes had no expression.

Alex said to her, 'I would like to introduce my wife. The *Signora* Ottavia Scott.'

Honeychile looked at the beautiful, mindless woman, then pityingly at Alex. Her heart was filled with sorrow for them both. Now, she finally understood why he had kept her at arm's length. She knew he would never leave Ottavia, that his love and his pity would bind him to her for ever.

'Ottavia cannot speak to you,' Alex said, looking bleakly at Honeychile. 'We are not even sure that she understands anything that is happening. But at least I know she wants to be here, in this house. Perhaps she lives in her memories of the past, when we were happy. I only hope so. I visit her as often as I can. I always hope it gives her pleasure to see me, but mostly she seems content just to sit out here, on the shady terrace, listening to the fountain and the birdsong.'

He helped his wife into a chair. Her blank eyes rested on Honeychile for a brief instant, then she turned and looked up at Alex.

'Ottavia, this is a friend,' he said, as though they were normal people, spending a normal afternoon together, taking afternoon tea in the garden.

His wife was not listening. She looked round agitatedly; then a little black cat ran from the garden. It jumped onto her lap and she put her arms round it protectively, holding it close to her.

'As you can see, Ottavia has a little friend to keep her company.' Alex's voice was gentle. He poured lemonade and held it to his wife's lips while she drank. Then he wiped her mouth with a napkin and sat beside her.

'Ottavia has been incapable of speech for fifteen years,' he said to Honeychile. 'And you had to see for yourself why I can never leave her.'

'I understand,' she said gently.

He shook his head. 'No, you do not understand. But now you will.' And looking at Ottavia, he told her what happened, all those years ago.

'It was a year after I had met with my father's other son,' he said, quietly. 'I had given him back his ships, his property, everything I had taken from him. I had repaid my debt and soothed my conscience. And I had, I thought, redeemed myself.

'I met Ottavia on Capri. She was on holiday there with her mother. She was young and fantastically beautiful, a magical girl with flowing black hair and sparkling brown eyes, full of life and interest. Her mother was frail, crippled with arthritis and Ottavia pushed her wheelchair up and down Capri's steep hills, hardly needing to pause for breath. Watching her, I thought she was indomitable.

'They were staying at the same small hotel I was, in the piazza. I would see her eating dinner alone every night, and when I asked the waiter, he told me the mother preferred to eat earlier and take a rest. Ottavia noticed me looking at her and she gave an encouraging smile, so I asked her if she would care to take a stroll round the piazza, perhaps have a drink in the café.

'She agreed, and we walked together along the little road that led along the coast, while she told me about her mother's illness and how she used to be so strong, and how sad it was for her.

'She was the daughter of a doctor, from Milan, who had died the previous year. She was nineteen years old and she had hoped to study medicine herself, but now she was just a nurse to her mother. Not that she grumbled, she loved her mother dearly. But there was a wistfulness about her, as she thought of what might have been.

'I couldn't take my eyes off her. She walked like a gazelle; she was so light and graceful. She was beautiful and caring and kind, and I fell in love with her that night. I was supposed to return to Rome and my work but I lingered in Capri to be with her. At the end of two weeks, when her holiday came to an end, I asked her to marry me.'

Alex closed his eyes, remembering. 'She just looked at me and I saw a love that matched my own in her shining dark eyes. She put her hand in mine, so trustingly, though she barely knew me. And she said yes.

'We were married the following week at the little church in Capri. There was no grand ceremony; her mother and mine were the only guests. She wore a pretty white cotton dress embroidered with flowers, made by a local woman, and she carried a bouquet of lilies bought in the market. There wasn't even time to get her a ring, so I promised that when we went to Rome I would buy her the most beautiful ring she could find. Meanwhile she picked out a little silver band from the local shop and that was the ring I placed on her finger that day.'

Honeychile's eyes were drawn to Ottavia's hand, still stroking the cat.

'It is the same ring she still wears today,' Alex said softly. 'She was too sentimental ever to change it. She said it would be bad luck.

'I remember how we laughed. How could bad luck ever find us? We were young, in love, a golden couple with everything we could want. At least we thought so, until a year later, she told me she was pregnant and I knew that we had not had "everything". That this baby would make our world complete.

'We were living in an apartment in Rome but Ottavia decided we should have a country house, now there was to be a child. So we went house-hunting and after a few weeks, we found Villa d'Ombrusco. Again, it was love at first sight for both of us. We bought it immediately and she spent the weeks of her pregnancy supervising its restoration. By the time our son was born, everything was ready.'

Alex paused. He leaned back in his chair, his eyes closed, as though gathering courage to go on.

Honeychile looked at Ottavia, still stroking her little cat. Her face was expressionless. She shivered, she did not want to hear what Alex had to say because she knew it was going to be terrible.

'I had forgotten all about my father and his son,' Alex said. 'I had put them out of my mind, finally. So I was taken by surprise when he came back for his revenge.

'I found out later that he went to the bandits who lived in the remote hill villages. He bought them grappa at the café, pouring liberally. He told them he was doing them a favour; that he knew of a rich ship owner with a wife and a baby son. He said that if the wife and son were kidnapped, the ship owner would pay a fortune for their return. Then he gave them money and went back to Rome. He knew that all he had to do was wait.

'My son was four months old when they came for them. Ottavia was just twenty-one. For two weeks, I heard nothing. The police could find no trace of them. I was frantic, distraught, I wailed and ranted and swore to kill anyone who harmed a hair of their heads. Then they sent a ransom note. I did exactly as they said. I did not tell the police. I paid the enormous sum they asked, and they sent me back my wife and child.'

His eyes were haunted as he looked at Honeychile, and she saw at last the depths of his grief. 'They had raped and brutalised her, then they cut out her tongue so she could not speak about it. Our son was dead. She was still clutching his little body to her when we found them, just the way she holds the cat now. And she had completely lost her mind.'

Alex got up and went to stand behind his wife. He put his hands protectively on her shoulders and she lifted her beautiful, blank face to him.

He said, coldly, dispassionately, 'The men who did it were hunted down like the wild animals they were. Later, when their bodies were found, their tongues had been cut out. No one knew who had done it. And, if they suspected, they did not say.'

Honeychile's eyes met his. 'And now you understand why there can be no future for us,' he said simply, with the guilt and sorrow plain on his face.

He kissed his wife tenderly on either cheek, then he called the housekeeper to come and look after her.

'We shall see ourselves out, Assunta,' he said, with a last lingering look at Ottavia, still clutching the soft little black cat. 'Take care of her for me.'

'Of course I shall, *Signor*,' she said, comfortingly. 'And I always will.'

They climbed back into the Mercedes and drove in silence down the hill. At the bottom, Alex stopped the car and turned for one last look. 'I used to do this every time I left them here,' he said. 'Ottavia would stand on the balcony outside our room and wave goodbye. She said it was so I would remember her when I was away, and that she would always be here, waiting for me.'

He sighed, 'I always stop, hoping that by some miracle, she will have remembered, and that she will be there, smiling and waving at me. But of course, she never will.' He shrugged sadly, as they drove off.

'So, Honeychile,' he said, after a while. 'What do you think now, of the smart, rich, successful Alex Scott? Now you know the truth: that he is a man with a heart full of secrets and guilt, that nothing can ever take away. Is he the man you thought he was?'

'He is more than the man I thought he was,' she said quietly. 'He is a man of honour, a man of courage who does not shirk his responsibilities and does not forget how much he loved. I only wish . . .' she hesitated.

He glanced at her. 'What do you wish?'

She had been going to say she wished he could love her as much as that, but she shook her head, and they drove the rest of the way in silence.

Later, that evening, the *Atalanta* was under sail power, heading lazily back to Positano. The beautiful Villa d'Ombrusco and its sad occupant seemed to belong to another world, light years away from the brisk reality of the sea and the sunlight. As she dressed for dinner, Honeychile wondered if this was the end of it all for them. She knew there were two choices in front of her: one, a life in the shadows as the mistress of Alex Scott; the other as the rich young Mountjoy widow, who would find herself a nice new husband and happiness in her children.

She looked at herself in the mirror; she looked young and almost childlike in a white silk dress. It was not the way she felt. She was no longer the naïve girl Alex had met. She was married and widowed; she had her own secret burdens of tragedy; she had born the brunt of gossip and public scorn. Now, she was a woman with nothing to lose.

She pulled off the virginal white dress and took out a gold sheath. The fabric was soft and supple with a dull shimmer of gold thread woven into it, and it clung to her like a second skin. She twisted a gold chain, stranded with diamonds, round her throat, and put matching diamonds in her ears. She swept her hair up at the sides, pinning it on top with a gardenia, and then she looked at herself in the mirror.

She smoothed her hand over the golden sheath. She *knew* that woman in the mirror. It was not the woman she once was, it was the woman she had become.

She did not need any perfume, the gardenia surrounded her with its fragrance. And she did not need shoes, not even sandals 'that would gleam as she danced' as the Sears catalogue had said, a lifetime ago.

Satisfied, she walked from her cabin, along the blue-carpeted corridor to the saloon. Alex looked up as she came into the room. He looked at her for a long time, then he smiled.

'What happened to my girl?' he asked shaking his head, ruefully.

'She grew up.'

He walked across, took her hand. He said, 'When I first saw you, I thought what a funny, plain little thing you were. Then you dazzled me at the Mountjoy ball. And now look at you. You're beautiful.

You are a woman of many disguises, Miss Honeychile Mountjoy.'

'You might as well know now,' she said calmly, 'that there is only one woman I want to be. And that's yours.' He began to protest but she covered his mouth with a kiss. 'I don't care about anything,' she said. 'I understand that you love Ottavia, and I hope you always will. All I want is for you to find room in your heart, in your life, just one small corner, for us.'

'Think about it, Honeychile,' he said, untangling himself from her arms. 'Just think about what it will mean; the gossip, the tarnished reputation, the fact that I can never marry you and no one will understand that it's not because I don't love you . . .'

'None of it matters,' she said. 'As long as you love me.'

He pulled her to him. 'You know I do,' he said, burying his face in the gardenia-fragrance of her hair, kissing her neck, her shoulders, her lips. 'If you only knew how much I love you.'

'Show me, Alex,' she whispered. And as he kissed her, she knew that her future was sealed. She might never become Alex Scott's wife, but she would always be the woman he loved.

The sound of the little gong being struck, signalling that dinner was about to be served, drew them apart. She tidied her hair as best she could and with his arm round her shoulders, they strolled to the after-deck, just as the last glimmer of molten-red sun flickered on the aquamarine horizon and was gone.

They sat in the candlelight, holding hands and nibbling on thin spears of green asparagus, on fresh crayfish and tiny perfumed wild strawberries, and they drank champagne and held hands and were content.

After supper, they strolled the decks, looking at the moonlit path on the indigo sea, enjoying the breeze and their nearness, through their linked hands.

At last they walked back through the silent ship to his cabin. He stopped at the door and looked questioningly at her. She opened it and stepped inside.

A green-shaded lamp cast a muted glow over the low bed, and on the beautiful Monet painting of the flower garden, in the little golden easel on the night table. The sea slapped against the sides of the ship, and it rolled gently as it cut through the waves. She began slowly to unfasten her dress.

* * *

Alex watched each tiny button as it came free, like a man mesmerised. And when, with a silken rustle it finally slid to the ground, he looked at the woman he loved. He held out his arms and she walked into them. Then he carried her to bed and covered her with kisses, and she knew finally, she had found the love and the happiness she had been longing for.

CHAPTER 39

The early June day was soft and balmy with a few blowy clouds drifting through a pale-blue sky. Starlings and wagtails chattered in the hedgerows as Laura rode the chestnut mare Billy had given her as a wedding gift, through the village of Swinburn. The carefully-tended gardens were in full bloom and she slowed the mare to a walk, admiring the hollyhocks in Frank Longbottom's garden, and the dazzling blue of his delphiniums that reminded her of the colour of Honeychile's eyes.

The village houses were built of square grey stones; there were lace curtains at every window and polished brass door-knockers that glittered in the sun. They were as familiar to her as her own home; she knew the inside of every one. As a little girl, she had baked jam tarts with Mrs Thompson and then eaten them, sitting on her immaculately-scoured front doorstep, with a big glass of milk straight from their own cows at Swinburn Farm. Years ago, she had gone upstairs at Number 3, to see Jennie Jakes's new baby boy, born the day before. She had peered at the lusty, yelling little scrap with its red face and said, puzzled, 'But I didn't know babies screamed,' and the little boy had obliged by raising his voice an octave and yelling even louder. Jennie Jakes teased her that it was her fault; she said he had almost driven them nuts with his yelling, until he was two years old and then he became as docile as a lamb. And now he was a sturdy sixteen year old, working at Swinburn Farm and doing well, too, she heard.

Laura had popped into every house along the street as a child and been treated to lollipops or glasses of sweet Dandelion and Burdock, and fizzy orange-red Tizer; Harrogate humbugs and Fuller's toffees. As they handed her the sweets they all said the same thing to her,

373

'Don't tell Mrs Swinburn, or she'll be after me for spoiling your dinner.'

Laura smiled. Her dinner had never been spoiled, and she had gained many friends. They had all been invited to her wedding. Everyone was coming, even ancient Mrs Hodgkiss, whose hip still bothered her, had said she wouldn't dream of missing it, and Ethel Aykeroyd was returning from her sister's in Barnsley for what she called, 'our wedding'.

Laura supposed it was 'their wedding' as much as hers. The villagers were her friends; they had watched her grow up with as much pride and affection as they had given their own children, taking her to their hearts because they had loved her father, Lorenzo, and because she was a 'poor motherless girl' and needed an extra bonus of love.

As she turned the corner by the church, she waved hello to Fred Roberts, the verger, busy pulling stray tufts of grass from the cracks in the flagstone path, getting it tidy for the big day, like the rest of the village. She bet there wouldn't be a weed left alive in Swinburn by Saturday.

She had taken Billy round to each of their houses, all forty of them. She had introduced him, and of course, Billy had loved it, and they had loved him. He had not even stammered once; he just shook their hands and said he had heard all about them, which was true, and that he was glad they were coming to his wedding because Laura had said they were like her family. He had listened patiently to old Tom Flaxman's stories about Laura's father when he was a boy; and had sat three year old Molly Yates on his knee, and not even flinched when she took her toffee from her mouth and dropped it on his trousers.

Billy had shared a pint of Tetley's Bitter and a game of darts in the Red Lion with the men, and he had been a genial and welcoming host at the reception they had held for all the village families, last Saturday night. They had served a four-course knife and fork supper in the village hall, gaily decorated with the red, white and blue buntings left over from the last coronation, that were always brought out for special gala occasions. The ladies wore their second-best hats (they were saving their new hats for the wedding) and floral dresses, and the men looked uncomfortable in what had probably been their own wedding suits and shiny boots. And the children, scrubbed to perfection, had run around underfoot, almost causing accidents as the trestle tables shook and tottered, spilling beer and hot tea.

The meal had been supervised by Jeannie who knew what everybody liked, and it was catered by the same firm that was doing the wedding. They devoured smoked Scottish salmon, roast Aylesbury duckling with all the trimmings, and chocolate profiteroles piled into great pyramids that drew gasps of appreciation and applause when they were carried proudly to the table.

Jeannie had sat at the head of the table with Laura and Billy opposite each other, half way down. After dessert she had tapped on her glass with a knife for silence. She had risen to her feet and made an emotional little speech, telling them how proud she was that they cared so much about her granddaughter. That she had not forgotten the love and kindness they had shown to Lorenzo, and to Adriana, and she was grateful that it had overflowed to Laura. Smiling a little tearfully, she said she was one of the oldest there. She had known some of them since she was a girl herself; she had been to their own daughters' weddings, births, christenings. And now it was her Laura's and Billy's turn and she was only glad that they could all come and share it with her.

She had sat down quickly before the tears could sneak up on her, to a storm of applause, and then Frank Hobbs had got to his feet and started to sing 'For She's a Jolly Good Fellow' and everyone else had sprung up and joined in. After that Ethel Wilde had sung her party piece, 'Jerusalem', in an ear-piercing soprano, and the more extrovert had got up and done their own songs or recitations of 'The Wreck of the *Hesperus*'; and all in all, it had been a jolly good party. One of the best, everyone had agreed as they had collected caps and children and made their way home through the soft summer night, to their cosy grey-stone homes where life and death and love had been celebrated for more than a couple of centuries.

Laura supposed it was the continuity of life at Swinburn that bound her to it; it never changed and she hoped it never would, so that her and Billy's children would be welcomed as Swinburn family, the way she had been herself.

She only wished Honeychile could have found the happiness she had. Not that she wasn't happy: she loved Alex and he adored her, but it might be many years before he could, as Uncle Mountjoy put it, 'make an honest woman of her'.

Of course, compared with the Prince of Wales running off with Mrs Simpson, Honeychile's romance with Alex was hardly noticed, even though Uncle Mountjoy had observed sadly that she would never be admitted to the Royal Enclosure at Ascot again. Laura knew Honeychile thought it was an insignificant price to pay for loving Alex. And after the tragedy of Harry's murder, everybody knew they were lovers. Only Honeychile had told her privately, they hadn't been then. That had happened later, on his yacht where, she had said dreamily, they had made love on a bed of moonlight as they sailed the blue Mediterranean.

Honeychile was already at Swinburn for the wedding, and Alex would be arriving that night. Anjou and her mother, Madame Suzette were coming tomorrow, the day before the nuptials, as were Uncle Mountjoy and Aunt Sophie, only they were all staying at the Old Swan, in Harrogate.

She nudged the horse into a trot and set off down the lane back to the Manor. The cow-parsley in the hedgerows was shoulder high, tangled with morning glories and dotted with clumps of bright blue cornflowers. The fields of barley on the left were a delicate green, and on the right the early wheat was ripening to the colour of Honeychile's hair. Bees droned by, heavy with yellow pollen, and a lark soared in the sky. Swinburn Valley in June was the loveliest place in the world, she thought contentedly, as she turned into the Manor gates.

She spotted Swayne patrolling the perimeter of the grounds, walking steadfastly forward, glancing right and left, on the alert for anything suspicious, though Laura couldn't think what he expected to find. Nothing criminal ever happened in Swinburn; no robberies or beatings or ghastly headless bodies in trunks; and nothing ever would.

His face was red from the sun and he looked hot and uncomfortable in his dark suit and tie, and heavy boots. The spoiled spaniel pottered along beside him, doing its best, she thought, to look like a bloodhound. She waved and called cheerily, 'How are you on this lovely day, Mr Swayne?'

He doffed his hat and said, 'Fair to middlin', Miss Laura, thank you.'

She laughed as she drew abreast of him, reining in the mare. 'You must have been spending time in the Red Lion. That's a Yorkshire expression you just used. And you, a southerner.'

He smiled, 'Born and bred, Miss. Not quite a cockney, but Clapham is close enough.'

'I trust the wedding presents are still intact? How could they not be, with your eagle eyes on them? I'm certain no thief could ever get past you.' She smiled, jokingly, but Swayne was hopeless, he had absolutely no sense of humour.

'I trust not, Miss Laura,' he said seriously. 'I keep my eye on them at all times, except for my half-hourly patrol of the grounds.'

'Well, it's too hot to be patrolling now.' She glanced sympathetically at his perspiring brow. 'Why not come indoors and have something cool to drink. You can always patrol again later, when the sun goes down,' she added, knowing how devoted to his duty he was.

'Thank you, Miss.' Swayne mopped his brow, gratefully. 'Perhaps that would be a better idea.'

'And Mr Swayne, I'm sure you would be more comfortable if you took off your jacket. Shirtsleeves will be perfectly all right.'

Swayne smiled as she nudged the horse and trotted off up the gravel drive. He took off the jacket, gave a huge sigh of relief, rolled up his shirtsleeves and whistled to the spaniel, rooting in the shrubbery. He was enjoying his job, here at Swinburn. He thought old Mrs Swinburn was a genuine lady, not like some of those titled society ones in London. She had brought up her granddaughter properly and Miss Laura was a credit to her.

He walked round the back of the house to the kitchen entrance, heaving another sigh of relief as he stepped into the cool kitchen. He hesitated; better check on Miss Honeychile first; make sure she was safe, though he didn't see as how she could be anything else, here at Swinburn. Then he would treat himself to a glass of Mrs Swinburn's good home-made gingerbeer. It was guaranteed to perk a fellow up on a hot day like this.

Honeychile was lying on a grassy bank in the shade of a willow tree. She was supposed to be reading a book, but she had been diverted, and instead was lying on her stomach, peering into the bubbling little stream at the minnows flashing by and the occasional brown-spotted trout, lurking beneath the flat rocks. She glanced up as the spaniel came bounding towards her, knowing that Swayne could not be far behind.

'Here I am, Mr Swayne, safe and sound,' she said, thinking it was really unnecessary for him to 'keep an eye on her'; but she knew Uncle Mountjoy had insisted. Swayne waved, acknowledging her, then he turned and headed for the kitchen.

She turned over onto her back, pillowing her head in her hands, staring at the infinite blueness of the June sky, thinking how serene life was here, and how different from the nervous feeling she always had these days, in New York. Alex was still worried about Jack Delaney. He insisted on round-the-clock bodyguards for her.

She had developed the creepy sensation of always being watched. Sometimes, she even thought she was being followed. She would be hurrying across Washington Square, or along Fifth Avenue and she would just feel eyes on her. There would be that warning prickle up her spine and she would swing round to confront whoever it was. And there would be nobody. Or at least, there would be dozens of people, none of whom seemed the least bit interested in her as they hurried past in that purposeful way New Yorkers had, as if they all had important appointments to keep and were already late.

So it was a relief to be here at Swinburn with Laura and Jeannie, lazing in the sunshine, with only Swayne to 'keep an eye on her', instead of a burly guard with a gun in the holster under his jacket. Even Alex had agreed that guards would not be necessary in England.

'Hey, lazy girl.' Laura flopped down on the grass next to her. 'I hope you're not bored?' she asked. 'Because if you are, I'm driving grandmother into Harrogate this afternoon. She's going to collect her "wedding dress", and of course the hat, from Rachel's on Parliament Street. I told her that Anjou's mother was the famous Madame Suzette of Paris and that she would make her the masterpiece of all hats for the occasion. But grandmother said, no, she had been patronising Rachel's for forty years, ever since they opened. And she wasn't about to take her custom away now, when everybody would read about it in the papers and know she had deserted them for the posher world of society hatmakers. She told me that she reckoned after putting up with her for forty years, Rachel deserved the credit.'

Honeychile laughed, 'That sounds like your grandmother, all right. And she's right. Besides, I'm sure Miss Rachel knows her style and what suits her, and she will look wonderful anyway.'

'We thought we might take a stroll round the Valley Gardens, then perhaps tea, at Betty's. Why don't you come along, it'll be fun?'

Honeychile thought how nice Laura was to ask her to join them when she had so little time left before the wedding to be alone with her grandmother. 'Thanks,' she said, yawning, 'but it's too hot and I'm too lazy even to move from this spot. Why don't you two go and have fun and tell me all about it when you get back.'

'Well, if you're sure you're not too bored, all by yourself?'

'Not bored, just lazy,' she reassured her.

'All right, but if you get hungry, just raid the larder. And if you feel like a ride later, try my new mare. She's still bouncing with energy, even though I rode her this morning. See you later,' she called, already on her way back to the house.

Honeychile resumed her prone position on the bank. She closed her eyes, listening to the gurgling stream and the bees buzzing in the clover, and the lovely 'silence' of the English countryside, alive with all kinds of subtle rustlings and creakings and dronings of a hundred tiny creatures. She thought sleepily, it was no wonder Laura loved this place. It was sheer heaven.

She dozed away the afternoon, then walked hungrily back to the house for tea. She had a cup of Earl Grey and one of Gladys's huge Fat Rascal scones, stuffed with cherries and almonds. After that, she took the mare for a ride.

They pottered along the country lanes, until they came to the hill behind the Manor, then she let her gallop. They stopped at the top while the mare snorted and caught her breath, and Honeychile admired the violet and peach sunset. She thought it was like a beautiful watercolour compared with the red-gold oil paintings in Positano.

When the sun was almost gone, they ambled back down the hill, through the lanes to the Manor. As she rode past the house to the stables in the back, she noticed Laura's car wasn't back yet, though it was already close to seven o'clock. She brushed the mare down, fed her, cleaned up the stable, then walked back to the house.

As she walked in the door the telephone was ringing. She ran to answer it, waving at Swayne in the kitchen having his supper, on the way.

She picked up the phone and said, breathlessly, 'Swinburn 231', wondering at the same time who the other two hundred and thirty Swinburn numbers belonged to, because as far as she knew the only other telephones in the village, were the vicar's and the pub.

'Honeychile?'

She smiled; Alex's voice still gave her that little thrill of excitement, and surprise.

'I'm almost there, *carissima*,' he said. 'I'm driving up. Right now, I'm in York. I'll stop for a bite of supper, then I'll be on my way. I should be with you in a couple of hours, at the latest.'

'I can't wait,' she said, 'And I can't wait for you to meet Laura's grandmother. You're going to love her.'

He laughed, 'If you say so, then I know I will.'

She told him she loved him, then put the phone down still smiling. It rang again, immediately. She grabbed it, surprised, thinking he was calling her back.

'Honeychile? It's Laura. Sorry about this, but I had a spot of trouble with the car. The mechanic from Jervis's garage is fixing it now, but it may take a while. So I thought I would take grandmother over to the Old Swan for dinner. She can enjoy her meal and check on the catering arrangements at the same time.'

Honeychile laughed, 'How was the hat?'

'Perfect. Of course, Grandma Jeannie was right, Miss Rachel does understand her style and it's exactly the right wedding hat for her. So is the dress. I told her she is going to outshine the bride at this rate.'

'Not a hope,' Honeychile said, because she had seen the wedding gown and she knew Laura was going to be a very beautiful bride. 'I'll see you later then.'

Honeychile went upstairs and took a quick bath. She put on a blue silk dress and brushed her hair, then went down to the kitchen to

380

say hello to Swayne. He had just finished his supper and Gladys was clearing up.

Honeychile thought, sympathetically, he had had a long day. 'Why don't you take an hour or two off, Mr Swayne,' she suggested. 'I think your devotion to duty deserves the reward of a pint of Bitter and a game of darts at the Red Lion. I shall be perfectly all right, and Alex and Laura will be here any minute. And I promise I'll keep an eye on the wedding presents for you.'

Swayne thought longingly of a pint. He looked at the spaniel, curled up with the black and white collies near the open back door. He thought that was carrying fraternization a bit too far; it would do the spaniel good to get away from those sheepdogs for a while, before it forgot who it belonged to and where it came from. Besides, it was quiet as the grave here. He had never worked in such a really quiet place before; it could get on a man's nerves, such quietness.

'Well, if you're sure you don't mind, Miss Honeychile,' he said.

'Of course I don't mind. In fact, I feel guilty that you are on duty so many hours. You should have someone to help you.'

'Tomorrow, the local constabulary will be sending a man over, Miss. And Saturday of course, for the wedding, we shall have a full contingent of bobbies.'

Still, he hesitated. 'His Lordship said I was to keep my eye on you at all times.'

She laughed, 'There's really no need. You enjoy your pint, Mr Swayne. As I said, you've earned it.'

Leaving Gladys doing the dishes in the kitchen, Honeychile went back upstairs. She turned on the lamp and looked round her, pleased. She loved her room. The brass bed had a porcelain panel set into it, depicting a crinolined shepherdess with three little lambs, and Laura had told her it had been here since the house was built, a couple of hundred years before. There was a polished mahogany dressing table with silver candelabra at the sides of the mirror, and a matching stool; and a pair of marble nightstands with shepherdess lamps topped with pink silk shades. The enormous old wardrobe was carved with swags and cherubs and sheaves of wheat, in a sort of glorious harvest festival medley, and in front of the Victorian green-tiled fireplace was a squashed looking armchair, slip-covered in a different chintz from the puffy eiderdown and curtains. The rose-garlanded wallpaper had faded to a pleasant pink; and so had the rugs. Nothing had been planned or matched, and yet it was just perfect.

Honeychile leaned her elbows on the windowsill, listening to the night sounds: a sheep bleating in the field; the leaves rustling in the breeze; the hoot of the barn owl that lived in the stable loft.

She remembered how lonely she used to feel at the ranch, listening to the sounds of the night. Now she was lonely no longer; she was the happiest woman in the world, except for Laura, whose wedding was in two days' time.

She thought how wonderful it would be if she could marry Alex, but life was not always that simple. They had both agreed to take their happiness while they could. They loved each other and their vows to each other were as binding as any marriage. One day, perhaps, he would be free to marry her. But remembering the poor, beautiful, mindless Ottavia, she knew she could never deprive her of the dignity of being Alex's wife, the *Signora* Scott.

'I'll be on my way now, Miss Honeychile,' Gladys called from the foot of the stairs.

'Oh, fine, Gladys,' Honeychile ran to the top of the stairs to say goodbye to her. 'See you tomorrow.'

'Bright and early, Miss. There's a lot to be done. Only two days to go until the wedding.' She hurried off, slamming the door behind her in the way that Jeannie Swinburn had been grumbling about for ten years now. Not that it made any difference, she said. Gladys was a slammer and that was all there was to it; she slammed doors, she slammed pots onto the table and pans on the stove, and nothing she could say would ever change her.

Honeychile stood for a moment, enjoying the silence of the house. Then she walked down the stairs and through the spacious black and white tiled hall, to the big dining room where the wedding presents were displayed. On the way she glanced at the longcase clock in the hall. The curlicued brass hands pointed to nine o'clock. Only another hour until Alex got here.

She turned on the light and what seemed like a mountain of silver glinted under the chandelier. The dining table was loaded with trays and candlesticks; toast-racks and goblets and cutlery in felt-lined mahogany chests. Trestle-tables covered in white linen cloths held more treasures and the massive sideboards gleamed with sets of fine

Spode and Royal Doulton china. Honeychile was certain that Saxton Mowbrey already had a surfeit of this stuff; she had seen it on her visits there, but Laura said they planned to buy a London house and all this would no doubt come in handy.

She turned off the light and went to the kitchen to see what was in the pantry; perhaps she might have a sandwich after all. She cut a slice from the loaf Gladys had baked that morning, spread it with butter made at the home farm, and added a slice or two of cucumber from the Swinburn garden. Then she leaned against the open doorway, eating her sandwich and thinking, amused, how English she had become.

Pools of light splashed from the windows onto the lawns and a pretty half-moon was rising over the church spire in the village. The sky was inky blue and everything looked peaceful, as though it were just waiting for Saturday's great day. She lifted her head, imagining she had heard a car in the distance along the lane, but there was nothing.

She whistled for the dogs but they didn't come running and she bet they had followed the spaniel and Swayne to the Red Lion. The spaniel seemed to have some suave city-dog attraction for them, though she couldn't for the life of her see why. It was as meek and mild-mannered as Swayne himself.

Closing the door, she walked back through the hall and up to her room. She tidied her hair, put on some lipstick and Chanel No.5 in anticipation of Alex's arrival, and then glanced at the clock, wondering where Laura and Jeannie had got to. It was already almost ten. She looked up as she heard a noise downstairs; that was probably them now.

She went to the top of the stairs and called, 'Laura, is that you?' There was no answer. Surprised, she ran downstairs and looked into the drawing room. Gladys had lit the lamps before she left, but it was empty. Puzzled, she listened again. There it was: a rustling sound. She wondered if it could be the dogs, coming home again, and she strode back through the hall towards the kitchen. She was half-way across when all the lights went out.

'Oh,' she said, stopping in her tracks and clutching her hand to her heart. 'It must be a fuse,' she told herself, realising she had no idea where the fuse boxes were. And then she heard the noise again.

Fear rippled suddenly up her spine. She stood, listening. She told herself not to be so foolish. She would just telephone Swayne at the Red Lion and tell him what had happened. She stepped cautiously forward into the darkness; she knew the phone was on the hall table to her right. She reached to pick it up.

A hand covered hers, slamming down the telephone. Jack Delaney had her in a stranglehold. 'If it ain't like old times,' he whispered in her ear. 'Me and you together, Honeychile. All we're missing is Rosie. And your husband of course.'

Her knees went weak with fear and panic. She just had time to think that Alex had been right and Jack was going to kill her, and then he hit her on the head with the kitchen rolling pin. The world spun around her for a second; then anger flooded her veins with adrenalin and hate. 'You bastard,' she screamed, twisting from his grasp and running to the door. He caught up with her, reaching out for her. She slammed the door on his hand, and fled unsteadily down the steps, into the night.

She heard footsteps on the gravel behind her and darted into the shrubbery. She stopped and waited a minute, listening. Her heart was pounding so hard she couldn't hear anything. She thought of Swayne at the Red Lion, and of Alex, driving from York: if she could hide, they would be here soon. She only hoped it would be soon enough to save her.

Close by, a twig snapped underfoot, making her jump. She dropped to her knees and crawled through the bushes, oblivious to the sharp stones cutting her, and the thorny branches ripping her arms; round the back lawn to the banks of the stream where she had spent a lazy, sunny afternoon, thinking how happy she was.

She stood behind the trunk of the big old willow, leaning against it, peering into the darkness. Her heart seemed to be stuck somewhere in her throat and her hands were slippery with fear. The stream gurgled busily and over it she could hear the sound of her own breathing. 'Alex, oh Alex, please come,' she prayed. 'I don't want to die and lose you now.' She closed her eyes, conjuring up his face, willing him to come and find her.

Then Jack grabbed her. 'No,' she screamed, 'no, no, no . . .'

In the distance, she thought she heard a dog bark. Jack hit her again. She dropped to the ground, clutching her head, feeling the blood trickling through her fingers. 'No,' she moaned, 'no, please no . . .'

There was a sound in the bushes and he looked away for an instant. Honeychile never knew how she did it; but she got to her feet and ran.

'Help,' she screamed, running along the bank of the stream, 'help me . . .' But she knew Jack was right behind her, he was gaining on her and she was weak.

There was a rustling in the undergrowth and with a deep growl, the spaniel launched itself at Jack. It sank its teeth into his arm with a satisfied sigh, as though it had achieved a life-long ambition. Jack gave a yell of pain, trying to shake the dog off, but it wasn't about to let go so quickly.

Swayne lumbered towards them through the bushes. He took in Honeychile prone on the ground and the spaniel with its teeth in the villain and he leapt into action. He felled Jack with a swift blow to the back of the neck, something he had learned in a stint in Hong Kong, in his police days. Then he dragged Jack's hands behind his back and clapped the cuffs on him with a satisfactory snap. He looked at the dog, still with its teeth in Jack's arm.

'Good work, old fella,' he said, pleased. Then he looked at poor Honeychile, bleeding from the head.

'I'm afraid I let you down, Miss Honeychile,' he said, regretfully.

Honeychile began to laugh; here she was half-murdered with Jack in handcuffs and Swayne was apologising for saving her. She would never understand the art of English understatement.

Then Alex was there and she was in his arms, held close to him and his heart was beating almost as wildly as her own. And she knew that now everything would be all right.

CHAPTER 40

Jerome Swayne almost stole the bride's thunder at Laura's wedding, because all the talk was of how he had saved Honeychile's life and caught the man responsible for Harry Lockwood's death red-handed.

It was a perfect June day. Tall white lilies adorned the altar; full-blown summer roses decorated every pew; and garlands of ferns and greenery were swagged along the stone walls of the tiny old church, filling it with their summery scent, and transforming it into a cool, shady garden. Billy and the best man, smart in their morning suits and silk cravats, waited at the altar with the vicar of Swinburn, the Reverend Mr Oates, who had known Laura since she was born. The tiny church was packed to the rafters; not another guest could have been squeezed in.

Lord Mountjoy was waiting in the front hall of Swinburn Manor for Laura. He took his watch from his waistcoat pocket, frowning as he looked at it. The bride was already three minutes late leaving for the church. He began to pace the floor, hands clasped behind his back, thumbs twiddling agitatedly. He told himself for the thousandth time he would never understand why women were always late. It was the simplest matter in the world to get yourself to an appointment on time. *Especially* to one's own marriage. He only hoped she hadn't gone and changed her mind at the last minute, because her grandmother Jeannie had already left for the church, and *he* simply wouldn't know what to do with her.

'Uncle Mountjoy.'

He swung round and looked at her, standing at the top of the stairs.

Laura had wanted hers to be a true country wedding, and now she was a perfect country bride in billowing white silk-taffeta with a posy of roses and lilies. She wore the diamond tiara that Mountjoy's own wife, Penelope, had worn for their wedding, as had countless Mountjoy brides before them. And her veil was the old Brussels lace his mother had worn when she married his father, overlaid with silk-tulle, embroidered with seed pearls.

Mountjoy thought his girl looked a vision of beauty. A lump came into his throat as she walked slowly down the stairs towards him. He took her hand, gallantly.

'You make a beautiful bride, my dear Laura,' he said, quite choked by an emotion he knew by now, was love. 'Billy is a lucky man. Yes, very lucky.'

'I think I'm the lucky one, Uncle Mountjoy.' She put her hand to his cheek, looking into his eyes, smiling. 'If it had not been for you, I would never have come to London. I would never have met Billy on the train that day. And I would never have known what a wonderful uncle I have. The very best in the world.' And she kissed him.

'Yes, well, maybe so,' Mountjoy agreed, deeply embarrassed but pleased.

He took her arm, and they walked down the steps and into the waiting carriage; an open landau from Mountjoy Park, its maroon and gold paintwork polished to a high gloss, and drawn by a pair of matched high-stepping bays from Billy's stable. The three border collies and Swayne's spaniel, sporting big red bows, trotted behind them, all the way to Swinburn Church. Like proper carriage dogs, Mountjoy thought approvingly, even if they were yapping at each other and panting in the heat.

The organ didn't so much peal as wheeze into Handel's oratorio, as the vicar's wife thumped the keys and the sweating young boy hidden in the back pumped for all his life was worth. The nine-voice choir, consisting of the local boys and girls, burst into song; the dogs barked vigorously outside and the babies woke and cried lustily.

All in all, Jeannie Swinburn thought, smiling at her lovely grand-daughter as she walked down the aisle to wed the man she loved, it was a true Swinburn wedding, and not too much different from her own to Josh, all those years ago.

Lord Mountjoy gave away the bride and then went back to his place in the front pew. He looked round him.

The front of the Church was filled with Saxtons and Mountjoys, though the Mountjoy contingent was a bit thin on the ground. There was Aunt Sophie, of course, regal in burgundy silk, anointed with diamonds and wearing a very big hat with a sweeping ostrich plume. And Jeannie Swinburn, looking charming in a deep-rose dress and matching hat. Then there was Madame Suzette, thin and Parisian-chic in a sea-green suit from Patou and the most beautiful hat, tilted forward with a little spotted veil over her eyes.

Anjou was wearing green too, the sort that matched her eyes, silk with too short a skirt and one of her mother's pretty little hats. She was also wearing the emerald necklace Mountjoy had given her, as well as an enormous diamond ring that must have cost a fortune. Mountjoy stared suspiciously at it as it caught the light, wondering where on earth she had got it from; he supposed she must have inherited it from that naughty grandmother of hers.

Honeychile. Ah, Honeychile. He looked at her, wondering how he could have coped if she had been badly hurt, or even worse, killed. The police had told him Delaney had confessed everything. What else could he do? Swayne had caught him in the very act.

Apparently, he had meant to stun her, then drive her to Westacre Crag. He planned to throw her over it to make it look like suicide. Thankfully, Swayne and the spaniel had foiled his plans.

Anyhow, here she was, safe and sound, looking beautiful in a yellow silk dress that was almost the colour of her hair, and the big Mountjoy pearls. Madame Suzette had kindly adapted Honeychile's hat, adding a touch of veiling to hide the bruises and the stitches in her forehead, and she looked almost her old self again.

She was sitting next to Alex Scott, her lover, and Mountjoy thought if love made her look that happy then what could be wrong with it? Besides, Scott had turned out to be a decent chap. Alex had told him the sad story about his wife and he had seen his dilemma. Though a man like himself, brought up the way he was, could not approve, he did understand, and even though the church could not, he had given them his blessing.

Behind the small Mountjoy contingent sat the entire population of Swinburn village, complete with children shuffling noisily in the heat, and a couple of babies who, thankfully, had stopped bawling. The men wore the whitest of white shirts and hot dark suits, and their wives were summery and cool in floral silks and competitive hats.

And in an aisle seat, near the door so he could still keep an eye on things, even though he was no longer on official duty, sat the man of the moment, Swayne.

All in all, Mountjoy thought as the organ wheezed into the Wedding March, and Laura and Billy smiled at him on their way back down the aisle, it was a beautiful wedding.

The reception marquee on the huge back lawn of the Manor was lined in pale yellow silk and ringed with rose trees in full bloom. The tables had matching yellow cloths with great bunches of pale yellow and pink cabbage roses. White-jacketed waiters poured 1920 Vintage Krug champagne, disinterred from the enormous wine cellar under Mountjoy Park, and the guests ate a delicious meal and mingled happily.

Unable to break the habit, Swayne stood in his 'at ease' position by the door, keeping an eye on things. The spaniel sat beside him, looking important in his red ribbon and all the guests stopped to say hello and jolly well done, and to pat the spaniel. Some of them remembered they would be having similar functions before too long, and said they would very much like Swayne and his dog to take charge of the security arrangements for them.

Before the ceremony Lord Mountjoy had personally thanked him and presented him with a cheque, the numbers on which made Swayne's mind boggle.

'There's no value I can put on life, Swayne,' Mountjoy had told him, sounding humble. 'I'm only glad you were there to help her.' He smiled and shook Swayne's hand firmly. He clapped him on the shoulder and invited him to the wedding as a guest, not a security man. 'Let the local bobbies keep an eye on the silver,' he had said. 'Come and enjoy yourself, Swayne. You've earned it.'

Pleased, Swayne took a cautious sip of champagne, wrinkling his nose as he did so and thinking he didn't know what they saw in it; there was nothing to beat a pint of Tetley's draught bitter, after all.

Then the wedding cake, five tiers, made by Betty's in Harrogate, was cut and the toasts were drunk, and Lord Mountjoy got up to make a speech.

He stood, looking around at his guests, clearing his throat. 'Yes, well, I'm not a great one for making speeches,' he said at last.

'But it is my privilege to do so today. I feel almost as lucky as the charming grandmother of the bride, Mrs Jeannie Swinburn,' he smiled at her sitting on his right, 'in being at my great-niece's wedding. In fact I'm luckier, because I only got to know Laura last year, and that almost by accident. Suffice it to say that I am proud and pleased that she is a Mountjoy, and that I was the fortunate man to give her away in marriage today, to another fortunate man, Billy Saxton.'

He raised his glass in a toast, 'To Mr and Mrs Saxton,' he said loudly, and everyone sipped champagne and broke into applause.

Jeannie Swinburn stood up next. 'I'm a happy woman today,' she said, 'but then I have always been happy, having Laura around, bringing her up.' She smiled, 'As you can see, I did a good job. She's a fine Yorkshire lass with a touch of Italian in the temper – better watch out for that Billy,' she added and everyone laughed. 'And she will make as fine a wife as she did a granddaughter.'

Then Billy stood up and thanked them both without even a hint of a stutter, until he proposed a toast to, 'M-m-m-my l-l-l-lovely w-w-wife,' and everybody laughed and cheered.

Watching them, Anjou wondered, a little jealously, whether she had made the right decision about wanting to be a mistress instead of a wife. She thought wistfully how happy Laura and Billy looked, and what a mess she had made of things. She was just thinking perhaps there was something to love and marriage, after all, when her eye caught Jakey Barrett's, the American friend of Billy's, and devastatingly good-looking. She gave him that smile. Old habits died hard, she thought with a pleased sigh. In September she would be a good girl and go back to the Sorbonne and work hard and get her degree. Until then, she was free and life was exciting.

It was time for the bride to change, but first she tossed her bouquet, and she made sure Honeychile caught it. They smiled at each other. Honeychile knew what Laura meant. One day, when God willed it, she would be a bride too.

In no time at all, Laura had changed into a cream-coloured suit and hat and she was sitting next to Billy in the Rolls. They were on their way to the railway station in Leeds, where they would take the train on which they had first met, to London. It was the first leg of their journey to Positano and Alex's yacht, the *Atalanta*, where they were to spend their honeymoon cruising the Mediterranean, and, like Honeychile, making love in a bed of moonlight.

The guests threw rose petals and rice and confetti and Laura turned to wave a last goodbye. Laughing, she blew Uncle Mountjoy a kiss, and she could have sworn she caught a glimpse of a tear in his eye, as he lifted his hand in farewell.

Everybody agreed that Laura was the most beautiful bride and it had been a wonderful wedding. But the party wasn't over yet. There was dancing in the marquee, and a lavish supper later, and finally a fireworks display that Lord Mountjoy always loved.

'It's a fitting end to a wonderful day,' Jeannie, sitting next to him on the lawn, said contentedly.

'Indeed, indeed,' he agreed, patting her hand. 'Laura's a credit to you, my dear.'

'And to Georgie Mountjoy, I think,' she suggested with a sly smile, making him laugh. 'I intend to come and visit you, you know,' she added, 'at that wonderful house in London I've heard so much about, and at Mountjoy Park.'

'Shall you really?' There was a pleased smile on his face as he regarded her. 'Well then, we shall just have to have another party, shan't we? Only this time it will be especially for you.' He laughed, enjoying the idea of her company and the party. 'I hope it will be the first of many we shall enjoy together,' he added.

Aunt Sophie took off her plumed hat and sank wearily into the chair next to them, as the last bombardment of catherine wheels and rockets and flashes and bangs faded into the blue night. 'One down, two to go,' she commented. 'We might have a long wait for Honeychile's nuptials, but still they are so happy.'

'And so in love,' Lord Mountjoy added, thinking that not so very long ago, he had barely known what the word meant. Now his life seemed filled with it.

'As for Anjou,' Aunt Sophie shrugged, 'that one is likely to keep everyone guessing; most of all, the young man who becomes her fiancé. I fear we shan't know until the last minute whether the girl will actually turn up at the altar, or whether she might run off with the best man.'

Mountjoy laughed, 'Little minx,' he said fondly.

Jeannie thought about Anjou: 'Don't worry your heads about her,' she decided. 'Anjou will fall on her feet all right; she has more sense than you credit her with. All she needs is time to grow up a little.'

'I dare say you're right,' Aunt Sophie agreed. 'Well, Mountjoy, the car is waiting to take us to Harrogate. I suppose this is the end of a wonderful day.'

'And the beginning of many others,' Jeannie said heartily, as she kissed all of them goodbye: Anjou and Suzette, Honeychile and Alex, Sophie, and William Mountjoy. 'We're all family now,' she told him, laughing.

As Laura had done, he turned to wave. She was still smiling and he said warmly to Sophie, 'A wonderful woman, wonderful. Didn't I always say there was something special about Yorkshire women?'

'I dare say you did,' Aunt Sophie replied, drily.

A few weeks later, Lord Mountjoy was sitting in his library, sipping his usual evening whisky and mulling over the meaning of happiness.

Mountjoy House was silent again, now that all his girls were gone. He had arranged for each of them to receive an equal share of his fortune; he had given them a great opportunity, and inadvertently, he had also given them his heart. In return they had brought him scandal and tragedy, but they had also given him their love and a great deal of happiness.

The telephone shrilled, breaking the silence. 'Hello,' he barked, picking it up.

'Uncle, it's me, Honeychile.'

'My dear, where are you?' A pleased smile spread across his face.

'I'm in Paris, with Alex. We are about to have dinner with Anjou and some new admirer she has in tow. A Frenchman this time.'

Lord Mountjoy groaned, 'A Frenchman,' he snorted, testily. 'What's wrong with a good solid English fellow I'd like to know.'

Honeychile laughed and the sound rippled in his ears like music. 'After all, Uncle, Anjou is French too.'

'So she is, so she is,' he agreed, smiling at his own foolishness. 'I suppose I must forgive her then,' he added, and Honeychile laughed again.

'I just wanted to tell you we shall all be arriving for Jeannie's party on Saturday,' she said.

'I'm glad,' he replied gruffly, 'wouldn't want you to miss it. Laura will be back so it's a joint celebration of sorts.'

'See you then,' Honeychile said. 'I must go now, or we shall be late.'

'I shall look forward to seeing you,' he said, reluctant to let her go.

'Me too.' There was a pause and then she added, 'Uncle Mountjoy, just one more thing. I love you.'

The receiver clicked in his ear as she rang off. He held it away from him, staring at it with a delighted smile. 'Well, I'm dashed,' he said, still smiling.

He sank back into his chair and took a sip of whisky, thinking about the children his girls would have. *His great-grandchildren*. Well, almost: he was sure old Georgie wouldn't mind him appropriating them as his own. And, come to think of it, Georgie couldn't have been such a bad fellow, after all.

One thing was certain: 'his girls' would come back to visit him. He had a lot to look forward to in his old age. He was a lonely man no longer.